Mark Within
Salvation

Onoma Series Book 3

Alisa Hope Wagner

Mark Within
Salvation

Onoma Series Book 3

Alisa Hope Wagner

Mark Within Salvation
Book Three of the Onoma Series
Copyright © 2017 by Alisa Hope Wagner
All rights reserved.
Marked Writers Publishing.
www.alisahopewagner.com

Scriptures taken from multiple translations of the Bible.

Author photo by Lori Stead of www.wetsilver.com
Cover images designed by Muhammad Ahsan Ayaz
Cover designed by Alisa Hope Wagner

ISBN-13: 978-0692907221
ISBN-10: 069290722X

Dedication

Daniel, my high school sweetheart and soul mate.

Isaac, my first-born son and prophet.

Levi, my brown-eyed boy and shepherd.

Karis Ruth, my cherished girl and graceful companion.

Christina, my amazing twin.

Acknowledgments

Every time I complete the process of writing, editing and preparing a book for publication, I'm reminded of how much work it takes and how much help I need. Writing a book is a solitary process, but preparing it for publication takes a team of friends. I am amazed at how each person who offers his or her time, energy and effort toward my book, shapes it in a unique and wonderful way. I am grateful for all the hands that have gently embraced my story and added a diversity of soul to it. I want to offer my heartfelt thanks to Patti Coughlin, Kerry Johnson, Shay Lee, Gina Martinez, Robin McNaueal, Faith Newton, Jennifer Smith, Daniel Wagner and Bernadine Zimmerman. I value all your encouragement, insights and corrections!

Moreover, the life of writing definitely involves my family. My husband and three amazing kids make daily compromises in order to give me the time to write. I don't take their sacrifice for granted, so I use my writing time wisely. Thank you to my husband, Daniel, and my children—Isaac, Levi and Kiki—for giving me a few hours every day to write books that honor God.

Finally, without Jesus Christ none of my writing would be possible. He is the one Who makes the fool wise, and I am a fool without the Holy Spirit's presence and guidance in my life. Thank You, God, for calling me a writer when I didn't yet deserve the title. But most of all thank You for calling me a Child of God when I could never earn it.

Introduction

In a single year, Ruth has fully embraced Colonial life with her fighter husband, Bear, and the existence she once found revolting has now given her true meaning and happiness. She and her growing family of dissident friends have discovered a way to infiltrate the World Government undetected, creating chaos in the system to loosen the government's increasing attempts for power and domination. Zach, Ruth's brother, and his tech-genius friend, Li, go on a journey to spread the web of Pastor Tom's underground communication network and unearth Neil Elder's disturbing plan to save on production costs in a world with limited natural resources. A hunt is unleashed for the culprits of the World Bank's first robbery, and the life of efficiency moves beyond production and into the realm of pomp, artistry and human ingenuity.

"Do not limit the limitless God! With Him, face the future unafraid because you are never alone." - Lettie Cowman

CHAPTER ONE

"This is a terrible idea," Zach said, staring out of the car window to the towering building across the street. His normally pale face flushed with apprehension. "What makes us think we can just leisurely walk into the World Bank, grab a bunch of jewelry and make it out of the city? Tom is out of his mind if he thinks we can get away with this. We are driving a gas-powered car. They will know we are Colonials. Bear will literally kill me—kill me!—if anything happens to Ruth! He will put me in a chokehold and squeeze until every ounce of breath has left my body!"

"You have been in the World Bank before," Ruth said, staring at her brother's profile from the back seat. She could see sweat trickle down his cheek. "Tom has prayed over it, and we have planned every detail. Jonah will be there too. I feel that everything will be okay. Bear would not kill you—though, he may put you in a chokehold," she said with a slight smile.

Zach looked back to his sister. "Your new-found wit doesn't humor me one bit. And you *feel* it? What happened to my sister who is all logic and no gut? What you feel doesn't make me feel any better. We should just leave right now before everyone sees you. Tom can find another way to raise the funds for his rebellion."

"What other way, Zach? Do you think it is a coincidence that I collected millions of dollars of jewels and that I still have my keycard? If it were not for the pearls that God had me put in my pocket a year ago, I would not be alive today. I needed funds to get back home. There are lives at stake. We need money to help people and to accomplish God's work and the funds for that are sitting in my vault."

"Look you two," Li said, as his eyes continually scanned the scene beyond the windows. "You need to make a decision now. Ruth's card expires tomorrow. The bank must let her in the vault. There is no precedent for this, and they won't want to make a scene. The last thing the World Bank wants is publicity from a dead, famous woman, especially Eve Pallue. And don't forget. All of our lives are at stake here. The World Government thinks I'm dead too."

"You're right, Li. We are all taking a great risk. I fear for all of us." Zach furrowed his eyebrows and turned fully to face his sister, gripping the headrest of his seat. "I've prayed. I have no clarity."

"Zach, I think you have no clarity because you are too emotionally involved. I know Jonah will be there, and the longer you wait, the more we compromise our position," Ruth said.

"I just wish God would give me a sign. I know I shouldn't have to always ask for one, but I need something. There is too much at stake. At least a single word!"

"Star!" Li blurted out.

Zach looked toward Li. His tan face dripped with sweat and his knuckles were almost white from clutching the wheel too tightly.

Li hesitated. "Star—I don't know. I just felt that word just now in my mind. Does it mean anything?"

Zach sat stunned for a few seconds. Suddenly, the anxiety on his face transformed to determination. "Ruth, let's do this. Li, we will be right back with millions worth of jewelry, so don't go anywhere."

"Yeah, right. I'll hold back from going to that café we passed on our way here," Li said, leaning his forehead on the steering wheel.

Zach opened his door and stepped out. He wore a tailored suit that Ruth had made. He slipped on his sunglasses and ran his hand through his blonde hair, causing his fingers to get stuck. He forgot that Pilar had put some sort of product in his hair to keep his hair from falling into his face. He untangled his fingers and hastily opened the passenger door to let Ruth out.

Ruth wore a black pantsuit that she had also made. Pilar came over early that morning and applied her makeup and curled her long hair into soft waves. She wore black, scuffed heels a size too big and carried a tattered briefcase—all items traded for at the last bazaar. As Zach led the way across the city street, she walked a few steps behind him.

Zach wished he could be accompanying Ruth as a Runner, not as her Bodyguard. He felt like a phony, and he tried to mimic the Bodyguards he had seen briefly in the past. They always carried themselves with confidence and slight cockiness. He prayed that Li's attempt to change his Runner status to Bodyguard status had worked. He knew Li was smart, but he didn't feel like betting his life on it just yet.

They arrived too soon at the doors to the World Bank, and Zach floundered at grabbing the handle to open the door for Ruth. Ruth gave him a brief, irritated look. Zach wondered if she was truly annoyed or if she was simply playing the part.

As they entered the expansive lobby, Zach was grateful that the vicinity was relatively empty. Most desks were void of personnel and only a few clerks stood behind the long counter toward the back of the lobby. A man saw them enter from one of the glass-enclosed offices and began to make his way toward the entrance. Zach knew this short, heavyset white man was not Jonah. He stopped feeling his heart pound. He was just about to tell Ruth to forget the entire thing when a deep, voice rang over the intercom.

"Simpson, you are needed in the security center immediately." The words boomed off the immense walls.

The man stopped abruptly. He gestured toward Zach and Ruth and said, "Wait."

He turned and headed toward the hallway situated between his office and the lobby counter. Suddenly, a large, dark man wearing a suit appeared from the hallway. He stopped for a moment, glancing momentarily where Zach and Ruth stood. He said a few curt words to the man before walking into the lobby. The other man disappeared down the hall.

Zach knew he was seeing Jonah for the first time, but he couldn't get over how intimidating the man was. When Ruth talked about him, he envisioned a large, sweet teddy bear. This man was a giant with a no-nonsense expression on his face. As he walked closer to where he and Ruth were standing, Zach couldn't help thinking that he was about to be tackled to the ground.

"How may I help you?" his voice rolled out like an ocean tide. "My name is Matt Coughlin."

"Uh—yes, I'm here to assist my client in opening her vault," Zach stammered.

"You nervous, son?" Jonah asked with a twinge of humor in his voice.

"No, sir. Not at all," Zach said.

"You know," Jonah said, as he grabbed the print identifier from the attachment on his belt. "There is no need to be nervous at the World Bank. We know and see everything here. We are protected from all danger and every threat."

Zach didn't know if Jonah was trying to be threatening or encouraging.

"Place your thumb here," Jonah said.

Zach instantly brought his thumb to the identifier, like he had done so many times in the past as a Runner. He silently prayed that his profile would come up as a Bodyguard.

Jonah stared at the screen and then back at Zach. "You're kind of lean to be a Bodyguard, aren't you?"

Zach smiled awkwardly. "Well, what I lack in mass, I make up in skill."

"I see that you are not carrying?" Jonah said, nodding to his belt.

"I have a leg holster," Zach said, patting his trousers.

"Let's just hope you don't blow off your foot," Jonah said.

Then Jonah's eyes reverted to Ruth, and he paused for a moment. "You look well this morning, Miss. How are you feeling today?"

Ruth said nothing for a long moment and stared at Jonah. "Well," Ruth said in T-variety. "Business."

"Yes, I'm sure you have business to attend to. Let me get your thumbprint, so we can get you started."

Ruth raised her right thumb to the print identifier. The scars on her hand became evident.

"What happened to your hand?" Jonah asked, concern rising in his voice.

"Accident. Infant," Ruth said, placing her thumb to the identifier.

Zach noticed that Jonah's countenance instantly changed. He now saw the man that Ruth had described. "She doesn't like to talk about it," Zach interjected, trying to repair the façade of generalities that was shattering.

The print identifier made a noise that Zach had never heard.

"It can't read your print," Jonah whispered. "You have no identity."

Zach looked at Ruth's hand. It had been burned, but the markings were so faded now that he was used to it. "What do we do now?"

Jonah stood for a second thinking. Suddenly, he put his print identifier back on his belt and gently took Ruth by the arm. "You will have to wait outside while Zacchaeus Daniels does his transaction."

"What do you mean?" Ruth asked confused.

"Do you have the bank card?" Jonah asked.

"Yes," she nodded.

"Give it to the Bodyguard. He will have to make the transaction for Eve Pallue."

Ruth fumbled her hand into her pocket and handed the card to Jonah.

"Give it to the Bodyguard," Jonah repeated. "Along with your briefcase."

Zach took the card and the briefcase. "How will this work?"

"I will show you to the vault in a moment. This woman must leave now for her own protection. I will escort her out. You wait here." Jonah carefully pulled Ruth by the arm and started walking toward the entrance. When he reached the doors, he opened them and turned his back to the cameras he knew were positioned on the ceilings behind him.

"Your identity is safe. God must want you to stay hidden. When you get in the car, hide on the floor of the backseat. The cameras can't see you there. I'll explain everything to Zach."

"Just tell me," Ruth said. "How did you survive? And how did you find me?"

"I fell to the flat under yours. There was nothing there. The water system kicked on and woke me up. I looked to the ceiling and noticed the fire was contained to a single area in your home, like it had been positioned to burn one way. By then crowds of people were leaving and the fire alarms were sounding. I made my way to the security room and it was empty. I wanted to see if you had made it out, but all the video cameras were off."

"Randall must have turned them off before he entered my flat," Ruth said. "He's good at starting fires and covering his tracks."

Jonah nodded. He continued, "I walked to the parking garage and noticed spots of blood, leading to where my truck was parked. Thankfully, my vehicle was gone, and I knew you had made it. I took off my shirt and wiped the blood leading to the stairwell, and the sprinkler system in the building covered your tracks up to that point. I found out later that you had fallen, leaving a tooth behind. I'm sorry you were injured so badly. When I finally arrived at Miss Christina's house, you were gone. I wanted to go find you, but I felt God tell me to stay. I buried Christina's body and took over her LPS. I then waited by the monitor for more than two weeks to find you."

"How did you know how to find me online?" Ruth asked.

"I waited for someone to search for one name—Naomi Watson. That's when I found Thomas Isaacs."

"Why didn't you tell me that you were alive?" Ruth asked.

"I didn't know who I could trust. You must not tell anyone who doesn't already know who I am. I'll continue my discourse through Tom. I have to finish my assignment on this end. Everyone has an important role to play, including you, Eve. Keep writing those articles. They are changing the environment around here."

"Do you think they will recognize me?" she asked

"Not one bit. They'll never know that you were here," he said.

"Then Eve is truly dead," Ruth said matter-of-factly. "My name is Ruth now."

Jonah nodded. "Ruth it is. Now, you better go. Charlie is in the vehicle?"

"Yes," Ruth nodded. "He goes by Li."

"Okay, he and Zach are now blacklisted. They must separate themselves from you and everyone they know until this thing is done. They have only a day or two before they go looking for them."

"Will you not get in trouble?" Ruth asked. "Won't they see the video of you and me at the vault when my pearl necklace broke a year ago?"

"No, I already took care of that. I've become quite good at erasing video feeds. God has already given me a plan. The only thing I need to figure out is how Zach got your bank card in the first place."

Ruth smiled. "He stole it from me, remember? When he installed my new Sleeper a year ago."

CHAPTER TWO

"**B**ear, she is in God's hands. We have planned everything out and prayed over every detail. She will be fine," Pastor Tom said yet again, watching his new friend walk the length of his office at Trinity Trading Center. He had known Bear only a short while, and he already liked him. The image he got from reading about him all over the news during his fighting days showed very little similarity to the man pacing before him today. Bear was raw and honest. There were no ulterior motives hidden in him. He was as exposed as a patient during open-heart surgery. Tom was both intrigued and humored that Bear and Ruth would fall in love with each other.

"I just got this woman in my life, and now you expect me to just let her go? I should never have agreed to do this! Ruth has no way of defending herself, and Zach can't protect her like I can. And do we really know this Li guy? Who is he?" Bear shouted. His thick midnight hair was pulled together at the nape of his neck. A few gray strands streaked the black like lightning. He wore a type of charcoal-colored gi that fighters wear, which Ruth had made specifically for him.

Tom sighed and continued looking at his HMS monitor. "There's no use yelling. The World News has said nothing about the bank. Eve's name has not even been mentioned. God's in control. He knows more than we do, and He loves Ruth more than you do. Just trust Him," Tom said. "Bear, please sit down."

Bear grabbed the nearest seat next to where Tom was sitting and dropped onto the chair. "It's so much easier to trust God when you don't care about the people involved."

Tom looked at Bear. "It is hard when God widens your heart. Loving people comes with a cost, but the love and joy repaid are worth the price."

"Now you sound like Ruth," Bear said.

Tom smiled. "Those are Ruth's words—from the latest article she sent me yesterday."

Bear straightened in his seat. "She sent that to you yesterday? She was only on her HMS for a second before we had to leave."

"Her writing is profound," Tom said and hesitated.

"What?" Bear asked.

"She's only been married for a few weeks, but I see a difference in her voice."

"Her voice is exactly the same," Bear said.

"No, not her actual voice. I mean her written voice. The feel of her words when you read them. She sounds more relatable now. And I know this may sound strange, but her writing reads more human. I think you have given her that."

Bear paused for a moment and then stared at the monitor. He fingered the creamy pearl strung on a single strand of nylon cord around his neck. Then he reached out both hands and placed them on the monitor. "God, if You are listening now, please shield my wife. Protect her somehow from being exposed. Hide her in Your hands and keep her secret. We are just starting our new life together, and we both have no clue what we are doing. We can't have this, not now. Let there be another way."

Tom watched Bear hold the monitor and whisper more words in silence.

"Amen," Tom said, as Bear brought his arms back to his side. "You know my wife made a necklace like that for Ruth before she left Trinity," he said, pointing to the pearl.

"Yes, I know," Bear said. "She made this one with her last pearl. The other one was buried with her mother." Bear's voice broke. "I can't let anything happen to her, Tom."

"Knock, knock," Cindy said from the open door of the office. "I brought you two a snack. I'm sorry if I interrupted something."

"Thanks, honey. You didn't have to do that, but I am sure hungry. We are fine. We were just praying for Ruth," Tom said, taking the two plates that his wife presented him.

"These pies are from Esther. One of her Efficientist from the farm brought them over today with a message that they are praying for Ruth. There's more upstairs. Esther heard that Bear's grandfather was a connoisseur of sweet treats, so she packed him a box full," Cindy said smiling. She placed her hands on her hips. "Any word about the team?"

"No, nothing yet," Tom said before grabbing his fork and taking a big bite. "Esther does know how to make pie."

"You're not hungry, Bear?" Cindy said after Bear set his plate on the desk.

"No, Cindy, but thank you for bringing it. I can't eat until I know that Ruth is okay," Bear said.

Cindy nodded. "You should have seen Li working on the HMS for hours every day before they left. The last thing he wants is for Ruth to get caught. He has the highest respect for her. Did you know that they met before she came here?"

Bear looked up at Cindy. "They did?"

"Yes, he had just become an Elite Efficientist before Ruth left. He had studied her—even writing one of his dissertations about her work. The last thing he would ever want for her is to get caught by the World Government. He felt a supreme weight to make sure she would be okay, which is why he was willing to risk his own life. He worked tirelessly to ensure that Zach would be labeled a Bodyguard instead of a Runner. That's never been done before, but he was able to do it. Everything that man could do on his end to ensure Ruth's safety has been done. The rest is up to the good Lord."

Bear got out of his seat. "That makes me feel a little better. I'm honored that Li took the time to keep Ruth safe."

"And one more thing," Cindy added. "He has been labeled dead by the World Government—killed in the Colonies. He is risking his life for this cause, so you can be sure Ruth is with two men who would do anything to keep her safe."

"Actually, three men. Matthew Coughlin—or Jonah as Ruth knows him—has already risked his life to keep Ruth safe. This man is someone you definitely want on your side. He's our eyes and ears right there in the epicenter of the World Government."

Bear got up and began pacing the floor again. "Yes, I hadn't realized all this. This is good. And when Ruth comes back home, I will keep her safe. Everyone knows the Shaman, but no one knows Bear. We may have to move, though. I've already been fixing my home for Ruth. She's picky and likes her conveniences, but I can build her another home. There is a village of Ka'to descendants up north. I may take her there with me. My grandfather won't want to leave, but he'll go where Ruth goes."

Tom watched Bear plan and pace. He was glad to have Bear in his widening fold of influence. Tom's expanding connections to this faith movement formed a giant, supernatural web across many colonies, and it was increasing rapidly. Tom was in awe of the position God had given him. He didn't deserve it, but he would steward it well. God entrusted him with so many talented people—all with special giftings. Tom was in the middle of an unfolding supernatural drama, and he couldn't help but love every minute of it.

Tom looked back at the monitor. "Wait a minute. There's news!" he exclaimed louder than he anticipated.

Bear jumped back into his seat. "What is it saying? I can't read any of it!"

"It's in T-variety. Hold on. Let me read it all the way through before I explain it all," Tom said, scrolling down.

Bear pointed. "Look, I see the car but only Zach and Li are in it. They took her! The World Government has Ruth!"

"No, just wait. I'm almost done," Tom said, swiping Bear's hand away from the screen.

Tom read for several seconds and then pushed away from the monitor. "I can't believe it," he said in a hushed voice.

"What? What's going on?" Bear demanded.

"Eve Pallue was never there," Tom said.

"How could that be?" Cindy asked, disbelieving. "They can't open her vault without her."

"A Bodyguard is allowed to open a vault for his or her employer," Pastor Tom said.

"Is that the rule?" Cindy asked.

"It must be. I can see why. A lot of Efficientists wouldn't want to go to the bank themselves. Zach had the vault keycard, so he would be allowed to open her vault as her Bodyguard."

"But Eve Pallue is dead. They would want to investigate first," Cindy countered.

"But look who was with them," Pastor Tom said, scrolling down the news feed.

"That's Jonah," Bear said, pointing.

"So, Jonah found a way to get Zach into the vault even though Eve Pallue is considered dead?" Cindy asked, amazed.

"Jonah may get in trouble," Pastor Tom said. "But I hope he had a plan. We need Matt Coughlin to keep his position in the World Government."

"So, Ruth is safe?" Bear asked, as hope filled his voice.

"Yes, it looks like God was listening to your prayer after all," Tom said, chuckling and patting Bear on the shoulder. "I don't know how, but both Ruth and Eve Pallue are nowhere to be seen in the bank robbery."

CHAPTER THREE

"**W**hat is the meaning of this?" Neil Elder asked, as Jonah entered the room. "And why are you carrying around a trash can?"

Jonah closed the door behind him. He was wearing the same suit he had on earlier at the World Bank. He set the trash can down by the door and walked to where Neil and Randall were standing by the LPS against the wall where Eve Pallue's once sat. He looked at both Neil and Randall. Randall had his gun in his holster. He knew that he would be dead within a few minutes if he didn't explain himself. God had prepared him on the way over.

"Oh, I just decided to take out some trash from the World Bank before I left," Jonah said with an easy smile that contrasted the tension that was in the room. "The upkeep on that place is appalling."

"We sent you to the World Bank to find a way to get those jewels to us! Yet, here I am reading that there has been a successful robbery at the World Bank. And Charlie Liu and this other guy, Daniels, have found a way to steal the jewelry from us. And you let him walk away with it all!" Neil shouted. "The only reason you are still standing right now is that you risked your life to save mine. So I have to believe this is part of your plan. Randall here thinks differently."

Randall stood with his hands on his hips without saying a word.

"You sent me over there to find a plan to legally get into Eve Pallue's vault, and I did just that," Jonah said.

"We wanted us to legally get in, not a Runner pretending to be Eve's Bodyguard who happens to have her old bank card from almost a year ago!"

Randall interrupted. "Zacchaeus Daniels was a Runner who stole that bank card from Eve Pallue, and you just let him and

Charlie Liu walk away with everything. They must have met at one of the factories and formulated this plan."

Jonah stopped. "That's how the Runner got that card?"

"Yes, he is a Colonial thief and you just let him slip away," Randall said with disgust.

Jonah laughed. "That makes everything perfectly legal then. Nothing wrong with a Bodyguard doing business on behalf of his client."

"But we know that wasn't Eve's Bodyguard. I was," Randall said.

"Now, before you do something too hasty, let me show you what trash I had to throw out of the World Bank," Jonah said, walking back toward the door.

Randall brought the gun out of the holster and pointed at Jonah. "Sorry, Matt. I no longer trust you or what's in that trash can."

"Just wait a minute, Randall. I think I know where this is going," Neil said, making his way to the front door where the trash can waited.

He reached into the can and began to open the drawstring of the large canvas bag within. When he finally opened it, he stared down for several seconds, letting loose a long whistle.

"Randall, put that gun back into its holster. I sent Matt here to do a job, and he has done it," Neil said, shaking his head.

Randall kept his eyes on Jonah. "Are you sure? What's in the bag?"

Neil leaned his back against the wall and pushed the trash can with his right foot until it fell over, spilling out sparkling metals and stones all over the entryway.

Randall's gaze moved toward the scattered jewelry, but he kept his stance facing Jonah. "How did you know they would be coming?"

"Last night, I was watching for any kind of movement in Eve's accounts, and I noticed a new Bodyguard—this Zacchaeus Daniels—added to Eve's profile. You say he's been here before?"

Randall and Neil looked briefly at each other before Randall quickly answered. "Yes, he's the one who delivered

Eve's new Sleeper—the one that was sabotaged and caused her Awakening. That must be when he got the bank card."

"That makes sense," Jonah said and continued. "I went looking for who changed Eve's profile. I knew it had to be an Efficientist—a top one from the look of it. The only person I could think who could break into Eve's profile is Charlie Liu, but he had been declared dead."

"Randall, you will have to take the fall for that. You labeled him too quickly," Neil said, stepping over jewelry and walking back into the living room.

"No, he won't," Jonah continued. "I reinstated Charlie Liu last night along with putting his money points back into his account. Sorry, I had to borrow them from you, Randall. But you can have them back now."

Randall stared at Jonah for several seconds before putting his gun back in the holster. "Were you able to clean up the mess you made moving my money around? And how did you know they would be coming today?" he asked.

"Yes, I covered all of my steps. It had to be today because it's the last day it could be emptied legally without the World Government getting involved," Jonah said. "Somehow, Liu and Daniels got together to pull off this plan. I let Daniels in. He put what he could fit into his briefcase, and I put the rest into the trash can. And he and Liu will take the fall when it's discovered that the Bodyguard profile had been falsified."

"The video cameras will be investigated," Neil said. "They'll see you coming out of the vault with that trash can."

"I went through the video feed and erased everything that needed to be gone. The World Bank will never know that I went into Eve Pallue's vault," he said, smiling.

"Was anyone else with them?" Randall asked.

"No," Matt said. "Just two men—Zacchaeus Daniels came into the bank and Charlie Liu waited in the car. By law Eve Pallue's Bodyguard can open her account with a bank card. How was I supposed to know that Charlie Liu could change Eve Pallue's profile? It's never been done before."

"Are you sure no one else was in the car?" Randall asked. "It seems impossible that only two men could pull off robbing the World Bank."

"Only Charlie Liu. I can send you the photos of both men," Jonah said. Then he added. "And they wouldn't have been able to pull off the robbery without my help. If Neil hadn't wanted what was in Eve Pallue's vault, those two men wouldn't have made it beyond the door, I assure you."

"You know, it's not going to be this simple," Neil interjected. "There will be an investigation. This is unprecedented, so the World Government will be obligated to lay some blame. Is there an account of how much jewelry Eve had in her vault?"

"No, she never listed everything she had. For all the World Bank knows, everything Eve Pallue owned could fit in the briefcase Daniels was carrying. And in regards to the investigation, I understand. I knew there would be repercussions. But I had an assignment to do, and I accomplished it," Jonah said.

"I'll demote you for now, but you will stay on my team. I'll see what deal I can work out. You are a hero in the hearts of the people for saving my life. I'm sure we can arrange something. You've done good, Matt. I asked you to do the impossible and you did it."

"Thank you, sir. It feels good to be trusted with such a sensitive assignment," Jonah said.

"Now, go back to the World Bank and make sure that everything is in order—nothing should be left undone. And then take the rest of the day and tomorrow off. I'll make sure this thing blows over quickly, and we'll get you back on a new assignment. I'm going to need you and that sharp mind of yours ready when you get back."

"I'll be ready," Jonah said. Then he walked around the spilled jewels, and opened the door slowly so as not to damage any of the priceless items. He carefully shut the door behind him.

Neil turned to Randall. "That name, *Daniels,* is sounding more familiar by the second."

"He's the man I hired to tamper with Eve's Sleeper," Randall said, dismissively. "He tampered with Trent's Sleeper before he died. You assigned me to find someone."

"Yes, but it's his last name that rings a bell," Neil said, walking to his LPS. "I've heard that name before." He was just about to put his thumb to the print identifier when Randall interjected.

"Okay, it's just a coincidence. But you hired me to quiet his father several years ago—Austin Daniels, the preacher."

"You hired the son of a man you were paid to kill? That's unnerving of you," Neil said and laughed. "Only you would want to meet the surviving son of the man you took out."

"He's the one who came to me," Randall shot back. "His mom was sick, so he needed to make money for her surgery. He was qualified and the other Runner working for us vouched for him. It's not my fault his father was making too much noise in the Colonies."

"I understand, and I'm not reading into anything. But let us just agree that Zacchaeus Daniels and Charlie Liu will take the fall. The World Government will want an investigation, and we will give them one. However, Liu and Daniels are not a serious threat. Matt is right. There was no way they could have pulled off that robbery without help." Neil said. "Choose someone on your team to go flush them out and silence them."

"I'll take the assignment. I can find them faster than anyone. Very few people on my team know much about the Colonies anyway. It's better if I do it," Randall said.

"Why would I send my best Bodyguard to the Colonies? I need you here," Neil said.

"Matt can watch over things while I'm gone. He saved your life. At least for that, he can be trusted. I won't be gone long. I'll find them and take care of them," Randall said.

"Are you sure you don't have a personal vendetta against this Daniels. He's just a Runner, you know? He's not worth walking away from everything you have here. Unless you enjoy the Colonies?" Neil asked, raising his eyebrows.

Randall's expression became rigid. "The World Government has just been robbed by a Colonial impersonating a Bodyguard. The only reason he got away was that we needed those jewels. But I will not let this worthless Runner live another moment thinking he bested me."

Neil hesitated but then relented. "Fine, just go quickly and get back here. I can see that you're letting your pride get in the way of your work."

"What will you tell Ada?" Randall asked. "She'll want to know why I left."

"I see you are getting attached to Eve Pallue's image consultant," Neil laughed. "Now you're letting love get in the way of your work. What's next? Religion?"

Randall grimaced. "It's not that. Ada is cunning, and she will wonder why I'm gone. She's acquired a lot of influence in the World News."

"Don't worry about her. I'll take care of it. You just go find those two men and get rid of them," Neil said. "Now I need to deal with the robbery of Eve Pallue's vault. You are dismissed," Neil said, sitting down at his LPS. "And I need to figure out what to do with all this jewelry. I know I have some buyers overseas."

Randall turned to leave.

"Oh, and one more thing," Neil said.

"What is it?" Randall asked.

"Don't use a fire this time to silence Daniels and Liu. I think a bullet in the head will do just fine," Neil said and turned back to the LPS screen. "Just make sure you get rid of the evidence."

"Yes, sir," Randall said, walking around the scattered treasure on the floor.

CHAPTER FOUR

"**W**e'll be at the Trading Center in less than an hour," Zach said, looking in the rearview mirror to where Ruth was sitting. "You okay, Ruth?"

She hadn't talked much on the ride home. He didn't want to bother her. He was learning his sister's moods. His mother who was usually good-humored would get into her quiet moods as well—usually when she was thinking about her daughter. Although Ruth and their mother looked very different, Zach could see some similar qualities in their personalities.

"Yes, I'm fine," she answered, staring at the sun's rays streaking through the trees. The large, fiery orb dropped toward the horizon, peeking in and out of foliage surrounding them. "I just wished I could have spoken to Jonah more. I had many questions for him. He was my first real attachment outside of *Life Efficiency*."

"Jonah wanted to talk to you too, but there just wasn't time. I only spoke a few words because I was trying to pack up the jewelry. His plan was brilliant, though. I'll check when we get to Pastor Tom's office to see if anything will be done to him. Bear will be relieved to know that you're still off the radar. It is better this way," Zach said. "I know God had planned it."

"Yes, but you and Li will have to leave," Ruth said, unlocking the briefcase and revealing the sparkling treasure within. "All for the contents of this briefcase."

"That was always the plan," Zach said and smiled. "Don't forget. You sewed pockets into my jacket and pants. I was able to fit quite a few pieces on my body and in that briefcase. I weighed about twenty extra pounds on the way out."

Li laughed. "Watching you empty your pants of all those rings and bracelets was something I never thought I would see. I'm surprised you didn't hide some in your underwear."

"What makes you think I didn't?" Zach chuckled. "I'm just saving that jewelry for later."

Ruth lifted a set of amethyst earrings. "I remember buying these," she said. "I completed my self-study on attachment disorder that I once struggled with because I was reared by multiple mothers."

Zach stopped laughing. His sister rarely discussed her feelings or her childhood, and he wanted to encourage her thoughts. "How many Mothers did you have after our mother?" Zach asked.

"I keep trying to count them, but their faces begin to blur. My father would hire a replacement anytime he thought I was getting too attached. They all had to sign a confidentiality agreement. Even if I searched today, I could not find them."

Zach and Li sat quietly.

Ruth continued. "I concluded in my research that a child should have only one Mother. The Mother may get attached, but the children will eventually grow distant and want their own lives. Producing would eventually shut out all emotions. If the Mother commits suicide after the detachment, she has at least served a purpose. Or so I thought."

Zach finally spoke up. "Do you still agree with that conclusion?"

"I know God does not," she answered. "He loves each person enough to die for her or him. If Mom had not nurtured me for the first five years of my life, I would not be able to form attachments at all today. My father made a gamble with my sanity. I am glad I got to see her one last time before she died," Ruth said. "Although it hurt watching her leave again, I believe it was good for me to have a relationship with her as an adult— even if only for a few weeks."

Li looked at Zach but said nothing. Zach returned his gaze to the road in front of him. The sun was lost behind the hills now, so he turned on the headlights. He looked back at Ruth through the rearview mirror once more. She was still searching through the briefcase of treasure.

"Can I ask you something, Ruth?" he asked.

"Only if I can ask you something in return," she stated without looking up.

"Do you know what you will ask me?" Zach wondered.

"No, but it will be in response to your question," she stated.

"Okay, fair enough. I was just wondering why Bear? I'm only asking because you've been so sheltered, and Bear is really the first man besides me you have met in the Colonies. So how did you know that you loved him?"

Ruth looked up from the jewelry spread across the backseat of the car. "Randall made advances toward me, and at first I liked him. But underneath his exterior, I sensed a lot of unknown. I believe he is not aware of what is inside of him. Someone like that is dangerous. They can commit acts and separate those deeds from their immediate consciousness. I know because I used to be that person."

"And how did that help you with Bear?" Zach asked confused.

"Bear has no unknowns," Ruth said simply.

"Bear is an open book," Zach mused. "Is that all?"

Zach heard silence and looked through the rearview mirror toward the backseat again. His sister's cheeks were reddening. "What is it?" he asked.

"I am attracted to him, as well," she answered quickly.

Zach laughed. "Well, I hope so, Ruth. Would be pretty sad to love someone who you don't find attractive. So what's your question for me?"

"I was going to ask you about Pilar, but I am fairly sure that you do not have a definitive answer."

Zach looked back at the road. "Some things get so knotted up that it's better just to start over."

Ruth nodded her head. "That's what I figured. Instead, I have a question for Li."

Li perked up. "Yes."

"Did Deborah and Esther tell you that I knew you were coming?" Ruth asked.

Li turned his head to face Ruth. "No, Pastor Tom told me."

"Do you remember that night at the PR event when it was your first time at our table?" Ruth asked.

Li seemed confused by her two dissimilar questions. "How could I forget? That was my first day as an Elite Efficientist, and I was replacing a man who had just died in an Awakening."

"When I sat down, you brought up the topic of Mother suicides," she said then paused.

"Yes, I think I remember that. I was simply trying to make a good impression."

"No, it was more than that," Ruth continued. "I researched you on the way to the event, and I discovered that your parents sent your Mother away after thirteen years of caring for you."

"Yes, that is true," he said hesitantly.

"She committed suicide. I thought you would have discussed your thoughts from your experience, but you never did. Why?" Ruth asked.

Li turned to stare out the window. He said nothing for several seconds.

"My parents were older when they had me. To them I was another project. Something to help them gain rank. They hired Ping before I was born to care for me. They brought her from the district of China. When I turned thirteen my parents sent her away without telling me. They agreed with your sentiments that she had served her purpose, and they wanted to lessen my attachments to her."

"How did you feel about her departure?" Ruth asked.

"Why is this topic important to you?" Li asked.

"The thoughts arose in my mind, and instead of burying them again, I am reworking them. That way I will have peace about the issue. I have learned the hard way that it is better to deal with heartache than to let it fester."

Li thought for a moment. "Yes, you are right. I didn't talk about the issue at dinner because I really haven't dealt with it in my personal life."

"Here is your chance," Ruth said.

Li exhaled a deep breath. "Okay. When I discovered that she was gone, I was devastated. I tried to find her, but my parents ensured that she would be untraceable. It wasn't until years later that I discovered she had killed herself. Ping wasn't simply a caregiver to me. She made me feel loved, connected and valued.

She was my world. When I lost her, I worked and produced to cover the pain. I thought if I could just become an Elite Efficientist, I could feel whole again."

"Did you?" Ruth asked.

"No, I came home that night feeling the same way I did when I was thirteen and Ping was gone," Li said. "When I found myself at Deborah and Esther's farm, I felt a little bit of what I was missing."

"Yes, I felt that too," Ruth said.

"What?" Zach asked, obviously enthralled by their conversation. "What were you missing?"

"Family," Li answered.

"Yes, family," Ruth agreed.

The three sat quietly while Zach continued to drive. He thought over the day. He couldn't believe that they had just successfully robbed the World Bank. He had a sudden thought. "Li, what made you say *star* back there before we robbed the bank?"

"I don't know. You asked for a single word and I felt *star* come to mind," Li said. "It was like an impartation or something. It's hard to explain. What did it mean to you?"

Zach stared at the road. "I opened the *Bible* before we left this morning and I read the first part of Genesis. I thought of how God made the sun, moon and stars. I realized that God is like the sun, He can only shine in the day. That is why He sent us Jesus, like the moon, shining in the night. And because of Jesus, we have the Holy Spirit, so we are like the stars shining in the darkness with Him. We have our own light of God in each of us. Li, when you said *star*, I knew that God was with us, individually and as a group."

CHAPTER FIVE

"**H**ere, *Aha-enah*. This is from the sisters at Trinity," Bear said, handing his grandfather a box containing pies.

"Thank you, *Ne'aw-ze*," the grandfather said, taking the box. "So how is our *baynit*? I see she has fallen asleep."

"Yes, I will carry her into the house. Pastor Tom wanted us to stay the night at the Trading Center, but I wanted to get Ruth home," Bear said, grabbing his overnight bag that contained his and Ruth's clothes.

"Here is a flashlight. I did not start a fire inside because I didn't know if we would be leaving right away. I am packed," the grandfather said, handing Bear one of the two flashlights he held. It was early in the morning and the sun still slept under the cover of the horizon.

"We won't be leaving, *Aha-enah*. Ruth's identity was not discovered. She will be safe here for now. You can unpack your things. We have a lot of work to do when the sun comes up. I want to finish putting the floors down for Ruth."

The grandfather's gummy smile could not be seen in the dark, but Bear knew his grandfather was pleased. He did not want to move up north.

"I am happy by this news. I prayed to God for such news, and He has answered my prayer. I think I like this praying. I will do it more often," the grandfather said, taking his box of treats and heading toward the house.

Bear shook his head. "Some prayers are answered right away and others take years," he said to himself. He put the overnight bag around his shoulders and walked to the passenger side of his truck. He opened the door.

"Are we home?" Ruth asked in a sleepy voice.

"Yes, my wife," Bear said. "Would you like me to carry you in?"

"No, I can walk. I need to stretch my legs. I feel like one has gone numb," she said, allowing Bear to grab her waist and bring her gently to the ground.

"I am glad we are done robbing the World Bank," Ruth continued. She carried a small purse that held the amethyst earrings that she wanted to keep. Pastor Tom insisted that she take several pieces of gold as well.

"I didn't realize that I married such a wealthy woman," Bear said smiling. "And intelligent, as well," he added.

"How about beautiful?" Ruth asked, smiling.

"I must admit. I find you more beautiful every day. I didn't like you being away from me," he said. He grabbed her hand and led her down the path to their home, lighting each step of the way with his flashlight.

"You were willing to give up your home and your life for me. Thank you," she said, looking around. The eastern sky was growing warm with light and Ruth knew the sun would be coming up soon.

"Yes, but now we can stay. I've always liked the burns on your hands. They reveal you have been through so much. But now I love them. They kept you safe," Bear said. "I know what it feels like having the world always looking at you, analyzing everything you do. That is why I left the fighting circuit. I didn't want us to have to go through that again."

"Honestly, I would have never have done it if I had not met you," Ruth said, making her way to the front door of their home.

"That doesn't make sense. We are married now. Wouldn't us being together make you not want to expose yourself?" Bear said, trying to prevent himself from feeling hurt. He was learning that sometimes it took him a while to understand Ruth's perspective on things.

Ruth stopped just before they stepped into the house. She reached up and felt the pearl at the nape of Bear's neck with her right hand and reached for her own with her left hand. "I told Pastor Tom before I met my mother that I would not help him with his cause. I was not at the point that I could sacrifice myself for others. I was like a baby who needed everyone's help."

"But don't I help you?" Bear said still confused. "I would have gone with you, but they said I needed to stay here. I couldn't take care of you if I exposed myself."

"No, it is not that. It is that you make me want to be less selfish," Ruth said, struggling to make him understand her thoughts. "You help me to feel beyond myself."

"Oh—I think I understand," Bear said, taking Ruth's hand into his own. "And I feel the same way."

The front door opened. "I have lit the fire," Grandfather said. "I am hungry. Are you two wanting anything from the box the old sisters gave me?"

"No," Ruth said. "The box of treats is yours."

"Good," Grandfather nodded. "Then, I'll be in my room if you need anything."

Bear and Ruth made their way into the living room. Ruth looked around. "It looks like Grandfather has been working on the floors while we have been gone."

Bear surveyed the living room. "You're right. All that is left is the kitchen. We'll finish that tomorrow. Then I'll get started making the cupboards," Bear said, glancing at the mostly bare walls. "I never noticed how much work needed to be done until you moved in."

"Would you build me that desk for my HMS? And now we have one of those old computers that Zach has given me. I need a more comfortable workspace."

"You need to start calling your brother Mark. He's going by his middle name now. And I better stop calling him your brother. I wouldn't be surprised if the World Government is already looking for them," Bear said.

"I am certain Neil will send someone to find them. I pray he will not send Randall," Ruth said, setting her small purse on the counter. "He is good at blending into the Colonies. I showed Pastor Tom a few photos of him and explained that he will probably be impersonating a fur trapper if he does come. Pastor Tom said he will spread the details about Randall."

"Is Pastor Tom certain that no one saw you at the World Bank?" Bear asked with concern.

"No, Jonah has erased my image from all the video feeds. But even if my image is found, I doubt if anyone will recognize me."

"You look nothing like my first impression of you. When I first met you, you looked near death," Bear said. "I had to talk to your brother—I mean Mark—about your well-being. Your mother's sickness and death had almost taken your life."

Ruth said nothing for a moment and reached for her pearl again. "I buried my mother with one of the pearls that helped me begin my new life. Cindy is the one who showed me how to make this chainless necklace. She also helped me begin my life as a seamstress."

Bear nodded. "She and Pastor Tom have a great marriage. They understand each other."

"They do. It was the first real marriage that I had ever experienced. I had not thought of it earlier, but they have greatly influenced my vision of marriage. I am grateful for our relationship with them," Ruth said, thoughtfully.

"Where will Li and Zach—I mean Mark—be going?" Bear asked.

"Pastor Tom has some key leaders that he wants Li and Mark to bring the old-style computers to. They will be driving to the different Colonies, making connections and spreading any news," Ruth said. "The computers need to be spread out, so my writings can stay hidden. Tom has been using his HMS to share my work, but he will eventually be caught. Too much relies on him. Having the computers in key locations will cover our tracks better and protect Trinity Trading Center."

"Tom told me that Li has been working on different viruses to sabotage the World Government. With your writings and Li's viruses, the World Government won't know what hit them," Bear said. "Finally, we can be on the offense."

Ruth smiled at her husband. "I hear you tell your students to always stay on the offense."

"You listen while I train my men?" Bear asked, raising his eyebrows.

Ruth laughed. "I cannot help it. I try to concentrate on my writing, but I hear you yelling at your students constantly. I am surprised they bring you goods in exchange for the beating you give them."

"I have to be harder on them than their enemy would be or else they will never win," Bear said.

"I am glad you trained Mark," Ruth whispered, becoming solemn. "If he has to fight Randall, I do not know if he would win."

Bear became serious. "Mark could win against an average person, but he would struggle against someone who is trained. Let's just pray it never comes to that."

"It will be different now that he is gone," Ruth said.

"You don't have to worry about them. They're kind of on one of those things Paul did in the *Bible*. You know with the other man. I think his name was Silas. They traveled a lot."

Ruth thought. "Yes, it is exactly like that. They are like Paul and Silas on one of their missionary journeys," Ruth agreed. "It was fitting that we circled them and laid hands on them while Pastor Tom prayed."

"You will miss Mark, won't you?" Bear asked.

Ruth thought and nodded. "I will, but I believe that we can find a way to stop the World Government's plans to absorb the Colonies into their system. With Li's virus attacks and my writing, we can definitely create a little chaos."

"I think it's funny that when this is all over, Li wants to own and manage a horse ranch. For someone who can create viruses out of imaginary numbers in the sky, he definitely loves to have his feet in the dirt and his hands working."

"I think that is most of us," Ruth thought. "I love writing, but I also enjoy sewing."

"Then I'm glad we get to stay here. You can write and sew in peace," Bear said. "I've done enough journeys in my life. I've gone all over the Colonies in the fighting circuit. I've even been to the city several times for some of those PR events. I'm ready to stay put, train my men and take care of you."

Ruth felt her cheeks blush. "I want to take care of you too," she whispered.

"Well, we both know you can't cook," he laughed.

"Yes, but you do look nice in the outfit I made for you," Ruth said, smiling.

Bear looked down. He was wearing another gi that Ruth had made, but this one was a deep blue. "I really like the fighting uniforms you've made for me. They are comfortable. The men are wanting some too."

"They like them because they are much more modest than what you used to wear when training," she laughed. "I almost never saw you in a shirt when I first met you."

"Clothes while training never felt comfortable until now," he said. Suddenly, relief swept over his face. He walked up to Ruth and clasped her slender jaw with his rough fingers. "I was so worried for you. I actually held Tom's HMS and prayed."

"Thank you," she whispered. "Do you think he knows?"

"Who?" Bear said.

"Zach."

"You mean Mark," Bear said.

"Yes, do you think he knows that Randall is the one who killed his father?" Ruth asked. "I am worried for him, and I will no longer be able to monitor his moods."

Bear said nothing and looked away for a moment. "He knows."

"He hasn't said anything," she said.

"I know," Bear said. "And that's what worries me."

CHAPTER SIX

Zach looked at the back of the van that Li was driving. They had carefully placed over a dozen old-style computers in the back along with other supplies. He had a list of towns and names of underground churches, but Pastor Tom had specifically told him that God would make their path. Zach scratched his jaw, feeling the beard already growing from his last shave when he disguised himself as a Bodyguard. He would be growing it out. That was the morning he said goodbye to Pilar. She hadn't cried. She only said that she would be praying for him.

Zach missed her. Seeing her everyday while he lived with her family had felt like heaven. He led *Bible* discussion from their home. People began to attend. Her father provided food for all the guests. It was like family—no sick mother, no missing sister, no dead father. He realized that he hadn't felt family like that since the church fire that changed his life. He needed to stop looking at the past. God was doing something now. Maybe God would eventually connect the past with his future, but he struggled with letting go. He looked over to Li driving and cleared his throat.

"What do you know about Randall, Ruth's old Bodyguard?" he asked nonchalantly. "Ruth said that he may be the one looking for us."

Li kept his eyes on the road. "He's ruthless. The only way we can outrun him is to outsmart him. If we were in face-to-face combat with him, we would die."

"Well, that's good to know," Zach said, sarcastically.

"We have his photos. We know what his bio will be. The first thing he'll do is stop at the Sleeper factory you worked at, but that will be a dead-end. He has no idea where I am because I never made it to my destination. The fact that Ruth was not exposed saves us a lot of trouble. She was connected to Pastor Tom, the sisters, me, Bear and you. As long as no one makes the connection between Eve and Ruth, we have nothing to worry about."

"Pastor Tom made the connection," Zach said. "He's an impressive Colonial."

Li nodded. "I truly believe that God has gifted him. I worked hard my entire life to get where I'm at, but Tom seems to dwell in a dimension that speeds up his understanding and ability. I've never seen anyone pick up on things like he does."

"It's called favor," Zach said. "He spends a lot of time in prayer. He gets knowledge straight from heaven, I think."

Li said nothing, so Zach continued.

"How did it feel having hands laid on you?" Zach asked.

"I felt something. I don't know how to explain it, but I felt determination rise up in me," Li said.

"It is weird being called Mark instead of Zach, but I'll get used to it. I'm kind of glad to go by my middle name. Zach comes with so much baggage. It will be nice to be free from it all for a time. My sister seemed to never have a problem being called Ruth. I don't even see her as Eve Pallue."

"Ruth is nothing like Eve," Li agreed. "But to me, you are still Zach. I'll call you Mark in front of others, but to your face, I'll have to call you Zach."

"Yeah, you're right," Zach said. "I still feel like Zach, but it will be fun to be someone else to people who don't know me."

"I can't make out that sign. What does it say?" Li asked, pointing to the right of the road.

"It looks like Chatfield," Zach said, getting out his map.

"Are we still near the Trinity River? Pastor Tom said that most of the towns will be around it."

"Yes, that's our first stop. Cindy's sister and brother-in-law run a small farm there. We will give them the first computer and test it out. They have an old HMS that was unplugged years ago. We need to see if they still have the connection capability. If they had it before, we should still be able to get access," Zach said.

"First of twelve," Li said. "We need at least seven or eight computers set up in order to infiltrate the World Government and cover our tracks, but twelve would be optimal. We have fifteen of them in the back. There's even an old-style laptop. I'll hang onto that one just in case. These old-style computers are so basic that they are almost untraceable."

Zach listened to Li, intrigued that they had found a way to sneak around online without being detected. He briefly looked out the window and saw something from the corner of his eye. "There's someone coming to the street! Do you see her?" Zach asked, pointing.

"Yes, she looks lost. What should I do?" Li asked, tensely holding the steering wheel.

"Pull over. Maybe we can bring her to Cindy's sister's house. They might have someone who would want to help her. She looks really young," Zach said. "No more than seventeen, I would guess."

Li pulled the van onto the grass on the right side just up the road from where the young lady had exited the woods.

Zach looked in the side view mirror. "She's stopped. She's just waiting there. Somethings wrong. I feel it. We need to pray."

"Prayer is good," Li said. "Okay, pray."

Zach bowed his head. "Father, I sense you want us to help this young lady. I promised You that I would be available to do whatever it is that You want. I know You love this child. Help us to help her. I pray this in Jesus' name, amen."

"She's been abused by men," Li blurted.

Zach looked at Li. "How do you know this?"

"I heard it," he said. "And she's not alone."

Zach looked back in the rearview mirror. "I don't see anyone with her."

"She has many with her," Li said, assuredly. "I think God's Spirit is talking to me."

"Great," Zach said. "I'm the one who has been in ministry for years, and you're the one who's getting prophetic ability."

Li closed his eyes. "She's hungry or else she wouldn't have come this far."

"Where are the people?" Zach asked. "We need to hurry up and decide what we're going to do. She's looking back towards the forest."

"All I see is an image of her, but she has many faces. Her body is the same, but her expressions keep changing. I don't understand it."

"Well, I do," Zach said. "Those aren't people with her. They're demons. Look at me."

Li opened his eyes. Zach noticed the astonishment in Li's face. He wanted to laugh but now was not the time. "This girl is not just under the influence of demons. I can guarantee she is full blown demon-possessed. And from what you've said, she is controlled by many of them. I used to help my father with freeing people. And I helped my mom with Bear when he came back. But I've never been the one in charge. We can't just leave that girl there. God has given her hunger to flush her out. I need you to take away all fear at this moment."

Li nodded his head, but his eyes were still wide with apprehension.

"Greater is He that is in you than the evil one in this world. I have seen it. They hate the name of Jesus. But it can't just be a name. There must be belief in the name we speak. We have to believe that the power of Jesus can break strongholds and save lives. The name of Jesus saved you from entering eternity without knowing your Creator, and that very same Name can save this girl from her enslavement to these demons. Do you agree?"

Li blinked his eyes. "Yes, that makes sense. If the name of Jesus is powerful enough to save me from hell, it is powerful enough to save this girl. It is true."

"I don't know what that girl has, but if my mom and I could help free Bear, you and I can help this girl. But you must walk in the authority of Jesus who defeated death. Do you understand?"

"Yes, I'm ready. I signed up for this. I wanted to make a difference. I thought I would only be setting up computers, but saving a girl from being demon-possessed sounds a lot like what Jesus did, so I'll do it."

41

Zach looked in the mirror once more. "Okay, we need to go. She's turning back. Turn off the engine and put the key in your pocket. Make sure to lock your door."

Zach got out of the van. He noticed that the clouds had darkened and covered the sun. Even though it was the afternoon in early autumn, the atmosphere seemed oddly dark and cool. He heard Li's footsteps catch up to his own and keep pace just behind him. As they got closer to the girl, he could see that her clothes were tattered and her hair was matted with dirt and briers. Her skin was filthy, and her face was gaunt.

She stopped and turned to face them. At first, her expression was blank, but suddenly a smiled appeared. "You two need some company?" she said in a sweet voice. "If you have some food to trade, I'll spend some time with you both."

When Zach and Li came up close to her, her smile vanished, and her sweet voice turned rough and low. "Never mind. I see that you two have nothing good for me."

The girl turned to leave.

"We come in the name of Jesus Christ, the Son of God who saves His people and sets captives free. I call on the mighty Lion of Judah, the Lamb of God, to bring the power of the Holy Spirit into this place! You can no longer live in this girl!"

The girl smiled again and said sweetly. "I don't know what you're talking about. I'm alone."

"That is not what God told me," Li said, taking a step toward the girl. "He told me that you have many evil spirits living within you. He said that you have been abused."

The girl's face twisted into anger. "You know nothing about me! People don't hurt me! I hurt them! Now leave me alone before I hurt you too!"

"We have food for you," Zach said. "We will give you something to eat if you let us talk to you just for a minute."

The girl stopped. The anger was frozen for several seconds and then replaced with thoughtfulness. Her voice changed to a higher pitch but continued to be rough. "There is nothing you can say that I haven't heard. You think there haven't been others who tried to pray for me? I asked to be filled with this power. I was tired of being abused by others. No one has touched me without my permission since I left."

"You left almost two years ago," Li said, looking over the young women's shoulder. "I see it. That house where they drugged you and let men touch you. I see you leaving. I see you alone."

The girl looked behind her. "How do you see that?"

"You asked God to help you. He sent you to another house. A house with a family. But you were too scared to go in. You didn't trust Him, so you walked away. You've been alone for almost two years."

"They would have just hurt me too!" the girl yelled. "That father. I saw him! He kissed his daughter when she was lying in bed."

"That's what good fathers do," Zach interjected. "They kiss their kids goodnight. Did he do anything else?"

The girl looked confused. "No, but he's a man. He could hurt her. He would hurt me!"

Zach looked at the young girl. She had been hurt over and over again by men. He thought it was interesting that God would send him and Li to help her. It was his father, Austin Daniels, who truly had a heart for the brokenhearted. He needed some of his dad's compassion. He prayed silently for help before continuing. "Jesus never hurt anyone. In fact, He loved them so much that He died to free us. Those demons with you do not love you. You think they protect you, but they are killing you. You're starving to death."

"They give me power to protect myself," she shot back.

Zach knew the girl was talking now. "Where do you sleep every night?"

"I sleep on the ground," she said.

"Do bugs get on you?" he asked.

"Yes," she answered. "What does it matter?"

"What do you eat every day?" he asked.

"I find stuff," she said.

"Where do you go to the bathroom?" he asked.

"Why are you asking me these things?" she yelled.

"Because I'm trying to show you that you are not being protected at all. You are simply being isolated. These demons who have you are evil. And they want to dwell in you because you have been made in God's image. God loves you. He wants to care for you, but you have to trust Him."

"But where was God when I was sold by my mother? Where was He when the men gave me those shots in my arm and touched me and hurt me? Where was God when I ran away!"

"He was in the forest with you that night, as you watched that family through the window. He was telling you to go to that family. They would take care of you," Li said. "And now He's telling you to trust us. We will take you to another family."

"They will hurt me!" she yelled.

"I will make sure that they won't touch you. Just give them a few days. If you don't like them, you can leave. But just give yourself a chance to eat real food. Sleep in a real bed. Wash in a real bathroom. There will be no shots and no men abusing you," Zach assured. "But you have to be willing to trust and take a chance. The worst that can happen is that you wind up back here."

The girl hesitated. "But what about the others?"

"Let's tell them to leave. You had them for a while. You know what they can do and how they protect you. But let us try something different. Did you know that God's Spirit can live inside of you instead?"

The girl's eyes widened. "Really?"

"Yes, and there is nothing stronger than God because He has created everything. You can have God's Spirit in you instead of those voices, and He will give you the strength to handle anything."

For the first time, the girl looked hopeful. "I feel them getting angry," she whispered.

"You have to be willing," Zach said. "I will ask God to move in and move those others out, but You have to be opened to God for Him to move."

The girl's face began to twist with rage. "Yes, hurry!" she screamed.

Zach's voice rose up, and he pointed his finger at the young girl. "You heard the girl! She wants you to leave! I command you demons to leave this girl now in the name of Jesus. The Holy Spirit is moving in!"

The girl's eyes fluttered. "But you don't know us," she said in a low voice that was unnatural for her.

"I sense anger," Li said hesitantly.

"I pray in the name of Jesus that the demon of anger leaves this girl now!"

The girl fell to the ground and began to writhe.

"And fear!" Li yelled.

"I pray in the name of Jesus that the demon of fear leaves this girl now!"

The girl kicked her legs and thrashed her arms.

"Should we help her?" Li asked.

"No, we can't touch her. It will cause the girl to mistrust us. It's not done. What else is there?"

Li closed his eyes. "I sense—something like dying in her," Li said.

"And the demon of death! You must leave this girl in Jesus' name!"

"No! No!" the girl screamed in the low voice. "We won't leave."

"Yes, you will!" Zach shouted. He stood over the girl and pointed at her again. "I have the authority and power of Jesus Christ who overcame Satan himself. You must obey me. Leave this girl at once and never return!"

The girl convulsed on the ground for several more seconds until suddenly, she stopped. Instantly, her face brightened and her body relaxed.

Zach and Li hovered over her.

"Is it done?" Li asked.

"Yes, it is," Zach said. "Honestly, she was a lot easier than some others I've dealt with."

"I find that hard to believe," Li said, looking at the girl sleeping peacefully on the ground. "It was like she wanted the evil spirits in her."

Zach nodded his head. "Yes, she did, which was why I needed to get her to want them to leave. It's hard to make demons leave if they have an open invitation. Right when she wakes up, we need to lead her in the salvation prayer. Then we need to get her to Cindy's sister's house."

"Move the evil out. Move God in. And find a loving family," Li said. "That's what happened to me—although, definitely not as dramatic."

"She's had a dramatic life," Zach agreed. He turned to Li. "You've had prophetic visions of her present and past. Now what about her future?"

Li thought for a moment. "I think she will help young women like her. She will return to the place she left and set them free."

"We'll give her that word of prophecy before we leave for our next stop. It could give her pain some purpose."

CHAPTER SEVEN

"So how's the move coming along?" Jonah asked after Dr. Linton opened the door to his flat.

"Come on in, Matt," Dr. Linton sighed and closed the door after Jonah entered.

"I'm settled in as much as I want to be. I didn't want to leave my house on the outskirts of the town. The last thing I want to do is live in the city, specifically in this building."

"Neil said you can visit your home on the days you have off. It's not like you're gone for good," Jonah said cheerfully. "I have to be honest. It will be nice to have the good doctor close."

Dr. Linton gave a half smile. "Randall left this morning. How do you feel about taking over his team for a while?"

"I think the team wasn't too happy about me being in charge, but they'll get used to me."

"You were the best pick," Dr. Linton said. "Too many egos on that team. I think you were everyone's second choice."

Jonah laughed. "Because everybody was their own first choice. I believe you're right."

Jonah walked down into the living room of the flat toward the balcony. He looked out the sliding glass door. "I've never been to a flat on the second floor. Didn't Neil offer you one close to his penthouse?"

"Yes, but I opted out. I'd rather be closer to the ground," Dr. Linton said, opening the sliding glass door. "Look, the stairs come right past my living room. I feel safer knowing that if something happens, I can get out quickly."

Jonah looked around. "It's also easy access for others. You better make sure your alarm is set every night."

Dr. Linton nodded. "The first thing I did when I arrived is figured out the security system."

Jonah stayed outside enjoying the early morning sun. "You don't trust the city much. Why did you ever want to leave the Colonies?"

"I've learned to trust no one. My parents were poor and did sharecropping on different people's land. No matter how hard he worked, my father always walked away from each crop he produced poorer than before. The landowners took everything. My sisters and I barely had enough to eat. I had to steal crops from others to feed us because my father wouldn't let us touch his crop."

"I never knew this," Jonah said surprised. "Why have you never gone back to visit your family?"

"I was ten when my youngest sister died. She was too young and hungry to fight off a simple infection. After her death, my mom took my other two sisters and went back to her hometown. My mom couldn't afford to take all of us, so I stayed," Dr. Linton said, pausing in thought.

"How did you afford to go to school?" Jonah asked curiously.

"A landowner took pity on me. He said if I could get accepted into a college that he would pay for it. I studied every night. After college, I got accepted into medical school free of charge as long as I repaid each year of school and training with a year of work. I only had a year left until I would be free before I met..." Dr. Linton stopped.

"That's when you took care of Eve Pallue," Jonah finished.

"Yes, I guess everyone knows about that," Dr. Linton said. "My final year was paid off by the World Government and I was free to work for pay."

"You don't sound too happy about it," Jonah said, looking at Dr. Linton.

"I was so restless to leave. If I would have just waited, I would have completed that final year already, and I would truly be free."

"You could leave anytime," Jonah said.

"I know too much. Randall would be on my heels if I left," Dr. Linton said.

"It's been a year. Don't you think you should know when your contract is up?"

"The only contract I have signed is one for confidentiality," Dr. Linton said. "There was never a contract for how long I would be required to work."

"Then you are free. You just need to have a chat with Neil about when you can resign. You can't forget that he is just a man."

Dr. Linton shook his head. "With the authority of the World Government behind him."

"The World Government looks intimidating, but it's a mess. Don't be ruled by fear or you'll make your condition worse."

"What's my condition?" Dr. Linton asked. "Since you seem to know so much."

"You've been enslaved to landowners, to your father, to the hospital and now to the World Government. I think you are your own problem. You are so used to being ruled that you don't know how to be free. Even now you are free, but fear has kept you captive."

Dr. Linton said nothing. He leaned on the railing of the balcony and looked down to the street below.

"Death is not freedom either," Jonah said. "You have no idea how to live as a free man."

Dr. Linton looked at Jonah. "Maybe you're right. I have lived in the Colonies and with these Efficientists and no one seems to know what the hell they're doing. They are all lost."

"Do I seem lost to you?" Jonah asked.

"You, I can't figure out. You are in the same boat that I am. We are both working for the World Government and we both know too much. But you have something more. I don't know what it is. I don't even know if I can trust you."

"Do you think I intend to harm you?" Jonah asked.

"No, I don't feel that, not like I feel with Randall," Dr. Linton admitted. "But I also don't know whose side you're on. You seem to pass right over everyone's sensor, like you're on another level. I don't know if you are oblivious to it all or just cunning."

"Maybe I'm both," Jonah said, laughing.

Dr. Linton looked at Jonah for several seconds before asking his next question. "I took care of Charlie Liu quite often when he became an Elite. We got along fairly well. In fact, he reminded me of myself—or, I guess, a version of myself if I would have grown up as an Efficientist. I would have never expected him to risk his rank, let alone his life. He's now a wanted felon for robbing the World Bank. I don't get it."

Jonah watched Dr. Linton struggle with his thoughts for a moment as he gathered his own. "Maybe he found that something *more* you mentioned earlier."

Dr. Linton pushed away from the railing. "Here's what really gets me. Charlie Liu robbed the bank with that man who worked at the plant, but the records show that Charlie never made it to the plant. In fact, the Runner factory was not on his itinerary. How did those two meet?"

Jonah rubbed his chin with the knuckles of his right hand and stood quietly. Dr. Linton fidgeted in the silence.

"Never mind. I shouldn't have brought it up. I've just been analyzing things that I should be ignoring," Dr. Linton confessed. "I'm trying to make sense of it all, but I'm only getting more confused."

"Zach Daniels. That's the man who was with Charlie Liu at the bank. He's the person you visited when you went into the Colonies several months ago, isn't he? I covered your tracks, so you wouldn't be found out."

Dr. Linton froze. His fingers held on tightly to the balcony railing. "His mother was sick. I was just trying to help him," Dr. Linton confessed. "How did you know?"

"I looked up the location before erasing the fact that you left without permission," Jonah said. "I knew you were probably just helping a friend."

"I wouldn't say we are friends," Dr. Linton said. "I've happened to take care of his family before."

"Did you meet anyone else in the Colonies while you were there?" Jonah asked, staring at Dr. Linton intently.

Dr. Linton said nothing, keeping his gaze on Jonah's face. "No, I didn't meet anyone else," Dr. Linton finally said. "Just Zach and his mother."

Jonah continued to stare at Dr. Linton for several seconds. "It's best you keep that information secret for your own safety. If Neil Elder finds out that you secretly visited Zach Daniels, he might accuse you of aiding and abetting him in the first robbery of the World Bank."

Dr. Linton shook his head. "You see what I mean? There's no one I can truly trust."

"And you think people can trust you?" Jonah asked.

"Why wouldn't they?" Dr. Linton asked.

"It depends," Jonah answered. "If you intend to harm or help."

"I'm a doctor. I help people," Dr. Linton said.

"Let's keep it that way, and people will trust you," Jonah answered. He looked back toward the sun rising in the east. "Well, I better go. I only wanted to welcome you to the building. Let me know if there is anything I can do for you. I'm always available."

Tom sat in his office, staring at the two printouts that came out of the printer attached to the old-style computer. He leaned back in his chair, allowing his thoughts to build onto the abstract construction in his mind. He loved being a mastermind behind the scenes. He thought stepping down from the pulpit would change his life, and in fact it did—for the better. Although he still secretly met with people within the Trinity Trading Center, his days of shepherding a small church were over. He now had the honor of shepherding a faith movement that would sweep across the world, and his bird's eye view was breathtaking.

"What are you staring at so intently?" Cindy asked from the doorway. "I've been watching you for almost a minute now, and I see excitement written all over your face."

Tom came out of his thoughts. "I just got two correspondences today. One from Jonah—um, I mean Matt. And the other is from Li."

"Did Zach and Li make it to my sister's house?" Cindy asked.

"Honey, we really have to use their new names. There's always a possibility that people are watching us, and if we say the names *Zach* and *Charlie Liu*, we'll compromise everything," Tom said. "I know it seems silly, but it's better to be safe."

"Okay, did Mark and Li make it to the house?" Cindy asked.

"They did—after an altercation with a young woman on the side of the road."

"Really? What happened?" Cindy asked, entering the room and sitting on one of the chairs.

"They ran into a girl who was demon-possessed," Tom began.

"Oh no," Cindy gasped. "Li is a young Christian. How did he handle it?"

"He was awesome. It seems that God has gifted him with prophetic abilities. He said he knew things about the young woman's life that were secret. God was giving him insights, so they could have an access point to reach her."

"Really, and he has absolutely no training?" Cindy asked unsure.

"That's the thing that is exciting," Tom said. "Do you know what I read today during my quiet time?"

"What?" she asked.

"I read about Matthew the Tax Collector. Do you know that he went from a reviled tax collector to an apostle almost overnight? Jesus called him, and he instantly left the tax office and followed Him, becoming one of the twelve disciples. No training—just blind faith."

"What does that mean?" Cindy asked. "Is Li called out like Matthew?"

Tom got out of his seat, holding the two printouts. He started to pace and reread the words that he had painstakingly deciphered before printing and deleting them.

"I feel in my spirit that God is raising up an army of Matthews. His grace is going to fall on everyone, gifting them everything they need to achieve His will. They'll be so lost and broken that they'll instantly jump into this new life with Jesus. Unlike me who it took years for God to rewire my religious thinking, these people will have no rewiring—just emptiness for God to fill."

Cindy sat silently for a moment. "Kind of like Ruth and Li. They gave up everything to follow Jesus."

"Yes, exactly!" Tom said. "Do you see? They lost everything at once, instead of losing it slowly over the years like I did. I'm not saying one is better than the other. But they will be able to achieve a lot more than us in a shorter amount of time."

"I don't know," Cindy smiled. "You are impressing me more and more every day."

Tom went to the chair next to his wife and sat down. "I enjoyed preaching, but I find so much joy in this," he said, holding up the printouts. "I love watching God's movements unfold before me. I see His Kingdom being established on earth."

"You've studied *Life Efficiency* from the backseat for so many years. I knew in my heart that your diligence and sacrifice each day would finally pay off," Cindy said.

"I never understood it before. Why did I have such a fascination with the World Government and what was going on in *Life Efficiency*? Other pastors would criticize my efforts or say I was secretly envious. But now I know God had given me this passion for a reason. And because of it, I have a perspective that very few people have, which includes a panoramic view of both Efficientists and Colonials and their interactions with each other."

Cindy reached over and stroked the side of her husband's cheek. "I never doubted you for a second. I didn't understand it, but I knew you were staying obedient to what God was leading you to do. Of all the pastors in the Colonies, Eve Pallue landed at your church."

Tom set the papers on his lap and took his wife's hand. "I couldn't have done it without you. None of this would have been possible without you by my side. You've made me a great dad, pastor and husband because of your belief in me. Thank you for never doubting me."

"Of course," she whispered, squeezing his chin before bringing her hand back. "Now, what does Matt have to say?"

"I have two monkey wrenches right now that I'm praying about. Well, more than that, but these two threaten the safety of our people."

"Is one wrench about Dr. Linton?" Cindy asked.

"Yes, I've already told everyone about him and that he knows that Ruth is still alive. Li wasn't happy about the news, but God really protected him because he never made it to his first stop. God brought him straight to the sisters' farm, which is a miracle of protection in itself. But now he's linked to Zach and Zach to Ruth. So Dr. Linton knows something is going on, but we had to take that risk."

"Okay, that sounds a little confusing, but I'm getting it. Is Dr. Linton a threat?"

"See that's the monkey wrench. Jonah—I mean, Matt," Pastor Tom said, looking at his wife. "Sorry, I just did what I told you not to do. Let me just use their real names for a moment because I'm getting confused."

Cindy smiled. "I would appreciate that."

"Okay, so Jonah knows that Dr. Linton went to visit Zach, and he has kept the information to himself. It's been months, and if Neil finds out that he went to the Colonies in secret, Dr. Linton might find himself caught up in a fire somewhere. Plus, Zach is now connected to the World Bank robbery, so the last thing Dr. Linton is going to do is expose that he knows Zach. This will keep Ruth's identity safe for now."

"Does Dr. Linton know that Jonah is on our side?" Cindy asked.

"No, never. Dr. Linton knows nothing about our side or our movement. No one must find out who Jonah is. Honestly, I don't even know who Jonah is. There is barely any information on this man anywhere. I can only find that he was Christina Straight's Bodyguard for many years and that's it."

"How could he possibly have gotten this close to Neil Elder without a clear background history?"

"God. That's the only answer I can find. This man has a lot of faith. Plus, he knows a thing or two on the LPS. He completely erased the fact that Ruth was at the World Bank during the robbery."

"Okay, so this monkey wrench is making a mess. I don't see a clear answer," Cindy said, shaking her head.

"You're right. There isn't one. And that's when I give it to God. He knows things that I don't know, and I won't mess them up just because I don't understand. If I try to fix the situation, I know I will only make it worse."

"Wow, I see your faith is growing," Cindy said. "This coming from a man who usually has to understand everything."

"I have to trust God because there are so many moving parts that are out of my control, but it feels good—the not fully knowing but trusting anyway."

"Okay, so that is one monkey wrench. Now what's the other?"

Tom picked up one of the printouts and inhaled deeply. "Zach knows that Randall killed his father in the fire."

"You mean, Mark," Cindy teased. "Everyone else knows, so I'm not surprised that he's figured it out. It's a horrible situation, but why is it a monkey wrench?"

"Because Zach is not talking about it with anyone—not his sister, not Li and not me. And if there is one thing I'm certain of, revenge of a loved one can be a powerful force."

"Do you think he's planning something?" Cindy asked.

"I don't think he consciously planning something. At least, I don't sense anything in his correspondence to me," Tom said.

Cindy paused for a long moment. "Do you think Randall knows who Zach is?"

"If he doesn't know, he'll soon find out," Tom replied. "There's too much evidence linking Zach to his father. And if he does know, he will want to finish what he started at the church fire."

CHAPTER EIGHT

Randall drove his truck carefully over the uneven terrain that led to the gas station and the small diner. Fur trading supplies filled the bed of his truck, and he didn't want anything tipping over. He needed gas, food and information. He'd been to this station before, and he was hoping to find a loose-mouthed Runner who wanted to talk. The diner was in close proximity to the Sleeper factory that Zacchaeus Daniels had worked at. Maybe he would find an old co-worker or just a town-crier.

Randall stopped his truck and put it in park. He held on to the steering wheel, analyzing his surroundings. The factory hadn't closed yet, so the diner was still fairly empty. He'd wait a few more minutes before he found a seat at a table inside.

He had been at the factory earlier that week and had spoken to the director who was over Zach Daniels' department. The man was an idiot. Randall couldn't believe he was an Efficientist. Being in the Colonies so long had turned his brain to mush. He'd received a notice on his LPS that Daniels was terminated from the management position at the plant, but he never thought to verify the information. Randall easily traced the notice, and it had come straight from the director's own LPS. Zach Daniels must have written the letter himself and sent it to the director. The factory records showed that he never came back to work after that day.

Zach Daniels' house was a bust, as well. A new family had moved in and had been living there for several weeks. If there had been any evidence of Daniels' life there, it had been trampled over by kids and dogs. The new tenants had never heard of Zach Daniels. They were new to that district, coming from a Sleeper factory miles away.

Randall wasn't upset, though. Finding Zach Daniels too easily would have been a disappointment, especially after he learned who his father was—Austin Daniels, the preacher who died in a fire, trapped in his church.

Randall heard a loud clatter and instantly reached for his gun in his hip holster. He looked into the rearview mirror and saw a Runner opening the large metal door to his box truck. He withdrew his hand and looked around to see if there were any passersby outside his windows. He was surprised at how jumpy he was. Working with Neil and heading his team had put him on edge. He would be called out quickly if he didn't relax a little bit. He needed a few more days to adjust to the Colonies before he did serious investigating. He would do a trial run today—just try to fit in and chat to a few people.

He thought back to the church fire. That was his first big job for the World Government. It seemed fitting that he was here now after all these years to completely finish what he had started. He knew that Zach Daniels was the main culprit of the bank robbery. He'd lost his father and his mother. He had a vendetta against the World Government for taking his father's life, and he had nothing to lose. He wondered if Zach knew what role he had played in his father's death. Probably not. From what he knew about Zacchaeus Daniels, he was indifferent and lacked ambition. The only reason that bank robbery succeeded was that Neil Elder wanted what was in that vault. Randall would make sure to tell Zach that bit of information before disposing of him.

Randall replayed the night that Zach tried to contact Eve Pallue. Was he trying to warn her about her Sleeper? He couldn't have possibly known she was in danger. No one had died in an Awakening up until that night when the Elite Efficientist, Trent, died. And how did Zach get his hands on Eve's bank card? She had kept it in her lock box in her room. He could have easily slipped in while she was working. Randall knew that Eve would get so immersed in her work that she would be oblivious to everything around her, including him. Zach probably used the bank card as a trophy to tell all his buddies about his time in the city with Eve Pallue. But Zach did appear to be extremely agitated that night. Maybe he was on some sort of illegal stimulant and his guilty conscience got the best of him.

He thought about Charlie Liu. He definitely did not seem like a guy who would rob the World Bank. Zach must have gotten to him somehow before he reached the factory. He still had the bank card and saw his chance for revenge and financial gain. He must have bribed spies at the factories to feed him information on incoming Efficientists. Only he and Neil Elder knew which stops Charlie Liu would be making, but Charlie must have notified the factory director of his arrival.

Zach had a bank card, so all he needed was an Efficientist to help him change his status to Bodyguard. Though he never thought Charlie Liu would turn criminal, he was impressed by his nerve. It took a lot of guts or stupidity to rob the World Bank. Now they had enough money to buy anything, pay off anyone and go anywhere. Honestly, Randall would be surprised if Zach and Charlie were still in the area. They could have bought a plane or ship with the jewels they stole and be halfway across the world by now.

Randall looked through the windshield at the diner and tapped his fingers on the steering wheel. He looked in the rearview mirror. He could see people walking in the distance and a few cars coming into the parking lot. He would leave in one minute. He leaned toward the passenger side of the truck and picked up the bag on the seat. He set it on his lap and opened it, fishing through the thick stack of papers. He finally found what he was looking for. It was a photo of Matt Coughlin walking with Daniels in the lobby of the World Bank. He flipped to the next photo. Charlie Liu sitting in the vehicle. He brought the photo closer. He could see no one else in the car with him.

Matt had done an excellent job erasing any video feed that would suggest he took the jewels out of Eve Pallue's vault and hid them in a trash can. In fact, there was almost no video left except for a few seconds of Zach and Matt walking through the lobby and a few minutes of Charlie Liu sitting in the vehicle. It was better to have too little video than too much, revealing the plan that Matt had accomplished. Neil wanted those jewels, and Matt delivered. But that was last week. Now he needed to focus on finding Zach and Charlie Liu.

Charlie Liu would be a dead-end. No one knew who he was in the Colonies. Zach's mother had recently died, and he had no siblings, so he needed to find a few of Zach's friends. He dropped out of Colonial college several years ago and had been a Runner ever since. Runners were liked in the Colonies because they interacted with famous Efficientists. People wanted to hear stories from the city. Zach had met plenty of famous people, so there had to be Colonials who had listened to him talk. He needed to find someone who knew too much and talked too often. Or he needed to find someone Zach cared about. But from what he knew about Zach so far, he doubted he cared about anyone besides his mother who had recently died. Zach had been childhood friends with a fighter called the Shaman who traveled the fighting circuit in Colonies. He had done a little research, but from what he could see, the Shaman had disappeared. The Shaman wasn't his real name, though. He would investigate some more tonight to find if he lived in the area and if he was still friends with Zach Daniels.

"Ruth, get up from that HMS and come outside with me," Bear said, pacing the tile floors of their living room.

"I am trying to understand this," Ruth said, motioning to the *Bible* sitting on the large desk that Bear and Grandfather made her. "I see something, but I cannot grasp it."

"Look, you've been sitting here typing for three days. Today is my day off, and I want to get out of this house. I'm tired of building things and fixing things in this house. I need to get out and actually feel fall coming."

"It is still warm outside," Ruth said, looking out the window. The trees lining the river still blanketed the sun, but she knew that soon the hot, yellow sphere would be rising above them all, heating up the day.

"It's several degrees cooler than just a week ago. You would know that if you would go outside. I can see your muscles atrophying before my eyes," Bear said, staring at Ruth's arms.

"I'm not asking anymore. Stop what you are working on, get dressed and come for a walk with me before it gets too hot outside."

Ruth stared at Bear for several seconds and then looked back down at her desk. "I am getting nowhere with this article anyway. I almost want to erase every single word of it."

"Don't erase it. Just save it, and let's go," Bear said, crossing his arms.

Ruth leaned back in her chair. "You look quite handsome when you are angry."

"Thank you for the compliment. Now get your tail up and get dressed," Bear said, resolutely.

"Okay," Ruth finally admitted defeat. "But I want to hear about what God is teaching you while we walk. I see you reading your *Bible*."

"Fine. You walk. I'll talk. Let's go."

Ruth quickly walked to their bedroom and got dressed in a pair of denim pants she had recently made and a plain white t-shirt. She scanned the vanity that Bear had built her. The make-up Pilar gave her several months ago was placed neatly in different baskets. Ruth powdered her face and carefully added the dark brown eyeliner around her almond-shaped, brown eyes. Then she took some tinted lip balm on her fingertip and smoothed it over her lips. She stared at her image and took some more lip balm and dotted her cheekbones, blending the pink hue like Pilar taught her. Finally, she grabbed the brush and pulled the bristles through her mid-length hair. She adjusted the small pearl that she always wore just above her collar bone on a thin nylon cord.

She reached for her brown, leather moccasins. She copied the design from Bear's moccasins. She remembered that she wanted to make him a new pair. His were over a decade old. She would surprise him with them. She slipped the shoes over her feet and walked back into the living room.

"I am ready," she said simply.

Bear stood in the kitchen, packing a small burlap bag with nuts and dried fruit. He looked up and gawked. "You look amazing," he said.

Ruth felt her cheeks become hot. "I am glad it does not take much effort to impress you," she said, trying to cover up her embarrassment.

"I almost want to keep you home now," he said, pulling the strings on the small bag and tying it closed.

"No, you made me get ready. Now I want to walk. Just keep us in the shade of the trees."

He laughed. "Of course, I will. Look how white you are. I wouldn't want you to burn."

Ruth smiled. Bear was always aware of the external elements of her surroundings.

The pair walked outside, and Bear set a brisk pace that Ruth could keep.

"Where is Grandfather?" Ruth asked.

"He ran some errands for me. He's heading to Levi's house. He trapped two rabbits yesterday, and he wants to make a trade."

"Did you save me the furs?" Ruth asked.

"They're in my storeroom as we speak. I cleaned and dried them this morning. I'll start the tanning process. How soft would you like them?"

Ruth thought about Bear's new moccasins. "Could you make them medium firmness but pliable enough to sew? I have an idea for them."

"Your wish is my command," he said, chuckling.

"What is Grandfather trading for?" Ruth asked.

"He says cornmeal and flour, but I think he just wants sweets," Bear said. "He's an old man. He deserves to have his small indulgences."

"I miss Pilar," Ruth said.

"You can have her over anytime. I know that since… Mark left, she has been really quiet," Bear said, stumbling over Zach's new name.

"Mark—I pray for him and Li every day. I am thankful that Pastor Tom keeps us updated. I miss Deborah and Esther too, but Cindy says that they have their hands full. I finally have a family and friends and we are all scattered now," Ruth said and became quiet.

"I'm glad you and I are together and here," Bear said. "Now watch your step. We're going to cross the river here because it's shallow."

"I don't want to get my shoes wet," Ruth said.

"See the path of rocks above the current?" Bear asked, pointing to large, flat rocks that formed a path across the river.

"Yes, I see them," Ruth said.

"Just follow my lead. The rocks should be fairly steady."

Ruth followed behind Bear. He moved from rock to rock with ease. While she had to wave her arms around to balance, he landed on each rock nimbly. He even skipped several rocks, jumping them by twos or even threes.

Bear finally made it to the other side and instantly turned around to face her. "Okay, just a few more and I'll help you to land."

"You make it look so easy," she said, catching herself from falling to the left.

"Don't talk. Just concentrate. You're anticipating too much. Just jump and counteract once you hit the rock."

Ruth finally made it to the last rock, and Bear grabbed her hand and brought her to the land. "What do you mean by anticipating?" she asked.

"I simply mean that you overanalyze with your head. Sometimes you just have to feel with your body."

Ruth nodded. "It is hard for me to stop thinking," she admitted.

"I know," Bear said, grabbing her hand and continuing their walk.

"Let me hear your thoughts," Ruth said, as she came aside Bear and kept his pace. "What have you been reading in the *Bible*?"

Bear scanned the area. Ruth knew he was looking for danger before he became slightly sidetracked by his thoughts. "I've been reading the Book of John. I really like it because Jesus is making everyone uncomfortable with His talk about being God's Son. He lost most of His followers at one point."

Ruth nodded. The entire book opened in her mind. As Bear talked, she could see the verses come up from her memory.

"Go on," she said when she noticed he was waiting for her to respond.

"Well, the one part that really gets me is Judas—the one who betrayed Jesus. He held the money bag. He must have been really trusted to have that position out of all the twelve disciples."

"Why is that?" Ruth asked. She had never reflected on that revelation before.

Bear looked at Ruth and laughed. "Of course, you wouldn't get that because you have no sense of money."

"I understand money," Ruth said.

"Yes, but you've never been in need, so you don't understand what it means to entrust someone with your money. You have to really trust him."

"I trust you," she said, defensively.

"Ruth, I know you trust me, but with money, it's not about trust with you. You really just don't care about it."

"Is that good or bad?" Ruth asked.

"It's neither. It's just who you are," Bear said.

"I always considered myself objective, but I guess no one can truly be objective," Ruth said. "I need to open my mind to more perspectives."

Bear nodded. "The only way you can do that is to get off that HMS and get around people."

"So why does Judas stand out to you?" Ruth asked. She was curious about what else Bear would say.

"When I first started fighting, I had a manager. He helped me after I separated from my dad. I worked with him for many years until I learned that he was stealing from me. I trusted him, and he betrayed me," Bear said and turned to Ruth. "The land is inclining. Do you want to take a small rest before going up?"

"No, but can we move a little slower as we go up?" she asked, panting. The walk was making her feel better, but she wanted to concentrate on what Bear was saying.

"Sure, I'll slow down a little."

"So, you were upset?" Ruth asked.

"You can say that. I broke his jaw," Bear said, becoming serious. "This man deceived me. I trusted him with all of my winnings. He smiled to my face all the while taking what was mine. Judas was trusted, but Jesus knew what he was doing."

"Yes, he told the disciples at the Last Supper," Ruth said.

Bear abruptly stopped. "And that's another thing that gets me."

"What?" Ruth asked, stopping next to him.

"That Last Supper deal—it's different in all four books—Matthew, Mark, Luke and that last one…"

"John," Ruth added.

"Yes, and that one. When Jesus was telling them who His betrayer was, they each say something different," Bear said.

Ruth could see stress coming across Bear's face, but she waited for him to continue his thoughts.

"One book says that Jesus put the bread into the bowl and handed it to Judas, and that's how they knew he was the betrayer. But another book says that Jesus and Judas reached into the bowl together. Another says that they were each holding bread when they both reached into the bowl. And the last one doesn't mention the bread or bowl at all—just that there's a betrayer. If the *Bible* is true, why isn't every story the same?"

Ruth could envision each story in her mind. The phenomenon of slightly different accounts was something she learned long ago as she studied history in her college prep classes as a young adult. She thought of how she could explain it to Bear.

"In each account is the betrayer the same man?" she started.

"Yes, Judas is the betrayer," Bear said.

"What other details are the same?" she asked.

Bear looked up and thought for a moment. "They were in the Upper Room. It was Passover. Jesus and His disciples were there."

"Yes, those elements are all the same," Ruth said, thinking. "Remember that I told you that I learned about you from reading articles I found from the HMS?"

"Yes," Bear nodded. "Instead of just asking me, you read about my personal life on the HMS. Those Efficientists loved to write about me."

Ruth ignored Bear's small jibe. "The Colonials wrote about you also. In fact, they were much more descriptive. I read several articles by them concerning one of your first fights. People were astonished that you won because you were losing at first."

"Yes, that's a ploy I used to gain more recognition," Bear said. "I would take a beating, so the win was more memorable for people."

"I never realized that was what you were doing," Ruth said, pausing for a moment. "You won by using an armbar, correct?" she asked and waited.

"Yes, that's right," Bear said, thinking.

"Every article explained that you won by using the armbar, but they were all a little different about how you got your opponent into the armbar. They were different because they were written by people with distinctive perspectives. They were all at various locations on the field, watching with unique viewpoints—both externally and internally," she said.

Bear moved the midnight strands that had gotten out from his ponytail away from his face. "Yeah, I used to notice that. When I would read articles about one of my fights, they were all a little different. But as long as they got the main details, like my win and who I won against, it didn't matter to me."

"Did you know that if the articles written about you were all the same, they would lose their validity?" Ruth asked.

"They would?" Bear asked.

"Yes, if they are all the same, then the writers were either copying each other or they had collaborated to write the same thing. Eyewitness accounts must all have a slight degree of variance for them to be true. As long as the main themes are the same, the viewpoints are each valid."

"The fact that these men each saw what happened between Judas and Jesus just slightly different makes the account true, not false?"

"Yes," Ruth nodded.

Bear stopped and thought. "Okay, I get that."

Ruth came alongside of him. "And remember, the Book of Luke does not mention the account at all—only that Jesus said there was a betrayer among them. There were lots of people in that room with Jesus. Peter and John saw everything that happened because they were sitting next to Jesus," Ruth added.

"Okay," he said crossing his arms. "Then I want to be close to Jesus, like Peter and John."

Ruth stared at her husband for several seconds. "I do too," she said. "And you are very much like Peter. He was a leader."

"What was John like?" Bear asked.

"He was more quiet," Ruth said. "He was a writer."

"You write a lot. I see you working for hours at the HMS," Bear said.

"I do write a lot," she whispered. "I only hope my words are making a difference."

CHAPTER NINE

"**L**i," Zach said, standing next to his friend. "Come on, we have to go before sunlight."

Li was kneeling on the floor and moving around what was once known as a *mouse* as he stared at the screen.

"I'm almost done," Li said. "I just need to cover my tracks a little bit."

"What's going on?" Zach asked.

"Pastor Tom sent me Ruth's latest article. It's good. I don't know how to explain it," Li said, looking up toward Zach. "It's more relatable somehow. Before her writing was poignant, but now I sense something else."

Zach looked at the old-style computer. "Did you print it out? I would like to read it."

"I didn't set up a printer for them. I have a few in the van, but I need to save them for some other names that Tom gave me. But I'll give you an overview of what she wrote when we start our next journey," Li said.

"What do you see that's different?" Zach asked.

Li held onto the makeshift desk and pulled himself up. His body was lean and several inches shorter than Zach's. He stroked the dark bristles growing around his chin.

"I think you would be able to explain it better, but I sense more of her humanity. It's almost like you can feel emotion as you read her words."

"What? Like passion?" Zach asked.

"No, it's not so much as passion, as it is—love. Yes, it's like you can feel a small bit of care or concern for her audience in what she is writing now. I have never seen that in her writing."

Zach thought for a moment. "It looks like Bear is getting to her."

"Bear and Jesus," Li smiled.

Zach looked at his friend, the Elite Efficientist. He had hated Efficientists for so long, but now his sister and his new friend were both Elite Efficientists gone rogue. Zach chuckled and gave Li a friendly slap on the shoulder. "God does have a sense of humor. My life was at a dead-end for years, and in an instant, everything is different. Jesus certainly enjoys changing the scene."

Li nodded. "I had finally attained everything I wanted and realized that none of it made me feel any better. Then my vision went blurry and I landed at the sisters' farm. I never thought twice about going back. Everything has changed, including me."

Zach looked out the window across from where the computer sat. "We better go. We said our goodbyes yesterday. She'll be in good hands here. I'm thankful Cindy's sister was willing to take her in. And she was thankful for the jewels we were able to provide her and her husband. They'll be able to do repairs on the farm and buy some equipment they've been needing."

"I left the girl a note," Li said. "I wrote everything that the Holy Spirit revealed to me about her. The farmer and his wife said they would give it to her when she wakes up today."

"I think that will help her. A word from God is valuable to someone who is in transition. It gives them hope to cling to during the difficult time of change. She will need all the hope she can get," Zach said. "Now let's get back on the road. I want to see what else God has in store for us."

"It's kind of exciting isn't it—the not knowing," Li said, grabbing his overnight bag that he set down by the desk. He carefully lifted an ax and wrapped it with a cloth before unzipping his backpack and placing it inside.

Zach nodded his head in agreement. "Are you really going to use that ax the farmer gave you? What else is in there? Rope?"

"He gave me several things that I've never used before. Maybe I'll get the chance to use them one day on my ranch," Li smiled and zipped up his bag. "I've learned that there are no coincidences. We gave the farmer some jewels and he gave us what he thought we needed."

"Well, I don't know if I'll ever use these cantinas that he gave me or the compass, but I put them in my bag. We are heading out to some remote places. You never know. Maybe we'll find ourselves in a tough spot," Zach said.

"It feels good to be needed for more than just achieving rank. I realize now that *Life Efficiency* is merely a distraction. It would have never given me real purpose. I would have eventually fallen away if God hadn't gotten to me first," Li said. "By the way, Pilar sent you a note through her computer at the house. I've hidden it, so we can print it out later. I really want to get my hands on one of the old flash drives. That way we could save the messages, so I don't have to hide them."

"Do you know what she said?" Zach asked. "Is there anything wrong?"

"I didn't read it. It's a short note, though. She knows not to put anything important into her notes to you, so we won't have to worry if people find them."

"We need one of those old flash drives, so you don't risk getting caught hiding letters," Zach stopped and thought. Determination covered his face. "I pray in the name of Jesus that we get not just one of those flash drives, but we get dozens. That way we can pass them out and people can save and spread the writings that Pastor Tom and Ruth share."

"So be it," Li said. "Now let's go start our next adventure."

Levi stared at his daughter, sitting at one of the counters in their kitchen. She was reading the *Bible* again, ignoring her afternoon chores. He wanted to help his firstborn girl, but he had nothing to give her that would heal a broken heart. Normally when he would walk into the kitchen to meet her, she would chat his ear off about all that was going on in town. Lately, though, all she did was read her *Bible* and pray. Ever since Zach left, she lost her assertive, contagious energy.

"What's God telling you today?" he asked.

Pilar looked up, startled. "I'm sorry, Daddy. I know that I'm supposed to cook the rolls you need for the breakfast deliveries tomorrow. I'll get started on them now."

"I don't mind getting them ready if you're occupied. I know when God's telling me something, it takes everything in me to keep myself from getting distracted."

Pilar closed the *Bible* and pushed it on the counter away from her. "That's the thing, Dad. God isn't saying anything to me. I keep bugging Him, asking Him what I should do. What does He want me to do next? There is so much I wanted before I turned thirty. But here I am with thirty just around the corner and nothing has changed."

"Now, Baby, you still have several years before you turn thirty. I'm not that old yet," Levi said with a low laugh. "Do you miss Zach that badly?"

"I do miss him, but that's not what's confusing me. I've prayed for him so long. I prayed so many hours that we could be together and start a family, but now that he's gone, there's this void."

"You miss him a lot?" Levi said. He wanted to be sympathetic to his daughter. He learned a long time ago that her stubbornness needed to go through its own process of understanding. He only prolonged the process when he tried to push it along.

"No, the void is not from him directly," Pilar started. "The void is between me and God."

Levi couldn't hide his confusion. "I don't understand. How does Zach leaving cause a void between you and God?"

Pilar got out of her seat and walked to the pile of dough rising in the large metal bowl. She reached her hand into the small burlap sack and pulled out a handful of flour, spreading it across the countertop. Then she pinched off a piece of dough and began to knead it into the flour.

"I'm embarrassed to say it," she whispered.

"What, Pilar? What's going on?" Levi said, walking toward his daughter. Unlike her mother, she was tall and could almost look straight into his eyes.

"I realized that my entire relationship with God has been built on my prayers for Zach. Now that he is gone, I don't know what to pray for. I've spent hours in prayer, begging God for this perfect relationship. But I never thought to just talk with God—just to get to know Him and to hear His voice. I thought I was doing so good—praying and seeking God. But it was for selfish reasons. It was to achieve the promises that I thought He had for me. Never have I prayed and sought Him just because of my love for Him. I'm so ashamed," Pilar said, setting the dough down and covering her face.

Levi took his daughter into his arms. She was strong and beautiful, and right now very vulnerable, which was not like her at all. He knew this moment was special, and he prayed a quick prayer for guidance.

"How long have you been a Christian, Pilar?" he asked.

"I don't know, Dad. Whenever I heard Zach and his father preach, like eight years ago maybe," Pilar said.

"So that makes you about eight years old," he said and lifted up her chin with his index finger. "Do you expect to be a perfect, mature Christian overnight without growing? Do you think you can bypass the years it takes to grow your relationship with God without making mistakes and learning from those mistakes?"

"No, but I hadn't realized how selfish I've been. I used to think I was such a good Christian girl—reading my *Bible* and praying and doing everything right. But all my motives were rooted to me getting my own way. I thought if I could be good enough, if I could work hard enough, then I could be worthy to have my dream life come true. I was so focused on what I wanted. Everything was fine when I could have my way," she said with fresh tears streaming down her face.

"And that pretty much sums up an eight-year-old," Levi said, wiping off her tears. "Jesus saved us when we were yet sinners, not when we were yet perfect. We come to God in our selfishness, and He gives us the perfect righteousness of Jesus. But it takes years to work that righteousness that God sees in the supernatural into the natural corners of our hearts and minds. Everyone who is born again is born an infant, and it takes time to grow into maturity. Some people are old like me, but still haven't matured. Do you know why?"

"Why?" Pilar asked.

"Because they won't humble themselves and admit their weakness. Yet here is my beautiful, strong daughter admitting that she has been selfish and wanting to grow up a little. I am not ashamed of you at all. In fact, I am so proud of you. God is going to use your humility so powerfully. You have such strength and now He can use that strength for His purposes and glory. Pilar, you amaze me," Levi said, placing both hands on either side of her cheeks that were dusted with flour. "I am so honored to be your father."

"When God exposed my selfishness, I felt so ashamed," Pilar said.

"How do you feel now?" Levi asked.

Pilar looked into her father's eyes. "I feel loved."

"Yes, when God prunes us, He will most definitely fill the hurt areas with peace and healing."

"Has this ever happened to you?" Pilar asked.

"Oh, Honey, so many times I have had to confess my selfishness. We have layers of it, which is why God is so gracious to expose them one at time. I've learned to receive it well, knowing that God was maturing me into someone better."

"You are pretty amazing too," Pilar said. "Our whole town is named after you. People respect your words."

"And that didn't happen overnight. I've come a long way from who I was, but I still have a way to go. I want to be my best self before Jesus calls me home," Levi said, squeezing his daughter's face once more before wrapping her in his arms.

"I think I know what to pray for now," Pilar said.

"What is that?" Levi asked.

"I'm going to ask God for His will, and pray for it," she said simply.

Levi held onto his girl. "I'll be praying that prayer too."

CHAPTER TEN

P ilar put her dad's truck into park. She was disappointed that she didn't see Bear's truck parked in front of his house. She only hoped that Ruth was still home—probably working on her HMS. She was grateful for the small, early cold-front that blew in. She had been working outside all day, and she hated visiting people's homes without freshening up before she left. But today she didn't have time to clean off or change. She needed to speak to Ruth and Bear right away. She grabbed the paper sack on the passenger seat next to her. She threw about a dozen leftover sweetbreads for Bear's grandfather. He would be expecting them.

"Ruth!" Pilar yelled before slamming the driver's side door after her. "Ruth! Are you home?"

Pilar ran up to the door and didn't bother knocking. If Bear wasn't home, she wouldn't be exposed to a compromising scene on behalf of her newlywed friends. "There you are!" Pilar said as she entered the living room. She saw Ruth right at her HMS as she expected. "Where's Bear?"

Ruth looked up from her HMS. "One of his men is fighting in the circuit. He left early this morning to take him, but he said he would be home later tonight. That's why he took his truck. He didn't want to be gone too long. He is returning as soon as the fight is over," Ruth said.

Pilar stopped. "Ruth, you know me too well. You answered my first question and the other three I had ready just after that."

Ruth smiled. "I do know you. Grandfather is trying to catch fish in the river. I am sure he saw your truck, so he will be arriving shortly for those sweets you brought."

Pilar looked down in her hands where Ruth was motioning. "Oh, yes. I'll set them here on the counter."

Pilar set the bag down and grabbed one of the chairs by the table and dragged it to where Ruth was sitting. "Okay, I just got word that Randall is in the area. He went to Zach's factory and was asking questions. He was also seen at the diner. He got some answers, mainly that Bear is Zach's best friend. So, he's going to be coming here. You need to get rid of this HMS and that old computer thing you have here," Pilar said, pointing to the computer.

"How can I get rid of them?" Ruth asked. "I need to keep writing. Pastor Tom says that my writing is causing lots of trouble for the World Government. After a year of writing, I finally feel like I am making a difference."

"Is it worth dying for?" Pilar asked in a serious tone. "Look, you don't have to destroy them. Just hide them. My dad hid ours. We have a secret storage room he built a long time ago where he would hide our surplus food from gangs that used to roam the area. You can't even see it because it blends in with the kitchen. So, Daddy put the computer in there."

Ruth got up and looked around. "How can I hide the generator, HMS and the computer. I will need my desk too. It would take Bear weeks to build something like that."

Pilar stood up. "We have to hide this stuff tonight," Pilar said. "Your days of sitting here in the open are over for now until we know that Randall has moved on. This man will kill you if he sees you working on an HMS. Pastor Tom says that you and Bear need to look like you have no online access. You will be less suspicious that way."

"I knew Randall was coming, but now that he is here, I am worried," Ruth said, turning off the HMS "I do not want him to hurt Bear. What if Randall tries to attack him because he is Zach's friend?"

Pilar leaned and looked at Ruth's face. "Bear is the best fighter anyone has ever known. If Randall wants to get information from him, he'll have to fight him for it. But it's best just to act like you have nothing to hide, which is why we need to get rid of these things," Pilar said pointing to the HMS.

"Do you think Randall has already been here?" Ruth asked, getting up and looking out of the window.

"No, not yet. I know for a fact that Randall is staying with that new waitress from the diner tonight. He was seen leaving with her when her shift ended. He may be occupied for the time, but he will come to this house tomorrow or the next day."

Suddenly, the door to the house burst open, and Pilar and Ruth screamed.

"Did anyone eat my sweets," Grandfather asked, eyeing Ruth and Pilar. He was holding a stringer with several fish dangling from it. "Sorry, I didn't mean to scare you girls. I saw your truck come in, Pilar. But I had just gotten a bite. I had to pull her in before I could get here. I was worried that someone might have gotten hungry and eaten one of my sweets."

"No, Grandfather. The bag is right there. We haven't touched any of it. But I can't let you have them yet," Pilar said.

"Why is that?" Grandfather asked. "Because I smell like fish?"

"No, that's not the reason," Pilar said, sniffing. "Though you do smell bad. It's because you need to help us get all of this into my truck," she said waving her hands over Ruth's desk. "And Ruth, we will need to find a reason for you to come to my house, so you can work."

Ruth stared at the HMS and thought for a moment. "I have an idea. You transport your father's baked goods to homes and businesses, and you sell your makeup on the side to your dad's customers. What if you were to sell my clothes along with your products? I can bring what I make to your house a couple of times a week."

Pilar hesitated. "It sounds good in theory, Ruth. But it gets difficult dividing proceeds. Sometimes people will pay me in a chicken or a favor or who knows what. It would be too difficult to split the proceeds of your work."

"I don't want any of the proceeds. You can keep them. What I need is help."

"What kind of help?" Pilar asked, interested.

"Bear is busy training his men, and he cooks sometimes. We both want a clean home. But I do not like to clean. I do not like to cook. I do not like to wash laundry. I do not like any of it."

Pilar laughed. "No one likes to do that, Ruth. It's just part of life."

"Yes, but I would rather sew another garment or create another outfit than cook or clean. If I could get help two times a week with washing and cleaning and a little cooking, I would willingly sew a wardrobe for that person or clothes to barter."

Pilar thought. "You know, my sister, Reyna, has been looking for some work. Javier has been working Daddy's fields with my younger brothers. He's doing a great job, and Daddy doesn't have to worry about the crops anymore, but I think Reyna wouldn't mind coming over here a couple of times a week, so she can get some new clothes. She can keep some. Sell some. Whatever she wants. I know she's been eyeing the pieces you've made me. Everyone is talking about those fighter outfits you've been making Bear. I bet she could sell those at the bazaar."

"Can we talk with her tonight? It would be wonderful if she could start this week," Ruth said. "I am supposed to do laundry with Bear soon."

"I think she would like that. And you can come over to my house while she cleans," Pilar said. "And work on your writing."

"Yes, I would want her to have the house to herself, so I have an excuse to visit you," Ruth agreed.

"There!" Pilar exclaimed, placing her hands on her hips. "We found our solution!"

Bear's grandfather went to the kitchen and placed the fish in the sink. He washed his hands with the water jug and dried them on the fabric of his pants before walking toward the HMS. "Let's get these moved, so I can eat. I'm hungry."

Pilar and Ruth watched Grandfather walk to the HMS and pull its power cord away from the generator. He then lifted the heavy machine easily into his arms and made his way to the open door. He disappeared outside.

"He's stronger than he looks," Pilar laughed.

Ruth looked toward her friend. She wanted to speak privately before Grandfather came back. "I am really glad you came over tonight. I had just prayed for help when you knocked on the door."

"What's wrong?" Pilar said, grabbing Ruth's hand. "Are you okay?"

"Yes, I am fine. I just have a question. But I want to talk with you about it in the truck on the way to your house. Grandfather will stay here in case Bear comes home early, so he can explain where I have gone," Ruth said, feeling the heat rise in her cheeks.

"Ruth, you're blushing," Pilar said, looking closely at Ruth's face. "Whatever you have to talk about is embarrassing you. I'm good with sticky topics, so I am glad I'm here. Let's get this stuff in my truck, and you can tell me all about it."

CHAPTER ELEVEN

"Where's your HMS and that computer thing?" Bear asked when he entered the living room. Ruth sat on a rug next to the fireplace. The small fire gave off only a soft glow, so she kept her hands close to the flames as she sewed each stitch of the fabric she was working on. She was wearing one of Bear's shirts. She had worn one of his shirts as a nightgown when she had no more clean clothes and had worn one of his shirts to bed ever since. Bear didn't mind. He even kind of liked it. It did make his pile of laundry bigger than hers, and he had a suspicion that was the reason why she did it.

Ruth didn't look up from her stitching. Bear could tell she was ending the sewing with a certain knot she liked to use, so he waited. After a few seconds, she grabbed the small knife from the floor next to her and cut the string. Then she placed the needle into a wooden box and folded the fabric on her lap. She looked up toward Bear when she was done. He loved the way the fire caused her cheeks to flush and the way the dark dilated her eyes.

"Pilar came over today, and we put everything in her truck and brought it to Levi's house. He has a secret room where we have hidden it. I will be writing at her house a few days a week," Ruth said. Then she asked, "Who won the fight?"

Bear looked back at the empty desk. "My guy won. Ruth, why would you move your HMS over to Levi's house? You write almost every day. I have to practically pull you off to get you to come outside with me. Can you get all your writing done? What does Pastor Tom say?"

Ruth grabbed her sewing items and got up. She walked to the kitchen counter and carefully placed them down. "Pastor Tom already knows. Randall is in the area."

Bear's body became rigid. He stared at Ruth for several moments, struggling with his emotion. "How could he be here so quickly? It's only been a little over a week. I thought they would send someone else to look for them. Was Li some kind of special Efficientist that they would send the best Bodyguard to find him?"

"No, I doubt they know Li's true potential. I think Neil Elder and the World Government underestimate him. I know I did. He can hack through every security system that the World Government constructs. Pastor Tom was good at hiding my writing, but Li is the best that I have ever seen."

"You don't think they know that?" Bear asked.

"Neil Elder would not send Charlie Liu on an assignment to a Colonial factory if he knew how valuable he was," Ruth said.

"So why did they send Randall?"

"He's here to kill…my brother," Ruth whispered, looking around. "We have to call him Mark or anything else other than Zach or my brother. Randall could be outside our windows now."

"That's it then. We should just leave," Bear almost shouted.

"Is that what God is telling you?" Ruth asked.

Bear felt his tense shoulders, and tried to force them to relax. "No, I felt like we should stay. I felt like he was telling me that we would be okay here," Bear admitted.

"Yes, that's what you told me. Let's not let fear cause us to doubt what God has told us," Ruth said.

Bear walked toward his wife. "I waited for you for a long time. I will not let anyone take that away from me," he said, folding her into his arms.

"Just trust God. We can't be led by fear. If we are going to achieve Pastor Tom's plan to compromise the World Government, we each need to listen to God and trust Him," she said.

"You smell clean, like water," Bear said, bending down and nuzzling Ruth's neck. He needed to change the subject. He disliked feeling inadequate, and thinking about the World

Government and Pastor Tom's ideas made him feel out of his element. Maybe he could distract himself.

"You smell like earth and sweat," Ruth said, smiling.

"It's been a long day outside," Bear said. "My fighter won and honored me with the first choice of winnings."

"What did you choose?" Ruth asked, looking up into Bear's eyes.

Black strands loosened from the ponytail Bear always wore and fell across Ruth's face, so he swept his fingers across her cheeks to move them out of the way. "Sorry, my hair is falling all over you. Honestly, I embarrassed myself today, but I did it for you. I even got heckled by some men in the crowd. But I noticed several bolts of fabric bundled up in the winner's pile, so I took them," Bear said. "I knew you would be pleased."

Ruth smiled and looked toward the door. "Where are they?"

"I wrapped them up in a tarp and placed them in the back of the truck. You'll like them. I know you like the fabric with the girly prints on them."

Ruth laughed. "They sell better when there's a design on them."

Bear looked at his gi that Ruth made. "I like mine plain and comfortable just like this one."

"I know," she whispered.

"Are you ready to go to bed? I've missed you," Bear said, kissing Ruth on the cheek.

Bear could feel Ruth's body become stiff in his arms. He instantly looked into her eyes. "What's wrong?"

Ruth's face flushed even more. She tried to look away, but Bear was holding her too close. "I'm unable to do anything with you for a few days," she whispered.

Bear loosened his grip. "Why?"

"It is nothing. I have just started my menstrual cycle."

Bear let go of her. "Oh, I forgot about those. You haven't been on one since we've been married."

Ruth fidgeted with her hands. "I forgot about them too. I have only had my menstrual cycle once in my life when I was young," she said matter-of-factly. "That is why I needed Pilar's help today."

"What do you mean?" Bear asked.

"When I had my first menstrual cycle, my father sent for a home doctor right away. The doctor put a birth control unit in me. It's a small mechanism that produces hormones and prevents your menstrual cycle for about ten years. I had it replaced in my twenties. And now I need another one."

"Why would you need it replaced if you're married?" he asked.

Bear looked at Ruth and she looked away.

"Ruth, you want to have a baby, don't you?" he asked. He had never asked her before. He just assumed. Everyone who gets married has children.

Ruth looked back at Bear. "I never wanted a baby. How can I take care of a baby when I can barely take care of myself?"

Bear let go of Ruth completely and stepped back a few paces. "You can't just decide for both of us. We are married. This is my life and my family. I'm halfway done with my thirties. I want to have kids with you now! All this time, I assumed we were trying to get pregnant."

"Why would think that?" Ruth asked.

"Because we've been having sex!" Bear said, walking up to her. "Every time we made love, I thought we might be making a baby. What was I doing? Wasting myself!"

Ruth's almond eyes sharpened with anger. Her chin jutted out and she pushed her hand against Bear's chest, moving him back a step. "Is making love with me just a way to have a baby? Do you not enjoy our intimacy? You cannot say you do not. I know you do. I like our life how it is. It is just now feeling normal. I am not going to add another human life to our marriage. What kind of parents would we be? My dad messed me up. Your mother messed you up. We are incapable of raising children!"

"Yes, like the rest of the world, we didn't have the best life growing up. But look at us, Ruth. We are so different. We are not the product of our childhood. You were Eve Pallue, but I don't see her. I see Ruth, my wife. You are quick to learn. Being a parent is hard, but we can do it together," Bear said. He felt himself almost pleading, but he didn't care. He wanted children. He had waited a long time to be at a place that he was healthy enough to protect and guide a family.

Ruth looked away. "Being a mom was never my desire, Bear. I cannot change who I am."

"That's the Efficientist in you talking, Ruth. You Efficientists would take all the young women from the Colonies and make them into Mothers. They would give their life for those kids, and then you would just dispose of them like trash. I know what you guys do to them. I've met my share of retired Mothers, trying to make a new life once their old one was ripped from them. But that's not how it's supposed to be. Pastor Tom and his wife do it right."

"That is exactly my point!" Ruth yelled. "How can you expect me to be a Mother when to me they are disposable?"

"Are you telling me that your mom was disposable?" Bear said, heat rising in his skin.

"No, but I sure was, and so were you!" Ruth yelled. "I will never have your child. I will never be a mom. All it will bring me is heartbreak and sorrow! Why can we not leave our relationship how it is?"

"My son will not bring you sorrow. He will bring you joy!" Bear countered.

Ruth crossed her arms. "How can you say we are having a boy when I will never get pregnant?"

"Are we not having sex anymore? Will we live as friends now and not lovers?" Bear asked, his voice becoming cold.

"You will just have to make sure you exit before you finish," Ruth said, her face blushing a deeper red.

It was Bear's turn to cross his arms. "I have done that with every single woman I've been with until I married you. I will not allow our marriage to look like a one-night-stand."

"Then I will need to go to the Colonial hospital to get birth control," she whispered.

"I won't let you," Bear said. "If you love me and believe in our marriage, you will not go behind my back."

"Will we live like friends then?" Ruth asked.

"I married a friend *and* a lover," Bear said.

"Yes, I am your friend and lover, but you never asked me to be a Mother."

Bear stared at his wife. She had always been flexible with new things and willing to bend for him. "Marriage leads to sex. Sex leads to babies. Didn't anyone ever teach you that in school? That is how God made it!"

"Then God will have to intervene," Ruth said with finality. "Because as of now, I will never be a Mother."

CHAPTER TWELVE

“What do you mean it’s gone? How can the entire *Unum Vernum* be missing? A book of that magnitude can’t just disappear overnight!” Neil shouted into his LPS. His gray hair was thinning, and his midsection had become thicker since he moved into Eve Pallue’s old high-rise flat. His breathing was labored as he tried to yell into the small microphone installed into his LPS. “Don’t people have their own copies on their LPSs at home? What do you mean they were all linked? Linked to what? The main copy. Did anyone think to print it out? No! No! It’s illegal to print out copies of other religious literature, not the *Unum Vernum*. This religious manuscript has been sanctified by the World Government. My team spent months finding the right material from all the world’s holy books to add to this compilation. You cannot tell me that it has just vanished overnight? I can’t believe this! LPS off!” he commanded.

Neil pushed out of his chair and paced the living room. His breathing became increasingly heavy, so he made his way to the kitchen and opened the cupboard next to the refrigerator. Reaching in, he grabbed various bottles and examined the labels until he found the one he needed. He hurriedly opened the bottle and choked down several pills. He set the bottle on the counter and leaned his palm against the cool surface, trying to catch his breath. He jerked his head toward the door when he heard a loud knock.

“Come in!” he shouted.

Jonah walked into the room, carrying several printouts. He took one look at Neil and stopped. “You’ve already heard about the *Unum Vernum*?”

“Yes, I’ve just been told that our entire book is missing, and no one seems to have a copy. How the hell does that happen?”

Jonah walked to the counter and spread out several printouts. Neil noticed his signature right away at the bottom of each one.

"These are the initial parameters of the *Unum Vernum* that you gave to the research team assigned to its development. You wanted absolutely no replication of this book. Every copy received was a direct link to the actual *Unum Vernum* saved to the World Government," Jonah began.

"Saved to the World Government. How could someone just steal it then? What are we? Just a network of systems on the Internet?" Neil yelled. His irritation was obvious, and he was frustrated with himself. He needed someone to blame, but his signature on all the printouts locked him in.

"Yes, that's about it. The World Government has no real location. There is no hard copy of the *Unum Vernum* because there is no place to put it besides one of the researcher's homes or a personal bank vault. But I doubt someone printed a copy of it because of the law prohibiting hard copies of religious literature."

"I look like a fool," Neil said. "Has the World News gotten wind of it?"

"No, not yet, but they will. Our only real reprieve is that Efficientists weren't all that interested in the book," Jonah said.

"Great. Your confidence in my work thrills me," Neil said. He slammed his fist against the counter. "We have to do something!"

"We won't get it back anytime soon. If someone did print it out, we'll have to send out a request for it. Then we will really look like fools," Jonah said, frankly.

"Well, I'm glad to see that you are taking some of the blame with me. I know what I've done to get you out of the World Bank fiasco," Neil said.

"No one needs to take the blame if we say that we pulled it," Jonah said.

"You mean we tell the World Government that we've taken it off the record?" Neil said. His face brightened, and he rubbed his injured fist with his other hand.

"Yes," Jonah said.

"But what reason will I give?" Neil asked with optimism.

"I don't know about that. I'm not the man in charge. I just know that whatever excuse you find, you need to give it to me now. I need to send out a statement before the World News finds the information from someone else."

"Okay, I see. Let me think for a minute. Tell them that we discovered a virus in the original copy," Neil said.

"One of the researchers will have to take the fall. There will be an investigation. We can't do that," Jonah said.

"You're right. Okay, let me see. We can't say we changed our minds. We will look ridiculous. What would Arthur Pallue say or even Eve? I know she's gone back on some of her research when she discovered a discrepancy. I would always think she was about to discredit herself, but she seemed to come back stronger, like she had the upper hand."

"Why don't you tell them it's a breach of security?" Jonah said.

When Neil looked at him blankly, he continued. "Having so many individuals linked to a single copy of a manuscript could be dangerous. One virus planted in the *Unum Vernum* will spread instantly to all the LPSs connected to it," Jonah said.

Neil paced the floor and scratched the side of his round midsection. "You know, you're right. I thought I would have more control if everyone linked to the *Unum Vernum*, but that really is a risk, not only to Efficientists, but to the World Government, as well. Do we have a lot of systems that are easily accessible by Efficientists?"

Jonah thought for a moment. "Most of our high-security systems must be entered with passwords, but we have a few low-security systems that can be accessed freely by outsiders—mostly our information storage, research and those sort of things. But if you are wanting to change the format of the World Government, we can do that later. Right now, I need to give a reason why the main book for the World Government's religion is gone."

"Tell them that the World Government is concerned about the security risk of having everyone linked to a single system. We have taken the *Unum Vernum* down for now and we will be reevaluating the format of the World Government. That's exactly what Eve Pallue would do. Then she would boost her rank by discovering a better way to organize the World Government, which is exactly what I'm going to do."

"Yes, sir. I'll get on that now," Jonah turned to leave.

"Matt, who do you think did this? Who could possibly erase the entire *Unum Vernum* linked to millions of LPSs without anyone finding out until it was too late."

"Could Charlie Liu have done it? I've researched his profile, but hacking and sabotage don't seem to be his specialty," Jonah said.

"No, Charlie Liu is a pawn. He would never know how to do this. He's probably halfway around the world now with his Colonial buddies and a handful of jewels. Randall is chasing the wind in the Colonies. No, I think we have a new culprit on our hands," Neil looked up to face Jonah. "I need you to find him. Do whatever it takes. Take whatever resources you need. But find who did this before he or she strikes again."

"Yes, sir," Jonah said and turned to leave.

"How did you do that?" Zach asked, turning to Li who was sitting on the ground with an old-style computer on his lap. "You just sent the *Unum Vernum* into obscurity. I can't find it anymore."

Zach sprawled on the floor with his head toward an HMS that was connected to the same generator as the computer.

"Shhh, don't say it so loud. Someone may be listening to us," Li said, cautiously. He looked toward the door leading from the cellar to the ground floor.

"These people are on our side. They're not going to say anything. We've been with them for days, helping them set up the computer and HMS," Zach said.

"Yes, I trust them, but a secret is hard to hide. If the World Police were to find them and question them, they wouldn't know how to conceal their knowledge. It's better to keep what I'm doing absolutely quiet, so no one is burdened," Li whispered.

"Well, burden me because watching you work was awesome. I can't believe you erased that entire book with all the links attached. I'm glad you erased it. Horrible religious counterfeit," Zach said still searching through the Internet.

"I didn't erase it because of its content. I erased it because it linked the World Government to people. With what I'm about to unleash on the World Government, I want as little collateral damage as possible. The fewer people linked to the World Government's systems the better," Li said and lifted the computer off of his lap and set it on the floor next to him.

"I can't believe it," Zach whispered.

"What?" Li asked, scooting next to Zach.

"I think your wish is about to come true," Zach said. "The World Government just released a statement about the *Unum Vernum*. They say that they have purposely removed it for security reasons, and they will be reformatting the World Government as a precaution."

Zach stared at Li. "They played themselves right into your hands."

Li smiled. "As long as they don't suspect these old-style computers, I'll be able to do what I want undetected."

"It's like a gift," Zach said.

"I lived my entire life obeying the rules and struggling to stay ahead. Now that I get to break the rules, everything is so much easier. It's like I was born to create chaos for the World Government."

Zach grinned and nodded his head. "And so you shall, my friend. And I'll keep us moving, so you can keep making a mess."

CHAPTER THIRTEEN

Esther looked over her garden. She allowed her tomatoes to ripen more this year. She had plans for them. Instead of simply selling them whole, she wanted to can them. Maybe even make some sauces. She was excited. The farm was full of Efficientists now, and she had many mouths to feed.

Esther looked up the path toward the house. She was glad she was alone for at least a little while. Deborah thrived on being around everyone. She loved being in charge and quieting disputes and directing all the questions. Deborah had taken most of the Efficientists to the Trinity Trading Center. For the next several days, the Trading Center would be hosting a bazaar. Lots of new faces to meet and lots of new products to look at. Esther had said that she would stay behind to watch over everything, but really she just needed to be alone for a while.

She looked at the sun just coming over the Trinity River. The glow of the great ball expanded over the green hills in the background. Mornings were her favorite time, especially since autumn was in full bloom. The afternoons were still warm, but the mornings felt cool with the north breeze flowing into what was East Texas before the Second Civil War. She wondered if her age was getting to her. She appreciated things that she once took for granted, like a soft breeze or the tickle of the grass along her bare feet.

She focused back on her garden. She had allowed a few willing souls to help her plant, and they had done a good job. Her garden had tripled since the previous year and more effort was needed to maintain it. She enjoyed the time just before harvesting. She could see the fruit of all her hard work—literally, developing before her eyes. She eyed the pumpkins. They still had several weeks to go, but it would be wonderful to have pumpkin pie. She envisioned the crust she would make and the whipped cream. Of course, she would have one of the stronger young men whip the cream. They were trying to use less electricity to stay off the World Government's view. More people meant more voltages being used. Almost all their electric appliances had to be turned off.

Esther turned when she heard the car coming up the gravel road that led to the ranch. It was too early for Deborah to be coming back home. Esther didn't recognize the truck. She didn't move—only watched for who the visitor might be. She saw the truck come along the side of the house. She waited, still unable to make out who the person was. The man got out of his truck and closed the door quietly, looking around. When he saw her, he called out.

"Esther, is that you?" he yelled.

"Who's asking?" she yelled back cautiously.

"It's Bear, Ruth's husband. We met a few times at the bazaar in Levington."

Esther strained her eyes as he walked toward her. Finally, she could recognize his dark hair pulled back and his Native American appearance. He wore some kind of matching fighter suit. He looked intimidating yet handsome. She could see why Ruth would fall in love with him. As he got closer, she could tell he was upset about something.

"What has happened? Is Ruth alright?" she asked when he approached her.

"Yes, she fine. Well, kind of. I need your help," Bear said, trying to cover his emotions.

Esther looked at him. She could see that he had been crying. He looked like a broken man, a married man. "Have you and Ruth gotten into an argument?"

Bear nodded. "Yes, and it's been almost two weeks and it's not fixed yet. I don't know what to do."

"Come to the house, and we'll sit on the porch. I do my best thinking there," she said.

"Okay," he said and walked beside her. "I know I shouldn't be here. I've compromised the ranch. I brought some items to trade with you, so if someone does see us, there'll be a reason for my visit. I just didn't know what else to do or who else to turn to. It's…sensitive."

"Well, alright then," Esther said, walking up the porch steps. "Just sit right there. That's where Ruth dear would sit. That sweet, little dove. I miss her so much, yet she was only with us for a few short months."

"Thank you," Bear said, sitting down.

"Can I bring you a cup of cold iced tea? We still have our refrigerator plugged in," Esther asked.

"No, I'm fine. But, yes, I am thirsty, but I don't want to be a burden," he said.

She could see he was wrestling with himself. "It's no bother. I'll be right back. I'm a little thirsty myself."

When she came back Bear was leaning forward and had his face in his hands. She took a loud step and he sat up. "Here's your tea. I sweetened it with just a bit of honey and lemon."

"Thank you," he said taking the cup. He tipped the glass to his lips and drank until all the liquid was gone. "That was very good. I didn't realize how thirsty I was."

Esther made herself comfortable. "Now, tell me what is going on. How is Ruth?"

Bear sat on the porch next to Esther's chair.

"You don't want to sit in a chair?" she asked.

"No, I would prefer to stretch out on the ground," he said, sitting next to her chair.

"I dropped Ruth off at Levi Jones's house early this morning. Ruth wanted to write, and I told her that I had something to do." He stopped. "I hope that wasn't lying."

"I think it's fine. Though, it would have been nice to see her. It's probably for the best she doesn't come here, but you might want to tell her where you've been," Esther said, waiting.

Bear nodded and closed his eyes. She sensed his tension, and she knew it wouldn't be long until he let it all out. She saw fresh tears forming.

"Ruth doesn't want to have children with me," he finally said. "We haven't been intimate since we had our argument almost two weeks ago. It's been agony. I feel like I'm losing my wife."

"I knew this would come up. You two didn't discuss it before you were married?" Esther asked.

"No, I never believed it would be an issue. I married her. She should have known that I wanted children—at least a son. Marriage is the start of a family," Bear said firmly.

"No, you are right. I agree with you one hundred percent," Esther said.

"Then why won't Ruth?" Bear said, pounding his fist on his knee.

Esther said a quick prayer. She could see this man was in pain, and he had taken a risk to come here. "You know when Ruth first came here, she was almost dead."

Bear's countenance calmed a little. "Yes, she told me she was burned."

"She was burned, dehydrated, broken, lost, alone, confused…she was like a baby in need of constant care and attention. God knew what her condition would be, so He had me and my sister at this farm all alone and ready to care for someone who was desperately in need. We doted on Ruth so much, and she just took it all in like a sponge. We asked very little of her. Our Efficientists who live with us now have chores and duties, but with Ruth, we just let her roam. Sometimes she would help us, but other times she would read books all day long or sew."

"Are you telling me she's unable to be married?" Bear asked.

"Yes, the marriage was a bit of a surprise to us. But mainly it just showed us how far Ruth had come. I truly believed that Ruth would not be able to keep a serious relationship with anyone—not even her mother or brother. She would write us when she was living with her brother, and I could tell from her letters that she was opening up and learning to not only be loved, but to love. When her mother died, I thought she would close up again, but she continued to love her brother and then you. It's nothing short of a miracle that Ruth is able to love you."

Bear sat listening intently. "Sometimes I do feel like she's detached from me, but other times, she is so vulnerable and open to me. It can get confusing sometimes."

"Ah yes, just like a teenager would be," Esther said. "Ruth is emotionally immature for her age. But it suits her since she looks so young anyway."

Bear stood up. "Honestly, I'm no better. It's taken me a long time to grow up."

"Yes, but you've had a good five or six years of really trying to be the man God wants you to be. My sister and I found your videos at the Trading Center. Someone brought them in. We got everyone together and watched them. I can see the growth in you from the very first one to the very last one. God was changing you slowly but surely. And now look at you. You have a wife that you love and you want a family. You've come a long way."

Bear knelt down next to Esther. "Why can't Ruth come with me? Why can't she understand where I'm at?"

Esther reached down and patted Bear's midnight strands. "You have about five years on her. I believe she can get where you are, but it will take a little longer."

"But look at me," he said. "I am almost thirty-six. How much longer can I wait."

"Abraham was old when he had his son. Thirty-six is not so bad. You still have a full life in front of you with your wife. Enjoy that time, and let God change Ruth's heart like He did yours."

"She is so smart in the *Bible*. Sometimes I think I am the one who is wrong, but then I feel like I know what I want. I know my desire for a son is from God."

"Ruth is smart when it comes to ideas of faith, but living out those ideas is an entirely different subject. She'll figure it out eventually, but making demands will only push her away. Just like a teenager would," Esther said, chuckling. "You will have to be the smart one in this case and live out your faith by putting your desires aside to save your marriage."

"Having a son is a hard desire to just lay aside," Bear said, wiping his eyes.

Esther lifted Bear's chin. "God sees the desires of your heart. You must trust that He will accomplish all His plans according to His will and timing. I know your heart is broken, but you have a chance to really pour into your marriage. Go be with Ruth. She is a precious soul who is capable of doing so much with the right person loving her. Go enjoy the wife of your youth," Esther said.

"Will you and Deborah pray for me?" he asked.

"We pray for you every day, but now we can be more specific. Now let's get up. I know that you better be getting back to Levington, and I want to see what you have in the back of that truck for me to trade. I have a few too many goats that I need to unload, so I'll see what I can get in exchange."

Bear got back up to his feet. "Thank you for listening to me. I'm usually not this honest with people I don't know well, but Ruth talks about you and Deborah sometimes when we lay in bed at night. You feel like family to me."

"Well, I consider you my son-in-law, so I hope you see me as family," Esther said. "Now come here and let me give you a hug."

Bear leaned down into the elderly woman and let her wrap her aged arms around him. She squeezed for several seconds before letting go.

"Bear, what are you lifting? I can feel every muscle in your body," she said with a laugh.

He smiled. "I mainly lift other men in spars. You would be surprised how heavy a body can be. I'm not as young as I used to be and my shoulders and knees don't move as well. But my men keep me in shape," he said. "Let me take you to the truck. I threw several things in from my shed. I didn't know what you would want, but I tried to get some things that would be useful on a farm."

Bear and Esther walked toward his truck. He threw back the tarp and exposed several items tied down with cordage.

"I can't think of anything we need for the farm. Deborah's at the Trading Center getting our canning supplies for the harvest," she paused. "What's in the box?"

Bear grabbed the edge of the truck, putting one knee on the truck bed. He reached in and slid the box to him. He lifted it up and jumped back to the ground.

"It's heavier than it looks," he said and placed it on the ground.

When he opened it, Esther gasped. "They're beautiful."

Bear smiled. "They're tiles. I used them to tile the wall in Ruth's new bathroom. I almost didn't use them because they're white tiles with pink flowers, but I knew Ruth would like them. She likes floral patterns. The tiles have each been hand-painted. I won them many years ago and just kept them to barter for something else. Somehow they always stayed in my shed."

"How many are there?" Esther asked.

"There are two more boxes just like this one," he said.

"I'll take them. Deborah will be overjoyed to know that we have the same floral tiles as our Ruth dear. Now, if you don't mind putting them on my porch, I will go lead you to your two new goats."

CHAPTER FOURTEEN

Randall peered through his binoculars and watched the truck pass by on the road back to Levington. He could see the Native American man they called Bear behind the wheel. He hadn't stayed long at the farm he had stopped at. He focused the binoculars. He could see two goats in the backseat of the truck. Maybe that's why he was driving more slowly. Randall could hardly keep up with him on the drive up here. It seemed a long way to trade for a couple of goats.

"The Shaman," he whispered. He had known about the Shaman for years. He'd even seen one of his fights when he was doing a job in the Colonies years ago. He was impressed by the physical aptitude and skill he displayed on the fighting grounds. That was one man he wouldn't want to get into hand-to-hand battle with. Randall had also found a few of his religious videos. They weren't much, but he could see the man was coming to some kind of spiritual awareness. Randall didn't get it. The Shaman left the fighting circuit at the zenith of his popularity. Even the Efficientists knew about him. It didn't matter, though. The Shaman was still physically strong and dominating. The young men he trained most evenings made sure of that.

Maybe that was why he was avoiding confronting him. He could easily shoot the Shaman, but that felt beneath him. He had been watching him and his wife for ten days and nothing interesting was happening. In fact, the couple had barely spoken one word to each other. He had checked their house while they were away and there was no HMS in there. No outlets for electricity either. A woman would come clean the house a few times a week, and the Shaman would drop his wife off at a house that doubled as the local bakery. There was a dark-skinned young woman that he found very attractive living there. She would sit with the Shaman's wife and talk with her. He wondered what they were saying. It didn't look like the other woman was married.

So far he had gotten barely any information from the Colonials. He couldn't find people who were willing to talk besides a few Efficientists he chatted with at the factory when he first began investigating. Everyone was nervous about the changes the World Government was making. He couldn't get anyone to trust him. He had spent the night with a waitress, and she was no help. She was too new to the area. He couldn't risk exposing his position. If anyone discovered who he was, he would lose his advantage. It was a fine balance of concealment and discovery.

Randall left the side of the road and walked back into the forest toward the ranch that the Shaman had just left. A few steps before entering the clearing to the ranch, he stopped and picked up his binoculars. There was that old woman wearing a lavender dress sitting on the porch again. She was looking at one of the boxes that the Shaman had given her. Their transaction went so fast. He had just come into this clearing when the Shaman reached into the back of his truck to grab the boxes for the old lady. Then she had led him to her barn and gave him two goats. He hadn't seen what happened before, but it couldn't have been much. It only took him about ten minutes to hide his truck in the grass and walk over there.

He wondered if he should stay close to the farm for a few days and keep watch. The old woman couldn't be living alone, could she? Randall looked around the forest. He would have to stay concealed. His truck was not a comfortable place to stay. He thought of the waitress's house. It was more tempting. She had invited him to stay every night since he got to Levington. Randall looked through his binoculars one more time. The old lady was reading something. He strained his eyes to read the writing on the cover. It was a *Bible*.

"She's not supposed to have that," Randall said softly.

But what was he going to do? Arrest her. Then everyone would know he worked for the World Government.

"This is a waste of my time. I'm going backward, not forward," he said to himself, putting down his binoculars. "I need to get back. This is a dead end."

Randall began walking back towards his truck. He needed to find a lead. He was supposed to be researching every night, but the girl he was staying with didn't have electricity. He knew there was something that he was missing. Some detail out there just waiting for him to find it. But he was getting distracted. Was he tired? Had he lost his drive to be the best? Neil would be contacting him soon. His portable had lost power several days ago. He should have gone back to the factory to charge it. Maybe that's where he needed to go instead of Levington.

The only way he would get answers from the Shaman was to interrogate him, which would force him to kill him at the end. The Shaman had many friends. His fighters alone that he trained numbered into the thirties. He would definitely blow his cover. He was the only new person in town. This case was a lot more difficult than the other ones he had been on. He always went after people who weren't hiding, but Charlie Liu and Zacchaeus Daniels were on the run. And from what he knew, neither of them had any family left. Somehow Daniels had gotten to Liu before he entered the factory and gave him his plan. Liu became an Elite Efficientist and realized it wasn't what it was cracked up to be. They should have never sent him to the Colonies in the first place.

Randall got to his truck and threw the binoculars through the window onto the passenger seat. He climbed into the front driver seat and slammed the door. He didn't want to spend another day watching the Shaman train his men or watch his wife sew. They knew absolutely nothing.

"I'll spend one more night with that waitress, and then I'll head back to the factory." He then wondered how much he should tell Neil once he got back onto the LPS. He didn't use his Portable to relay important details because they were too easily hacked. Neil had known Randall was following Zach's friend, but Randall hadn't told him that the friend was the infamous Shaman. "Should I tell him?" he whispered to himself. "No, he'll just tell me he's too high profile a target. Neil doesn't need to

know everything," he said with finality. He put the truck into drive and spun his wheels along the rocks.

Deborah held tightly onto the steering wheel and watched as the truck from the forest finally drove off. She had left some of her bartering items at the farm and once she dropped off the others at Trinity Trading Center, she decided to quickly drive back home. She was about to turn onto the gravel road that led to her farm when she saw a truck in the distance driving off the road and into the forest towards the farm. She didn't recognize the truck, and something told her not to go home.

She stopped her van and backed it up to where she could barely see where the truck had left the road. Then she waited. After about fifteen minutes, she almost choked when she saw another truck pull out from the gravel road that led to the farm. She caught a quick glimpse of a man with tan skin and black hair. The only one she could think of was Bear, Ruth's new husband. The truck did look familiar. She could see two of her goats in the backseat of his truck.

A moment later, she saw a man in the distance appear with binoculars, standing where the first truck had hidden itself in the forest. He was looking at the second truck drive off. Then he disappeared back into the woods. She waited for what felt like an eternity. Was he going after her sister? Was he robbing the farm? Who was that man? That's when she saw the truck finally leave. She waited another minute or two to make sure the first truck was truly gone for good before she slowly drove her van back onto the road and took a right onto the gravel road that led to her farm. As she pulled up, she could see her sister reading her *Bible* on the porch. There were three boxes at the foot of her rocking chair. Something was definitely wrong. She needed to grab her sister and get back to Trinity Trading Center to talk to Pastor Tom right away.

CHAPTER FIFTEEN

"You went to the farm!" Ruth yelled, jumping into the truck and slamming the door as hard as she could. Bear looked at Ruth shocked by her greeting. "How do you know that? I only just got back," he said. He'd come back to apologize for their fight, but now he was in trouble again.

"Pastor Tom contacted me on the computer while I was on the HMS almost two hours ago. He said that Deborah had forgotten what she was going to bring to the Trading Center and was going back home when she saw a man in a truck pull off onto the side of the road and into the forest. She decided to wait and that is when she saw you leaving the farm. Then that man watched you drive off, went back into the forest—I'm guessing to watch Esther who was alone!—then he also left."

Bear's body tensed. "A man was following me?" he asked in disbelief.

"Yes, and you led him straight to the sisters' farm! Why would you compromise their position?" Ruth asked with tears flowing down her cheeks. "Deborah and Esther mean a great deal to me. I don't want Randall getting to them. He will torture them for information and then burn them alive!"

Bear said nothing for several seconds. He looked straight through the glass windshield, thinking. "He has been watching us, Ruth. I knew it. I felt something strange, but I just thought it was because of our argument. I've been on edge every single day."

Bear suddenly stopped. "He's been in the shed."

Ruth stared at Bear. "How do you know?"

"Some of the locks were switched. I just thought that I had absently mixed them up, but I've never done that. They are always in the same order."

"Pilar made me move the computer and HMS to her house. He's probably been here too. Why hasn't he done anything yet?" Ruth said. "Did he follow you here?"

Bear looked at his wife. He could see desperation in her eyes. Her breathing was rapid, and her entire body was flushed. She had been upset since their argument and this was only going to make things worse if he didn't act soon.

"I saw a truck a while back, but it turned off. It looked like it was heading to the factory. Let me get you home," he said and put the truck into drive.

"What am I going to do?" Ruth whispered. "Zach is gone. Pastor Tom hasn't communicated with him or Li for days. Now Deborah and Esther are compromised and Pilar too. You aren't speaking to me. Randall is after me again…" Ruth buried her head into her hands and began to cry. "Why does loving people hurt so much? Life was easier when I had no one."

"Ruth, Randall is not after you. If he has been watching us all this time, he has no idea who you are. Even if he followed me today to the ranch, all I did was trade Esther a few boxes of tiles for two goats. He didn't see anything but a trade," Bear said. An image of him kneeling and crying next to Esther came into his mind. He just hoped Randall hadn't seen that.

"But why did you go there?" Ruth asked turning her tear-streaked face to him.

Bear turned to look at Ruth and felt his heart surge with sorrow at the sight of his wife's face. "Because I love you!" he almost shouted. "Because I didn't know what to do. And I didn't know who to turn to. Because I've never been married before, and I have no idea what I'm doing. Because you and I are so different, but I want us to work out!"

Ruth stared at Bear as he turned back to look at the road. "What are we going to do? From Deborah's description, the man could be Randall."

Bear said nothing. He felt his jaw clench. "He's a wuss."

"How could you say that?" Ruth said.

"He's watching us from the shadows. He won't confront me because he's afraid of me. He knows I'll pummel him. I want to do that. I want to kill him for going into my home, breaking into my shed and watching my wife," Bear said with anger rolling in his voice.

"He doesn't know who I am or else he would have gotten to me already," Ruth said. "He needs to blend into the Colonies, but no one is talking. Pilar told me that a man has been seen at the diner and factory. People are scared of the World Government. They don't know who to trust."

Bear nodded. "The World Government's trying to tighten the reins, but their efforts are backfiring."

"I'm scared for Deborah and Esther. And what about the Efficientists staying with them?"

"Deborah did the right thing not going home until he had left. If she saw him following after me, he didn't think the farm was worth staying for. Ruth, I promise you that I would never want to endanger the sisters. I brought stuff to trade, so my visit looked legitimate. I didn't stay more than fifteen minutes— twenty at the most. What he saw was a simple trade. If he would have been suspicious, he would have stayed at Trinity. All I can say is that God is looking out for us."

Ruth said nothing. Bear could sense that she was putting her emotions aside in order to analyze.

"He's been watching us since our argument," she said finally.

"He hasn't seen much then that's for sure," Bear said, thinking over the last several days. Even though he had hated Ruth's silent treatment, he realized now that it was perfect timing. Silence meant nothing was revealed. They hadn't mentioned the name *Zach* in days.

"Jonah promised me that he would conceal my presence at the World Bank," Ruth said. "He's become good at covering my tracks."

"I'm grateful to that man now on many accounts," Bear said deep in thought. "There has to be a way to repay him."

"You are repaying him," Ruth whispered. "He trusts you to protect me."

Bear let Ruth's words linger in his ears. He had seen the images of Jonah. He was a formidable man. He had never respected a man whom he had never met, but he respected this

Jonah—a Bodyguard of sorts—who had taken care of Ruth when she needed it most. Now it was his turn.

"Levi has friends that work at the factory," Ruth added. "They'll let us know if Randall returns there."

Bear drove slowly through the beaten path to his house and parked the truck. So much was happening, and he had been so stuck on what he wanted. A family right now was impossible, and may never be possible. "I think Randall is finding it hard to fit in. He can't compromise his position, so he's going back to rethink his strategy. One of the men I train is a Runner. He should be coming back this week. I'll have him go to the factory and take a look around. I can talk to Levi tonight after I train my men. We can see if his friends will keep an eye out for Randall."

Bear got out of the car and walked around the front. He opened the passenger door and helped Ruth out. "You did your makeup today," Bear said, wiping the black under her eyes that had smeared from tears.

"Pilar wanted to try a new product on me," she whispered.

Bear could feel Ruth's skin shiver under his touch. "I'm sure it looked good. Did you write today?"

Ruth shook her head. "No, I had nothing to write. Instead, I researched family."

A rush of energy went through his body. "What did you find?" he tried to say nonchalantly but failed.

Ruth looked into Bear's eyes. "I found that it means something different than what I feel inside. My thoughts are wrong, but I don't know how to change them."

Bear brought Ruth into his arms. "I love you. I need you. These past few days have been unbearable." He began to kiss her neck and chin.

"But I still do not want children. I want to be with you. I do not want anyone else right now. I know it sounds selfish," Ruth said.

"Then that's what we will do. It will just be me and you until something changes. I'm fine with that. In fact," he leaned in to kiss her lips. "I'm more than fine with that."

Ruth draped her arms around Bear's neck. He missed her touch. Missed her attention. "What did Esther tell you?" she asked.

"She told me what I needed to know," he whispered and kissed her lips again.

"No one is watching us now," she said, sliding her hands down his shoulders and around his waist. "When do your men arrive for training?"

Bear looked toward the sun. It was still high enough in the sky. "Not for a while yet," he said, scooping her up. "I need you now. The past few days have been hell."

CHAPTER SIXTEEN

"I've only seen images of mountains," Li said, staring toward the west. He wore a backpack on his back with a cantina jutting out of one of the pockets. "I have never felt so small—or tired."

Zach matched Li's gaze to the left. Before them golden layers of large rocky earth piled into the hazy blue sky. "Those are the Guadalupe Mountains of what was New Mexico. I'd seen them a few times when I was a Runner, but never from this angle. I think we are more north than I was expecting us to be."

Zach reached into his pocket and took out a small compass. He held it in the middle of his palm and stayed still, watching the metal pin move north. "Maybe we should head south a little. I know the factory is around here somewhere. I could get there easily from the road. Too bad we had to turn off to hide the van in the forest."

"You said there is a neglected area of the factory that we can work from," Li said.

"The entire basement is storage for retired Sleepers. It has electricity. If we can get there, we can decide our next move," Zach said.

"We won't be able to go back until Randall thinks we are gone. I will have to create new names for us, and we'll have to create a new life for a time," Li said. "It will be easier for me than for you. You have family."

"I know. We both made this choice," Zach said.

"The air is so much drier here," Li said, stopping his walk.

"Let's rest here for a moment," Zach said. He looked at the rock figures in front of him. They looked like large, stone men wrestling on the ground. The path in front of them was dusty, yet dotted with yellowish shrubs and weeds. On the left horizon, he saw a forest, crawling toward the great rocks.

"Maybe we should head to the forest," Li said.

Zach turned his body around to get a full 360-degree view of their surroundings. He too carried a backpack that held the few precious jewels they had left and an old-style laptop that they had been saving. It fit perfectly into the large pocket of the backpack. He had been in lands like this before, but he never actually explored them. He would watch the scenery as he passed by in his truck, delivering goods from the factories. He used to consider himself somewhat of a nomad as a Runner, but now he was realizing that he never took the time to really travel beyond the safe windows of his truck. "I know the factory is in this area, but we may be several miles off—maybe even a hundred miles off."

"Should we retrace our steps and try to make it back to the van?" Li asked.

Zach thought for a moment. He could feel the balmy breeze roll over his skin. Fall had come faster than he expected, and they were much farther north and closer to the mountains. "I'm fairly certain that our van is gone. We hid it as best as we could, but it will be found eventually," Zach said. "We only had a few computers left. They won't be worth much to anyone, but they'll take the van. I'm just glad we were able to set up twelve computers. That will be more than enough."

"But the van's tire was blown. They'll just leave the van if they can't drive it," Li said, hopefully.

"Whoever takes it will probably have a spare tire handy. I regret not bringing one. I didn't feel like we had enough room, and I thought we wouldn't get too far from civilization. But here we are. The tire is blown and now we're lost."

"Thankfully, we took the jewels with us," Li said, starting his walk again toward the mountains. "And that farmer from our first stop gave us a few supplies. I was saving that ax for when I started my ranch, but it looks like I'll be using it now."

"The jewels can be useful, but if we don't refill our cantinas soon, we won't make it more than a few more days. And I'm getting hungry myself. Do you have any more of that chicken jerky from our last stop at that ranch?"

Li shook his head. "No, we ate it all for breakfast. But I still have a few biscuits left."

"I can't eat one more of those biscuits. They didn't taste good when we first had them—God bless that young lady who made them for us—but they taste like dirt."

Li laughed. "You're starting to sound like an Efficientist. I had to get rid of my cultured palate long ago."

Zach turned to face Li. "What are you talking about? You lived with Deborah and Esther. Their table spread is known for miles as the best."

"That's true. Their cooking is good. But it was still different for me. The water tasted like it was contaminated. I had to force myself to drink it, fighting my gag reflex all the way down. It wasn't until later that I realized I was drinking minerals that were good for me."

"Well, if we find water out here, it will have more than minerals. There will probably be some organic material. Hopefully, nothing toxic. We can try to boil it, but we have no way to start a fire. We should have stayed at the ranch a little longer. There was no reason to keep heading west," Zach said, feeling his voice trail off. He didn't want to admit it and scare Li, but he didn't know what they were doing out there.

"It was nice of them to let me ride a few of their horses. The rancher gave me more pointers that Pastor Tom never taught me," Li said, reminiscing. "But you felt the Holy Spirit tell you that it was time to leave, so we did. I trust you."

"I know it must have been hard for you that first day we got to the ranch and you saw all those horses. We spent most of the day installing the computer," Zach said. "I've never seen you work so fast and there were lots of complications. And that virus you sent out to the World Government. That was even better than erasing the *Unum Vernum* nonsense."

"I don't know which I enjoyed more: riding the horses or sending out that virus. I wonder how all the Efficientists reacted to the socialization of their ranks?" Li wondered, smiling.

"You have a gift of hacking and causing chaos, my friend," Zach said. "And I'm glad you're on our side."

"You have a gift as well," Li said. "I enjoyed your *Bible* discussion the last night at the ranch. It reminded me of my time with Deborah and Esther and the others when we would open the

Bible and discuss it. You explain the *Bible* well. I feel the Spirit of God when you teach."

"My father was more of a preacher type. He liked to be on stage and talk in front of hundreds of people. I prefer the small group setting, especially in homes. I like seeing the faces of the people I'm talking to. I like to listen to their viewpoints. I don't want to be the only voice that's heard," Zach said.

Li nodded. "Your preference is perfect for what's happening now in the Colonies. Church has been outlawed. All we can do is meet and talk."

"My father gave his life for the church," Zach said and stopped. His thoughts instantly went to Randall, and he could feel his heart rate pulsating.

Li looked towards Zach. "Are you okay?"

Zach blinked his eyes, refocusing on the situation. "Yeah, I'm fine. I was just thinking about my sister and Bear. I want to hear from them. Let's continue our walk."

"Did you read that note from Pilar?" Li asked, picking up his pace to match Zach's.

"Yes, she's just keeping me informed about everything. I miss her—a lot more than I thought I would," Zach said.

"Are you worried about her and Ruth?" Li asked, hesitantly.

"No," Zach shook his head. "Randall will take one look at Bear and walk the other way. He needs to stay hidden. Bear is too strong and too well-known. He'll look for another way to find us."

"Bear is extremely threatening looking—though, he's not much taller than I am. He has more muscle in his hand than I do in my entire leg. I've watched videos of his fights. If I had to face him for battle, I would instantly feign death," Li said without hesitation.

Zach laughed. "I've fought him a few times when he condescends himself to train me. He likes to tie up his right arm when he fights me. I do fairly well, but I really think he's going easy on me. He's always easier on me than his other men."

"He must care about you," Li said.

"No, it's not that. I think he knows that I'll never do a real fight, so I won't have the chance to embarrass him," Zach said.

"Are you able to take him down?" Li said, intrigued.

"No, of course not. I always wind up with bruises and sprains. I'll hurt for several days, but that's Bear taking it easy. His other men don't fare so well when they fight him, so they rarely ask to spar," Zach said. "But he'll point them out at any given moment, and they'll have to fight him."

Li leaned forward and shielded his face from the sun with his hand. "Do you see that?"

Zach looked toward the tree line to the left. They had gotten closer and the land surrounding them was greener. "Something's moving," Zach squinted his eyes. "It's a herd of horses."

Li's voice heightened with excitement. "If I could get a few of those horses. We could ride them."

Zach stopped and stared at Li. "Do you think you could train wild horses?" Zach asked, unbelieving.

"Pastor Tom worked with me as much as he could. I have done more than enough research on how to work with horses and start a ranch. I know I could train two wild horses for us," Li said unable to hide his eagerness.

"But how long will it take?" Zach asked.

"Honestly, it can take months, but we'll just have to do it in days. We will continue to train them as we head south. We can get anywhere we want much quicker, and we won't be restricted to the road," Li said.

"How are we going to get two horses?" Zach said. The possibility of traveling more efficiently was enticing. He had ridden horses before, but never bareback. "And can we ride them without a saddle?"

"It won't be comfortable, but we can trade some of our jewels for two saddles when we find the town. That farmer gave us rope. Do you think it will be thick enough?" Li asked, pulling off his backpack.

"He gave us an ax, two cantinas, a compass and that long bundle of cotton rope—all items I thought we would never use. I prayed for flash drives, and God gave us survival gear instead,"

Zach laughed. "I guess God knows what we need more than we do."

Li took out a large bundle of inch-thick, cotton rope from his backpack. "That will work, right?"

Zach nodded. "It looks thick enough as long as the horse doesn't try to yank it too hard."

"Let's travel more to the west as we walk to the tree line, so we don't startle the horses. I bet there is a source of water that keeps the horses close. I have that ax. We will cut down trees and make a pen. Then I will start a fire and you and I will get two horses," Li said with confidence.

"You make it sound so easy," Zach said. "Have you ever started a fire?"

"I started them with Deborah using flint," Li said.

"But we don't have flint," Zach said. "I could start a fire easily if I had what I needed."

"You can tear apart a Sleeper and rebuild it. I've already rebuilt the computers we gave away. Between the two of us, we will figure out how to use the power source of that laptop and make a fire," Li said.

Zach began walking, veering left to stay far from the horses. "Okay," he said. "I trust you."

"Good," Li said, keeping a brisk pace.

"No word from the boys yet?" Cindy asked when her husband slipped into the bed.

Pastor Tom leaned into the pillows stacked against the backboard. "Not a single word. It's been a week and I have no idea where they are at. Last I heard, they had reached a ranch toward the border of where Texas used to meet up with New Mexico. Li will love that. I couldn't spend too much time training him on the horses Deborah and Esther got him, but he learned quickly. I know he was doing a lot of his own research on the side, using the HMS in the office."

"He wants to have his own ranch someday," Cindy said. "Such a different life than what he has ever known. Well, now that he's out in the Wild West, maybe he's getting his chance to experience what it's really like."

"Zach said something about a factory he wanted to get to that was further west. I don't know. I feel they are okay, but I've told everyone to keep praying for them. They need one miracle after the other," Pastor Tom said. "I really didn't understand why Zach wanted to keep going. They had already connected enough computers. He said something about this being his final stop. I guess he knows that they can't come home yet."

"Your plan has worked out perfectly, but now they're still on the run. Seems like God is doing something bigger than we could have imagined. Do you think they'll be okay?" Cindy asked.

Pastor Tom looked at his wife. "Zach has street smarts and Li is almost as smart as Ruth—even smarter when it comes to technology. If they work together, I know they will make it through anything."

"And what about Randall?" she asked.

Pastor Tom looked up at the ceiling. "I think he's gone. Our people at the factory say he hasn't been back for a few days. I think he found something. Or he's going back to get reinforcements. Li's last virus on the World Government has the World News in an uproar. He must have done it at the ranch," Pastor Tom said and tried to stifle a laugh. "I can't believe that he made everyone's rank the same. Neil Elder would be livid."

"How did Li know how to do that?" Cindy asked in awe.

"That's what is ingenious about these old-style computers. Li can creep around undetected. By the time the World Government catches wind to what's going on, it's too late. The Efficientists with low ranks now have more. And the top Efficientists now have less. It's like all the ranks were pooled together and divided equally. Serves them right. That's what they're trying to do to us."

Cindy leaned back against her pillow. "I can't believe that they're trying to stop the bartering system in the Colonies. They want to give us all equal money points. Don't they realize that many people will stop making things and growing things? They'll just live off of the allotted money points."

"That's exactly what they want. Once Colonials take their money points, they'll stop working. And when we stop working, nothing will get done. Then the World Government will have the excuse they need to take over everything and give us mandatory jobs. Neil Elder's *Colonization Plan* is the scariest thing I've read so far. He's talking about dominating people. Eve Pallue wanted to direct people, but Neil is looking for a totalitarian rule with his Ten Regional Magistrates. It's all about power."

"That is why we need to pray," Cindy said. "We need Li and Zach to stay safe."

Pastor Tom nodded his head. "Each of us is playing our part, but I firmly believe that Zach and Li have one of the biggest parts to play."

CHAPTER SEVENTEEN

"**W**hat in God's name are we doing, Li?" Zach asked, holding one of the homemade torches that he and Li made using a large stick and pieces of dried bark.

The two men stood at the edge of the forest where they had been staying for the last two days. It was late afternoon, and the sun's course was beginning its descent toward the west.

"I'm getting two horses," Li said, resolutely.

"You may be claiming the impossible," Zach said.

"No, I'm calling into being things that are currently not," Li said. "Isn't that what you have said to me before?"

"Okay, what do you need me to do?" Zach asked.

"You'll have to walk back through the woods and get beyond the herd. Then use the char cloth that we made and reflect sunlight on it from the DVD that we found in the laptop to light the torch. Wave the fire and try to push them down the tree line toward me. I will try to get two of them in the pen we made."

"I still can't believe we started a fire by using that computer battery and bits of wire," Zach said, nodding at the fire that Li and he made two days ago. "Then we made char cloth from the small hard drive and material from our jeans. I'm impressed with all that we've done. Too bad it came at the cost of our only form of communication."

"I hated to tear the laptop apart, but I knew we could use a lot of the components. I'm glad we thought to bring it. We may not be able to communicate, but once we get those horses, we can get anywhere," Li said.

"If we hadn't found that pecan tree, we wouldn't have had the strength to do all this work. We found water. We made fire. We made a pen. Look at us! We're mountain men," Zach exclaimed.

"Now all we need are horses," Li said, looking toward the horizon. The mountains piled to the east of him. The forest sprawled out in front of him and to the west. In front of the mountains, the land unfolded like a rugged canvas. "I can do this. I can live off the land. I was dreaming of owning a ranch, but I feared I couldn't handle it. Now I know. I was meant to be out here. I love the mountain air."

"Once we find the factory and finish this thing, I'll help you start your ranch," Zach said. "You've done so much for us. That's the least I can do."

Li looked at his friend. He knew Zach meant the words he had spoken. "I would appreciate your help. If I can somehow sabotage the money point system, I think the World Government will fall."

"Is there a way to do that?" Zach asked.

Li thought and gazed at the landscape. "I don't know, but somehow we need to find a way."

"If you could infiltrate rank, you should be able to do the money points, right?" Zach asked.

"The money points system is the most guarded aspect of the World Government. Honestly, I would need help from the inside."

"I wonder if Jonah could help," Zach said.

"I don't know. I have looked him up, and there's very little record of him. He's a complete mystery," Li said, as his gaze fell on the horses.

Zach matched Li's stare. "They're all just standing around. If you could choose, which one would you want?"

Li's eyes scanned the herd and lingered on the black and white dappled horse standing over the herd, keeping watch. "I want the black and white one that is standing."

Zach looked and shook his head. "I think he's the leader. He'll be hard to train. I'll just take one of those lazy ones lying about."

"Are you ready?" Li asked, looking back at Zach.

"I think I have the easy part. You're the one who has to catch them. Right when I get them moving this way, I'll run back here and help you. Okay, I'll head back into the trees and walk along until I get far enough away from them. Then I'll try to sneak up behind them and light my fire before chasing them this way," Zach said, trying not to sound anxious.

"I'll be ready," Li said.

As Zach walked back into the woods with his torch, hard drive holding the char cloth and DVD to reflect the sun, Li went back to inspect the pen that they built. Luckily, they had found several dead trees. He used his ax to shave them into spikes, and he and Zach drove them into the ground, forming a large rectangle enclosure.

Li noticed the ground was littered with pecan shells around where their small fire was dying down, leaving only a few embers. When they first arrived, they found the large pecan tree. They had tried to open the shells with their hands, but they quickly found rocks to break them open. They had eaten about a pound of pecans each until they realized how thirsty they were. Then they found the small creek only a few hundred yards deeper into the forest. Zach tested the water and drank it straight from the source, but Li wanted to heat his up first. Once they got the fire started, he allowed his cantina to heat up the water, and he quickly sipped his water hot.

Li looked back toward the herd of horses. They still rested in the field. The day was the coolest day of the season so far, so they warmed in the sun, allowing the cold air to temper the heat. The dappled leader looked around before reaching toward a small patch of yellowing grass. He nibbled along the grass edges, keeping his eyes toward his herd.

Li looked around, wondering if he had forgotten anything. He spotted his backpack laying with Zach's against the tree where he and Zach had slept the last few nights. They had gathered leaves to make a small pallet. He and Zach had discussed everything from their lives to the *Bible* while staying warm next to each other. He thought it interesting that they had met Ruth the very same day over a year ago. Zach met her that morning while setting up her Sleeper, and he had met her that evening during his first PR event with the Elite Efficientists. The circumstances that led them under that tree started the day they both met Eve Pallue. All their paths collided that day, and the effects of their meeting still continued.

Li realized that he should move the backpacks out of harm's way before the herd came running in. He quickly grabbed them and decided to hang them on a thick, short branch located on a tree further back. All the small, insignificant things they owned seemed so valuable now that they were in the wilderness alone. He glanced at the cotton rope that he placed near the pen. He had cut the long rope into half, getting about 12 feet of cord on each rope. Then he made a simple halter at the end of each rope—a trick that Pastor Tom had taught him if a halter wasn't readily available. The cotton rope was tightly woven, so he hoped it would hold the horses. He watched many videos of different cowboys breaking in wild mustangs for their ranches while living with Deborah and Esther. He never dreamed he would be breaking in horses so quickly, but now was a good time to learn.

Li was ready. He felt like the years of sitting behind an LPS with his parents hovering over him had culminated in this moment. He would no longer allow people to dictate what he would do. He didn't care about rank, money points or producing. He wanted to live his life the way God intended him to. He felt more alive than he had ever felt. The only missing link now was a horse. He didn't want just any horse. He wanted the lead horse. He would be proud and stubborn, but nothing less would satisfy Li.

Suddenly, a penetrating whistle cut through his thoughts. He looked toward the herd, but instead of lazy horses resting in the sun, he saw a multitude of pounding hooves coming his way with Zach waving his torch like a rattlesnake shaking its tail behind them. Li grabbed his homemade torch and lunged toward the small dying fire. Without thinking he picked up one of the embers and placed it on his torch, burning the tips of his thumb and index finger. The torch quickly began to smoke, and a small fire ignited. He ran back to the clearing. He couldn't tell if time had halted or accelerated, but he felt as if the pulse of adrenaline rushing through his body was giving him supernatural strength.

Zach was doing a good job veering the horses toward their campgrounds. Li had a sudden thought that he had watched too many horse videos and had tricked himself into thinking he could be a cowboy. But it was too late now. He had no choice but to become what he never imagined possible—a cowboy. An all-black mare was the first horse to make it toward him. Li quickly decided to ditch the torch, throwing it into the small fire. He opened his arms wide and walked slowly to the horse who had tired out by now. She reared up, and he quickly moved to the side. He then waved his arms and angled his body in the direction of the pen. She bucked and kicked her hind legs back but continued moving in the direction of the pen. Finally, she made it through the wide space, and Li closed the rickety door that they had made using twigs tied together with thin, long strips of bark. She walked the length of the enclosure, breathing heavily. When she could find no way out, she subsided her steps and stopped altogether.

Li turned his attention back to Zach. The black and white stallion had turned on him and reared up on its hind legs, kicking its forelegs at Zach. Li grabbed one of the rope harnesses he had made and began running to Zach's position. By the time he got there, the horse's ears were pinned back, and he was pawing the ground. Li knew he was about to charge. Li yelled out and swung the rope he was holding into a circle. The stallion looked at him and lost focus of Zach.

"I got your mare!" he yelled at Zach without taking his eyes off of the stallion. "Go back and try to get the rope harness on her. She's fairly docile."

"You sure you don't need me here? This one is aggressive!" Zach yelled out.

"No, I've got him. Just make sure the mare is okay," Li yelled.

Zach slowly backed away from the horse and made his way into the forest. Li continued to swing the rope and call out to the stallion. The horse turned his body to fully confront Li. His ears were still pinned back, but he was no longer stamping the ground. Li stopped swinging the rope. He placed the harness into his right hand and opened both arms wide, walking slowly

117

toward the stallion. He locked eyes with the animal. The horse's dark brown eyes matched his own. They were both scared and in a new situation with no idea of what to do next. Li continued to talk calmly to the horse.

"Shhh, Xīnnián," Li said in Mandarin. He and his parents were not fluent speakers of their heritage language, but he did know how to read and write it. He didn't know why the Chinese word for New Year came to his mind, but he wanted to name this stubborn stallion New Year because that's what they were experiencing now—a new year, a new season, a new life together. The horse seemed to respond to the name. His ears relaxed a little, but he still stared intently at Li's movements.

Li continued to speak to the horse in a calm voice, calling him by his new name. He envisioned coming up to the side of the horse's shoulder, and wrapping the harness around his neck and then looping the rope around his muzzle. It would be simple if the horse would cooperate. The horse no longer feared Li, but he was still guarded. Li knew the stallion had fierce strength. He would have to win the horse's trust and assert his authority over him somehow.

Li got to an arm's length away from the horse, and reached out his left arm, bringing his right hand with rope close behind. When Li's fingertips slid through the stallion's black mane, the stallion reared up again. Li stood his ground. His adrenaline poured into his veins like gun powder ready to explode. When the horse landed, Li threaded his left hand through the black mane, gripping tightly. This made the stallion lunge into a sprint. Li felt his feet slide from underneath him, and his right hand dropped the rope and reached over the stallion's shoulder, grabbing hold of thick cords of black mane on the other side. Li held both arms against the stallion's body, trying to bring his feet off of the ground. Li wouldn't let go, but he didn't want his feet to get trampled.

The horse continued running, but as Li held on, the stallion began to buck. Li felt his body fling against the horse's left shoulder like a flag. He tried to relax his muscles, while keeping his fists closed. The stallion continued to buck for several seconds until he realized that the hands were not going to let go.

He began to run straight, and Li took the opportunity to push his feet off the ground, throwing his right leg over the stallion's strong back. Li wrapped his arms around the stallion's neck and gripped his torso with his legs. He kept his head down by the horse's neck and began to try to talk in a calm voice again. The horse's run became a trot and he began to veer right toward the tree line. Li didn't move until the horse came to a complete stop. As Li hugged the horse's neck, calling him by his new name, Xīnnián, he knew that he had done it. He still had a long way to go, but he was now a cowboy with his own stallion. What was impossible had become possible.

CHAPTER EIGHTEEN

"I found where they are heading," Randall said through the microphone of the LPS.

"Where?" Neil's voice rang back through the speaker.

"It's a factory in the New Mexico Territory. Near the mountains," Randall said.

"How do you know for sure?" the voice shouted back.

"I found an encrypted note sent to Zach's old LPS. I interrogated the Colonial who took his place, but he has no idea who Zach is. His story holds up. He only just arrived at this location a few months ago," Randall said.

"Send me the exact location," the voice demanded.

Randall quickly typed a few keys on the LPS and sent the location of the factory to Neil who was waiting on the other end.

"This factory is no longer a part of the system. I have taken it over for research," the voice almost shouted. "There is sensitive information at this facility, and Daniels and Liu must not be allowed to get there. You need to stop them now."

Randall sat back in his chair. He knew Neil Elder was keeping something from him. His voice sounded anxious.

"I saw that you and Ada went to the PR event last evening together," Randall said.

"We only went as mutual professionals. You know how she likes to attend the Elite outings. Hurry up and finish your job and then you can take her," Neil said.

"I would appreciate it if you stayed away from my things while I do your dirty work," Randall said stiffly.

"Fine! She's all yours. Just get to that facility and stop those two from sabotaging my work. If information gets out too soon about what's going on there, I'll hold you responsible!"

Randall didn't like being on the other side of the threats. "Give me full access to all the factories from here to there to take what I want. I need food, water and fuel. It will take me two days to get there. Don't worry about Daniels and Liu. I'll take care of them. Let the facility know that I'll be coming. Send me the names of those in charge to my Portable. I'll be back to my regular duties within the week. Off."

Randall signed out of the LPS, and stared at the printout. It was only a few short sentences. It read like an SOS. They were in trouble and needed help. They would be at the factory in a few days. Too bad they didn't realize that the factory was now private property of Neil Elder. Whatever research Neil was doing there, it must be important.

Randall grabbed his jacket from the chair and his Portable. He was tired of impersonating a Colonial. He was more than glad to leave this place. Watching people didn't have the thrill it used to. He wanted to be back at his job, in the public eye, with Ada Armel by his side. The quicker he got this job done, the quicker he could get back to the city.

"What is it? What's wrong?" Cindy asked, watching as her husband paced the floor.

"I just got word from Levi. His men from the factory spotted Randall. He found something, and he's gone," Tom said.

"What does that mean? What could he possibly have found? We don't even know where they are."

"That's just it. Randall interrogated the man who took Zach's management position, but he didn't know anything about Zach or Li. But one of Levi's men saw Randall holding a printout. Randall got provisions and left in a hurry, heading west. He wouldn't just leave unless he had information," Tom said. "We haven't been using that LPS. We've never used it to relay any information."

"Then there shouldn't be anything on it," Cindy said.

"But there was," Tom said. "I keep thinking over and over again in my mind. Did I miss something? I don't even know the code to that LPS—neither does Li. The only person who could possibly get in it is—" Tom stopped.

Cindy stared at her husband as fear flooded his face. "You don't think Zach sent something?"

Pastor Tom grabbed the chair facing the old-style computer and sat down. He typed several keys and waited. The old computers seem to take an eternity to load. Finally, he found what he was looking for. "I can't believe it."

Cindy squinted at the screen. "It's a bunch of gibberish."

"No, it's a coded message from the laptop that I gave Zach and Li," he said.

"What does it say?"

"I can't crack the code. It can only be done on an LPS," Tom said and then looked toward his wife. "But I'm pretty sure Zach has revealed their final location."

Shock spread across Cindy's face. "Why would Zach reveal where they will be?"

"Because he wants to confront the man who killed his father," Tom said simply.

CHAPTER NINETEEN

"**T**hank you, Reyna. My home looks beautiful as always," Ruth said as she entered the living room of her house. The day had been cool and she wore pants and a light jacket. Even though Reyna had been working in the house, she looked beautiful. Pilar and Reyna always wore makeup and clothing that enhanced their looks. "Is Bear here?"

"No, he went off with Grandfather to set up animal traps in the forest," Reyna said. "Grandfather particularly loved the sweets I brought him this morning. I'll have to remember that he likes banana bread."

Ruth looked toward the kitchen counter. "I smell something baking."

"I made you two pot pies, of sorts. I soaked the jerky that Bear had stored up. He let me in the shed today. I can make a lot with what he has in there. I added some dried beans and a few other vegetables and made a pie crust. I have the coals heated up low, so I've been letting the pies bake for over an hour now. I think they are just about done," Reyna said, walking over to the counter and grabbing a thick towel. She opened the coal stove and brought out one of the pies. "Yep, they're done."

Ruth walked over to the pie while Reyna got the other one out of the oven. "I see the shine on the crust. Did you bring over eggs?"

"See, and I thought you couldn't cook," Reyna giggled.

"I choose not to cook, but I've watched the sisters enough to know that an egg wash was used on the crust," Ruth said. "Bear had mentioned that he wanted to get a few chickens for the house."

"I can get some for you," Reyna said. "Dad has plenty. You know, my dad's birthday is coming up. I bet he won't miss a few chickens, and I would really like to get him one of those outfits Bear wears. My dad says they look comfortable," Reyna said.

Ruth was getting better at bartering with people. "You bring me four chickens and I'll make Levi a gi. And I will also make him one from Bear and me for his birthday," Ruth said.

"Only if I can bring you six chickens instead," Reyna said.

Ruth smiled. "I would appreciate it."

"Then we have a deal!" Reyna exclaimed.

"Bear was resistant to the idea of having someone helping us at home, but I think he really likes everything you do for us," Ruth said. She knew that making people feel appreciated was valued in the Colonies, and she was learning how to express gratitude.

Reyna smiled and Ruth could see a lot of Pilar's features in her expression.

"I love coming over here to help you and Bear. It's so peaceful here compared to my dad's house. There is always someone there and something going on. It's quiet here, and I can think while I work. Besides, you and Bear are easy to clean after. You barely make a mess," Reyna said.

Ruth looked toward her desk where all her sewing supplies were neatly organized. "I'm almost done with that outfit I am creating for you. I have added a little surprise. I made sure to ask Pilar first, and she says you will love it," Ruth said.

"I can't wait to wear it to the next bazaar. Everything you make is so perfect. I've gotten so many compliments on the outfit you made me as a wedding gift," Reyna said.

"I am glad," Ruth said.

"Any word from Zach today?" Reyna asked.

Ruth's expression instantly faltered. Pastor Tom had contacted her today and told her his theory of what Zach had done. "Yes, I have received some news from Pastor Tom."

"Did something happen to him and Li?" Reyna asked, fear restricting her voice.

"Nothing so far, but we do know that Randall has discovered where they are going," Ruth said and paused.

"Where are they going?" Reyna asked.

"That's just it," Ruth said. "We don't know. I have a letter that Zach sent to his previous LPS at the factory, but I can't decipher it unless I use an LPS. He sent it specifically so that no other machine could decode it," Ruth said. "Pastor Tom and I tried for an hour, using his HMS and my old-style computer. Maybe Li could do it, but he's not here. The only one that knows what Zach wrote is Randall."

"Why would Zach send a letter that no one could decipher besides Randall?" Reyna said and suddenly her expression turned to shock. "He wants to be found!"

Ruth nodded. "That's the only conclusion we could find."

"Does Pilar know?" Reyna asked.

Ruth nodded again. "I have never seen her so angry."

"What are you going to do?" Reyna asked.

"I have to talk to Bear first, but Levi has already gotten us a way into the factory tonight. I'm going to find out where my brother is and go get him."

"You two will stay in this truck! I'm the one doing the delivery!" Pilar almost shouted. She was fed up with taking the backseat in all of this, watching all her friends risk their lives while she stayed at home praying. It was time for action.

"You cannot decipher the letter, Pilar," Ruth said. "Let me make the delivery, and I will get to Zach's old office."

"I will not have you walking into that factory alone," Bear said in a tense whisper. "I can't believe I agreed to this."

"Will you two stop talking!" Pilar shushed. "Ruth, I know everyone in that factory. They know my family and they trust me. I will get in there, and I promise I will find a way to sneak you and Bear in. Just let me make this delivery to the night crew. Give me about ten minutes to chat with people and find my contact. I will come back and get you and bring you straight to the office. I need to see who's working today. I need to see if there are any Efficientists in there. Trust me. I might not be good with all this technology stuff, but I've been in almost every home of every worker in there. Let me do what I'm good at," Pilar said.

Pilar and Ruth sat in the front seats of the truck while Bear monitored from the back seat. When Pilar first found out what Zach had done, compromising his position and his life, she had a long talk with God. And for the first time in years, He told her to act. She had been waiting idly for so long that she almost forgot what it felt like to actually do something. The man she loved was miles away, and she would do everything she could to help him.

"I know all those men too," Bear said. "I could just as easily talk with them."

Pilar turned and looked at Bear without intimidation. "Half those men in that factory fear you and the other half idolize you. Your presence here is probably the least helpful to our mission. Now stay here and wait until I come to get you. Both of you. Bear, hand me those two boxes next to you. I need a reason to go in there, and a midnight snack from my father to the workers is more than appropriate."

Bear lifted one of the boxes, handing it to Pilar. He then handed her the other one. "Do you need help?" he asked.

"This is not my first rodeo," she said. She stacked the two boxes in her right arm and opened the door with her left. Then she got out and slammed the door shut with her foot. Bear and Ruth watched Pilar as she walked to the lit entrance of the factory.

Ruth and Bear sat silently together. "She said it," Ruth whispered.

"What?" Bear asked.

"*This is not my first rodeo*. When I met Zach for the first time when he installed my new Sleeper, that is what he said. My mother used to say it," Ruth said.

"Why is it important?" Bear asked.

"None of the Varieties use clichés or expressions. When Zach used it, I felt that it was familiar. I could not understand why. I looked it up to get the meaning, but that did not help with what I was feeling. I did not understand it at the time, but I do now. Zach looks a lot like our mother did when she was young. He has a lot of her same mannerisms. His presence in my flat in

126

the city and the expression he used is probably what helped me remember my mother. My near-death experience is what unleashed the memory into my awakened state. Before she only existed in my dreams."

"She's thinking about Zach," Bear said, understanding.

Ruth nodded and looked back toward the window. "She was so angry when I told her Pastor Tom's theory."

"She better get to him before I do," Bear said. "Because I'm just as angry. All this talk about me letting go of how my father and mother mistreated me, and he won't let go of this Randall guy."

"Zach will lose if he confronts Randall," Ruth said. "Randall has already attacked him once. The only reason he did not kill Zach was that I told him not to," Ruth said.

"Zach will be prepared this time," Bear said. "He wouldn't have sent that letter unless he had a plan. I just hope it doesn't end in death."

"We need to get into that factory. I have to know what this letter reads," Ruth said. "Zach robbed the World Bank. He set up all the computers for Pastor Tom. I hope I am wrong, but I feel like he did all of this to send this letter to Randall."

Bear leaned back in his chair. "That would make sense. I wondered why he would so willingly compromise your safety. He wants revenge."

Bear and Ruth sat quietly, watching for Pilar to exit the factory.

"He deceived me," Ruth finally said. "He behaved so innocently, like he was ready to do something great for God. All the while he was planning his revenge against Randall."

"Ruth, sometimes revenge gets stuck so deep in your soul that you deceive yourself. That's why God cut me off for so long from others. I didn't know how far gone I was until all I had was time."

"Tranquilizers," Ruth whispered.

"What?" Bear asked, leaning toward the front seat.

"I remember a conversation I had with Zach about Li. Li was thinking about starting a ranch, so Zach did some research on my HMS. He left some of his research on the screen. One in particular was how to care for sick or injured horses. I read briefly about horse tranquilizers," Ruth stopped. "Their last stop before we lost contact with them was a horse ranch."

Bear looked at Ruth for a long moment. "He's going to try to tranquilize Randall and then kill him? He has no idea what he's getting into."

Ruth looked at the factory from the window. "Where is she?"

Suddenly, Ruth saw movement. She looked toward the back of the factory away from the entrance. There it was again. A hand was waving from a low window that was set just above a large trash receptacle. "There she is!" Ruth said, opening her door and getting out into the dark parking lot.

"Where?" Bear asked, getting out as well.

"Her hand is waving from the window," Ruth said, as she jogged briskly into the night.

Bear caught up with her. "Don't tell Pilar. She'll find out eventually, but she doesn't need the stress of it all right now."

Ruth looked at Bear. "We are in agreement."

CHAPTER TWENTY

"I told you that I would come through for you," Pilar said after Bear squeezed his body through the small window and climbed down the ladder. "Here, put the rod back into the window," Pilar said, handing Bear a metal rod. Bear grabbed the rod and climbed halfway up the ladder, fitting it into the two grooves—one on the upper ledge of the window and the other on the lower ledge—so it blended with the other rods that guarded the entrance to the window. "I'm guessing this window has been used before," Bear said, climbing back down.

"The workers use it to smuggle stuff they want out of the factory. They never take too much because they don't want to get caught. Just a few boxes of canned goods or components for an HMS."

"Are you the only one here?" Ruth asked.

"I brought the food, chatted with a few of the workers and in exchange I was given a map and a few descriptions. I escorted myself to the ladies' room and have been gone for almost five minutes now. As long as we hurry up, I won't be missed," Pilar said and turned to Bear. "Do you remember Zach's old office?"

Bear thought for a moment. "Yes, it looks over the factory floor."

"Okay, the door is unlocked. Go in there. Decipher the letter. And meet me back in my truck. I have to leave through the entrance now, so I don't look suspicious. I don't want my dad or my family to get in trouble with the World Government. Make sure to go right back to this room and put back the rod in the window before you leave. Use this map," Pilar said, handing the map to Bear. "The cameras aren't working in these specific areas."

Bear took the map. "Okay, we'll meet you outside in fifteen minutes."

Pilar turned to Ruth. "Find where he is. I think he's up to something. I told him I was concerned for him in my last letter, and he never responded."

Ruth and Bear watched as Pilar quietly sprinted toward the stairs like a cat sneaking at night.

Ruth looked at Bear. "She knows."

Bear opened the folded paper. "Follow me," he whispered.

Ruth moved behind Bear, following his movements. He wore a charcoal-colored gi that she had made him. He made almost no noise while he moved and his breathing was quiet compared to her labored breaths. She realized that she needed to exercise more. She was still winded from running through the parking lot, crawling through the window and climbing down the ladder. Both Bear and Pilar had to help her—Bear pushed her up and Pilar helped her through the opening while trying to keep the ladder balanced.

Bear and Ruth made their way up the stairs about a minute after Pilar went through the door. But instead of turning left, they turned right. Bear immediately led them into another stairwell and by now Ruth felt dizzy.

"Bear," she whispered and stopped.

He immediately turned around. "What's wrong?"

"I have to slow down. I'm out of breath," she said.

"Really, Ruth?" he said in a frustrated tone.

"I sew and type all day," she said in a hushed, irritated tone. "You can just go to the LPS without me and find the information we need."

"You know I can't do that," he whispered back.

"Exactly. You have strengths and weakness and so do I. So slow down!"

Bear leaned against the cold cement wall. "Point taken. You know, you are cute when you're tired and mad."

Ruth rolled her eyes like she had seen Pilar do hundreds of times. "Just go slower," she said and continued.

Bear laughed as she passed him by, and he quickly skipped a few steps to get back in front of her. "We are almost there. His old office is by the stairs. I always wondered how he was getting so much stuff out of the factory. He was getting it through the window."

Ruth didn't like to think of her brother stealing from a factory. She remembered all of the cans of food he would take home. He would tell her and their mother that it was surplus. She was finding out more and more that her brother had a lot of secrets.

Bear took another right as they got to the final step. He dragged his right hand against the wall until it reached the door handle. He pressed his left hand gently on the door and turned the knob with his right. A soft click sounded. Bear opened the door for Ruth, and she walked straight to the desk and sat down in the chair.

"Close the door, so the light from the LPS does not shine through," she said.

Ruth took a printout that Pastor Tom had forwarded to her from her pocket and unfolded it, laying it on the desk next to the LPS. She gave a few short verbal commands. At first the LPS wouldn't turn on, but she kept typing and giving short verbal commands. Finally, the screen glowed to wakefulness. She continued to type and give commands, opening several windows at once.

"Ruth, you're fast at all of this. Are you reading everything? I see at least a dozen windows open," Bear said, bending down to get a better look at the screen.

"I am trying," she said.

Bear got the cue. "Okay, I'll be quiet."

Finally, Ruth's hand stopped and her eyes scanned all the images and words she had brought up to the screen. Less than thirty seconds later, she closed out all the windows and the screen went black.

"What did you find?" Bear asked.

"I found everything," Ruth said.

"Let's get out of here. You can tell us in the truck," he said, opening the office door once more. He looked left and right and then exited into the hall. He could see the desolate factory below. He closed the door quietly when Ruth came out. He then retraced his steps down the hall, taking lefts until they made it to the stairwell. When they got to the basement, they jogged to the back of the large room where the windows let in dull wisps of light. Ruth started up the ladder first, and Bear followed behind her. She handed him the metal rod, and he reached down and softly let it hit the ground before climbing back up to help Ruth.

"Okay, take my hands and I'll drop you down," Bear whispered to Ruth. He grabbed Ruth's petite frame and carefully pressed her legs through the opening, keeping his hips and torso taut to prevent the ladder from moving. He lowered her as far as he could and dropped her to the trash receptacle below. She landed softly.

"Can you make it down to the ground?" he whispered from the window.

"Yes," she said looking around. "I'll just grab the edge and dangle my feet before dropping. It's not too far."

"Okay, run to the truck. I have to get the rod and put it back in the window after I crawl out. I'll be right behind you," he said and climbed back down the ladder.

Ruth got on her hands and knees and slowly crawled backward to the ledge of the trash receptacle's closed lid. She grabbed the ledge and lowered her body. She felt her head start to spin and she forced herself to take several deep breaths. Her body dangled for less than a second before she had to let go. Her feet hit the ground and she felt her body roll, dispersing the force of the impact. She then got up and sprinted to the truck. She felt her adrenaline pulsing through her body. She saw Pilar's figure waiting for her behind the steering wheel. She needed to sit down and rest. When she finally got to the truck, she opened the passenger door and jumped in. Her breathing was so heavy that she couldn't say anything. She looked at Pilar and saw fear in her face. Instantly, she knew something was wrong.

She heard a click as all the doors locked. "Drive right now or I'll kill your friend," a man's voice said from the backseat.

Ruth instantly recognized the voice. It was Randall.

"Drive now!" Randall said, grabbing Ruth's hair and pulling her head back toward the gun he held in his right hand.

"I'm trying!" Pilar screamed and struggled with the keys in her hand. Her hands trembled, and she had difficulty putting the key into the ignition. When she finally turned the key, Randall yelled again and Ruth screamed in pain as her head was pulled further back. Before she could push the gas, the window to the backseat exploded. Bear's bloodied hand was clawing at Randall's face.

"Ruth! Get out! Get out!" Bear yelled.

Ruth couldn't think. She grabbed at the door lock and pulled it up. She tried to open the door but her labored breathing and the shock of Randall's presence caused her to hyperventilate. She instantly felt her vision spin like a cyclone. All she could hear before she went unconscious was Randall's voice screaming, "My eyes! My eyes!"

"He needed bait. Plain and simple," Bear said. His voice was tense but controlled. "Levi is amassing a small army to get Pilar back. He's just waiting for Ruth to wake up, so he can get the location out of her. Most of my guys have already said they would join him to rescue her. You don't understand. My men want a fight. They have been trained to fight."

"They can't do that," Pastor Tom said. "They will compromise everything we are doing. We have the key to bring the entire World Government to their knees, and they will compromise it. Not only that, they will cause the World Government to bring their own army against us, and it will devastate the Colonies."

"You can't tell a father that he can't go get his daughter back," Bear said, trying to keep his voice down. "He doesn't care about your cause. His baby girl has been kidnapped."

"There is something greater at stake here. Pilar means nothing to Randall. And from what you've told me, he's injured," Pastor Tom said. "We just need one or two men to follow them. You can do that, Bear. Take Levi with you."

Ruth opened her eyes. She was lying on the couch in the living room, facing the door. She could see Pastor Tom and Bear standing near the kitchen. Bear's right hand had thick bandages wrapped around it. He wore a fresh gi and his hair was wet from washing. She no longer listened to what they were saying. She could only watch Bear. He stood like a bear ready to attack. He was lean and strong, and she could see the grey streaks in his midnight hair that was pulled back at the nape of his neck. She centered on one thought. He was completely hers, and she loved him. He damaged his right hand for her, and she knew he had risked his life going after a man with a loaded weapon. No matter all the small things he did that irritated her, she finally felt completely surrendered to him. She could see his breathing become quicker, so she refocused on what they were saying.

"I can't be responsible for what Zach does or Levi does or even what Randall does. I have a wife and a grandfather that I am to look after. I want children. I can't be this vigilante anymore. Pilar is my friend, but I have to protect my home. Right here is where I'm called to be. I need to safeguard the people that God has given to me."

"No, no, you're right. Zach has gotten himself in this mess. He will need to figure it out. But Levi can't just declare war against the World Government. We need to contact Zach or Li somehow. When they get to the factory, we must find a way to let them know that Randall has taken Pilar," Pastor Tom said.

"The factory is gone," Ruth said, trying to sit up.

Bear looked over to her and swiftly made his way to the couch, kneeling next to her. "You don't have to say anything," Bear said, stroking her face. "Just rest."

"How did I get out of the truck?" Ruth asked.

"Bear smashed his hand through the window, breaking almost every little bone in his right hand," Pastor Tom said, walking toward the couch.

Ruth looked at Bear's hand. "I'm so sorry."

"It's only a hand. I would have gladly given it up and more for you," Bear said. His frustration loosened and tears formed.

Ruth savored the weathered look of his face, which was so opposite her lineless appearance—even though they were only a few years apart. His face carried emotion, while hers appeared blank. She could see the hours of stress and anger were finally catching up with him. "I love you," she whispered spontaneously.

Bear grabbed her chin with his left hand. "Randall is hurt. He was blinded by the glass. I wish I could have shoved the glass ten times harder into his face and killed him right there."

"Bear, we can't harbor thoughts of trading evil for evil," Pastor Tom interrupted.

Bear looked back at him. "It was not evil that made me punch my fist through that window. It was love."

Pastor Tom stared at Bear. "You're right. I'm sorry again. I would have done the same thing for Cindy. Obviously, I'm out of my expertise in this situation."

"How did he get Pilar?" Ruth asked.

"He freed himself from my grip and grabbed Pilar's neck before she could get out. He put the gun to her head and made her drive. Thankfully, you unlocked your door before passing out, and I was able to pull you out as they drove off," Bear said.

Ruth tried to imagine the scene in her mind. "You used your left hand to get me out?"

Bear nodded. "It's a good thing I train with both hands because my right hand became useless quickly. That's how Randall slipped out of my grip so easily. I would never have let go of him if the bones in my right hand weren't all broken"

Ruth stared into Bear's eyes and instinctively reached up to wipe the tears along the side of his face. "Thank you," she whispered.

"I'm going to leave you both. I know you're tired," Pastor Tom said tentatively. "I'm going to go talk with Levi before driving back to Trinity and try to help him through this, though, I feel like I have little to offer him. Ruth, what did you mean when you said the factory isn't there anymore?"

Ruth pushed herself up higher against the sofa cushions. "Zach must not know that the factory is no longer there," she began. "It was taken over by Neil over a year ago."

"What's there?" Pastor Tom asked.

Ruth looked toward the fireplace. "No one knows the real reason why my father and Neil split."

"Neil was your father's protégé—supposed to take his place," Pastor Tom said. "But they had a falling out, which is why he had you."

"Yes, they worked together for years until they had a severe disagreement, which correlated with Neil's family business before entering *Life Efficiency*. His family owned miles of farmland in the Colonies," Ruth said.

"Yes, I heard about that, but then they lost it all, which is when Neil's parents sought out your father. Neil was about twelve or so," Pastor Tom said, intrigued. "What happened?"

"Neil's family used forced labor on their farms," Ruth said.

"What does that mean?" Bear asked.

"They owned Colonial slaves," Ruth said, simply. "The World Government did not know about it, but they never thought to research how the family was producing so many crops. Efficientists ate their food and never thought about where it came from. His family hired overseers to go into the countryside looking for nomadic and poor Colonials to enslave them. Some of the people were so destitute that they came willingly. They would be fed and sheltered, and in exchange they would work. But the overseers began to mistreat the people and they revolted. Instead of letting them go, Neil's father killed them all—hundreds of Colonials died."

"What?" Pastor Tom said. "I've never heard of this."

Bear got up from the couch. "My grandfather has told me rumors of this, but I didn't believe him."

"The World Government covered it up because it was an embarrassment. My father began to teach Neil, but they split years later when Neil wanted the World Government to institute forced labor again."

"I can't believe this," Pastor Tom said. "So there are Colonial slaves controlled by Neil that the World Government doesn't know about it? Oh no—this is all part of Neil's *Colonization Plan*, isn't it?"

Ruth nodded her head. "The factory that Li and Zach are headed to is a forced labor camp. It is one of several that Neil has put into operation since I have been gone. He has kept them all secret for now."

"I can't believe you found all that out on the LPS you were on for less than a minute," Bear said, astonished.

"Yes, I know where the old factory is. I know that Zach does not know what he is walking into. And I know that he has taken horse tranquilizers from the ranch that he last visited," Ruth said. "And I do not think that Randall knows about the forced labor camps."

"You think Randall's in the dark about all of this?" Pastor Tom asked.

"Yes," Ruth said. "I found a communication from Neil's LPS to the only LPS at this forced labor camp," Ruth said and became quiet.

"What did it say?" Pastor Tom asked.

"Neil wants Randall dead," Ruth said.

CHAPTER TWENTY-ONE

"You did it!" Zach said, walking tentatively to where Li sat on the horse's back. "Here, I brought the rope harness you dropped."

Zach watched Li ride the black and white horse bareback, amazed at the sight. Li wouldn't let go of the fierce horse. Zach feared his friend would be hurt, and he would have to cancel his plans. Maybe he even wished for it a little bit. He had sent the letter to his old LPS at the factory, and he knew that Randall would find it. His path would soon cross with the man who murdered his father. He knew his heart wanted revenge, but he was torn between what he knew was right and what he wanted. He only hoped that God would intervene somehow.

Li brought his right leg from over the horse's back and dropped both feet on the ground. He kept hold of the horse's mane. He took the rope from Zach, and pulled his handmade harness around the horse's neck and muzzle. He held the other end of the rope tightly and began stroking the horse's mane. "Were you able to get the harness over your horse?" he asked.

"Yes, and I'm pleased to announce that she's timid and docile. I've named her Lazy Dusk, but Lazy for short. It's seemed fitting for her. I think she's already tame," Zach said, smiling proudly. "She's nibbling on grass in the pen. I broke open a few pecans for her. She seemed to like them. But I think she's thirsty."

"You're probably right. I'll bring Xīnnián to the pen and let him rest a bit. Then we can bring them one at a time to the creek," Li said. He stroked the horse's face.

"What's his name?" Zach asked, looking confounded.

"Xīnnián," Li said quickly.

"I couldn't catch that. Say it again, but break it down in syllables that I can understand," Zach said, listening intently.

"I named him *Xin Nian Kuai Le*," Li pronounced phonetically.

"Is that Chinese?" Zach asked.

"It's Mandarin for New Year," Li said. "I don't know why it came to me. I feel like it's a new life for me and for him."

"I like it," Zach said, crossing his arms and grinning. "But I can't say it. I'll just call him Xin for short if that's alright by you?"

"Xin…I think it sounds good," Li said, petting the horse's shoulder. "Now let me see if he'll let me lead him with the rope."

Li held the rope tightly in both hands and took a step. The horse didn't budge at first, but Li whispered his name and stroked his head again. Then he tried another step, and this time the horse began to walk. Li walked slowly at first, but he picked up speed as they got closer to the camp. Zach opened the pen door, and Li led Xin into the pen next to Lazy.

Xin seemed excited to see the black mare in the pen with him. He reached his muzzle toward her and sniffed and rubbed her face with his.

"I think they're a couple," Zach said. "Let's just hope it's not mating season."

"No, mating season is over, but I believe Lazy is too young to mate. She still has a few more years until it's safe for her."

Zach reached through the tall, wooden spikes of the pen and began to stroke Lazy's back and side. "Well, just make sure you keep Xin away from my girl," he said with a smile. "I wouldn't want any accidents."

Li smiled back. "I'll try."

Zach watched his friend pet Xin and whisper his name. Li truly enjoyed being with the horse. Zach wondered if they hadn't already begun to see the small beginnings of Li's ranch. He really wanted to help Li begin his dream. He even wondered if he could trade his life at Levington for a life in the wilderness. Instantly, he thought of Pilar. She had written him. She sensed he was up to something. She was right. He got her letter the day he left the ranch with horse tranquilizers in his backpack. He wondered if the rancher would realize that they were missing. Probably so. How could he talk with such passion about God and His Word—all the while harboring thoughts of revenge in his heart? He couldn't unleash himself from hurting the very man who destroyed his life.

"Zach, did you hear me?" Li asked again.

"I'm sorry," Zach said refocusing on Li. "I was thinking about Pilar. What did you ask?"

"I asked if we should leave in the morning? We need to buy saddles for these horses. Do you think you can get us to that town you have visited?" Li asked.

"What about the factory? I need to send correspondence to Pastor Tom," Zach said. He worried that Li would try to sidetrack his plan.

"We can still go to the factory," Li said. "But we need to get saddles and supplies first. I think we should go into the town at least for a day and get cleaned up. We have to buy new clothes, eat a decent meal and get better harnesses and ropes for our horses. We should have more than enough jewelry to get everything we need."

"The town is very remote. No one will own an HMS. Pastor Tom and the others are probably worried about us. They have no idea where we are or even if we are okay," Zach argued.

"You know I almost always agree with you in these situations, but we can't go to a World Government factory looking the way we do and half-starved. Pecans are nice, but we need real food. I've had to tie wire through the loops of my jeans to keep them up, and I've noticed you pulling yours up quite a bit. We have to eat, get cleaned up, buy supplies and then we can go. One day won't make a difference."

"But what if it does?" Zach pressed.

Li stopped and stared at Zach. "Is there something about the factory that you have not told me?"

Zach realized he had pushed too hard. "No, not at all. I'm just worried about Pilar and Ruth. You're right. One day won't make a difference. I've thought back over our trek out here, and I believe we are only twenty or thirty miles from the town. The factory was only a day's walk from the town, so it won't take us too long with our horses."

"We shouldn't ride the horses too hard tomorrow. We will have to alternate walking and riding them, which will prolong our journey. It may take us up to two days to make it to the village, so we need to take as much water and pecans as we can and fill up before we leave in the morning."

Zach nodded his head. "Let's leave just before dawn, so we can get as much ride time as possible."

"I know you miss Pilar. You weren't able to respond to her latest letter, and I realize that must be frustrating. I only met her briefly, and she's an amazing person." Li said.

"She is an amazing woman. I don't know why she still loves me. I've put her through a lot. Sometimes I just want her to find someone else. She told me she went on a few dates, but they never worked out. She says she'd rather have me with difficulty than another man with ease."

"Why do you keep her at a distance?" Li asked.

Zach heard Li's words and knew exactly why he kept her at a distance. If she knew what was inside of him, she would try to bring it to light and speak some sense into him. But he knew what he was planning was wrong, and he would have to deal with the consequences later.

Zach finally looked at Li and lied. "I don't know why."

"Can you just give them two days? If I haven't heard from Zach and Li by then, you can go get Pilar," Pastor Tom said. He was sitting at Levi's large wooden table still dusted with flour from the previous night. He could barely get Levi inside the kitchen, so he could talk with him. Levi's anger and pain caused his normally gentle features to become hard.

"Please, Levi. Listen to Pastor Tom," Maria said. "I want her back too, but you will make things worse for her."

Levi pounded the thick table with both fists and stood up. "How could I make it worse by bringing her home?"

"You don't understand. The place Randall is taking her is a forced labor camp. It won't be like the factory here in Levington. It will be gated and guarded by men with machine guns. And Randall's eyes are wounded. Even if he can see a little, he will still have glass in his eyes. Bear made sure of that. And don't forget about your daughter. She is the strongest young woman I know. I won't be surprised if she's halfway home by now."

"But how can I know that?" Levi said, trying to control the volume of his voice. "What if she's calling out to me right now?"

"Can you please sit down?" Pastor Tom asked, motioning to the chair.

Levi continued standing. "I have at least ten men willing to come with me right now. I could already be there. My baby girl could already be home!"

"Maria," Pastor Tom said, turning to Levi's wife. "What do you think your daughter would want?"

Maria looked at her husband and thought for a moment. "Just before she left last night with Bear and Ruth, she had said that God told her it was time for her to act. I know my daughter, and sitting on her hands is very hard for her. So, when God told her that He was about to use her, she was so excited. I can't shake the feeling that God is using her somehow in this situation. And I know my daughter. She would rather do something and be scared than do nothing and be bored."

"You would leave your daughter to the wolves?" Levi asked his wife.

"No, Levi," Maria said, grabbing her husband's dark hands. "But our daughter is strong, and she loves to be in control. I can almost guarantee that she will take control of this situation. That man has been blinded and injured. Pilar is a fighter. I feel it in my heart that we will see her soon. And you have another daughter and two sons here who also need you. I need you. It does none of us any good if you and Pilar are both gone, and the World Government targets the rest of us."

142

"But this is the man who killed Zach's dad and who tried to kill Ruth. He has a gun. He's ruthless," Levi said. His rigid features began to soften, and tears streamed down this face.

"Levi, the hardest thing for a father to do is let go and trust his Heavenly Father. Regardless of what I'm saying, what do you think God wants you to do? What do you think He's telling you?" Pastor Tom said.

Levi sat back down in the chair and his head fell into his hands, smothering his cries. Maria walked over to him and wrapped her arms around his large shoulders.

Pastor Tom prayed silently.

After less than a minute, Levi brought his head back up. "I'll give you forty-eight hours," he said in a firm voice. "If Li and Zach haven't contacted us by then, I will go get my baby girl. I don't care what the World Government knows."

CHAPTER TWENTY-TWO

"**K**eep driving!" Randall's voice shot up from the backseat. "I will shoot you if you pull over! Go in the seat for all I care."

Pilar had enough. She had been driving all night. She was tired and needed to relieve herself. She could have already jumped out of the truck at any moment, but she didn't want to be lost outside at night. As weird as it sounded to her, she feared the dark woods more than the man in the backseat. Randall, this man whom Zach had become obsessed with since he discovered his identity, was wounded. His eyes were filled with glass, but his left eye could still see her. He had dozed off more than once, but Pilar continued to drive. She knew that—although this was far from what she had imagined—this was what God had released her to do.

"Look," she finally said. "I could have easily left you two hours ago when you fell asleep. But I didn't. I kept driving in the direction you told me to go. But now I need to relieve myself. I will not mess myself or my truck."

"Fine," Randall said, roughly. "But you will need to go fast, and I will not let you out of my sight."

"Whatever," Pilar said and began to pull the truck to the side of the road. It was early morning and the tip of the sun was peering over the horizon. She slowed the car off the gravel road and stopped along the grass. She looked around the area. It was different from her home further south. There were more hills and large trees with yellow and orange leaves dangling from them. She got out of the truck, and she heard Randall follow behind her from the backseat. She couldn't help but roll her eyes.

"Do you expect me to pee in front of you?" she asked turning toward him.

He cocked the gun he held in his right hand. "You better," he said.

144

Pilar noticed that he held a piece of ripped shirt in his left hand against his right eye. His face and chest were covered with dry blood. "Your right eye looks like it bled a lot through the night."

"I didn't realize the Shaman would put his fist through my window, now did I?" Randall said, derisively. "Don't you worry about me. Once I get to the factory, I will get a home doctor to make me as good as new. People do as I say where we're going. Now do what you need to do."

Pilar walked around the truck, looking for the low bush she had seen from the window. "I'm going to squat behind this bush. Don't worry. I'm sure you'll have a good shot if I try to run."

Pilar walked to the bush, ignoring the gun that followed her steps. She didn't care who was looking. She needed to relieve herself. The pressing on her bladder had escalated over the last fifteen minutes of driving. She faced away from Randall and quickly pulled down her pants and squatted. She was irritated it took her body a few moments to respond, so she imagined she was back at her house in Levington, listening to her family working in the kitchen.

When she finally walked back around the bush, she saw that Randall was leaning against the truck, working on a Portable. Randall had the gun in his left hand pointing in her direction and typing on the Portable with his right hand. She had a better view of his right eye. He could barely blink because pieces of glass were protruding out.

"Just stand there while I finish this," he said. "We should be there in a few hours if you continue to drive straight."

"We are almost out of gas," Pilar said.

"I saw that you have three extra gallons of gasoline in the back. You are very prepared," he said. "That will be more than enough."

"You're right. I do," Pilar said. "My father always makes me take it for emergencies."

Pilar thought for a second and made a quick decision. "I also have food and water and a medical kit back there," she said. "I can take a look at that eye for you. I can tell the glass is really hurting you. The longer you leave the shards alone, the more they will bury themselves deeper."

Randall pushed himself away from the truck. "What do you know about first aid?" he asked.

"I know that I have tweezer in that medical kit. I can pull the glass out. And we can flush both eyes out with water that I have," Pilar said.

"The glass in my right eye hurts, but I have a tiny sliver in my left eye that's digging in. I can feel it," he said, walking up to her.

"That one may be too far gone for me," she said. "I can look, though."

"And why would you even volunteer?" he asked, suspiciously.

"Simple," she said, standing straight and crossing her arms. "I want to live. You let me live, and I will pull the glass out of your eye before you become blind."

Randall pointed the gun to her face. "You know who I am don't you? I waited at that factory to see which people would try to get that letter that Daniels sent. I thought the Shaman might come. Didn't think he would bring his wife. But then you showed up too. I knew you dated him in the past, but from what I gathered, you two were not together anymore. So I was surprised to see you there last night. Would you make good bait for Daniels?"

"We aren't together. I doubt he would do anything for me. He doesn't love me. I only helped Bear because he needed a way to get in the factory," Pilar said. "Bear doesn't even care much, but he felt obligated. I'm sorry. There's not much bait when it comes to Zacchaeus Daniels."

Randall nodded. "I thought as much." He stood thinking. "What do you know about Charlie Liu?"

Pilar opened her arms. "I have never heard that name before."

"You know, that Daniels has it in for me. I should have killed him when I had the chance, but I listened to a woman just like you, and I will not...." Randall stopped talking. He screamed out and covered his left eye. "It hurts!"

"You keep forgetting that you're wounded and you roll your eye around. You're going to lose that eye if you keep doing that," Pilar said. "But if you don't want me to take the glass out, then I'll just get back into the truck and drive you to the factory. Hopefully, they can get a doctor there in a few hours. We are far away from any hospital."

Pilar began to walk toward the truck, intending to get back into the driver's seat.

"Stop there. Even if I let you take this glass out of my eye, what makes you trust that I will keep my end of the bargain?" he asked.

Pilar shrugged her shoulders. "A man of honor never goes back on his word. Are you a man of honor?"

"Okay," he finally said. "Get this glass out of my eye and I will not kill you. But that doesn't mean you're going to be safe. I'm sure the World Government will want to keep you silent."

"Whatever you say," Pilar said and began walking toward the bed of the truck. She placed her hand on the truck and pushed off the tire with her feet, landing inside the bed of the truck. "Here is the emergency kit and water. And I have a box of stored bread. I'll get the gas when we are done," she said and pulled the handle on the tailgate, opening it. Then she sat down and scooted the medical kit and water toward her.

"Come here," she said, dangling her legs over the side.

Randall placed the Portable in the backseat and walked toward Pilar. He held the gun tightly in his hand. "Let me also make you another promise. If you hurt me or run away, I will hunt down every single member of your sweet family, including your precious sister, and kill them all. Do you hear me? Don't do anything stupid."

"I won't, so now lean your head against my leg and be still," Pilar said, patting her left thigh.

Randall dropped his gun hand by his side and leaned his back against the tailgate. Then he slumped his head back against Pilar's thigh. He was still covering his right eye with the piece of material.

"Remove your hand so I can do this. Now, I said I would take it out. I didn't say it wouldn't hurt. Glass in the eye is one of the worst pains ever, so be ready," Pilar said, opening the medical kit. "Good, we have gauze and tape. And here are the tweezers."

Pilar placed her left index finger over his eye and her thumb under it, stretching his eyelid open. He kept wanting to squint, so she had to keep the tension. "Stop moving your eye. You're making it harder."

"Make it quick!" Randall shouted before standing still.

Pilar saw the biggest piece and gently grabbed it with the tweezers, making sure she had a good grip. Then she pulled quickly straight up from his right eye. Randall yelled.

"Stay still. Let me get the other one," Pilar demanded.

Randall relaxed again, but his breathing was labored. Pilar didn't want to make a mistake. She knew this man could either thank her or scream at her. She carefully went to the other piece of glass in his right eye. It was thinner but more deeply imbedded. She grabbed the glass close to the eye, so the shard wouldn't break apart. When she had it firmly, she pulled straight up again. Randall yelled again and brought his head up.

"It's bleeding!" he yelled.

"I know," Pilar said, jumping off the tailgate. "I got them both out, so they'll bleed a little bit. Come back here, so I can wash it out and bandage it. Then I can take a look at your left eye."

"You won't touch the other one," he yelled.

"Fine!" she yelled back. "At least let me wash that one out, so you'll stop being angry!"

Pilar noticed that Randall kept his gun hand down as he looked at her. "Wash them. Bandage them. And then drive me to the factory," he said, firmly.

"Fine," she said.

CHAPTER TWENTY-THREE

"**I** brought that old computer back for you," Bear said. He looked at Ruth lying on her side in their bed. She was reading the big *Bible* that one of the sisters had gifted her before they had met. She wore a white nightgown she had made after they were married. He liked it on her. It was simple, but feminine. It wasn't until you looked closely that you realized how well it was made—one intricate stitch after the other over a thin contour of lace. It reminded him of Ruth. She was simple, but feminine, and you didn't realize how complex and truly magnificent she was until you looked closely.

"Are you sure that is wise?" she asked, getting up on her elbow. He noticed her deep chestnut hair had grown several inches since their wedding. It looked beautiful draped down her pale shoulders and onto the white sheets of the bed.

"I would rather hide this thing here than have you go over to Levi's house right now. Zach has a little more than twenty-four hours to contact Levi before he declares war. Randall's not here, so I'm not worried about him seeing you. Besides, Grandfather and I have set traps all around this house. No one is getting here unnoticed."

"Did you tell the men that you train?" Ruth asked. "I would not want them to get hurt."

Bear sat down on the bed next to Ruth. "I will, but I've canceled training until we figure out what to do about Zach and Pilar. They know better than to wander around my land anyway. They'd be more scared of me than a trap."

Ruth smiled and continued to read, turning one of the thick pages. "What are you reading?" he finally asked.

Ruth looked up. "Nothing really. I am skimming, taking in verses as I see them."

"What are you looking for?" Bear asked, leaning in to see her book. "You're reading Isaiah."

Ruth looked back at the page. "Not really," she said and closed it. "I think I am waiting for God to give me an answer, but I am not finding it."

Bear raised his eyebrows. "I thought you said that the *Bible* has all the answers."

"Yes, it does have revelations that can apply to our lives, but—" she said and paused. "I think I already know the answer. I guess I am looking for more proof other than what I feel inside."

Bear had never seen Ruth so lost for words. He wondered if she was going to ask him for help or information. He couldn't tell what she was doing, but she looked confused, which was rare to see in her. "Are you upset about Pilar?" he asked.

"Yes, but that is not the answer I am seeking. I did pray for her. I have dealt with Randall, and I know he cannot be trusted. Pilar is stronger—stronger than I was. If anyone could outwit Randall, she will."

Bear couldn't help himself. He touched Ruth's shoulder and stroked it gently with the tips of his fingers. He had been alone so long, but she was worth the wait.

"I am struggling with family," she said.

Bear instantly brought back his hand. "I thought we already decided on that," he said, trying not to sound gruff.

"I know that I had decided and you yielded," she admitted. "I apologize. I know that must have been a difficult choice for you."

Bear said nothing. He would not accept an apology for his compromise, but he wouldn't argue over it either. He knew it was part of marriage, but it still didn't make it easier.

Ruth watched for his reaction, but he didn't give one, so she continued. "I notice that all the families in the *Bible* were not perfect and they had many troubles. Honestly, their troubles seem beyond our own, especially when the kings' sons began to overthrow the throne. They were selfish and brutal. I see my father's power like a throne, and I tried to fulfill his expectations all the while people were always trying to overthrow it."

"People like Neil," Bear said. He enjoyed when Ruth talked. Much of the time he felt like she was a stone vault, but it was the rare times of openness that he clung to.

"Yes. He continued to chase my rank. I always had to be one step ahead," she said. "Like you, when you were the best fighter in the circuit. Fighters would always try to take your position."

Bear chuckled. "Always, and they never could, which is why I retired to train others."

"I think family is supposed to be the opposite. Instead of the constant challenge, family should be a place of rest and safety."

Bear leaned his elbow into the sheets and faced Ruth. Their bodies were aligned on the bed. "I guess that is how family should be. I don't think you or I were raised like that, but that sounds just about right to me."

"I see that there are healthy families and unhealthy families. Deborah and Esther—although they had no children of their own—provided a very healthy family for me. Pastor Tom and Cindy have a healthy family. Pilar's family is healthy. The world I have seen so far has many healthy families—not perfect, but healthy."

"What's the difference?" Bear asked now intrigued.

"That's what I have been asking myself," Ruth said. "When I looked at all the healthy families around me, I sense one thing. There is an element of selflessness. It is like they put the needs of the family above the needs of the individual. It does not mean the individual is not important, but the individual's needs are incorporated into the family's needs as a whole."

Bear thought about his mother. She lived a very selfish life. She consumed herself with her own grief and covered it up with drug addiction. He knew she loved him in her heart, but that love did not go into her day-to-day actions. There were times she wouldn't feed him or wash him. He had to learn at an early age how to care for himself.

"I can see that," he finally said. He didn't want to say too much because he enjoyed listening to his wife speak what was on her mind.

Ruth stared at him from her side of the bed. "I can see you are not understanding my point," she said.

"Yes, I do," he said slightly irritated. "I heard everything. Selfish people have horrible families. I see exactly what you're telling me."

Ruth sat up and crossed her legs. "Yes, that is was I said, but I am telling you something."

Bear got up and faced Ruth again. "What? I understand. I see what you're getting at," he said, trying not to sound defiant.

Ruth reached out and gently lifted his bandaged hand. Suddenly, he saw tears streaming down her face. "I mean that you are the most selfless man I have ever met," she whispered through her tears.

"Oh," he whispered back. He let Ruth pet his injured hand. Normally, he didn't like to baby himself, but it felt good coming from his wife. "God had to do a lot of work in me. I used to be very selfish—much like my mother."

"Yes, but that is not you anymore. I feel like I am still very selfish inside, but I know God can change me like He changed you. And..." she stopped her words.

"Ruth, what's wrong? Are you upset about what Randall did in the truck? I got to you as fast as I could," Bear said. He didn't understand why Ruth looked so sad.

Ruth shook her head. "No, I am trying to tell you that I am willing to start a family with you. I guarantee that I will not be perfect, and I still have a lot of selfishness in me, but you have given me a healthy family here with you and Grandfather. I trust the home that you have provided for me—enough to bring a new life into it."

Bear stared at Ruth, questioning if he had heard her right. "Do you mean you will have a baby with me?"

"Yes," she said, firmly. "I want us to have a baby. I do not know what is going to happen with Randall or Pilar or Zach and Li, but I do know that I love you. And for the first time, all I care about is our family."

Bear shot up out of the bed. His face flushed red and he felt he had the strength of ten lions. He stared at his bed with his wife looking up at him. She wore no makeup and a plain white nightgown, but she never looked more beautiful. He couldn't help but scoop her up in his left arm. As she clung to his shoulders, he dried her tear-dampened cheeks with the gauze on his right hand. "Do you think we will have a boy or a girl first?" he asked.

"I would prefer to have a boy," she said.

Bear's smiled widened. "Why? Because you know I'll train him well?"

It was Ruth's turn to blush. "Yes, but also I have trouble enough trying to be a girl. I would rather not train someone in an area in which I already have difficulty."

"Okay then!" Bear said excitedly. "We will have all boys."

Ruth grabbed his face. "Let us have one first and see how we do."

"Whatever you say," Bear whispered, nuzzling her neck. "I just want a family with you."

CHAPTER TWENTY-FOUR

"**Z**ach, I see the town ahead," Li said, holding the looped rope he'd made into reins. He looked back at Zach. His mare, Lazy, was eating again. He realized she was probably less than two years old and still growing. "Do you see it?"

"Yeah, I see it. I just don't know how long it will take Lazy to get there. I think I'll get down and walk her. It may be quicker."

Li watched Zach pull his foot over the mare's bareback and land on his feet. "You ride her well," Li said. He stayed on his horse's back. Xin was strong, and he wanted the stallion to get used to his weight.

"Thanks. I had a friend whose family attended my dad's church when I was young. He taught me to ride his horse. He would ride her to church every Sunday," Zach said and became quiet.

Li watched his friend walk in silence. Zach had been quiet during their ride all day yesterday. Now it was only late morning on the next day and they were almost to the town. They got there quicker than he had anticipated. The horses had done well, getting accustomed to their human counterparts. But it seemed that Zach was going slow on purpose. He didn't ride his horse fast, and he would let her meander and nibble on grass as he rode her.

"Is everything okay?" Li asked. "We are almost to the town. We will get our supplies and rest up. We will be at the factory by tomorrow evening at the latest."

"I know," Zach assured. "I just feel out of sorts. We are far from home. We are almost done with our mission. I'm just wondering what is next for me."

"We aren't done yet," Li countered. "I still have to find a virus that will bring the World Government to their knees."

Zach looked up at Li but kept walking forward. "I know. And after that you'll start your ranch. I guess I'm just struggling with the meaning of it all. I feel like we'll get rid of one evil and another one will pop right up behind it."

Li watched Zach as he looked back at his mare, calling out to her. Zach was right. There will always be evil in the world, which is why there also had to be good. Li waited for Zach to look back up at him, but he kept his head down. Li turned his head back toward the town. He hoped they would find someone willing to help them once they arrived.

They walked in silence for another thirty minutes until they reached the town. There were only a few buildings, but Li could see more houses in the distance—each on its own acres of land. He saw what looked like an old-style church, but there was no cross on the steeple. There were not many people along the dirt road, but he did see a small crowd at one of the buildings. It looked like a diner.

"Let's get something to eat first. I'm starving," Li said without looking back at Zach. He knew Zach would just follow behind him. He rode up to the diner and saw a wooden fence about ten feet from the entrance. There was already one horse tied up to it. He glided off of Xin, and used the lead rope to bring him toward the fence. Xin was cautious of the small building, so Li petted his muzzle and whispered to him before tying him up. Zach brought Lazy to a small patch of grass, and she was content to be tied up while she nibbled.

"Zach, are you ready? I need you here with me. I know you're worried about something, but now is the time to be alert and attentive to the people around us. We need help, and these people need to trust us."

Zach nodded his head. "Yes, you're right. I'm here with you. Let me do the talking. I've been to this town before, so I know what to ask for."

"Good. I will follow your lead," Li said. He walked behind Zach as he went up the stairs and through the entrance to the restaurant. They chose a table with a window overlooking their horses. The small crowd thinned out as people went off to their own homes. Li began to recount the days to see what day they were on. It was Sunday. He wondered if that was why the town looked so desolate.

The man who watched them enter came around the counter and to their table. "I'll be closing the restaurant soon. We close for dinner on Sundays. But I can make you what we have left. Y'all from around here?"

Zach smiled. "No, we're from Levington. It's a town southeast of here."

The man shrugged. "Never heard of it."

"Do you follow the fighting circuit? We're close to where many of the fights take place," Zach said. Li could tell he was used to this conversation.

The man's eyes brightened with recognition. "Oh, y'all near enchanted rock?"

"Well, that's about a day's walk from us, but we do have many of the fighters close to us. In fact, you know the Shaman?"

The man nodded enthusiastically. "That fighter is old school. I thought he was done fighting, but when I heard he was fighting again, I wanted to go see him. But I can't leave the diner. I don't trust anyone. Too bad we don't get those fights up here."

"Well, he's my friend. In fact, he just married my sister," Zach said.

Li watched Zach talk. At first, he couldn't understand why he was being so forthcoming with information about his life, but when he saw the ease wash over the diner owner, he knew that Zach needed to be honest, in part, in order to gain trust. He thought it would be best if he didn't say anything. The last thing he wanted known was that he was a stowaway Efficientist.

"Wow! What are you doing way out this way?" the man asked.

"Well, I used to be a Runner, but I quit my job. I don't like where the World Government is heading. Now me and my friend go to different houses fixing up HMSs. In fact, we just left a ranch south of here. I've been to this town before, about three or four years ago, but our van got a flat and we had to ditch it," Zach said, waiting for the man's reaction.

The diner owner leaned in toward the table where Zach and Li were sitting and began to whisper. "Y'all are lucky that the World Government didn't *gather* you. They might have taken you into one of their labor camps."

Li looked at the man. "What are you talking about?"

The man looked at Li, noticing him fully for the first time. "Who are you?" he asked suspiciously.

"Don't worry about him. He's my friend from the factory we used to work at. We both quit together and decided to make our own business," Zach said. "Now what did you say about labor camps?"

"Can't believe you boys haven't heard that the World Government has been starting them forced labor camps. The old folks tell rumors of labor camps from when they were younger, but now they're as real as anything. These guards gather up any people who live out on their own. People and families who live away from factories and who don't have them HMS thingies," the man said. "They make 'em work the farms and do the things that machines used to do. If you're poor and alone, it doesn't matter what you look like, they'll get you. That's why I'm surprised you two didn't get gathered."

Li still couldn't believe what he was hearing. "Why haven't you and this town been gathered?" he asked.

"There is strength in numbers. They won't gather you if you live around other people. And as long as at least one person has an HMS, you'll be fine. When the gathering began, our pastor—I mean, um, Rohan, got one for the town. He keeps it at his shop."

Zach leaned in. "My father was a pastor until the World Government burned him and his church to the ground. You don't have to hide information from me. I know very well what the World Government does to pastors who hold church." Zach's voice changed. Anger overthrew his casual demeanor instantly.

"I heard about churches being burned down after the World Government banned dispersing religious material. I'm sorry your father died," the man stopped and thought for a moment. "Pastor Rohan doesn't hold church anymore. He doesn't want to jeopardize the people of our town. But his shop is always open for people who need a good word from him."

"What kind of shop does he own?" Li asked.

The man smiled. "He draws portraits of families. He also has other paintings he does." The man leaned in and whispered, "He also has an old printing press in the basement where he makes copies of different books of the *Bible*. They are available for anyone who needs them."

"You think we could talk with him?" Li asked. "We have family waiting to hear from us. It would be sure nice to contact them with the HMS."

The man stood up. "He might if he trusts you."

"Where did you say that labor camp was located?" Zach asked.

"You said you were here a few years ago running some things. Did you happen to go to the factory about thirty miles out?" the man asked.

"Yes, that's where we were going to try to stop. I might know someone who still works there and will let us finish some work," Zach said.

"Don't bother," the man said. "That factory has been closed down. It's now a labor camp. They farm the land around the factory."

"I can't believe it. There's actual slavery that the World Government has organized?" Li said in disbelief.

The man looked at Li. "You better believe it and stay far away, or they'll gather you. Let me get you two lunch and then you can go see Pastor Rohan yourselves. He'll let you know what's been going on."

"We don't have much to trade for the food," Zach said.

"I don't need anything from you," the man said. "I'll feed you what I got left in the kitchen in remembrance of your father—a man willing to die for what he believed in. It gives the rest of us some hope."

CHAPTER TWENTY-FIVE

Rohan Gupta wiped his sweaty, tan palms on his jeans. He had the windows open to allow the cool, fall breeze to glide into the basement, but working the old printing press for so long exhausted his limbs. He had recently come into several large stacks of cotton paper, and he wanted to print as many of the Four Gospels as possible. The World Government erased all digital copies of the *Bible* when the *Unum Vernum* had been released. Thankfully, he'd thought to print the *Bible* out on his HMS before it was gone forever.

Rohan instantly felt his mood lift when he thought of the *Unum Vernum* being erased. His mind replayed the *Bible* story of the idol, Dagon, that kept falling down in the presence of the Ark of the Covenant. That's what happened to the One World Religious Book—it had fallen face-first into oblivion. Rohan prayed blessings over the person who made that horrible excuse for religious literature disappear.

He moved the two large, blackened daubers into the ink that he spread over his cement island. He then pounded them together, spreading the ink evenly over the stretched goose leather. When he was satisfied, he pounded the daubers on the two metal plates with several chapters of Mark on them. He only had two more plates to go after this Gospel. When the ink was laid, he placed the cotton paper on the tympan and covered it with the frisket to protect the outside areas of the paper from getting inked. Then he closed the tympan with the cotton paper securely inside and moved it under the press, turning the handle to press the ink onto the page. More sweat began to form on his forehead, dripping from the shaggy strands of his dark brown hair. He let go of the lever, and distributed the moisture from his brow onto the back of his hand.

Just as he was about to open the tympan, he heard the clopping of horses' feet. He looked up toward his front window and saw the black legs of a horse. He didn't recognize the horse or the voice of the rider. He stopped moving and waited to see if the rider would pass by. Instead, two booted feet stomped onto the ground. Rohan knew that he would soon have a visitor, and he didn't know if his guest was friendly or not. He pulled off his apron and went straight to the basin of water and hand towel he kept in the corner for such a time.

Zach sniffed the air. He smelled ink. The factory he'd worked at had a small printing station for the different labels and pamphlets printed for the items he'd delivered. He looked toward the small house and saw windows just above the ground, leading into the basement. He couldn't see inside, but the air pouring out smelled of sweat and ink. Zach didn't stare too long. If the printing was being done in the basement, it probably wasn't legal. He continued to tie Lazy to the tree next to Xin.

"Do you smell that?" Zach whispered to Li, swinging his backpack over his shoulder.

"Yes," Li answered. "What is that? Paint?"

"No," Zach said, shaking his head. "That's ink, but it smells different—not like at the factory. It smells like ink made in the Colonies from organic material. There's a sweetness to it, like sap."

"I really hope this pastor trusts us. I'm no longer hungry, but now I feel filthy. I need to wash off. Are you going to be as honest with him as you were with the man at the diner?" Li asked.

"No," Zach said. "I'm going to be more honest. This man owns an HMS. We need to use it to let everyone know we are okay. We have to see what's going on at the old factory." Zach had hoped to lead Randall away from his friends to him, so he could finish the plans he had been mulling over since he found his father's killer. Now that the factory was no more, he needed to see how much Randall knew. He couldn't plan his next step in the dark.

Li leaned in toward Zach. "If he has an HMS, he probably knows who we are. Our images have been placed all over the Internet. We don't know what his reaction will be."

Zach looked toward the basement window again. "This man is either working for the World Government, keeping an eye out for people to gather for the work camps or he's a pastor and can help us. Either way, we have no other options but to take a step of faith."

"You're right. We are in a desperate state, and—" Li stopped, sniffing the air. "We stink."

Zach lifted his right arm and inhaled. "I knew I smelled sweat. No wonder the owner of the diner was pushing us out so quickly."

"Now that we are in town, I really want to take a bath," Li said, shifting the backpack on his back.

"Let's go see if this pastor can help us. Maybe there's something we can do for him in return," Zack said and began to walk toward the entrance of the house.

Just as Zach was about to knock on the door, a brown-skinned man, descended from India, tugged the door opened. "Greetings," he said in a light tone. "Welcome to my art studio. I am normally closed on Sundays, but I can see you two are visitors. How may I help you?"

Suddenly, the man's smile vanished. "Wait a minute. I know you two. You are Zacchaeus Daniels, the pastor's son who robbed the World Bank," he said, pointing to Zach. "And you are Charlie Liu, the Elite Efficientists who helped him," he said moving his finger to Li. "You two look horrible. Are you on the run? Is anyone chasing you?" he said, darting his eyes up and down the dirt road.

"No," Zach said, holding up his hands. "No one knows we are here, but our van broke down and we've been walking, trying to find a village to get supplies, take a shower and send communication."

"Come in! Come in!" Rohan said, excitedly. "You never know who's watching around here. We are too close to the labor camp. Something will have to change and soon."

161

Rohan led them through the small hall of his home. Framed paintings littered the walls from the baseboards to the ceilings. Zach glanced at a few. There were many portraits of people. They reminded him of his father. Austin Daniels loved to take photographs of the members of his church. Zach remembered many occasions when his father would be in the darkroom for hours, developing film of the portraits he took.

Rohan stood next to several wooden chairs in the living room. "I apologize for the lack of furniture. My wife went to stay with one of our sons and his family for now. She insisted on taking the couch," he said smiling. "We have a new granddaughter. She's a beautiful girl. Here let me show you," he said, walking to the back wall of the living room where more paintings resided. He carefully handled a large one that hung in the center of the wall.

"This is my daughter-in-law and my granddaughter. She is only one week old here. She is now almost three months. Can you believe it?" he asked and stared at the painting for several seconds. Zach saw the love on the man's face.

"Why are you not with them?" Li asked, setting down his backpack against one of the walls.

"Ah, yes," Rohan said. He walked back to the wall and hung the painting back up. "I was there for a little more than two weeks before I returned back here. The problem is that this town is too close to the labor camp. Several families have already left, but there are dozens of families still here. If their numbers dwindle too much, the World Government will gather the people left behind. I'm in a predicament. I want to be with my family, but I don't want to leave the people God has called me to minister," Rohan said, sitting down in one of the chairs and motioning for Zach and Li to have a seat.

"So you are a pastor, like the diner owner said," Li acknowledged.

"I have been the pastor here for forty years this winter. I have seen my people through everything. I've adapted every time the World Government placed new regulations on me and the church. God has always given me a new strength to continue my work, but now— I feel lost about what to do. I don't know where to go or who to turn to. In fact, I was in my basement printing out the Four Gospels for the town's people before I left. I told God to open a door or I would have to go back to my family."

Zach noticed that Pastor Rohan's smiled broadened. He looked to be about the age his father would be if he were still alive—late sixties or early seventies. But there was an energy and vigor in him that was ageless. "Has God given you a door?" Zach asked.

The old pastor leaned forward, placing his hands on his knees. "I don't know. You tell me. I have two men in my living room. One is an Elite Efficientist who could possibly disperse rank or even erase entire books from underneath the World Government's nose. And the other is the son of a man whom I greatly respect. A man who loved God and his people enough to fight against injustice. And several weeks ago, these two men robbed Eve Pallue's vault at the World Bank. You know," Rohan said standing. "I've looked over the World News's explanation of this robbery, and it still makes no sense. It's too clean cut. There is no way you two could have pulled off that robbery without divine intervention."

"What conclusions are you coming to?" Zach asked, leaning back in his chair. The pastor obviously had a love of the drama, so he would play into it a little.

"Well, I am glad you asked," Rohan said, enthusiastically. "You two have been on the run ever since. And by the looks and smell of you, you haven't taken your riches to live out your days in luxury. So to me, you two look like one gigantic, open door."

Li looked at Zach, unsure of how to respond. "It's okay," Zach said. "I think we can trust him."

"I go by Li now if you don't mind," Li said.

"So you are a Christian?" Rohan asked.

"Yes. God got ahold of me on my way to the Colonies," he admitted.

"He'll do that, you know. God wants to use His people to share His Word, but if no one can be found, He'll just do it Himself. That's what He did with me. I was just minding my own business when God sent a young girl to me who loved Jesus. Since I loved her, I had to love Him too," he said chuckling. "It was kind of a package deal. How did you two meet?"

Li looked at Zach again, so Zach decided to get the explanation over with.

"We met through a mutual friend named Pastor Thomas Isaacs," he began.

"I've never heard of him," Rohan said.

"You may not know him personally, but you've seen his work on your HMS. He's the one starting some kind of faith movement through the Internet."

Pastor Rohan sat down. "You mean he's the one writing the articles that the World Government keeps erasing?" he asked, stunned.

"He writes a few of them, but most of them are written by others. He is basically the webmaster, connecting all the dots." Zach didn't want to mention his sister. Bringing Eve Pallue into the light was unnecessary.

"So, it is organized. I thought so, but it didn't seem possible," he said. "How are you able to spread the communications so efficiently without getting caught?"

"Li here is a genius when it comes to that," Zach said.

Pastor Rohan looked at Li with appreciation in his countenance. "Are you to thank for erasing that religious monstrosity from my HMS?"

"You mean the *Unum Vernum?*" Li asked.

"Exactly that. That phony counterfeit of religious material," Rohan said with disgust.

"Yes," Li said plainly.

Pastor Rohan got up again and walked over to Li. He reached out his hand and shook Li's hand with vigor. "In all my days of ministry, I have never been so overjoyed than I was on that morning when I saw that the counterfeit had fallen. I reread the World News report over and over again. The thought of its demise has been my companion since my wife went to live with our son. Thank you. You have made this old man happy."

Zach saw a glint of red rising up in Li's bronze checks. He hadn't seen Li so embarrassed. Rohan released Li's hand and patted him with force twice on the shoulder. He then walked back to his seat and sat down, anticipating the rest of the conversation. "So why did you rob the World Bank?" he asked.

"Pastor Tom wanted funds to support the undercover ministry we were starting. We discovered a way to communicate without the World Government finding us," he said.

"What? How?" Pastor Rohan asked, his eyes wide with curiosity.

Li decided to take over. "We use old-style computers and get them into the system. The World Government can't see us because it doesn't know to look for us. We've already set up about a dozen of them. We had a laptop we could offer you, but we had to use it to make fire when we found ourselves stranded."

Pastor Rohan slapped both of his knees with his hands. For the first time, Zach saw black ink smeared on his palms. "Just look what I have!" Pastor Rohan said, getting up. He walked to a small closet they had passed in the hallway. He opened it and bent down, grabbing hold of something. He popped back up holding an old CPU.

"It's been here all along. My youngest son used to work on everything mechanical. We have old video games, music players, you name it! I got this as a trade for a portrait, thinking my son would want it. But he said he didn't have time. You know how those young kids are after they get married and have a few babies, so I put it in my closet waiting for a time to get rid of it."

Li stood up and took the large CPU from Rohan. "You are strong for your age," he said.

"Ministry keeps me fit as a fiddle," he said, pounding his abdominals.

"Do you happen to have the screen and keyboard to go with it?" Li asked.

"Ha! I have more than that. I have a printer too," he said, placing his hands on his hips. "And a bunch of these small flash drives, I think my son called them. You see! I prayed for an opened door, and I've got it!"

Zach looked at Li. "Well, we prayed for flash drives."

"We can set up the computer to get you connected with Pastor Tom's communication," Li said, holding the large CPU.

"But before we get started, can we take a bath and get some sleep? I'm suddenly feeling very dirty and tired."

The man looked from Zach to Li. "I guess ministry can wait a bit. It is Sabbath after all. I just so happen to have two extra beds and a pump for water and a large basin in the bathroom. The water will be cold, but it will be clean," Rohan said and opened his arms. "Zach and Li, you are welcomed as guests in my home."

"Li, go ahead and take a bath first," Zach said and turned to Rohan. "Pastor Rohan, would you mind if I just send a quick note from your HMS to let everyone know that we are okay. I would hate for them to worry any longer."

"It's in my room," Pastor Rohan said. "Follow me."

CHAPTER TWENTY-SIX

"Have you gotten word from anyone yet, Reyna?" Levi asked his younger daughter. She had been staring at the screen of the HMS for over an hour

"Just wait, Daddy. Pastor Tom said he would send word to the HMS regardless if he heard from Zach or not," Reyna said.

"Where is Javier?" Levi asked.

"He's packing to leave with you," Reyna said. "Daddy, if you and Javier leave, how will we finish harvesting the wheat? How can my younger brothers and I possibly run everything with you and Pilar gone? Regardless of the fact that you're taking my husband, we will be lost if something happens to you."

"He volunteered to go," Levi said defensively.

"That man would do anything for you," she said. "You are not young, Dad. He's not going to let you take on the World Government alone."

"Look, Reyna, I know this is not the best situation, but Pilar needs me," Levi said loudly, pressing his fist on the desk where the HMS sat. He turned his attention to the screen. "Come on, you stupid thing! Send me something."

"Just be patient, Daddy. They'll contact us," Reyna said.

"If that man had taken you, I would be doing the exact same thing. I will protect my family," Levi said. He hung his head and begun to rub his temples. "My headache won't go away."

Reyna sighed. She got up and walked over to her father. "Daddy, you don't understand. It feels like I should be fearful because Pilar has been kidnapped. But I'm not scared. I know my sister. She is strong. Besides she wouldn't want you to compromise not only our family, but this entire town, to go on some rescue mission."

"I'm so tired. I haven't slept. I keep having dreams that she's calling me," Levi said.

"Do you think those dreams are from God or from your fear?" she asked, rubbing his shoulders.

"I really don't know. It feels like my heart has been stolen from me. My first-born, strong-willed girl is gone. I want her back home," Levi said, letting his cheek fall onto his daughter's hand. The tears came out so easily now.

"Ruth says that Neil Elder has put a death sentence on Randall. They may do the job before you even get there," Reyna said.

"Or they may just kill them both out of convenience," he said back.

"Can we pray for her, Daddy? Let us ask God to not only protect her, but to help her fight," Reyna said.

"Okay," Levi mumbled through his tears.

Reyna bowed her head next to her father's. "Dear Father, nothing surprises You. I know that You are as we speak walking with Pilar, protecting her and guiding her into the plans that You have for her. Please, God, give us peace and comfort to know that she's okay. Show Zach and Li how to bring her home. It is in Jesus' name we humbly ask these things. Amen."

"Amen," Levi whispered.

A bleep sounded from the HMS as the screen came back to life. Levi shot his head up and turned to face the screen. He scooted his chair closer, so he could get a better view. "It's Pastor Tom!" he yelled.

Reyna read over her father's shoulder. "Li and Zach are in a village thirty miles from the factory. I've told them that Randall has Pilar in her truck and that he's hurt. They are planning to get her. I will keep you informed."

"Oh, thank You, Jesus!" Levi said.

Reyna stood up straight. "I guess now Pilar's getting what she's always longed for."

Levi looked up at his daughter. "What is that?"

"Zach's full attention," she answered. "Between him and Li, I don't think there's anything they can't do."

Levi nodded his head. "They did rob the World Bank," he acknowledged. "Too bad Bear's not with them. He would definitely defeat Randall."

"Don't forget, Daddy. Bear did wound Randall. With glass in his eye and the long drive that they are doing, he'll be really sick by the time they get there. I bet Pilar is just waiting for her opportunity to leave. And Zach will be the most determined to get her back because, whether he will admit it or not, he still loves Pilar."

"You told Randall where we were going! Why?" Li asked. Li had bathed and was wearing an old outfit from one of Pastor Rohan's sons. He walked to the living room where Zach had called him. "I knew you were pushing to go to that factory too much."

"Keep your voice down," Zach said. "Pastor Rohan is finishing the *Bible* prints in the basement." Zach strung his fingertips through his blonde beard. It had grown over an inch since they'd been gone. "Because our mission is done, and he will not stop hunting our family and friends. I thought if I could bring him to us, at least it will give everyone a break."

"No, there's more to it than that," Li said. "You were bringing him to the factory for a reason. You know I have a plan to bring the World Government down, and you have compromised it. There's something else. You've become quiet ever since we left the ranch," Li stopped. "I've got it! You kept asking the rancher about the horse tranquilizers. Let me see your bag," Li said, holding out his hand.

Zach stood still. "I don't have any tranquilizers."

"You say that," Li snapped. "You're lying. I can see it. You are harboring revenge for the death of your father. I see it in you now. That's what you've been holding back."

"It doesn't matter now, does it?" Zach shot back. "Randall has taken yet another person that I love, and he will kill her if we don't do something."

"You said that Pastor Tom wrote that Neil wants Randall dead," Li said, thinking. "Randall must not have known about the labor camps. Neil doesn't trust him. He doesn't trust anyone.

Looks like your wish to see Randall dead will come true after all," Li said, looking to Zach.

Zach said nothing. He still hadn't bathed. He felt dirty on the outside and inside. He needed just to wash it all clean. Finally, he looked back to Li. "I'm sorry for withholding information from you. Yes, I stole some of the horse tranquilizers. I didn't know how I was going to do it, but I was going to trap Randall and tell him how he destroyed my life. And then—I don't know what I was going to do next. I can't shake this anger against him."

Li walked to Zach. "Randall didn't kill your father. He was simply a man doing what he was told. He is a pawn. Neil Elder may have ordered it, but what I'm coming to realize is that he is too just a pawn in a bigger, more sinister plan. The darkness created in you is the ultimate goal. Pastor Tom is always telling me to let things go or the enemy will use it against me. You have to let it go. Murder will bring you down to their level."

"I thought I had let it all go," Zach said. "Ruth came into my life, and I needed to protect her. Then she married my best friend. And I then find out that the man who tried to kill my sister, who also happened to beat me to a pulp—is the very same man who killed my dad. Something in me just broke."

"I can't work with you if I can't trust you," Li said. "Give me those horse tranquilizers."

Zach shrugged his shoulders. "I don't even trust myself. That's probably why I keep Pilar at a distance. But now she needs me."

Li stood watching Zach's movements as he thought through everything. Finally, Zach walked to the chair where his backpack was. He opened it and reached into the very bottom, pulling out the thin box that held the jerky. He opened the box and pulled out something folded in fabric. He walked back to Li. "Here they are."

"Thank you," Li said. "Now how are we going to get Pilar back?"

Zach reached back into his backpack and pulled out a bag. He opened it up and drew out a diamond tennis bracelet. "We'll use this," he said handing it to Li.

"What am I going to do with diamonds?" he asked, holding up the bracelet, watching the diamonds scatter lighted dots of rainbows across the wall.

"I'll use what's left in this bag and trade for some saddles and supplies. You get on this HMS and contact Jonah. We need to get you reinstated back to an Elite Efficientist," Zach said, counting the leftover jewels in the bag.

"It's no use," Li shrugged. "They already know my face."

"But they don't know the true story of how Neil Elder wanted to provide for the labor camps, so he needed to tap into a source of wealth that couldn't be documented. You're not a criminal. You're a hero, bringing gifts to the leadership at the labor camps for their hard work and dedication," Zach said.

Li watched the diamonds wave to and fro in his hand. "You think that will work?" Li asked, intrigued.

"Those diamonds will make anything work," Zach said.

"I could trade for an entire ranch stocked full of horses and supplies," Li said, wistfully.

"Yeah, until the World Government decides they need your land," Zach added.

"We have to bring them down," Li said, balling up the bracelet in his fist.

"I'll wait for Pilar on the outside. She knows I'm here, so she'll try to get away once they arrive. You get on the inside, give the gift to the head guy and collect as much data as possible. I have a feeling we're going to need it in the future. I want to see just how many labor camps there are."

"I'll need a car and a driver," Li said. "The more legitimate I look, the better it will go."

Just at that moment, Rohan opened the door that led upstairs from the basement and entered the living room. "I'm all done with my printing. What else do you boys need from me? I'm ready to help."

Li and Zach both looked at Pastor Rohan and then each other. "I'll see about getting Rohan upgraded to a Bodyguard."

"Good thinking," Zach said.

CHAPTER TWENTY-SEVEN

Jonah only had a few moments to spare before he had to take Neil to his PR Event tonight. He hated this aspect of his job. Now that Randall was gone, the eye of the World News was on him. He was the hero who saved Neil Elder. He despised the attention, and his face suffered from smiling, so he reverted to a stoic look, which the World News coined "watchful." He wanted Randall to come back, but Pastor Tom had already informed him that Neil had marked him for death. This was not good news because Randall had been a screen for him, shielding him from Neil Elder.

Jonah opened the small safe located in his room. He took out the old-style laptop, and plugged it in next to his HMS. He waited for it to turn on, and he reread the correspondence from Pastor Tom before opening the new letter from Li. Although Jonah didn't quite understand what was going on, he understood that a lot was at stake. Li and Zach were developing a rescue operation for Pilar, and they needed Charlie Liu reinstated and a Bodyguard position created for a new name, Rohan Gupta.

Randall had kidnapped the founder of Levington's daughter, Pilar, and he would declare war against the World Government to get her back. Not to mention Pilar was the love interest of Zach. Jonah couldn't quite fit together all the relational puzzle pieces of what was going on in the Colonies. This small rebellion had grown extensively.

Now he had to worry about a group of men fighting Randall and maybe waking up the World Government to what was going on behind the scenes. This would not be good for the plans that Li and he were working on to bring the World Government down. Jonah finished Li's letter and thought of the other bit of news that Pastor Tom had relayed to him. Neil Elder had begun labor camps. Jonah felt his fist ball up on the desk. His mind quickly dealt him images of enslaved people. Jonah calmed his breathing. He knew something like this would eventually happen again, and he believed he had prepared himself for it, but the bitter taste in his mouth caused him to have a moment of rage that he didn't know still survived in him. Christina Straight warned him long ago that anger may sneak back on him.

An alarm sounded in Jonah's living room and he looked toward his security camera. It was Dr. Linton. Jonah quickly unplugged the laptop without turning it off. He walked back toward his safe and placed it inside, shutting the door and spinning the handle. "Open," he said, and the door to his flat opened.

"I'm sorry to bother you," Dr. Linton said. Jonah noticed dark circles under his eyes. His face looked thinner—almost gaunt, and he had an image of Christina Straight right before her death rise in his memory.

"Dr. Linton, you don't look well at all. Are you sick?" Jonah asked.

Dr. Linton hesitated. "Yes, of sorts. Not physically— though, I wish it were physical. I can't sleep. I'm a secretive man, and I normally wouldn't discuss my problems with anyone, but I can't live like this anymore."

"I wish there were something I could do to help. Did you have that talk with Neil Elder that I mentioned earlier?" Jonah asked. "About your contract being up?" Jonah didn't want to lose Dr. Linton, but it might be better for all concerned if he retired into a small Colonial village somewhere.

Dr. Linton put his hands in his pocket. He squirmed from side to side as Jonah watched him. "See, here's the thing. I'm having thoughts of suicide, so I don't know where to go from here. I don't know if the thoughts are from my work here or just from who I am inside. My life has never been like this. I've always had goals and something to aim for. I've always thought that if I could get where I want to be, then these feelings would go away. But here I am, and they are still here, haunting me."

Jonah watched Dr. Linton. He knew he was telling the truth. He at one time had been in the exact place Dr. Linton now found himself—finally getting what you thought you needed and realizing it didn't take away the pain. "Can I recommend a Life Therapist to you?" Jonah asked, knowing the answer.

"No, no. I don't need a shrink. They won't understand or maybe they'll label me emotionally impaired," he said.

"I have some reading that may help you or at least distract you," Jonah suggested.

"You do?" Dr. Linton asked. "I'm desperate for anything to help me sleep at night."

"Everything I'm about to give you is illegal. They are documents that have started an underground faith movement of sorts that Neil is trying to stop. Many Efficientists have been reading them if they can find them."

"I've heard about those documents. They are hard to find," he said. "And very illegal."

"I happen to have all of them. Maybe you'll find your own peace and your own truth by looking at the truth others say they have found. But I have to warn you, most of the writing is very difficult to follow. Most Colonials wouldn't understand it."

Dr. Linton's uneasy expression was replaced with offense. "I am a medical doctor. I am sure that I would follow the writing perfectly fine," he said walking to Jonah. "Where are the documents?"

"I'll give them to you," Jonah said. "But you'll get in trouble if they are found on you, so be careful."

"The last thing I want to do is get caught with anything illegal," Dr. Linton said. "I'll make sure to keep them safe in my flat."

Jonah walked toward his safe, but turned to Dr. Linton before punching in the code. "Would you mind looking the other way for a moment?"

Dr. Linton exhaled and rolled his eyes but turned to face the door. "Okay. I can't see anything."

Jonah pressed the key code into the safe and opened it. He bent down to grab the stack of papers on the floor of the safe. Once they were safely in his left arm, he shut the safe with his right hand and turned the handle again. "You can turn around now."

Dr. Linton's eyes opened wide. "How long has this movement been going on?" he asked. "That stack of papers is almost two feet thick."

Jonah looked down at the stack of printouts. "I've been collecting them since I got here."

"There must be a lot of different writers. You say they're Efficientists? I know a lot of people have dropped rank and have gone into the Colonies," Dr. Linton said.

Jonah went to the kitchen and grabbed a large paper sack that he kept from his different deliveries. He placed the papers inside. Then he put a few bananas, a loaf of bread and a jar of honey on top of the stack. "There are a few different writers," he said, thinking of Eve Pallue and Pastor Tom.

Jonah walked toward Dr. Linton and handed him the bag. "Here are the groceries you wanted. I hope you enjoy your banana and honey sandwich." He looked at his watch. "I have to get going. I have another PR Event to attend. Happy reading to you. I want to hear your thoughts."

Dr. Linton held onto the bag with both hands. "I would rather read these than attend a PR event. I think I have the better end of the stick."

Jonah's expression became stoic in preparation for his long night. "I believe you are right."

CHAPTER TWENTY-EIGHT

Zach watched as Rohan drove off in his car with Li in the back seat. In less than three hours, they had gotten all the supplies they needed. Li and Rohan were both wearing suits. An image of Pastor Rohan wearing a thirty-year-old dark, brown suit that was three inches too tight came to mind. He hoped that the labor camp guards wouldn't notice. Li's horse, Xin, had been tied to a tree in Rohan's backyard with food and water. He would be good until they came back. Zach looked at the saddle on Lazy, and fitted his new cowboy hat onto his head. "I've got a cowboy hat, and you have a saddle. Looks like we're the real deal now," he said, securing the saddle once more.

"C'mon, Lazy! Let's go find Pilar," he said, throwing his right leg over her back and sitting on the saddle. Luckily, Rohan had a neighbor who was more than willing to trade two of his saddles, harnesses and ropes for the jewels. Zach suspected that the man and his family were getting ready to leave town. Zach had only a few jewels left, and he would keep those to help Li start his ranch. Rohan's car finally disappeared over the horizon. It wouldn't take them long to get to the factory. He would take the road in the other direction and backtrack a little. Rohan said that there was an intersection that Randall and Pilar were headed to since they were coming up from Levington. Zach wanted to head them off before it was too late.

"Come on, Lazy," Zach said to his mare. "You've eaten and gotten some rest. Let's get to work." He gently tapped his heels into her side and she began to trot. Zach lowered his body and tapped his heels again. "Let's see how fast we can get there."

"Wait a minute," Randall said. "Describe it to me again." His right eye was covered with a gauze patch and his left eye was almost swollen shut, giving him very little visual range. He held the gun in his right hand, and the truck keys in his left hand. Pilar noticed that he looked fatigued. His face was flushed and sweat was covering his body. He was very sick.

"It doesn't look like the factory that we have back home," Pilar said, looking through the binoculars. "There is wire fencing around it all with some kind of looped wiring at the top. I'm guessing to keep people out or maybe in. I see guards with guns around the parameter. And people walking in lines and getting into trucks."

"It sounds like a prison camp, but I've never heard of one here," Randall said.

"It couldn't be," Pilar said. "I see kids too. Little toddlers with their moms. I even see a few moms with babies in their arms. They are wearing normal clothes—not uniforms. But the clothes look ragged."

"Are the kids getting into trucks?" Randall asked.

"No, they are outside. I see white bundles on the ground. It looks like cotton. They're picking through it."

"Neil didn't mention anything about actually creating labor camps," Randall said. He walked back to the truck and leaned against it.

"Are you sure this is where Zach said he would meet you?" Pilar asked.

"Yes, I'm sure!" Randall yelled. "Do you think I'm an idiot? If it weren't for my eyes, you would be gone right now!" Randall yelled, kicking the tire of the truck with his foot. "I can't believe this. Why didn't Neil tell me?"

"Should we go to that town just west of here that I saw on your Portable? Maybe someone there can help us," Pilar said.

"You would just love for us to go the Colonies wouldn't you? I'm sure Daniels is waiting to ambush me there. That's it! I can take it from here!" Randall yelled and brought his gun up to where Pilar was standing.

"You promised me!" Pilar yelled, ducking.

"I lied!" he shouted back.

Pilar instantly began to run away from her last position. She heard shots coming from behind her, but Randall's aim was off because of his damaged sight. Pilar was planning on leaving Randall anyway when she found the factory, but she wanted to wait to get supplies—at least the food and water that her dad always made her keep in the bed of the truck. But she realized that more than supplies, she wanted her truck back. She ran behind a large bush and looked back to the road. She could see Randall struggling in the front seat. She realized that he was trying to find the right key to start the ignition. Thankfully, she had a lot of keys because of all her deliveries. She looked back to the terrain behind her unfolding like an everlasting, yellow haze. She would rather fight Randall than walk alone in the wilderness.

She rounded the bush and began to run back toward the road. She didn't have much time. The driver's side door was still open. She could see Randall handling the keys with both hands. The gun must be on the passenger seat because she didn't see it on the dash. She crept around the back of the truck and duck-walked to the back-passenger window. She popped up quickly and looked through the window toward the front passenger seat, catching a glimpse of the gun. She slinked to the passenger door and grabbed the door handle, taking a deep breath. She would open the door and grab the gun before he could. She counted in her mind. One. Two. Three. She jerked the door open and snatched the gun just as Randall reached for it.

"Drop my keys and get the hell out of my truck!" she yelled, holding the gun to where his left eye could see it.

"You have no idea what you're doing," Randall said in calm voice.

Pilar leaned back and took a shot in front of Randall's face. The bullet raced in front of him and out the opened door. "My daddy taught me how to use a gun. You shot at me twice and I shot once. I still have plenty of bullets to take you down!" she yelled. "And I will gladly put you out of your misery!"

Randall lifted both hands. "Fine, I'll get out." Randall got out of the truck and stood.

"Move back ten feet!" she shouted.

Randall smirked. "Don't forget," he said. "I know where you and your family live. If you're not going to kill me, I'll be back for you."

178

"From what you've told me about your boss," Pilar said, crawling into the driver's side and then looking at Randall. "I seriously doubt that you'll be around much longer." She slammed the door shut and put the truck in reverse, pulling the truck back in a cloud of dust. She saw Randall's Portable next to her. It still had the map opened. She turned west on the shambled intersection and began her quest to find Zach. "Please, Lord," she said. "I pray he did not go into that factory."

Pilar had to drive slowly because cracks in the road would cause her tires to slam into the hard dirt. She had driven her truck for so many years, and she knew that two of her tires were getting low. She looked at the gas gauge. Her gas tank was almost empty. If she could just make it to town, she would easily find Zach if he was there. Small towns don't keep secrets well. Pilar continued to cautiously drive, weaving right and left on the road to avoid big rocks and other debris. She could tell that this road wasn't used often.

She looked back down at the Portable. The screen was black. It must have turned off after being idle so long. She tried to wake it up, but it stayed off. She couldn't use the Print Identifier because it would go into lockdown. She would give it to Li when she saw him. Maybe he could turn it on. Pilar looked back at the road. She knew she had a turn off to the right coming up, but she couldn't remember when. "Great," she whispered. "The last thing I want to do is get lost out here."

Pilar stopped the truck. She reached in the backseat and grabbed the binoculars—another thing her father insisted that she keep in her truck. "I'll have to thank Dad when I get home," she said aloud. She always thought he went overboard with his safety rules. When she first began making deliveries, he insisted that she come home after every delivery. He would only give her the goods for one house at a time. It wasted time and money in gas, but he had always been overprotective. "He's probably upset at himself for letting me go to the factory with Bear and Ruth," she whispered. "I need to contact him first thing."

Pilar got out of the truck and jumped into the bed of the truck. She brought the binoculars to her eyes and began to survey her surroundings. "I don't see anything," she said. She looked back toward where the factory was, and it was lost under the horizon. "I'll just have to keep driving straight and stop every ten minutes to see if I can see the town." She jumped back onto the ground and got back into the truck, keeping the binoculars on her lap.

Pilar continued to drive straight, watching every inch of the road for the large cracks cutting into the hardened dirt. The gas gauge was on empty. Randall had used all her extra gas trying to get them to the factory. She knew she had some more miles left in the tank, but didn't know exactly how much. Her father would always fill her truck up every night regardless of how much she drove it that day. She stopped after what felt like ten minutes and got back out of the truck, holding her binoculars. She scanned the area again, but still she did not see anything, so she got back in the truck.

She continued driving. About five minutes into her drive, her truck began to jolt. "Oh no," she said. "That's not good." She kept the truck going for about a minute more until it began to coast. It didn't coast for long because the old road slowed the pace. Finally, Pilar put the truck into park. "Dang it!" she yelled. She got out of the truck. Her first impulse was to grab the gun she had placed on the passenger seat. She feared Randall might have already gotten to the old factory and sent out people to go after her. She put the gun into her jean pocket and quickly got back onto the bed of the truck. "He's walking and half blind. There's no way he has gotten there already. I've only been driving for less than thirty minutes. I still have time," she said to herself.

She scanned the horizon again, looking back from where she came from. She wiped the sweat from her dark skin. "I probably look a mess." She hated looking disheveled almost as much as being lost. No one was chasing her yet. She looked in front of her. Suddenly, she saw a dark spot moving to the east to where she knew the factory was. She held her breath, waiting for the spot to become more visible. It was a white and black dappled horse, and someone was riding it.

Pilar dropped her binoculars. She needed to signal to the rider somehow to come to her. She looked around the bed of the truck. She saw the broom she used to clean out the truck bed after her deliveries. "I need a white flag," she said. She looked around and saw nothing she could use. Suddenly, she set the gun down and unbuckled her bra from under her shirt. She slid the white bra out of one sleeve. "Well, I guess this will have to work." She tied the bra to the end of the broomstick. She held the broomstick above her head, waving the bra back and forth. Then she took the gun in her right hand and pointed it away from her toward the ground and shot out three distinct shots. She put the gun back into her pocket and continued to wave the white bra.

She squinted her eyes toward the black dot. It seemed to be coming to her. She looked down to where she set the binoculars and picked them up. She held the broomstick tight in her left hand and brought the binoculars to her eyes with her right. She could see the rider now. He was a white man with a light-colored beard and a cowboy hat atop shaggy, light hair. "Probably from the town," she whispered, dropping the binoculars back down. "God, please let him be one of the good guys."

Pilar continued to wave the flag, watching the man and horse getting closer. She felt the gun against her hip. There had to be at least four shots left, probably more. Randall's gun was nice, and she thought he would make sure it was fully loaded before he began his stakeout at the factory. As the rider drew closer, he brought the horse to a slow trot. She couldn't distinguish his face. The cowboy hat had produced a shadow that reached below the man's nose. She usually could tell the character of someone just by looking at them. She felt funny waving her bra in the air, so she just held it still. She didn't want to bring it down and let the rider think her intentions were wrong.

When the rider finally got in front of the truck, she waited for him to speak. He sat on his horse for several seconds. The sun was bright above him, and her eyes began to water from too much sunlight reaching her pupils.

"Pilar, why are you waving your bra at me?" came a familiar voice.

Pilar dropped the broomstick. "Zach, is that you?" she asked.

"Who did you expect to rescue you?" he asked. She couldn't see it, but she knew he was smiling.

CHAPTER TWENTY-NINE

"Pilar, you must be the easiest woman to rescue. I swear you make it look easy. I can't believe you shot a bullet across Randall's face," Zach said after he got Pilar down from his horse.

"He's wounded. You can thank Bear for that," Pilar said.

"So he broke the window with his fist," Zach said in amazement. "He must really love my sister."

"It must be nice to be so loved," Pilar said, dusting herself off. "I need to clean up. I feel horrid."

Zach stared at Pilar. This was the most disheveled he had ever seen her. Her black hair was windblown, and her bronzed skin smelled of sweat and earth. He waited for her eyes to meet his. She had green eyes that shone brightly from her flushed cheeks. "You look beautiful to me," he whispered coming close to her.

"Why did you leave that note for Randall to find?" Pilar asked, concern filling her expression. "He could have killed you."

Zach kept his eyes locked on Pilar's. "I told myself it was to protect you and Ruth, but really I wanted to see him. When I met him the day I met Ruth, I didn't know he was my dad's murderer. I had always just blamed the World Government for the fire, but for the culprit to have a face and name—I don't know. It did something to me."

Pilar took Zach's hand. "Reopened the wound."

"Maybe. Or it just unearthed it," he said. He stroked Pilar's cheek. "I've missed you. It was nice staying at your family's house those weeks—seeing you in the kitchen every morning. Sharing coffee with you. I liked it."

Pilar's face softened, but suddenly she turned to the horse. "Let me get everything I brought," she said, grabbing keys and Randall's Portable and gun. "Do you mind getting the gas can? I want to take a quick shower and then go get my truck. You say the pastor here stores gasoline in his backyard?"

Zach watched Pilar. He realized that she no longer trusted him. He could see why. He had played with her emotions for too long. "Yes, we used some to fill up the pastor's car before he and Li went to the labor camp."

"We should hurry up then. I want to be back when Li gets here. I want to see exactly what they're up to in that old factory. I just hope he doesn't run into Randall."

Zach grabbed the gas can that dangled from his mare's saddle. "Follow me to the back, so I can tie up Lazy. Then I'll show you where the bathroom is. He had a water pump, so you can fill up the bathtub. I saw some women's clothing in this closet when he got me some clothes. I'll try to find something that will fit you."

Zach held the new lead rope he had traded for and began to walk Lazy around the house. Pilar walked next to him on his right side.

"Do you think Li will be able to get into this Portable?" she asked.

"I'm sure he can. He still has his, but he left it with Pastor Tom. I bet he'll be glad to have this one. We wouldn't have gotten lost if we had it."

"Yeah, but you wouldn't have wound up here. And Li wouldn't have gotten his horses. I still can't believe you two were able to catch wild horses. I wish I could have seen it," Pilar said. "When you rode up to me on your horse, I had no idea it was you."

"Did you find me attractive?" Zach teased.

Pilar smiled. "Actually, I was so embarrassed by my appearance that I couldn't think of anything else, but now that I look back on it, you did look like someone out of a western story."

"Why, thank you," Zach said. "And here's Li's horse."

Xin stood, resting in the shade of the large tree in the backyard.

"Wow!" Pilar said. "He's huge and beautiful."

"You should have seen Li jump on his back. He was pulled several hundred yards while the horse continually bucked and reared up. I was sure Li was going to get hurt, but he finally got on Xin's back and held on tight. It was really spectacular. I always thought Li's vision for a ranch was kind of a childish daydream, but he can really do it."

"Li has a lot of heart," Pilar said. "When I met him, I thought he was going to be all brains, and I wouldn't relate to him. Are all Efficientists like Li and Ruth?" Pilar asked. "I love them both so much already. They're like family to me."

Zach thought for a moment. "Only the ones who lost everything, I guess," he said. He tied Lazy next to Xin. "Let me bring you into the house and show you around. Pastor Rohan has an old printing press in the basement. I mean this thing is several hundred years old!"

"Didn't your dad have one of those?" Pilar asked, trying to remember.

"No, he wanted to get one, but he would just use the HMS to print things, which is one of the reasons he got in trouble with the World Government."

Pilar put her hand on Zach's shoulder before he led her to the house. "I know I've told you this before, but I am sorry about your dad and your mom. I don't know what I would do without my parents."

Zach felt Pilar's hand linger. "You would have done a hell of a lot better than I have," he said, honestly. "I think I've been selfish. I'm an only child with parents who coddled me. It was hard for me to let it all go. I've let my dad's death get in the way of everything."

"Randall didn't look good when I left him," Pilar said. "I cleaned out his right eye, but I couldn't get the glass in his left eye. It was too small. He looked like he had a fever, and he was very weak and almost delirious. He would have to walk all the way to that old factory. I don't know if he'll make it," she said.

Zach took her hand in his. "Even if he does make it, he won't ever leave."

"Why?" she asked.

185

"I got a message from Pastor Tom. Neil Elder has put a death sentence on Randall. They'll kill him when they find out who he is."

"How do you feel about that?" Pilar asked.

"I want to say he's getting what he deserved, but then again, we shouldn't rejoice when our enemies fall," Zach said, letting go of Pilar's hand. "Besides, it was probably Neil Elder who ordered the execution of my father. I've done the research. Neil was placed in charge of fighting the Efficientist Christian Sect when the Apostle, or Christina Straight, was writing those articles. He thought it was a Colonial starting the movement, so he began to execute anyone who he thought would be a potential candidate. Little did he know that the Apostle was living in the same city as him and just down the street. It's interesting that she helped Ruth find salvation right before she died, and now Ruth has taken over her work."

"There are so many things that can take your life. I would rather lose my life for the Gospel than for any other reason," Pilar said. "Your dad is a martyr and people still remember him."

"You're right," Zach whispered. He paused for a moment, watching Pilar stare at him, wondering what she was thinking. She was a strong woman, but she seemed different now. Maybe a little broken. "I'm glad I found you."

Pilar smiled. "Me too. Now show me where I can wash up. I'm starting to feel uncomfortable in my own skin."

"Follow me," Zach said, grabbing her hand again and leading her into the backdoor of the house. "I'll show you where the bathroom is. There's a pump that hangs right over the tub. Very convenient."

"Will you let my dad know that I'm okay? I'm sure he's worried. Also, tell him thank you for forcing me to carry all those extra supplies in the back of my truck. I don't think I would have made it without the food and water and gas he provided. Oh, and for making me learn to shoot a gun. That came in real handy."

"I'll relay the message to Pastor Tom. He'll send it through the computers to your dad. I know he'll be relieved. You know,

Pastor Tom had quite the challenge keeping your dad from rallying up a posse and coming up here to get you."

"Of course, he would," Pilar said, smiling. "I'm his baby girl."

Reyna heard her father yell from outside. She instantly dropped her box of baked goods and ran toward the noise. "Dad! Dad! What is it?" she yelled as she entered the kitchen.

Her father was staring at the HMS that Ruth had left with them.

"Zach has her! Zach has my baby girl!" Levi yelled at the top of his lungs.

"What's going on?" Maria said, entering the door at the back of the kitchen.

"Pilar is okay. Zach found her. She got away from Randall. She took his gun! She shot at him and drove off with the truck. I can't believe my baby girl," Levi mumbled, tears pouring down his face.

"Let me read the letter, Daddy. I can barely understand you," Reyna said, sitting at the chair in front of the monitor. "Look, Dad. They said that all the supplies you made her keep in the truck kept her alive. The food, the water and the extra gasoline. You did help her!"

Maria walked to her husband who was now on his knees, crying and praising God. "You see, my dear. You did rescue Pilar. In fact, you saved her life. All those times you made her keep freshwater and food and you kept her gas tank full with more gas in the back. You saved her. You gave her a chance to live!"

"Oh, thank You, God, for protecting my baby girl. Thank you for making her strong like me. I should have trusted You, Father. You knew she would be okay. You knew she was a fighter," Levi prayed.

Maria held onto her husband and looked toward Reyna. "Is she coming home now?"

"It looks like Li is investigating that old factory that they've turned into a labor camp," Reyna said, reading the end of the note. "Pastor Tom will keep us updated." Reyna closed out of the letter. "Pilar is fine and she's with Zach and Li. She'll be more than okay. She's actually getting to do something, which is what she's been praying for."

"Should we tell Ruth and Bear?" Levi said, getting up with the help of his wife.

"No, I'm sure Pastor Tom sent the information to the computer that they brought back to their house after Randall left," Reyna said, sighing with relief.

"Now let's just pray the threat of Randall disappears," Levi said.

CHAPTER THIRTY

Li sat in the back of the car and waited for Pastor Rohan to open his car door. After a moment when Rohan did nothing, he finally spoke up. "You have to open my door. Remember everything I told you. Always look around like you're inspecting, but never say anything unless I speak to you first. Keep the gun in the holster behind your jacket. Don't show it. It's so old, they'll question whether you're a real Bodyguard or not."

"Yes, okay," Pastor Rohan said nervously. "I hope I parked in the right place. I see other cars, but there are no signs." He got out of the car and scanned the area. A security guard holding a Portable strode over to meet them.

Li got out of the car, motioning for Pastor Rohan to close the door. He crossed his arms when the security guard approached.

"Are you Randall Hunt?" the security guard asked.

"No, my name is Charlie Liu. I've been assigned to speak to Ted Stanton. He's the man in charge of the facility," Li said in Long English. He was going to pick a Variety, but thought better of it when he heard the security guard speak.

The man looked at his Portable. "I wasn't informed of any other visitors today."

"It was a last-minute arrangement. The document was sent to this facility about an hour ago."

The man continued to work on the Portable. Li could tell that he was not proficient at working it. "Do you need me to guide you? It may go more quickly. I am not used to waiting so long," Li said in a haughty tone.

"Okay, I see it. Is this your Bodyguard?" he asked.

"Affirmative," Li said.

"He looks kind of old to be a Bodyguard, doesn't he?" the man questioned.

Li straightened his back and stared at the security guard. "This man knows more about protection service than you and all the security guards here will ever know. Insult him one more time, and I will leave. When I return to the city, I will have a conversation with Neil Elder about this facility and its personnel."

"Sorry, I didn't mean to offend," the man said, eyeing Pastor Rohan. "Follow me. Mr. Stanton is in his office."

Li followed the security guard with Pastor Rohan behind him. Li noticed sweat dripping down Rohan's face. He wiped his own brow with his sleeve to hint to Rohan to wipe his. Pastor Rohan noticed the gesture and wiped his forehead. It was a cool day, but Rohan's face was flushed. Li just prayed no one would notice.

The security guard walked them passed the checkpoint to enter the facility gates. The first thing Li noticed when they got through the gate was the smell. He almost reached to pinch his nose. He knew it was a mixture of sweat and urine and human feces. He looked around and saw people wearing rags and other tattered clothing. There were no men. He only saw women and small children. There were piles of cotton, and the women and children were pulling thin fiber strands along great looms.

Li walked closer to the security guard. "Why are the machines not in use to make the fabric?"

"No disrespect," the security guard said, "But you don't know much about what's going on here."

"That is why I am here. The World Government leaders want me to inspect the work and see if there are any areas that we can help," Li said, hoping to get some information out of the man.

"We could use the help. They want us to use human labor because the machines that normally do this work take energy, and that gets expensive. Human labor is supposed to be cheaper, but I'm telling you that these people take a lot of money to manage. They almost live just as good as we do," the security guard said.

Li looked around at the human depravity that he saw, and he greatly doubted the man's words.

"The people tire out too quickly. We've been doing this now for almost a year, and we have too many sick and dying. Mr. Stanton doesn't know what to do with all of them," he said. "He's hoping to get some answers today. The medic can't keep up with them. We either need to release them or just take them out of their misery."

Li thought quickly. "That will be one of the things I'll address to Mr. Stanton." Li quickly looked at Pastor Rohan. He could see tears welling up in the pastor's eyes and his mouth gaping at the sight of the people. "This smell is horrible. You may want to cover your face with a handkerchief if you think you'll be sick."

Pastor Rohan looked at Li confused. But he quickly recovered. "No, I am fine," he said, closing his mouth and sniffing back his tears. Rohan kept his eyes forward as they continued to pass the people.

The security guard led them into a building after pushing the code to open the door. He pressed the eight numbers quickly, but Li memorized them. They began to walk up several flights of winding stairs.

"Are there no elevators?" Li asked.

The security guard shook his head. "No, elevators take energy. The only thing we have at this facility that uses energy is the security system. We have no cameras on site. Just alarms if there are trespassers or someone tries to escape. And we have a few HMSs, Mr. Stanton's LPS and our Portables that are powered by generators. The electricity has been shut off since the labor camp took over the factory. You should be glad you didn't come in the summer. Hot as hell. Made me wish for the old days when I worked for the factory."

"I know you have had some setbacks, but I was told that this labor camp is doing better than the others," Li said, trying to get more information.

"Of course we are. Those other labor camps—I think the last count was six of them—they aren't doing well at all. They treat the people too good—getting showers and three meals a day. They might as well be working for the government. They let the families be together at night. They're just waiting for a revolt," the security guard said. He stopped at the last step. "Here we are—top floor—level five. Follow me."

Li walked just behind the security guard into the empty top floor. There were no lights beside the sunlight streaming in through two windows. The other windows were boarded up. He saw a glow from an HMS screen behind a slightly opened door to an office. The security guard went to the door and spoke through the opening. "Sir, I'm here with Charlie Liu."

"Come in," a voice behind the door said.

Li walked in behind the security guard. The first thing he noticed was a gun on the man's desk next to the LPS. The man sat in his chair, eyeing him.

"Wait here a minute, will you Officer Jackson?" the man asked. "I have a few questions for Mr. Charlie Liu."

"Yes, sir," the security guard said, standing at attention.

"I just got this letter only moments ago that I will be receiving another visitor to my facility, but you are not the man I was expecting," Ted Stanton began. "I'm a little confused because I've seen your face in the World News. What I've read today, and what I've read over the past several weeks seem to contradict each other."

Li was ready. "Neil Elder knew that this facility and the others he's investing in needed more funds. I found a way to provide those funds," Li said, reaching into his pocket and bringing out a long strand of diamonds. "This is an unofficial gift to you. And I'm on unofficial business. But Neil Elder sends his best regards, unofficially, of course, and says to keep up the good work."

Ted Stanton got up from his desk and walked around to the bracelet, grabbing it and bringing it close to his face. Li instantly knew that he was a low ranking Efficientist who had been working in the Colonies probably all of his adult life. He was a short, fair-skinned man with thinning, brown hair flecked with grey. After inspecting the diamonds for several seconds, he looked toward the security guard. "Officer Jackson, please stand right outside my office and shut the door."

"Yes, sir," the security guard said, exiting the office and closing the door behind him.

Ted looked back at Li. "You know, Mr. Liu, that entire story of the World Bank robbery didn't sit well with me. I knew something seemed fishy. I applaud your ingenuity," Ted said, walking back to his chair and sitting down. He placed the bracelet in his shirt pocket, patting it before continuing. "I was expecting a Randall Hunt today. I was asked to quietly get rid of him. Should I still be expecting him?"

"That is out of my area of expertise," Li said. "But I can do a little research and let you know."

"So you don't know everything," Ted said. "That's good to know. I've learned that it's best to keep some of the details to yourself. Too much knowledge makes for too much power."

Li said nothing.

"Are you here to inspect operations?" Ted asked. "I know you didn't come all this way to give me a gift."

"Yes, I was told you were having trouble with the sick," Li began.

"Oh, yes," Ted began. "What do we do with the laborers when they are no longer useful? Do we let them go, so they can spread information about our facility? Do we keep them here, and take care of them for the rest of their lives? Or do we quietly dispose of them, which is what I've been trying to get approved? Look, you gave me a Colonial medic who has no equipment and no electricity to use equipment even if he had any. Right now, we have over twenty people laying on cots on the first floor. What am I to do with these people?"

"That's why I am here. To help find the best solution," Li said.

"And just today," Ted said, getting out of his seat. "I get another sick Colonial passed out on my doorstep. What do my security guards do? They bring him in and give him to the medic. And now I have another sick mouth to feed and care for."

"Was the Colonial a woman or a man?" Li asked, thinking of Pilar and Randall.

"What difference does it make?" Ted asked. "It's another expense!"

"It does matter when I make my report to Neil Elder that a woman found this place so unintimidating that she willingly went to it," Li said, forcefully.

Ted brought up his hands. "Sorry, I didn't mean to disrespect. It was a man. He actually looks to be in good shape if it weren't for his eyes."

Li instantly knew that Randall was here. "You can't fix him up and use him?"

"The medic had to remove his left eye. His right eye had been damaged but someone thought to clean it. Even if he heals, he will still be a burden," Ted said. "Which is why I need to know what I'm to do with these people once their labor is of no more use to me."

"I have an answer," Li said, smiling. "Which will suit us both. But I'll have to get on your LPS right there and do a little manipulation."

"Will I get in trouble?" Ted asked, warily.

"Remember those details you were mentioning?"

Ted Stanton grinned. "Yes, I do."

"This will be one of the details that we won't mention to anyone. I'm doing some research that requires human participation, but—how can I say this—it's hard to get volunteers. And you have a surplus of volunteers. Let me alleviate your burden, and I will pay you in more trinkets," Li said, making a mental note to contact Pastor Tom about the rest of the jewels he had hidden at Trinity Trading Center.

"Ah, I see where this is going," Ted said. "By all means, have a seat," he said, swiveling the chair toward Li. "It's already on and ready."

Li sat down and erased all the documents of his arrival. He quickly looked to see if Neil had read it. No readers. He knew Jonah must have sent his reinstatement documents through the old-style laptop. He sent a report about Randall dying in an accident at the factory to Neil Elder from Ted Stanton. Finally, he sent a quick note to Jonah while the director inspected the bracelet in his pocket. "There you go," Li said, standing up. "I was never here. And if you can contact all the other facilities and let them know to bring their sick here, I'll make it worth your while. Just let them know that you're handling the surplus population. And don't worry about Randall Hunt. I just took care of him for you."

"Well, this has been worth my while after all," Ted said, reaching toward Li's hand and shaking it vigorously.

Li allowed his hand to be shaken. "Now just to be sure. I only need the people who cannot work anymore—the really sick, lame and dying. If I hear about any mistreatment of our labor force, our deal is off. Being productive for the World Government is still our primary concern. This little detail we have together is just a side note. Is that understood?" Li said. He did not want their deal to create more harm to the Colonials.

"Yes, I agree. I am still expected to meet my quota. When do you want me to arrange the delivery of the people?" Ted asked.

"Give me a few days to prepare my research team," Li said, thinking. "But let me take that newcomer you got in today. The man who lost his eye. Is he conscious yet?"

Ted shook his head no. "He's pretty bad off. Will pack him up for you, but I doubt if he'll make it."

"I'll take my chances," Li said.

The man raised his eyebrows. "Oh, I see. One more volunteer for your experiments?" he laughed.

"Why waste a perfectly good candidate?" Li smiled back. "Now, show me to the first floor."

Jonah finally made it back to his flat. He walked straight to the safe and typed in the passcode. He spun the handle open and reached down to get the old-style computer. He held it in his left hand and opened it with his right. He didn't have time to sit. He needed to erase the document he sent to the factory. The laptop was excruciatingly slow. Finally, when the screen turned on, he tried to find the document. It was gone. He kept looking, but no trace of it could be found.

Suddenly, he noticed two notes from an LPS at a factory. One was addressed to him at the computer, but he found another addressed to Neil at his LPS from the director of a factory. He cracked into Neil's account first, which was quite easy from a computer that was unnoticeable. Ted Stanton, the director, informed Neil that Randall had died in an accident at a factory. Jonah wondered if that was true. He opened the other note Li had written directly to him, which must have bounced through the network of computers that they had set up. Jonah read the note written in T-Variety. Randall was alive but injured, and Li was taking him. But what Jonah read next caused his breath to instantly release from his lungs. The factory in question had really been transformed into a labor camp. The World Government, championed by Neil Elder, was now using human labor to save money.

Jonah closed the laptop. Anger rose within him—an anger he hadn't felt in years. Labor camps were starting once again in the Colonies. He had to stop them.

CHAPTER THIRTY-ONE

"**T**hat's the second one I sent home today," Grandfather said. "Those men need you, *Ne'aw-ze*." Grandfather closed the door after Bear entered the living room. They both carried a stringer of fish.

"*Aha-enah*, it's only been less than a week. They can survive without me for a short time. I'm trying to let my hand heal first," Bear said, lifting up his right hand. He then took Grandfather's stringer along with his own in his left hand and brought them both to the sink.

"I don't think you understand the honor you have that men, strong men, would want to be led by you. You take your position for granted too easily," Grandfather said. He then looked at the kitchen counter and saw a familiar box. "Is Reyna here?"

Ruth looked up from the old-style computer. "She was here just for a short time today. She brought the box of baked good for us to celebrate Pilar being found."

"Why did she leave so early?" Bear asked, looking around.

"She cleaned for two hours but then had to leave. She is making Pilar's deliveries, so she is busier than before. Grandfather, she brought you extra today," Ruth said, smiling. "People love to spoil you."

Grandfather walked to the counter and lifted the lid to the box. He raised his eyebrows in anticipation of the sweets he saw. "Would any of you like to choose something before I go to my room?" he asked rhetorically.

"No, *Aha-enah*. Leave so I can be alone with my wife," Bear said in mock aggravation.

Grandfather closed the lid and gently placed the box under his arm. "The fish would make a good stew for tonight, *Ne'aw-ze*. Make sure to make it spicy. I want to taste what I'm eating," Grandfather said, heading to his room at the back of the house.

"Yes, *Aha-enah*. I know how you like your fish stew," Bear said, chuckling. He looked toward Ruth when Grandfather closed the door. "You know, he has had more sweets now that we are married than he's ever had. I think he looks out for you for the sweets."

Ruth smiled. She was getting used to Bear's sarcasm. "No, he looks out for me because I make him comfortable clothes."

Bear laughed. "He is the best dressed old man that I've ever seen. I know of a few widows who have their eyes on him."

Ruth's expression turned to concern. "Do you think he would leave us?"

"He's too set in his ways," Bear said. "He's content here. I'm sure he'll die in this house and in his bed with sweets all around him."

"I don't like that thought," Ruth said. "I just want everything to stay the same for a while."

Bear moved to the chair where Ruth was sitting. "What are Zach and Li up to?" he asked, looking at the small screen. "I still can't believe that Li tamed a wild stallion. I heard him speak of owning a ranch, and I wanted to laugh. But I guess only God knows what people are capable of."

"When people lose everything, they find themselves," Ruth said.

"Any word on Randall?" Bear asked.

"I don't want to tell you," she admitted.

Bear's serene expression disappeared. He leaned closer to the screen. "Why? What happened?"

"I've already deleted the communications," Ruth said. She watched Bear straighten up and wait.

"He can't be still alive?" he asked.

"He is," Ruth nodded.

Bear stood and crossed his arms. "Tell me what you know."

Ruth turned off the computer, and took a breath before speaking. "Randall walked to the old factory after Pilar left him. He passed out near the facility, and they found him. They brought him in and did surgery on his left eye. They removed it. Li went to the facility and made a deal with the director for all the sick and injured. Jewels for lives. Zach and Li are going to stay there for now and try to rescue as many people as possible. There's a pastor helping them—Rohan Gupta. Pastor Tom will use the computers to find homes for the people. Li is looking for a way to erase the World Government's money points, but they want to learn about the other labor camps first."

Bear listened intently. When Ruth was finished, he began to pace the floor behind her. He stopped. "I have two questions. Is Pilar staying with them?"

Ruth nodded. "Yes, she wants to help them. Levi has given his consent for her to stay."

"Okay," Bear said. "And you still haven't finished the story about Randall."

Ruth looked up at Bear. "Li rescued him from the labor camp and brought him back to the village where the pastor lives. They are caring for him, but they don't know if he'll make it."

Bear stopped. "And what does Zach say about this?"

Ruth briefly looked at Bear's hand and back at his face. "He hasn't said anything, but he's the one staying up at nights, caring for Randall."

"Well, it finally happened, Pastor Tom," Deborah said as she opened the door. "They've turned off our electricity."

"Good thing fall is in full swing or our houseguests would be miserable. Best just to slowly ease them into real Colonial life," Esther said. "How are Cindy and the kids?"

Pastor Tom looked at the two aged sisters, wearing their floral printed dresses and their hair up in buns. At one time, they had felt like pests, but now he valued their thoughts and efforts more than anyone other than his wife. "They're all fine. Our oldest is now fourteen. I can't believe how fast time goes by."

"You're telling us," Esther said, taking his coat and hat. "One minute I'm a teacher and my sister's a nurse. Then we run a small orphanage. Finally, we are a part of a movement fighting the World Government. Things have certainly changed!"

"Where are your houseguests?" Pastor Tom asked, looking around.

"They are bringing in the grapes!" Esther exclaimed. "We would have let you know, but we really didn't need help this time. We have more than enough hands with all of our Efficientist friends. They're sleeping three or four to a bedroom. Deborah and I now share a room."

"But we'll do anything to make sure no one is left behind. We've gotten many declarations of salvation, and we're still working on the rest," Deborah said. "Come to the kitchen. Esther and I were just making some fresh bread."

"I had to use the wood burning stove. I was nervous at first, but I feel like the bread has a nice smoky flavor to it," Esther said.

Pastor Tom nodded and smiled. He was used to Deborah and Esther jabbering on. He wouldn't interrupt them until they asked how Li and Zach were doing. "That will be nice. Cindy was going to make me lunch, but she knew that you two dears would have something for me."

"Of course she did," Deborah said. "My sister always has something ready for company."

Pastor Tom followed the sisters to the kitchen. He sat down at the familiar table. He watched as Esther cut a thick slice of bread.

"I know you like the ends of the loaf. Can I dribble a little honey over it?" Esther asked.

"Yes, please," Pastor Tom said.

"Here, I'll get it," Deborah said. She opened a large glass canister on the counter. Pastor Tom could see the thick golden liquid glinting in the sun streaming in through the open kitchen window. She lifted the honey dipper and waited for Esther to bring the plate of bread to her. Then she poured a large portion of honey all over the bread. Esther took the plate and laid it in front of him.

"My, doesn't that look good," Pastor Tom said. He lifted the bread and brought it to his lips, taking a generous bite. Esther and Deborah both waited for his reaction.

200

"I'm telling you, Esther," he began. "You cooked mighty good with the electric stove, but this here is something special."

"It's like a new adventure," Esther said. "I'll have to bring out my old recipes."

Pastor Tom continued to eat as the two sisters sat down. He knew they were getting ready to listen.

"So, Pastor Tom, we know you didn't come all the way out here for a friendly visit," Deborah began. "Our HMS no longer works, so we can't communicate with you or Ruth or Li, and now we feel like too much is happening, and we need to be caught up."

"For some reason," Esther chimed in. "Deborah and I have been praying and praying—specifically that hearts be open and that the love of Jesus just shines through."

"Can I get a glass of water?" Pastor Tom asked. "This honey is delicious but sticky."

"Oh dear, where are my manners?" Esther said, getting up. "The water hasn't been refrigerated, but it's still cool."

"That's what I'm used to," Pastor Tom said. "Thank you." He took several large gulps of the water to wash the bread and honey down. "What's the last you heard?" he asked after Esther sat back down.

"The last we were told was that Pilar, Bear and Ruth were going to Zach's old factory to get on his LPS because he had sent a letter there about where he was heading," Deborah said. "Which doesn't make sense. He should have just sent it to one of us."

Pastor Tom realized that so much had happened in such a short period of time. The sisters had only just lost electricity a handful of days ago, but they were several steps in the dark. "Okay, let me see if I can get you caught up, so you can gear your prayers to what we need now."

"Randall was waiting for them at the factory. He kidnapped Pilar in her truck, but Bear smashed his hand through the passenger window and saved Ruth, damaging Randall's eyes," he began. He heard gasps from both ladies.

"Don't worry. Bear's hand is healing, and he's taking it easy. Ruth and he are still in Levington, and they don't have to worry about leaving anymore."

"Why is that?" Deborah asked. "Did something happen to Randall?"

"Has Pilar been found? Did Levi go get her?" Esther asked, anxiously.

Pastor Tom raised his hands in mock surrender. "Hold on. A lot has happened in a few days, and things have become more complex than I could have ever imagined. Let me just try to get it all out, and then we can discuss the details."

Esther and Deborah immediately stopped asking questions and waited for Pastor Tom to speak.

"Randall was wounded, and Pilar got away from him in her truck. Randall's eyes were infected and he was very sick. He walked back to the old factory where he was supposed to meet Zach, but he passed out. The security guards brought him in, but a medic had to take his left eye. Zach found Pilar. Li and another pastor, Rohan Gupta, went to the factory, but it's not a factory. It's—" Pastor Tom's voice trailed off.

"What?" Deborah asked. "What is it?"

"It's a labor camp," he said. Both women gasped again, so he quickly said the rest. "Neil Elder has decided that human labor is cheaper than using machines. He has around six labor camps—all with Colonials with two things in common. They are nomadic and poor. They call it *gathering*."

"They're gathering Colonials?" Esther asked in disbelief.

"Yes, they started gathering people in labor camps when Neil Elder took over Eve Pallue's position in the World Government. And if this works, I'm sure Neil will try to establish labor camps in the World Government, and they'll be used all over the world. It's all part of something he's calling the *Colonization Plan*. The other nine magistrates must not know about it yet. Randall didn't know about it either, which was why Neil told the facility director to kill him."

"So Randall is dead?" Deborah asked.

Pastor Tom shook his head. "No, they thought he was a Colonial. Li struck a deal with the facility director that he would trade jewels for the lives of the laborers who are sick and dying. Otherwise, they would begin to terminate them. The first life that Li rescued was Randall's."

"Does Zach know?" Esther asked.

"Yes, he's been caring for Randall, so your prayers of an open heart and Jesus' love are mandatory right now," Pastor Tom said.

"I can't believe there are labor camps. I thought that was just a myth to keep kids inside," Deborah said.

"From what Li has written, the camps are horrendous. The people are living in filth and slaving all day—little kids even. Whole families have been gathered. But we're going to figure out how to get them out. I have several jewels left stored away, so at least we can get the sick out. I'm leaving tomorrow to meet up with Zach and Li and Pastor Gupta. I'm bringing Li's Portable too. He has Randall's, and he said they will help in bringing the World Government down."

"Is Cindy okay with you leaving her and the kids?" Deborah asked.

"Now that Randall has been found, we have some time. She'll be fine. I'll only be gone for a few days. I need to see first-hand what's going on over there, and I want to have a chat with Randall Hunt."

"Can Ruth and Bear visit us now?" Esther asked.

"I don't see why not. The sooner the better, though, because things are going to start happening. You can go over to my office anytime this week and use my HMS and generator to talk with Ruth. I'll let Cindy know, and she'll help you contact Ruth's old-style computer."

"We'll go tomorrow," Deborah said.

"I better be going," Pastor Tom said, getting up. "I have to start packing. But," he stopped. "I mainly came over here to ask you to pray."

"Yes, we will be praying for everyone," Esther said.

"Well, I need you to pray specifically for something we need desperately," Pastor Tom said, looking at the sisters. "We have the funds and we have the ability to communicate—thanks to Zach and Li. Now we need to find homes for these displaced people."

CHAPTER THIRTY-TWO

"How's he doing?" Pilar asked, walking into the bedroom where Zach was sitting on the chair. The morning sun was streaming in through the windows. For the first time in a long time, Zach looked like the young man she had met so long ago—innocent and weightless. His blond beard crept across his face in soft waves. His blue eyes shone from his tanned face.

Zach looked at the bed. "His fever finally broke. The infection in the left eye socket looks better too. I seriously didn't think he was going to survive when Li brought him here two days ago."

Pilar shut the door and leaned against it. "How do you feel?" Zach hadn't spoken much in the two days that Randall had been here. He watched over him, barely eating or sleeping. She hoped this third morning would be different. Maybe he would speak to her. He looked different, like he had surrendered. Pilar knew that look because she had recently experienced it herself.

Zach kept his eyes on the bed. "I don't know. It's kind of weird," he said. Then he looked up at Pilar. "The tranquilizers that Pastor Rohan used on him the first night he came here when he was thrashing around—I stole them from the last ranch we were at. That's why I sent the letter to my old LPS. I wanted him to find me, and I was going to use the tranquilizers on him."

"What were you going to do after you gave them to him?" Pilar asked.

"I honestly don't know. I don't even know if I would have gone through with it. But here he is," Zach said, turning his attention back to the bed. "The man who murdered my father. I'm torn. I want to ask him if my father was conscious when he set our church on fire. Did he hear his screams as he burned to death? But then I think of my dad and what he would want me to do."

"And what is that?" Pilar asked. She didn't want to push the conversation, yet she knew that this time Zach was willing to share his thoughts. She wanted him to keep talking.

Zach leaned back into his chair and looked at the ceiling. "I know exactly what my father would want. He would tell me to forgive and tell this man about Jesus. I opened Pastor Rohan's *Bible* today that he left on my nightstand. I read Jesus' words about loving your enemies. It sounds so easy in theory. But now I have a face to go with my pain. It's not some World Government conspiracy. It's an actual man lying on this bed."

Zach moved back up in his chair. "I remember speaking to Bear about his mother. He had such hatred for her. I would tell him to forgive, but it was hard for him. He would take care of her—all the while she would mistreat and neglect him. I see now how foolish I've been. I had easy words with little understanding."

Pilar pushed off the door and walked toward the bed. She stared down at the figure. She had heard so much about this man. She feared him and what he would do to her family and friends. But now he looked thin and weak. "I look at him and think back on all my fear. So much of it was due to my lack of trust in God."

Zach got out of the chair and walked toward Pilar. "How do you feel?"

Pilar looked at Zach's face. She wanted to touch his beard, but she resisted the temptation. "You know, when I was running away from him, I realized that I feared being helpless and lost more than I feared him. I looked at the emptiness around me and decided to go back and get my truck. Maybe I sensed that he was sick. I could see it in him. Bear got Ruth out of my truck, but he injured Randall enough to make him less of a threat to me," Pilar said.

"Ruth says that Bear broke almost every bone in his hand and tore his skin apart. He hasn't trained his men since the injury. I think it's good he's taking a break," Zach said. "Now we have time to figure out what we are going to do about the labor camps."

Pilar felt tears sting her eyes. "Li said the conditions for the Colonials there are horrible. Pastor Rohan has been praying nonstop. I see him pacing outside with his arms up begging God for help. I can't believe this is happening."

"It seems that human labor is now cheaper than machines," Zach said. "I knew the bottom would drop out somehow."

"What do you mean?" Pilar asked.

"Colonials are starting to leave the factories. Even Runners are becoming hard to come by, which was why I was always so busy. The Colonial villages, like your dad's, have been thriving. We don't need the World Government anymore except for HMSs, but even those weren't so necessary, except to follow what all the Efficientists are doing according to the World News. But no one cares about what they are doing anymore," Zach said. "I guess Neil Elder realized he was about to lose his workforce, so he decided to take them against their will."

"People don't watch the World News since Eve Pallue died. I think Colonials are more interested in their own lives now," Pilar said. "This must be a backlash to the falling ratings of the World Government."

Zach looked at the man sleeping soundly in the bed. "If Randall didn't know about the labor camps, they must be very secret. Will you forgive him for taking you?" Zach asked.

"Yes," Pilar whispered.

"Pilar, he tried to shoot you," Zach said.

She looked into Zach's blue eyes and saw his deep concern for her. "I think Randall was delirious when he shot at me. It really came out of nowhere. Besides, my dad says sometimes you have to do what you know is true regardless of how you feel."

Zach walked up to Pilar and put his arm around her waist. She leaned her head against his shoulder. "When I found out you had been taken, I felt fear gripping me. But somehow I knew that I would find you. When I heard those three shots and saw your truck, it was one of the best moments of my life."

"Will you forgive him?" Pilar asked.

Zach sighed. "The funny thing is that I feel forgiveness already inside of me. It's like God is giving it to me freely, but I'm having trouble accepting it."

"Well, you better accept it," she said. "Because I have a feeling that Randall is at a crossroads. The World Government wants him dead. He has no place else to go. He'll need people on his side."

"You're right, but there's only one problem with that," Zach said, staring at the unconscious face of Randall.

"What is that?" Pilar asked, looking at Zach.

"He has no idea Eve Pallue is still alive," Zach finished.

"What are we going to say?" Pilar asked.

"I don't know. Pastor Tom is on his way. We'll decide once he gets here. All I know is that Randall can either be a liability or an asset. I just don't know which he'll turn out to be," Zach said, keeping his eyes on the unconscious figure who continued to sleep next to the *Bible* on the nightstand.

CHAPTER THIRTY-THREE

R uth startled from her sleep. "What?" she asked. Bear was sleeping next to her, fidgeting. She could hear him speaking, but didn't understand. He didn't answer, so she spoke louder. "Bear, what are you saying." The room was completely dark. The moon was behind clouds, so no light came onto the bed.

Bear's voice became louder. Ruth still couldn't discern his words. He began to sway side to side in the bed, bumping up against her. "Bear, wake up," she whispered. "You are dreaming."

Bear's breathing became more rapid, like he was wrestling one of his men. He began to thrash harder and speak louder. She fumbled her hand to his chest. His body was soaked with sweat, but she knew it wasn't warm in the room. The crisp, autumn air bristled in through two windows. Ruth realized something was wrong. He was usually a very deep sleeper, worn out from the day's activities.

Ruth got onto her knees and tried to shake Bear awake. "Bear!" she shouted. "Wake up!"

Bear's hand flew out and struck her across the face. She felt an instant sting. She fought off the shock. She needed to help her husband. It seemed as though he was fighting off attackers in a dream. Ruth got low to the bed and crawled onto Bear's torso, avoiding his flailing arms. She clung desperately to his body, knowing that she couldn't stop his movements. She only hoped she could hang on to him without getting hit again.

"I demand in the name of Jesus that you who are attacking my husband must flee from here. You are banished because the Holy Spirit lives in him. You are not welcome here."

"They're hurting me!" Bear screamed. "Get them off!" He began to pull at Ruth with his left hand, trying to get her off of him.

The door to the room tore open. "What is it?"

She heard Grandfather's voice, but she couldn't see him. "Help hold down his left arm!" she shouted.

Grandfather went straight toward the bed. She could feel him grabbing for Bear's left arm, which was swinging. Bear's right hand was wrapped in gauze, so it could only beat against her side.

"I demand by the holy and powerful name of Jesus Christ that every one of you leave my husband now! He is forgiven. He has been washed clean. There is no darkness in him that you can feed on! Listen to my voice and the authority I have as co-heir with Christ, the Firstborn of my brothers and sisters, you will leave now!" Ruth shouted. She now sat erect on his chest. Bear's left arm was pinned by his grandfather and his padded right hand beat against her ribs. She felt the pounding lessen.

Bear screamed. Then his hands went limp. The beating on her ribs stopped, and Grandfather fell against Bear's left arm onto the bed. She listened to Bear's breathing. It was slowing down.

"Should I start the fire and bring in candles?" Grandfather whispered in the dark.

"No," Ruth said. "Let him sleep."

"What happened?" he asked.

"I think he was attacked by demons," she said.

"But I thought Zach's mother stopped those dreams," Grandfather said.

Ruth placed her hand on Bear's chest. She could feel the calmness of his strong heart returning. "He's harboring unforgiveness. Demons can attack any area of our lives not submitted to God."

"Who has he not forgiven?" Grandfather asked.

"I think himself," Ruth said. Then she laid her body against Bear's. She placed her head against his heart, listening to the steady beat. He always liked it when their bodies touched. It calmed him to know she was there. "Go back to bed, Grandfather. We'll see you in the morning."

Bear's eyes opened. He was surprised to see the sun so bright already coming in through the windows. He must have slept in. He felt a strange weight on his chest and looked down. Ruth's long brunette hair was scattered around him. She was sleeping with her body completely on his with her legs and arms tucked closely around him. He smiled. She must have been cold. He leaned up higher on his pillow, so he could get a better look at her. He began to stroke her hair that was strewn across her face. He pulled several strands aside, so he could see her countenance. His hand suddenly stopped when he saw a blue bruise across her cheek.

"Ruth," he said, grabbing hold of her body and sitting up. "What is on your face?"

Ruth tried to open her eyes, but the right one was swollen shut. "What?" she whispered, barely awake.

"Ruth," he said again louder, lifting her face to his. "You've been hit. The entire right side of your face is bruised. What the hell happened?" he demanded.

"Ouch!" she yelled out. "Do not grab me so hard."

Bear looked to the right of her body where his arm was holding her up. He instantly noticed that the bandage around his hand was unraveling and there were spots of browned blood. He lifted her white gown to reveal her torso. "You have bruises all over your body!" he said. "Ruth, what's going on?" He felt a sickening in his stomach. He tried to think over last night. He'd had a nightmare. Something terrible had happened. He stared at Ruth's face and tried to remember.

"I remember you yelling over me. I was being attacked— just like I was six years ago—tormented by those demons that came to me when I smoked peyote as the Shaman. You said something—" he thought, trying to remember. "You said the name, Jesus, and they left me."

Ruth tried to open her eyes again, but only the left eyelid lifted. "Yes, you were spiritually attacked and I prayed over you. Grandfather came to help me."

"Did he do this to you?" Bear shouted, looking towards Ruth's face. "Did you fall? Why are you so beat up?" Bear looked at Ruth's expression and he knew instantly he had done this to her. "I did this to you?" he asked.

Ruth scooted back down and grabbed ahold of his torso again. "Let us just go back to sleep," she whispered. "Everything's fine now. We'll talk about it when I am awake."

Bear felt Ruth grab hold of him. He wanted to believe everything was okay. But he couldn't stop the sick feeling in his stomach. He remembered too many mornings when he would wake up next to a woman, beaten and bruised by his hand. He'd promised himself and God he would never touch a woman in that way again. But here lay his wife, the person he loved more than anything in this world, and his handprint was across her face.

"Ruth," he said, not wanting to believe the truth. Tears began to burn his eyes. "I did this to you."

"You were asleep," she whispered. "You were not aware of what you were doing."

Bear pounded his left hand against the back of the wall. "No! No!" he shouted.

He pulled Ruth off his body and got out of bed. "No! God! No!" he yelled louder, pounding his fists against the wall again. This time he punched through with his left hand.

The door opened. "What is going on in here!" Grandfather demanded.

Bear looked at his grandfather. "*Aha-enah*, you let me hit her? Why didn't you stop me?"

"I did, *Ne'aw-ze*, but you were asleep. I held down your arm, so *baynit* could pray those demons away from you," Grandfather said, walking to Bear and putting his hand on his shoulder. "You were asleep. You didn't know."

Bear threw Grandfather's hand off him. "You should have stopped me. Look at my wife! Look at her face! She can't see out of her eye. Her body is bruised! I hit her with my own hands!" he yelled, staring at Ruth who was sitting on her knees in the bed. Her face was flushed and wet with tears, which made her look more wounded.

"Bear, please, calm down," Ruth said. "Let us talk about this. I promise you. It will be better."

"No," Bear said, taking two steps back away from the bed. "No, you shouldn't be near me. Stay away from me!" he shouted. He walked out into the living room. He looked around at the house he had made for Ruth. What was he thinking, starting a family? He was cursed. He couldn't be a good husband, let alone a good father. He needed to get out. He lunged toward the door and yanked it off its hinges. He let the door fly onto the ground and he began to sprint through his property toward the river. He could hear the footsteps of his wife behind him.

CHAPTER THIRTY-FOUR

He couldn't let her catch up with him. She would see his shame. She would know that he had hurt women—many women, more than he could count, who reminded him of his mother. He beat them and left them.

"Bear!" he heard Ruth's voice behind. "Please, wait for me! I am unable to keep up!"

He ran harder. He made for the river. She wore no shoes and wouldn't be able to follow him through the current, and she would just go home. His feet were tough and used to maneuvering through the slippery rocks.

He splashed through the icy water. The coolness eased the heat radiating from his body. He leapt to each stone, balancing just before he made another leap. He was across the river in seconds. Then he ran up the hill to put the shame behind him. When he finally made it to the top, he heard a shotgun exploding through the morning air. He stopped. The shotgun went off again and a third time. He knew it was his grandfather's. He looked back. He could see the entire river. He saw a figure shrouded in white, tumbling across the rocks with the current. It was Ruth.

"Save her!" the voice of his Grandfather yelled. He was standing near the water.

Instantly, Bear's feet began to tear through the air. His arms pushed him faster with every swing. Ruth's body stopped against a large rock. She was trying to get up, but her wet nightgown pulled her with the current. Bear felt the cold splash of the water again and he was by her side a moment later. He scooped her up out of the water. Her entire body was drenched and shivering.

"Ruth, are you okay?" he asked, holding her body to his.

"Do not leave me!" she cried.

"I'm sorry. I won't ever leave you again," he said. His body balanced easily in the water, and the current made its way around his legs. He held her until the shivering subsided. He walked her back to the shore where his grandfather waited, holding the shotgun on his shoulder away from them.

Ruth finally stirred. "You did not mean to," she said. "You were attacked. I felt them. You were trying to get them off of you."

He stared at his wife's bruised face. She looked at him full of forgiveness and love. It broke him. "I thought those demons were gone. Naomi prayed over me by the Blood of Jesus. I felt them leave, but last night, they came to me. I don't understand why," he said, clinging to her body. "I'd rather lose you than hurt you."

"We are both hurt," she said, trying to smile. "We'll heal together."

"Yes, but you're hurt because of me," he said, gently stroking her bruised cheek.

"And you are hurt because of me," she said, reaching for his bandaged hand that was now soaked. "You risked your hand to save me. Let me take risks too."

"But why is this happening again?" he asked. "I thought that they couldn't touch me anymore like that."

"The enemy cannot go where forgiveness has been," she whispered. "What are you holding onto?"

Bear looked at the bruise across his wife's otherwise flawless face. "I don't want to tell you. I don't know if you could have read about it anywhere," he said as his voice broke.

"What?" Ruth asked.

"I used to beat women," he said, lowering his head against Ruth's shoulder. "I would hurt them and many wouldn't leave. They let me abuse them until I got rid of them. I abused them because my mom had hurt me so much. Since we've been married, their faces keep coming to me. I never paid for those sins."

"Were any of them seriously injured?" Ruth asked.

"No," he whispered. "Just bruises like the ones you have. But more than anything, I tore their self-worth apart with my words. How can I be a husband and father when I've done these things?" he asked, his voice tumbling into tears.

Ruth shifted her body, bringing her legs around Bear's torso. Grabbing his jaw with both her hands, she forced his face up so his eyes locked with hers. "When I was Eve Pallue, do you know what I did?" she asked, not waiting for an answer. "I told other Efficientists to send the Mothers of their children away. I explained that their value had been used up, and they were no longer worthy. Many Mothers committed suicide because of my decree. How am I worthy to be a mother when I devalued the life of those Mothers?"

Bear stared into Ruth's good eye. The golden rings within the light brown hue shone brightly in the morning sun. She continued. "Women died because of my words. No, I did not force them to commit suicide, but I invited them. But I have to let that go. Jesus has already taken that sin and erased it. If I choose to carry it, the enemy can feed on that darkness."

"I understand, but I'm not like you, Ruth. You have the ability to freely let things go. It's hard to explain," he said, spotting the giant shed he built beside his house. "Your brain is like my shed. I get rid of things and I keep things. Once something is gone, it's gone for good. But my mind is different. Everything is intermingled. I feel it all as if it was yesterday. When I look at your face," he said, gently stroking the bruise again. "I see every woman that I have ever hit. I feel the weight of my sin falling on me again and again. I don't know how to dump those memories out of my shed."

Ruth wound her arms around Bear's shoulders and pressed her good cheek against his neck. "Bear, like anything it takes discipline. You did not become the best fighter in the Colonies overnight, and I did not become the top Elite Efficientist overnight. My mind is extremely trained. Just like your body is."

Bear thought about her words. "Yes, you're out of shape," he said, chuckling.

"And so are you," she said, offering up a half smile.

"Do you forgive me?" he asked.

She whispered back. "Yes, I do. And on behalf of the women you have hurt, we also forgive you. You must now forgive yourself, so the enemy cannot stay there in that wound anymore. If we are going to start a family, we will have to let go of our family wounds."

"Do you want to start a family with me?" Bear asked, feeling his heart race again.

"I am considering it," Ruth said, leaning her head against his neck. "Now get me home."

"*Aha-enah*," Bear said to his grandfather, standing near them.

"Yes, *Ne'aw-ze*," Grandfather said.

"Do you still have some sweets leftover in the box that Reyna brought?" he asked.

Grandfather grinned. "Yes, my stomach ached from too much, so I had to leave the rest. Would you like them?"

"Yes, I will get them and bring them into our room," Bear answered, as he began to walk back to the house. "And make sure no one disturbs us all day."

Grandfather watched as they walked away. He adjusted the shotgun on his shoulder. He looked up at the sky and felt the autumn sun warm his face. "So that is it, God. That is how we forgive others," he whispered. "Thank You for showing me."

CHAPTER THIRTY-FIVE

Pastor Tom poured the fuel into the tank of his car. When it was done, he opened the rear car door and placed the canister on the seat next to the others. He counted. "Well, that's it," he said to himself. He closed the door and reached through the driver's side window. He leaned in and grabbed Li's Portable. He turned it on using his thumbprint. He was glad that Li had thought to add his print to the Portable too.

He analyzed the map shown on the screen. "I'm almost there," he said aloud. "Li knew exactly how much gas I would need. Always good to have the smart ones on your side." He walked back to the driver's side and opened the door. He got in and set the Portable on the seat next to him. "Let's get there before it gets too dark," he said. He looked in the back seat where he had several computers stored. Most of them weren't working, but he hoped he had brought enough parts for Li to get them in running order.

He began his slow drive through the rough terrain. There was once a road here, but it had become broken and overgrown with age. He had seen photos of Old America before the Second Civil War. It looked so established that people thought it would never crumble. Pastor Tom looked at the desolation around him. "Little did they know," he whispered.

A few minutes later, he saw the labor camp in the distance. There would be a turn off to the village any second now. He kept driving, but suddenly stopped. He peered out the window, looking back. He had passed it. The turn off was hardly noticeable because the last of the sun's light was vanishing. He backed his car several feet and then turned down the new road going west. He had to drive even slower. The empty gas jugs in the back seat were bumping up against each other.

He looked in the distance and his heart froze. There were several large trucks, driving in a line. "Are they coming this way?" he whispered. He slowed the car to a stop and watched the trucks. He wished he had thought to bring binoculars. There were a few at the Trading Center. The trucks seemed to be going toward the labor camp. Finally, he remembered what Li had told him. The men get shipped to the fields every morning. "They must be just coming back," he said. He grasped the Portable next to him and checked the time. "It's almost 7:30 at night, and they're just getting back. I can't believe this," he said, anger rising in his voice. "We need to stop this slavery right now before Neil Elder makes this horrible idea global."

Pastor Tom put the car back into drive. He moved the car a little faster this time, letting the jugs in the backseat tumble. After ten more minutes, he finally saw the village in the distance. "It's too close," he whispered. They were only miles away from the labor camp. "No wonder families are leaving. I can see why the pastor was torn about leaving them."

As he came into the town, he saw a man on a large, black and white horse gradually coming toward him. "No, that can't be," Pastor Tom said. He stopped the car and looked out the window. "Li, is that you?" Pastor Tom asked in disbelief.

"Yes, sir," Li said, leaning down from his horse. "And this is Xīnnián, but you can call him Xin," he said. "Come, Pastor Tom, follow me," Li said, taking the reins and moving the black and white stallion back in the opposite direction.

Pastor Tom stepped gently on the gas pedal. "I can't believe my own eyes. Li is a real cowboy. I can't wait to tell Cindy. She was right. All those days she forced me to help Li ride that horse. I wanted to give up. I thought there was no way he could be a cowboy, but just look at him. Note to self: always trust your wife," Pastor Tom said, chuckling under his breath. "Okay God, You got me here. Now guide me in what I need to do next. I don't have much time, so You have to be very specific. I need to know if Zach can be trusted, and I need to know what to do with Randall Hunt. Also, I want to show my appreciation to Rohan Gupta. I don't even know the man, but from what Li has told me, he is a man after Your heart. Also, God, I feel like that printing press can be used for something, but I don't know what yet. Show me. Keep me open to the possibilities around me. I pray this in Your Son's name, amen."

Pastor Tom followed Li as they passed a small diner. He saw that, though it was dinner time, the diner only had a few patrons. A few minutes later, Li stopped in front of a small house. The house was hard to distinguish in the dark, but he could see the silhouette. When Li slid off the horse, he put his car in park. He grabbed the Portable and his overnight bag. He only had one change of clothes. He wasn't planning on staying more than a few days. He opened the door and got out.

"Is that my Portable?" Li asked.

"Yes, I brought it. Thank you for the map and directions. I got here quickly with just enough gas."

"Pastor Gupta has more gasoline in the back. We'll make sure you have enough to get home," Li said, leading his horse to the house.

"How did he get so much fuel?" Pastor Tom asked.

"He says God told him ten years ago to start collecting as much as he could, so he began to save every gallon he could get," Li said.

Pastor Tom sniffed the air. "Is that the printing press I smell?"

"Yes, Pastor Rohan has been working on printing the Four Gospels from the *Bible*," Li said.

"I see," Pastor Tom said. He noticed that Li wasn't going to the front door. "Where are we going?"

"I have to tie Xin up for the night," Li said. "Isn't he a beauty?"

Pastor Tom could barely make out Li's expression, but he could hear the pride in his voice. He reached out to pet the stallion's muzzle. "He's a great horse. I'm amazed at how you were able to ride him. You really impress me, Li. Cindy knew all along that you would make a good cowboy."

"She's the one who told me I could be a rancher in the first place," Li said.

Pastor Tom stopped. "Really?"

"Yes, I told her that there was nothing I enjoyed at Deborah and Esther's ranch. I didn't like the goats or the gardening or the cooking or any of it. That's when she told me that I should be a cowboy," Li said. "She told me that someone was looking to get rid of their horse, and I should persuade the sisters to trade for it," Li said.

Li stopped and tied the horse to the tree. Pastor Tom noticed the other horse grazing on the grass. Xin went straight to the other horse and snorted a greeting.

Pastor Tom spoke up when Li turned his attention back to him. "Cindy never told me that she's the one who suggested it," Pastor Tom said.

Li smiled. "She wanted you to train me, but she thought it would sound better if I asked you myself."

"She did, did she?" Pastor Tom said. "That woman of mine is full of surprises."

"Have you heard from Randall?" Ada asked. She wore a black suit dress and sat at the table of the PR event. Her food was hardly eaten, but she was on her second glass of wine.

"No, it's been days, and he hasn't contacted me," Neil said. The facility director had written him, telling him that Randall was indeed dead. Randall was gone for good, but he would let Ada know later. He hated that he felt conflicted about losing his best man. Hopefully, Matt Coughlin would take up the slack. "Besides, we are not supposed to speak about that topic in public."

Ada flung her blonde, shoulder-length hair behind her shoulders. "What does it matter," she said. "No one cares for these events anymore. The polls for the Elite Efficientists are way down. There is nothing to see, and the World News ratings have plummeted. People have stopped watching us on their HMSs and LPSs because we are boring. If you don't do something quick, we will lose all public interest."

"That's not my area of expertise," Neil said. "I have to deal with the other magistrates. I'm trying to run a World Government. Can't you do something about it?" he asked. He was getting tired of her whining. He wondered what Randall ever saw in her besides her looks.

Ada continued to sip her wine until the red liquid disappeared. The waiter instantly came to refill it. She covered her glass before he could pour the wine. "Did I motion for another glass?" she asked sternly.

"No ma'am," the waiter said.

"I never drink more than two in public events. Go find yourself another empty glass to refill," she said, shooing him away.

The waiter backed away from the table and left.

She leaned forward. "How can I use my expertise when I am so limited. You give me no funds and no authority to do anything! I can't plan an event when I have to stay accountable to everyone. I have no team. I have no resources. I am limited, and look what is happening. Everyone is losing interest in us, and I am not to blame!"

Neil leaned his elbows onto the table. "Fine, do what you need to do," he said and looked back up to Ada. "But whatever you do better be good. I want the polls to go up, do you hear me? I can't have any more Efficientists dropping rank and moving out to the Colonies."

Ada smiled sweetly. "You have my word," she whispered. "Just make sure I have the right funds and the ability to pick my team, and I'll have those ratings up by the first of the new year."

"That's only a few months away," he said.

"I have everything already planned. I was simply waiting on you," Ada said. She took the napkin from her lap and dabbed the corners of her mouth. "I better get some sleep. Tomorrow is going to be a fun-filled day." She set the napkin on her plate and motioned for a waiter. "Leaving," she said. He pulled out her seat and helped her up.

Neil watched as she walked to the door, which was promptly opened by one of the Bodyguards waiting outside. He waved to the waiter. "I'll take another," he said, motioning to his empty glass.

CHAPTER THIRTY-SIX

Bear wore only his sarong and the single pearl that Ruth had given him on their wedding day. His tan skin glinted in the morning sun. That morning had been warmer than the other mornings, and the heat matched the way he was feeling. He balanced the large piece of wood with his left hand on the flat rock he used to split logs. He then grabbed the ax on the ground next to him with his left hand and brought it over his head. Finally, he brought the ax down with force and precision, watching the wood split into two. Splitting logs was normally a job for one of his younger fighters, but today he felt the need to work up a sweat.

He woke up early, looking at his wife's bruised face before going outside. The swelling around her eye had gone down, and the blue tones were fading to an unpleasant yellow. Guilt gripped him when he looked at her. He forced himself out of bed. Mornings were the hardest for him. They were quiet and full of thoughts and emotions. He was too idle. He needed to train his men again. He dropped the ax and looked at his right hand. Ruth had put a fresh bandage on it the night before. He tried to clench his fist, but most of the muscles wouldn't cooperate. He had broken many bones over the years, but he struggled losing the strength of his right hand.

Everything had changed. For five years, he waited on God to change his circumstances, and now that they were, he felt insecure in them. He was scared to sleep. Every time he would begin to dream, he would wake himself up. He was losing weight. He'd put on his sarong and had to tighten it several inches. He needed to talk to someone. Zach was his first choice. Most of the men he trained were intimidated by him—either because of his fighting skills or notoriety or both. Zach was one of the few people who never saw him as the Shaman. He knew

Zach would be honest. He could write Zach, but he communicated better face-to-face.

Bear looked around at his surroundings, making sure no one was in sight. He began to walk. "Okay, God. I'm talking to you," he began. "I need strength to overcome this guilt I have. I think I've had it for a while now, but I've been keeping myself busy. But now I have nothing but time."

He stopped, thinking. "Ruth says that I need to let go of what I feel. The only problem is what I feel is so much a part of me. Does that make sense? How do I cut something out of me that's already a part of me?"

Suddenly, an image of a fighter who fought in the circuit with him came to mind. The fighter had a small bump on the back of his neck. At first, he had ignored it. But after a few days of fighting, the bump grew and became red and painful. His friend tried to squeeze the bump, thinking it was a large pimple. But the bump, which they later learned was a boil, became infected. And the fighter became feverish. They finally contacted a medic. The medic cleaned the boil and lanced it. Then several times a day he put a warm, wet cloth on the infected area. After about a week, the boil and the infection were almost unnoticeable.

"Why are You giving me this image?" Bear said. He wanted to hear God speak. "Are my feelings of guilt like a boil on me?" Yes," he thought. "That's exactly it. The feelings may be a part of me, but they're like an infection. God is getting rid of the infection."

Bear continued to walk with the image of the fighter in his mind. "Yes, You have lanced it. It took me seeing my wife's bruised face to feel it. Now what are you doing?" he asked, trying to relay the metaphor to his life. "You are allowing me to rest while you put a wet, warm cloth on the infection. I see now," he said. "I see now!"

Bear needed to run. He wanted to watch the world around him turn quickly across his view. As he ran, he brought up the face of every woman he could remember from his past. When he saw each face, he said two simple words: *Forgive me.* Each time a new face appeared, he said the statement again: *Forgive me.*

When he got to the river, he took a right and began to run alongside it. The chant of the current repeated with him: *Forgive me. Forgive me. Forgive me.*

His footsteps became lighter. The sun's rays streamed in through the trees, lighting his path of freedom. Finally, the image of Ruth's face appeared, and he slowed to a stop. The face of an innocent girl with the strength of a thousand women. He tried to say *Forgive me*, but she wouldn't take it. She simply said back, *Forgiven.*

In that moment, he knew that his wife had forgiven him before the sting of the slap had set in. She wrapped her body around his in complete trust, even though her eye had been swollen shut. She knew about his abuse of women, but that did not affect the way she looked at him or responded to him. Her forgiveness was absolute and complete. He once believed that she had difficulty showing emotion, but now he knew that her passion dwelled in the place of forgiveness for herself and others. He needed to get back to her.

Bear turned and began to walk briskly back down the river. The current of the water now seemed to applaud his freedom. "Thank You, God," he whispered. "I am forgiven. I will no longer carry this infection. You lanced me at first, but now you are tender with me. Thank You for giving me Ruth. If I would have known how much I would love her, I would have easily waited fifteen years for her. The five years You had me stop seeking relationships with women seem so small compared to my love for her."

His feet veered from the river, and he walked up the hill that lead to the clearing of his home. "I must contact Zach and see if there is anything they need. I may not be able to train my men right now, but I can help in some way." He looked at his shed. He had plenty of food stored up that he could share. In fact, some of it needed to be consumed soon. He would go through his shed today and see what he could give.

He looked back at his house and stopped. Ruth stood in the doorway, wrapped in a small blanket she had made. He tried to read her face. Though she showed very little emotion, he knew something was wrong by the way she waited for him. He quickened his pace.

"What is it?" he asked. This time seeing her bruised face did not spark guilt, only love. He saw the single pearl that she wore around her neck, and he knew that they were bound together for life.

"I got on the computer to make sure Pastor Tom made it to the location," Ruth began.

"Is he okay?" Bear asked. "Did anything happen on his way?"

"Yes, he's fine. There were no problems. They have a lot of plans. I'll tell you about them later," she said.

"So what else did you find?" Bear asked, seeing anxiety actually appear on his wife's face.

"The World News posted today that Ada Armel—she is the one who used to work for me and who began dating Randall. She has been given approval to plan something she's calling, *Grand Opus Gala*. She is gathering talented, learned and interesting people to share and demonstrate their life's work to the world. It's happening the first of the year in about two months. But she will have PR events continuously until that time. There are a hundred names on the list of Efficientists and a few Colonials from all around the world, and they have all been summoned. They will begin preparations for the three-night Gala starting New Year's Eve. The Gala will be mandatorily shown on every LPS and HMS around the world.

"It sounds to me that the World Government is getting desperate," Bear said. "They're trying to get people back on their HMSs again."

"That's exactly what they are doing," Ruth agreed.

"So why does this bother us? You have your old computer thing. We won't need to watch it."

Ruth shook her head. "Yes, we will."

"Why is that?" he asked.

He watched Ruth fidget. He hadn't seen her this uncomfortable in a while.

"You are one of the hundred representatives that have been summoned," she said.

"What?" he asked in disbelief.

"I read over every name. The Shaman is on the list," she said.

"Why would they summon me?" he asked, incredulously.

"You are the best fighter, and you have done PR events in the city. I clicked the link to your name, and they had a video of your last fight at Enchanted Rock. Millions. You have millions of views and the World News just updated less than an hour ago. By the end of the day, everyone—Efficientists and Colonials—will know your face and will have researched your entire life, like I once did."

He looked around his property. "You think they will try to come here?" he asked.

"Yes," Ruth said, simply. "Ada has already sent formal invitations to each *Grand Opus Gala* representative. We should be expecting someone from the World Government here any day."

"But what about Randall? I'm sure he told them I was Zach's friend," Bear said. "I don't understand how my name could be on that list."

"I do not know either. But Randall woke up this morning. Pastor Tom and Zach are getting ready to talk with him," Ruth said. "It does not matter, though. Your name is on that list, and with the views your video has received, Ada will insist you come."

"I'll just tell them I'm unable to make it," Bear said, and held up his hand. "Look, I'm injured."

"You have no choice," Ruth said, gently taking his bandaged hand.

"They can't make me go to the Efficientists' Gala!" he yelled.

"If you do not attend, you will be marked by the World Government as an agitator," she said. "And you, me, Grandfather and this entire village will become targets."

Bear looked at his wife. She was calm, taking the punches as they came to her. "I will not leave you here by yourself. You have to go with me. I don't want to be without you."

"I fear that I will be recognized. I have not so far, which is God's protection," she whispered.

"You look nothing like the Eve Pallue that I used to watch on the HMS," Bear said. To his eyes, she looked better than the Elite Efficientist he used to fantasize over. "No one will recognize you."

She looked away for a brief moment. "Ada might. She has seen me without makeup."

"Randall has seen you without makeup, and he didn't recognize you," he said.

"Ada is different. She is trained to see things. But we have time to consider our options and plan what we will do next. I will contact Jonah and wait to see what Randall does. But we will need to get ready."

"Ready for what?" he asked. "I'm used to people knowing me. I fought on the circuit for years."

"No," she said. "Once you are on the World News, everything changes. You are now known globally."

"You really think this Gala thing she's doing is necessary?" Jonah asked. He stood in Eve Pallue's old flat that was now occupied by Neil Elder. He noticed that Neil seemed unusually happy this morning.

"Look, it is out of my hands now. Ada already had her press conference announcing the Gala to the World News, and she has plans to do PR events up to the time the Gala airs on every LPS and HMS across the globe," Neil said, turning from side to side in the swivel chair.

Jonah didn't want to give in. "But we've had attacks on the World Government. Randall is gone. We need to build a better team with all this publicity we're going to get. What if this Gala is a distraction, keeping us from seeing what's going on around us?"

Neil jumped up from his seat. "You see, that is what is so brilliant about this entire situation. I should have listened to Ada before, but I underestimated her. This *Grand Opus Gala* is a distraction, but not for the World Government. It's a distraction for the rest of the world. The PR ratings have jumped up. Thousands of unused HMSs have been turned back on. I just finished talking with the other magistrates, and they are excited as well. It seems that Ada has done her research. She had chosen key individuals from all around the world to be representatives at the Gala. She's even chosen some exceptional Colonials. That woman is brilliant."

"There were a lot of names on that list. The security risk to you has just increased by a hundred-fold, at least. I don't have the manpower to handle what Ada is suggesting we do," Jonah said.

"How many available rooms do we have in this building?" Neil asked.

"Less than a dozen. I'm going to have to quadruple my team. I'll have to interview, hire and train dozens of new Bodyguards. I can't do all this alone," Jonah said, thinking. "Maybe I can promote the team I have now to senior rank, and put teams underneath each of them. That would alleviate the burden. Then I can assign each team to different phases of the Gala."

Neil clapped. "That's the thinking I want to hear from you. We have the funds now to do anything. This will be our chance to build and strengthen our manpower."

"I can double up the flats in this building and assign the new personnel three or four to a flat. But where do you want the Gala representatives to stay?"

"Get with Ada and just pick out one of Arthur Pallue's smaller buildings. The World Government owns those now, so we can do whatever we please. Have Ada spend a little money to spruce it up. We want to show the world that we know how to treat our guests."

"Yes, sir. Anything else?" Jonah asked.

"Yes, when you choose a building for the Gala representatives, go ahead and move Dr. Linton and Ada over there."

"Do you have a new doctor in mind for our building?" Jonah asked.

"I'll find one. Just keep your eyes on Dr. Linton. He's harmless enough, but I still like to know what he's up to," Neil said. He went back to his LPS. "I better get some work done. There's a lot to plan."

"Do you mind if I move to the new building, as well? Most of the threats will be in that building. I'll have Bianchi take over here. He'll have his own team. You like him, correct?"

Neil looked up and thought. "Okay, but only until this Gala thing is over. Then you move back here. Send Bianchi my way when you leave here. I want to discuss a few things with him."

"Yes, sir," Jonah said. He wanted to ask one more question, and he thought this would be the perfect time since Neil was in an unusually good mood.

"What about Daniels and Liu? Should we keep looking for them?" Jonah asked.

Neil didn't look up from his LPS. "Before Randall's accident, he still hadn't found them. He did hint to something, but I think he was just desperate. He'd lost his touch. Too much publicity made him soft. As for Daniels and Liu, those two are gone for good. They probably bought a villa near the coast somewhere, and they'll stay quiet. They didn't get enough jewels to make them a threat. Forget about them, and stay focused on building our team and preparing for Ada's Gala. Make sure you watch her spending, will you? I think she can be a tad excessive."

"Yes, sir," Jonah said. "I'll get started right away." Jonah turned and walked toward the door. When he first found out about the Gala, he was nervous. But now he had a different idea about what God was preparing. The only problem he could see was that one of the Gala representatives was the Shaman. He had not yet met Ruth's new husband, but he was about to.

CHAPTER THIRTY-SEVEN

Zach watched as Pastor Tom softly closed the door behind him. He had been talking to Randall for over an hour. He had so many questions that he didn't know which to choose first. He had spent the last three days caring for Randall, but when he saw him waking up, he instantly left. He was thankful that Pastor Tom arrived so quickly. There was no way he could determine his own reaction to this situation. His emotions were unpredictable.

"What happened?" he whispered as soon as Pastor Tom came close enough to him.

"Let's talk about it in the kitchen," Pastor Tom said.

They both walked into the kitchen. "Where are Li and Pilar?" Pastor Tom asked, looking around.

"They took the horses for a walk. Pilar has taken a liking to Lazy. I think she may take her from me," Zach answered, trying to sound cheerful.

"And Pastor Rohan?" Tom asked.

"He went to get food. He wasn't prepared for a house full of guests, but I think he's enjoying having us here."

Pastor Tom sat down. "Rohan Gupta. You know, I've heard of him. He's been doing ministry since I was a kid. He's a wise man. I'm glad I brought those computers. He's taking one, and when Li fixes the rest, he will be passing the rest on to his sons and a few other people he has in mind. Our computer network is growing."

Zach sat down and listened absently to Pastor Tom's plans. Pastor Tom enjoyed networking. It was a gift he had, but Zach didn't want to talk about future plans. He wanted to talk about Randall.

"I can see that's not what you want to talk about," Pastor Tom continued.

"I want to talk about Randall's plans," Zach said. "What if he goes back to the World Government? What if he lets them know where we are?"

Pastor Tom shook his head. "He won't be doing that. The World Government has declared him dead from an accident."

"I know that," Zach said. "Li sent the document, but what if he decides to ignore it?"

"Neil wants him dead. He's lost an eye. The life he had is gone. There is no way they'll give it back to him. Jonah has taken his position," Pastor Tom said.

"You didn't tell him about Jonah or Ruth, did you, Pastor Tom?" Zach asked, trying to quench his fear.

"Of course not," Pastor Tom said. "I simply told him about Jesus."

Zach stopped. "That's what you did for an hour in there?"

"I listened about his life and then told him that God loves him and has plans for him. People in his position are more willing to listen."

"What condition is that?" Zach asked.

Pastor Tom leaned back in his chair. "Brokenness," he answered. "A near-death experience seems to open people's eyes and ears to eternity."

"Did you tell him about Li and me?" he asked.

"He already knows that you two helped him escape the camp. He's been in and out of consciousness for the last three days. He remembers Li and Pastor Rohan bringing him into the house, and he remembers you taking care of his bandages and giving him water to drink."

"What does he say about that?" Zach asked.

"He doesn't understand it," Pastor Tom said. "The system of God's kingdom is vastly different than the system of the world's kingdom. I hope you don't think that I'm patronizing you, Zach, but I am proud of you. You could have acted in revenge, but you acted in mercy instead. I think you've done what many people couldn't have done."

"What is that?" Zach asked.

"Forgiving him," Pastor Tom said.

Zach looked away and rubbed the long strands of his growing beard. "I have to be honest with you, Pastor Tom. The forgiveness wasn't mine."

"What do you mean?"

Zach leaned forward, placing his elbows on the table. "It was like God gave me the forgiveness. I saw Randall's face, and instantly the feeling of mercy was shoved into my spirit. I didn't want to accept it at first, but when I did—" he stopped.

"It felt good," Pastor Tom finished.

"Yes, it felt like I was free from something I didn't know was weighing me down. I felt like a child again. It was almost too easy. I still don't fully believe it, which is why I want to speak to Randall myself. I want to see if that mercy is real."

"Well, he wants to talk to you," Pastor Tom said. "But I wanted to talk to you first and make sure you are working in the right system."

"I think for the first time in a long time, I'm truly in God's system of doing things. And you know what the funny thing is?"

"What is that?" Pastor Tom asked.

"God's system is simply love. Just loving someone puts you into that system. I feel it now, like really. And not just for the people who love me, like Bear and Pilar. But I feel it for the World Government and all the people who give their lives to something that keeps them blinded and controlled."

Pastor Tom smiled. "That's why what we are doing is so important. We may not be able to free everyone, but we can certainly show them the door. Randall is waiting for you if you would like to speak to him. I haven't told him anything about what we are doing. I don't know when or if we can ever trust him. His presence here is full of unknowns. We will just have to take it one step at a time."

"Okay," Zach said, getting up from the table. "Then I will take the next step."

Zach walked toward the back bedroom where Randall had been staying. When he got to the door, he took a deep breath before softly knocking.

"Come in," he heard.

Zach prepared himself. He knew anything could happen. He said a quick prayer for strength before opening the door. When he walked into the room, Randall was up, looking at the mirror above the chest of drawers. A bandage was wrapped tightly around his head and across his left eye. He was the same height as Zach, but stockier with several more pounds of muscle. The hazel hue shone from his right eye, and his light brown hair spread down past his ears. He looked nothing like the pictures from the PR events he had seen. Zach realized that there would have been no way to take Randall down himself without cheating.

"It's pretty hideous," he said simply.

"What?" Zach asked.

Randall looked into the mirror at Zach's reflection. "My eye or my empty eye socket. It's completely hollow. I just saw it."

"It looks a lot better than it did three days ago," Zach said.

Randall said nothing. He walked to the bed and sat down. Zach didn't move.

"You can sit in that chair. That's where I've seen you the last few days. Always sitting in that chair. Sleeping or looking out the window," Randall said.

Zach walked to the chair and sat down.

"You know, your friend had a lot to say about faith," Randall began.

"He's a pastor. That's what he's called to talk about," Zach said.

"Every time I would ask him a question, he would somehow veer it to this Jesus. Always Jesus," Randall said. "Like I'm so broken that I would fully embrace this God Man."

"I have," Zach said.

"You never mentioned Jesus when I first met you," Randall said. "If you had, I might have realized who you were sooner."

"And who is that?" Zach asked.

"The son of a troublemaker pastor who wouldn't follow orders," Randall said.

For a second Zach felt anger, but forgiveness instantly overcame him. He realized Randall was testing him. "My father obeyed a system beyond this world's system."

"I know, and it cost him his life," Randall said. "Your father's disobedience called me out to start something I didn't want to start."

"You mean a fire," Zach said.

Randall didn't flinch or look away from Zach's position. "Your father was my first of many fires. I was called by the World Government to stop the disobedience, and I did it."

"You did what my father could not do," Zach answered simply.

"What was that?" Randall asked.

"You obeyed the world's system when it contradicted God's. That is what my father could not do. You call it disobedience, but he called it obedience."

Randall said nothing but continued to stare at Zach. Zach stared back uninterested in looking anywhere else. Finally, Randall turned away. "Which is better: To die in obedience of God's system or live in obedience of the World's system?" he finally asked.

"That very same system you decided to obey wanted you dead," Zach said. "So your obedience backfired, after all. That's how the world's system works. You compromise to live, but that compromise will eventually kill you. I know because it almost killed me."

"Yet you live," Randall said.

"No, not killed me physically. It almost destroyed the purposes that God has for me."

"Now you are sounding like that pastor. He seems to think that we were all created for a purpose," Randall said. "He even thinks I have a purpose, and that this Jesus loves me and died for me."

"He did," Zach said. "He saved your life, didn't he?"

"You and Charlie Liu saved my life," Randall said.

"No, we didn't," Zach said. "I wanted to kill you. That's why I sent that letter. I wanted to drug you and kill you."

"You should have. That would have been justice," Randall said.

"Justice," Zach repeated. "God's justice is perfect. He is uncompromising. If He weren't, he would be a corrupt God."

"Yes, but I live," Randall said. "Isn't that corruption?"

"God is also a loving God. Which is why Jesus, that name you seem to mock, is so important."

Randall looked back at Zach with his right eye. "Why is that?"

"God is both just and loving. All of us—you, me, Pastor Tom—are flawed. None of us is perfect and deserving of mercy. We all are broken. God cannot have a relationship with us because to do so would corrupt His justice."

"You're not making sense," Randall said.

"See, that is God's system. It doesn't make sense to the world's eyes. God loves us too, and He wants a relationship with us."

"But you just said that He can't," Randall said, becoming irritated.

"God is very imaginative, so He found a way," Zach said.

"How?" Randall asked.

"He left His throne as King of the Universe, came to this earth and became human. He lived the perfect life, and took our jail sentence and gave us His freedom. Jesus became the bad guy, so we could be the good guys. Now we can have a relationship with God because we are no longer corrupt. We have been perfected," Zach said. He felt God's Spirit pouring into His words. His spirit was lifted as he talked to his father's murderer.

"This Jesus. He became the bad guy for me?" Randall said.

Zach sensed hope in Randall's countenance. "The *Bible* says that Jesus took all the bad stuff we have done."

Randall shifted on the bed. "Okay, so me starting the fire in that church that night—Jesus took that?"

Zach instantly thought of his father. He wanted to ask if his father was awake while the fire burned around his body. He pushed the image aside. "Jesus became my father's murderer the day He died on the Cross." When those words slipped out of

Zach's mouth, he felt his spirit break. "Jesus took the sins of the world on His shoulders. He became a liar, a thief, an adulterer and a murderer for us all. The *Bible* says He took those sins into the grave and left them there. He rose back to life three days later with the victory over all injustice paid in full."

"But I still feel the weight of what I've done," Randall said.

"Because you still carry your sins," Zach answered.

"How do I get rid of them?" Randall asked, anxiously.

"You have to ask Jesus to take them and to give you His salvation. You have to accept Jesus into your heart," Zach answered.

"I don't understand that," Randall said.

"I mean, you accept Jesus' payment for the sins of your life. And then you make Him your boss," Zach said, saying it in a way he thought Randall might understand.

"I just say, *Take my sin, Jesus*?" Randall asked, disbelieving. "It seems too easy."

"It is too easy. But that's God's system of forgiveness. He did the hard stuff for us, but we have to take it," Zach said.

"Well, I want it," Randall said. "I want to be free of my old life. I can't go back to it now. I've been blacklisted. What do I need to say? Tell me."

Zach got up and walked up to Randall sitting in the bed. He placed his hand on the man's shoulder. "Repeat my words."

"Okay, I'm listening," Randall said.

"Dear God," Zach started, waiting for Randall to repeat after him. "I know I deserve punishment for all the wrong things I've done. I understand that Jesus paid for my sins, so I could have a relationship with You in this life and when I die. I ask for Jesus' payment for my sins. I accept His forgiveness. I want you to be my boss. I will try to obey your system and not the world's system. Thank You for saving me from eternal payment of my sins. I know now that I am free from who I used to be. I pray this in Jesus' name. Amen."

"Amen," Randall repeated. "I feel it. I feel something's different inside of me."

Zach smiled. "I feel it too," he agreed.

Zach sat back down in the chair. He wanted to ask the question about his father's death, but knew he couldn't. Instead, he asked another question that he thought Randall might answer.

"Why did you not confront my friend. I know you watched him and his wife for several days?" Zach asked.

"You mean that Shaman fighter?" Randall asked.

"Yes," Zach answered.

"He and his wife barely spoke a word. I overheard them talking only a few times, but they never said your name," Randall said.

"Did they say the name Mark?" Zach asked.

"Maybe, it sounds familiar," Randall said.

"That's my middle name," Zach said and smiled.

"I should have looked into that," Randall said. "Middle names are not important to Efficientists."

"But I still don't understand," Zach pushed. "Why did you never question him or confront him?"

Randall sat, thinking. "I never allowed myself to ask that question."

"Why?" Zach asked.

Randall stood up. "I did research before leaving to the Colonies. I discovered that the Shaman was a family friend of yours when you were young. I was surprised because I had met him once when he was doing a PR event in the city."

"You met Bear?" Zach asked.

"Yes, that's what I heard his wife calling him, *Bear*. It's fitting," Randall said, pausing. "I met him when I was still a low-ranking Bodyguard. One of the Efficientists brought him in and showed him off. He inspired me. He was aloof. No one could touch him. He was unimpressed by the gifts and accolades they gave him. I respected that. The night before I left, I watched his last fight. I knew I could never subdue him. I would either have to kill him or stand clear of him."

"So you chose to stand clear of him?" Zach asked.

"Yes, and I lost my eye because of it," Randall said, walking back to the mirror. "That's how I know that I can't go back. I've lost my touch."

Zach walked to the mirror and looked at Randall's reflection. "Or maybe you've just gained something," Zach contradicted.

"What?" Randall said, turning to Zach.

"Your heart," Zach answered.

CHAPTER THIRTY-EIGHT

"That's the weakness I see in the Colonies," Rohan said. "There are some small villages like this one, but a lot of the people are nomadic. They fear what happened in the Second Civil War, so they stay away from people. But they are the ones getting gathered by the World Government."

Rohan and Tom were walking through the dirt streets of the small village. They passed several houses that were abandoned.

"Their fear is isolating them," Tom agreed. "You know, I get it. People can do evil things. It does seem safer to separate yourself, but really our strength as a church will be found in numbers. That's why I feel the need to network as much as possible," Pastor Tom said.

"I helped build this town. The houses were here before, but we moved in and cleaned things up. We had everything we needed. We met for church and the families thrived until that *Life Plethoricity* nonsense was written," Rohan said.

Pastor Tom thought of Ruth. "Neil Elder was making laws before *Life Plethoricity*. We were banned from reproducing any new religious documents. The World Government was slowly adding one restriction after another, trying to gain more power."

"Yes, you're right. I guess the squeeze from the World Government was so slow at first that you didn't even notice it. One compromise and then another. As Colonial villages got stronger and more organized, the World Government created more restrictions," Rohan said.

"It all comes down to power and control," Tom said and stopped. "Was this your church? I see a steeple missing its cross."

Rohan looked up. "Yes, this is where I ministered for many years. I think that's why I couldn't leave. Or maybe I was waiting for my guests to arrive," Rohan said.

"You miss your wife and family?" Tom asked.

"I do. Once I get Zach and Li established here, I'll go to them. I have the computers now, so I can keep communicating with you and the others. I'm glad to be a part of this faith movement you have created."

"God's creating it," Tom insisted. "I'm just here for the ride. Li was able to get five computers working. That will give you and your sons each one, and you'll have two more to pass on."

"I have a few people in mind," Rohan said. "Restless pastors like myself, feeling like they need to be a part of something greater."

Tom thought of the printing press in Pastor Rohan's basement. "What will you do with that printing press?"

"I'm done making hard copies of the Four Gospels. Without pastors being able to preach, I fear the people will not have the shepherds they need to guide them," Rohan said.

"The shepherds are out there. But the church will resemble the Book of Acts more than anything," Tom mused.

"That's it!" Rohan exclaimed. "I should be printing the Book of Acts. It needs to go with the Four Gospels. Of course, it does! It's church flourishing under the oppression of a world government."

"I think you're right. I can help you if you want. I'm fascinated by the process. I watched some old videos on your HMS yesterday. It really is a two-man job," Tom said.

"It is a two-man job," Rohan agreed. "I would value your assistance."

"What will you be doing with it when you leave?" Tom asked.

"I don't know. I can't bring it with me. Why? Do you need it?"

Pastor Tom continued to walk next to Rohan. "I don't know why, but I feel the Holy Spirit is going to have me use it for something. I can't think of anything now, but I know it will come to me. I was hoping I could take it back to Trinity Trading Center. I would like to trade you something for it."

"You've already given me the computers. I feel that is a fair trade," Rohan said.

"Yes, but you're leaving the computer that your son didn't want and your HMS. You are doing far more for us than we are doing for you," Tom said.

"I'm just glad those things aren't going to waste," Rohan said.

Pastor Tom knew that Rohan would not want to take a gift easily. "I brought some of the jewels that we had from Ruth's vault," he began. "I'm giving most of them to Zach and Li to use for bringing the sick out of the camp. They will need help finding homes for them and teaching them. I will use my network to find them homes, and Li, Zach and Pilar have agreed to minister to them."

"I still am having trouble believing that Eve Pallue is living as a Colonial now, and she's the one who's been writing those articles. If I didn't trust your word, I would say it was impossible," Rohan said.

"Very few people know the truth about her, and we want to keep it that way. I only told you because I see you as a leader of this movement that God is preparing. He will use you in mighty ways," Tom said.

"Who would have thought: A seventy-three-year-old pastor finding a new calling in life. God is too good to me," Rohan said, turning to Pastor Tom. "Thank you for trusting God and starting this movement. You give yourself very little credit, but you are an apostle in this new church that God is establishing."

Pastor Tom allowed himself to take the compliment, something his wife was always telling him to do. "Thank you for your words. I came alive when the persecution began. It's like I was created for this time."

"And you have been," Rohan agreed.

"So, about those jewels. I want to give you just a few in exchange for the printing press and for your house and the rest of the gasoline in your backyard. You can use them to establish a northern location for our movement."

"You mean start a trading center like the one you have in Trinity?" Rohan asked.

"Exactly," Tom said. "It doesn't have to be as big, but you will need a cover for your ministry. Your sons can get involved. The jewels I have for you will be more than enough to establish a fair-sized trading center," Tom said.

Rohan thought for a moment and continued to walk. "I see what you're getting at. If our movement is to grow, we will need to establish another base."

"Yes, I am at the max of my capability. I know we need to expand, but I need more leaders, like you," Tom said. "Which is why I was completely honest with you about Ruth, Jonah and everything. I need to share what's going on and get sound advice from someone who knows as much as I do."

Rohan nodded his head. "Thank you for trusting me. I will do it. I will establish a trading center and be available for whatever God has next. I only have a few more years left to live, and I'll make them the best yet."

"Thank you," Tom said. "Now let's get back to the house and print out the Book of Acts. I want to head home tomorrow, but I need to make sure that Zach and Li have secured someone with a little medical ability first. They are about to have a houseful of sick guests. There's still lots to do and very little time left."

The two men walked back to the house. As they turned the corner, Pastor Tom saw a familiar vehicle on the driveway. It was Esther and Deborah's van. "What are they doing here?" Tom began to run, and Rohan following behind him.

Tom made it to the door and pushed it open. When he entered the living room, he saw Deborah sitting on the couch, wearing her floral dress with her hair pinned up in a bun and sipping from a teacup. He recognized three other Efficientists who were houseguest at her ranch sitting next to her. Pilar and Zach and Li were also in the room. Someone must have said something funny because they were all smiling. "What are you doing here?" he asked louder than he'd anticipated.

"Well, that's a fine way to say hello," Deborah said.

"But you're not supposed to be here!" Pastor Tom said.

243

Deborah placed her teacup on the end table next to her. "I most certainly am," she said. "I go where God calls."

"Why would He call you here?" Pastor Tom asked confused.

Deborah gently straightened her skirt and stood up. "You are about to have a house full of sick people here. Have you forgotten that I am a nurse?" she asked.

Pastor Tom fumbled. "No, I didn't. I just thought you and Esther were busy."

"The harvesting season is almost over. Esther has plenty of help. I am needed here. I will help those poor souls who have been forced into labor camps. And you see I have brought my three volunteers," she said, motioning to three young people with her. "They wanted to go and be of some use, so here we are."

Pastor Tom stared blankly for several seconds. "You mean, you are here to help heal the sick?" he asked.

"That's what I said," Deborah reiterated.

Pastor Tom's face broke into a wide smile. "Now, Miss Deborah, my dear, you are an answer to prayer!" he shouted. He walked over to Deborah and gave her a brisk kiss on the cheek.

It was Deborah's turn to be flustered. "Oh, Pastor Tom, I'm just trying to stay useful. Plus, we stopped at Levington before we came. Ruth and Bear donated food and clothes. Pilar's family donated food and bags of flour. Reyna packed a few bags of clothing for Pilar, knowing that she would be here for a while. The back of my van is filled to the brim. I'm surprised we got it all in there. And I brought as many medical supplies as I could. We at least have enough to get started."

"I didn't think to ask you. I should have, but I was so rushed to get here," Pastor Tom confessed.

"Well, I didn't think to offer until you had already left," Deborah said.

Pastor Tom couldn't help but allow a goofy smile to appear across his face. God had taken care of everything he was praying about. "By the way, have you seen our first patient yet? Zach did a good job caring for him," he said, thinking of Randall.

Zach stepped forward from where he had been standing with Pilar. "He's gone."

"What do you mean *gone*?" Pastor Tom asked surprised.

Li chimed in. "I found a note. He said not to worry. He wasn't going back to the World Government, but he needed to find his family. He also apologized for everything, including what he stole."

"What did he steal?" Pastor Tom asked, quickly.

It was Pilar's turn to speak. "He stole my truck," she said. "Again."

Deborah watched as the group began moving the items from her van to the house. These were the times that she appreciated her age. She wasn't expected to lift a finger, which suited her fine. She needed to save her strength for the sick people who would be coming in two days. She watched as Zach carried a bag back toward the house and followed him. After Pastor Gupta directed him, he set the bag down on the floor in the back room.

Deborah took the opportunity now that they were alone. "Zach, do you mind if I could speak with you in private? I need to discuss something of great importance with you," she asked.

"Sure thing, Miss Deborah. What's up?" he asked in his normal, nonchalant manner.

Deborah noticed a door leading to the backyard. "Can we go in the backyard. I don't want to be overheard," she said, pointing to the door.

"The van is almost done being unpacked," he said. "I could use a little break. We can check on Xin and Lazy. Pastor Gupta was able to get them a stack of hay. I want to see how they've been enjoying it," he said, walking to the door and opening it for Deborah.

"Thank you, dear," she said, as she walked outside and into the cool air. She enjoyed the mountain wind. It was drier than the air on her farm.

Deborah heard the door shut behind her, and she waited and watched as Zach petted and whispered to the horses. "Those two are the wild horses Pastor Tom told me about. All that time

Li spent with that old horse on the ranch paid off. Don't despise small beginnings," she mused, distracted briefly from the horrible news she needed to relay to Zach.

Zach plucked out a few handfuls of hay and allowed Lazy to nibble from his outstretched hand. She didn't eat much, so he brought his hand to Xin who ate the rest. When he was done, he wiped his palms on his jeans and turned to Deborah. "Okay, Miss Deborah, what news do you have for me?"

Deborah squirmed under Zach's carefree smile. She hated to be the bearer of bad news, especially when it was about Ruth. "I was glad to visit with Ruth before coming here," she began. "She's adjusted well to Colonial life."

"Yes, but she does have Bear cleaning up the place. You should have seen it before. No floors, an outhouse, barely any shelving or furniture. He's really worked hard to make it a home for her. I think he even rigged some kind of water system," he said, chuckling. "I've never seen Bear so intent to please anyone. Heck, he's even donated stuff from his shed to us. I've never seen him do anything like that before."

Deborah couldn't laugh along with Zach.

"Is something wrong with her?" Zach asked, noticing her mood didn't lighten.

"Yes, and I don't know how to say this. It was quite shocking for me. When I asked Ruth about it, she just said it was an accident, but how can I believe her?" Deborah asked as tears began to form around her eyes.

"What's going on?" Zach said, coming up to Deborah.

"It's Ruth. She had a black eye with lots of bruising on her face. I asked her about it, but she said that she fell into the river. I've been around many bruises and this one is from a hit across the face. And when I hugged her, she cringed, like I hurt her ribs. When I asked her to pull up her shirt, she again said she fell in the river. And the worst of it is that I know she's lying to me."

"No! It can't be." Zach couldn't imagine Bear harming his sister in any way. An image of the fierce fighter he used to be—the Shaman—filled his mind. Bear loved Ruth, but would he harm her in anger?

Deborah fell into weeping. "Is Bear capable of hitting a woman?"

Zach placed his hand on Deborah's shoulder. "Deborah, may I use your van for the day?"

Deborah sniffed and looked up to Zach. "Why?"

"I'm going back to Levington to get my sister," he said. "I'll take her back to Esther at the ranch. Just let Pilar and Li know I'll be back before the sick people arrive in two days."

Deborah nodded. "Okay, I'll let Esther know you are coming."

CHAPTER THIRTY-NINE

"Matt, I need more workers. I want this lobby to dazzle with decadent early 19th-century aristocracy decor! I want a ballroom that would make the Regency Era proud! I want that dingy, abandoned conference room to be transformed into the *Grand Opus Gala Ballroom,"* Ada spoke loudly over the construction noise to Jonah, who stood at least two feet taller than the tip of her head. Dust from the work filled the air, but they stood at the rear of the construction in front of several opened windows. "The representatives will be arriving soon. We have no more than two weeks to pull off a historical miracle! People around the world will be watching this event."

Ada wore a velvet, burgundy spencer jacket over a knee-length muslin dress adorned with wine-colored velvet flowers down the front. She had created an entire line of clothing that she named, Regency Mélange, a mixture of Regency Style for modern times. She knew the World News would be following her every move, and she would use the publicity to sway the polls, like Eve Pallue once did. She noticed the World News setting up for filming and interviews by the sliding glass doors. This was her moment. She would outshine all the stuffy Efficientists with their faces stuck on the LPS screens. She was going to show them that life was not just about productiveness; it was about beauty, entertainment and pleasure while experiencing the best that the world had to offer in human innovation, creativity and imagination.

"You have over two dozen workers here. How many more do you need?" Jonah asked.

"My ballroom must have vaulted ceilings. I had to move the residents living on the third floor whose apartments were taking up my ceiling space. We have six apartments being demolished as we speak, so that's taking half my crew. I need at least a dozen more men. Neil has given me full authority concerning the *Grand Opus Gala*, and I will do what it takes to get it done well."

"Okay, I'll keep looking for more workers. And are you sure you need mahogany wood planks? They are pricey."

Ada laughed and looked up to Jonah. "You haven't received my document today?"

Jonah sighed. "I've received several of them already," he said, holding up his Portable.

"But have you received the newest one? I have had a donation from the magistrate in Central America, and he will be providing the floors for my ballroom. West Indian mahogany— only the best! The only problem is that he wants to attend with several guests, and I wasn't planning on any visitors besides the representatives."

"Let me get this straight. You have been given the best wood for the ballroom floors, yet I read an invoice on my Portable this morning that you are flying in an artist who works with chalk to draw on floors?" Jonah asked.

"Yes, silly. Chalking the ballroom floors was quite fashionable, but only for the very rich. They chalked the floors in exquisite patterns before the dance, and the hostess invited all her VIP guests to enjoy the artwork before the dance began!" Ada said, excitedly. "I've always thought I was born in the wrong era. The times today are boring and bland, but all that is about to change."

"Don't you think all of this is a waste of money and people's time?" Jonah asked.

Ada stared up at Jonah's dark, strong face. He looked intimidating, but she had since learned he could be a softy. She had conversed with him after PR events on several occasions. He even took her home once when Randall stayed behind with Neil. "I don't criticize your work," she began. "I just lost my boyfriend to a factory accident for no good reason. Instantly, his life is gone. You both protect people every day and for what? To watch them sit at their LPS screens all day? Don't fault me for wanting to bring beauty and imagination to this world. I want to showcase the talents of one hundred amazing individuals. People want to work toward a greater cause. They want to believe in the World Government, but the ratings are falling. Because, honestly, there is no sense learning so much if you don't experience anything at all! Therefore, if I want to spend a little money and make things special and exquisite, you should be willing to help me. If not, go back to Neil and ask him to reassign you."

Jonah said nothing and stared at her for a long moment. She felt embarrassed under his gaze, but she knew he wasn't judging her.

"Okay, I'll help you in whatever way I can. But I really think Neil sent me here to watch you and make sure you don't go overboard," Jonah said.

Ada threw her head back and laughed. Her freshly-cut chin length blonde hair moved flawlessly around her round face. "Too late for that! And don't worry about me over-spending. I wrote a short piece on the gift from the Central American magistrate for the World News, and I believe the others will be sending more gifts very soon. If I can get the European magistrate to create the chandeliers that I have designed, my full vision will be complete!"

"Are you sure you'll get them?" Jonah asked.

"Completely. And if not, Neil will buy them," she said, looking at her Portable and turning it on. She wanted to go over her checklist again.

"Can I ask you a question?" Jonah asked.

Ada kept her eyes on the screen as she scrolled through the collection of Regency Era jewelry images she had stored. She needed to check on her crew making her clothing line and see about developing the jewelry pieces she had in mind.

Jonah cleared his throat. "I read over the profiles of the 100 representatives you've chosen. I'm impressed by the uniqueness of the talents you have chosen."

Ada looked at Jonah. "It seems a lot of people are impressed by my list. I just chose the things that intrigue me the most. Honestly, though, I had to add some names that I wasn't fascinated with—like most of the math and science representatives—but I knew they would be important to the fullness of the *Grand Opus*."

"I was surprised to find that you'd added a few Colonials," he added.

"Yes, that was a last-minute decision. I had to take off ten Efficientists from the list, which was a hard choice. But I knew that if I wanted to get the Colonials involved that I would need to include them. When Eve Pallue was alive, she was able to draw everyone's attention, but I doubted if one person could have the same effect that she had. That's when I decided to dedicate ten percent of the representatives to the Colonials. I really do think it was a brilliant decision."

"Yes, I think you're right," Jonah said. "But I'm curious. Why did you choose the fighter?"

"You mean the Shaman?" Ada asked.

"Yes, his name didn't seem to fit the list," Jonah said.

"Before Randall left, I saw him watching a video of a Colonial Circuit fight. There was a Native American man with a Mohawk beating his fists into another man's ribs. It was brutal and I wanted Randall to turn it off, but when the fight was over, the Shaman took out a drum and began to pound on it and sing. It was quite mesmerizing. He captured the entire audience with his voice. Do you see how many views his videos command?"

"I did, but the video you're describing is not the one you posted by his name," Jonah said.

"I know," Ada smiled. "I didn't want to give everything away. I'm going to have him sing and play when he gets here. I haven't decided if I want him to fight yet. I don't know if my ballroom should be bloodied, but then again, the viewers may love it. The Shaman may be the highlight of my Gala!"

"I noticed that you didn't choose any religious people to be representatives," Jonah said.

Ada looked away and exhaled. "I was going to, but after the *Unum Vernum* debacle, I didn't want to get into religious debates. Plus, that faith movement has taken a lot of Efficientists to the Colonies. I doubt Neil would want me to give center stage and precious time on the World News to a bunch of religious folks—no matter how talented they are. By the way, have you seen Dr. Linton lately? I need him ready to check the incoming Gala representatives."

"There was a last-minute change in plans. He won't be working the Gala now. Dr. Wharton will be taking his place."

Ada let out a frustrated sigh. "I must be notified of these changes. I have a lot of people that I'm trying to coordinate." She held up her Portable and started scrolling through the different files.

"I just discussed it with Neil before coming here. We both agreed that he is currently unfit to represent the World Government on this level."

"He does seem stranger than usual," Ada said, as she continued working on the Portable. "And he looks like he's not sleeping. I didn't want him working the Gala in the first place, so honestly, I'm relieved."

"That makes two of us," Jonah said.

"There!" she said and smiled. "The switch has been made. No harm done." Then she turned and looked back to the entrance where the World News was setting up. "That reminds me, what am I going to do about the other requests to come to the Gala?"

"Who's asking to come?" Jonah asked.

"Almost everyone!" she said. "I thought that since the Gala would be broadcast on the World News that people would watch it from their homes. But the Central American magistrate wants to come. And I have a feeling most of the magistrates will. Then there are other highly ranked Efficientists around the world who will pay their own expense to attend the Gala."

"Neil will not want all the magistrates to be one in place at the same time," Jonah said. "And that would create a very dangerous situation for me."

"Oh, I know. What if I split them up? Three different magistrates for each of the three nights. Then of course, Neil will attend all three nights because he's funding the Gala. That will be perfect. We won't have all of them at the same time, and Neil will feel superior, which he adores."

Jonah hesitated. "But you will still have to limit additional guests. I already have to worry about the security of a hundred representatives and their families," Jonah said.

252

Ada suddenly clapped. "I've got it. I will have a VIP silent auction. I will give one hundred VIP tickets to the *Grand Opus Gala* to the top bidders. And that will give me additional funds!"

"A hundred is too many. But you can do thirty," Jonah said, sternly.

"Matt, I must have at least eighty!" Ada pleaded.

"Okay, fifty and no more," Jonah demanded.

"Deal!" Ada exclaimed. "Perfect solution. Matt, I should use you as my sounding board more often. You have ironed out many of the frustrating wrinkles in my vision."

"It's the least I could do since you've just quadrupled my workload," Jonah said, sarcastically.

"You know me," she added. "Always here to please. Okay, I better go. The World News is signaling me. I've made them wait long enough for my interview. I will announce the fifty VIP tickets to the *Grand Opus Gala* right away. Please ensure I have the additional work crew by tomorrow morning, will you?"

"I'll do my best," Jonah said.

Ada straightened her jacket and smoothed her dress before she squared her shoulders toward the entrance where the paparazzi lined up around the World News cameras. They had all set up behind the roped-off section of the building near the entrance. She had watched from her LPS monitor as Eve Pallue reluctantly addressed the World News over and over again in the past. Now it was her turn.

"Where's your Bodyguard?" Jonah asked, looking around.

"I put him in charge of moving the residents out of the apartments that were blocking the vaulted ceilings of my ballroom. Most of them did not want to be relocated," she said.

"Ada, you cannot be without a Bodyguard," Jonah said. "Look at the line of cameras. You've put yourself at risk."

"I was left with no choice. I don't have enough workers," she said sternly.

"Fine, I'll walk out with you, but after this interview, bring your Bodyguard back. I'll make sure you have more workers tomorrow," Jonah promised.

"Thank you, Matt. You have proven to be a valuable part of my team," she said. "You may lead."

Jonah sighed and began walking toward the row of cameras. Ada followed behind him.

CHAPTER FORTY

Ruth sat at the desk, staring at the old-style laptop. Her long, auburn hair was pulled behind her ears. A soft blanket was wrapped around her body. She felt slightly irritable while using the computer. It was extremely slow compared to the HMS, and Ruth remembered thinking that the HMS was slow compared to her LPS. She could only type or use the single mouse pad with her index finger. No voice commands. And if she opened too many windows at once, the computer would slow down even more or come to a complete stop.

She scrolled down the World News and clicked on the video of her previous image consultant, Ada Armel. She listened intently to her interview. She glanced toward Bear who was fixing one of his animal traps on the floor in the living room. "Jonah is guarding Ada," she said.

"I thought he protected Neil since Randall has been gone," Bear said, not looking up from the thin wire he was wrapping around the trap door.

"He does. I wonder what has happened," Ruth said. "And all the magistrates will be attending the Gala. That has never been done before. It is a security risk."

"Maybe that is why Jonah is there," Bear said, looking up from his work. "The video stopped. Who's the blonde?"

"She was my image consultant. She's the one coordinating the Gala. This computer is so frustrating," Ruth said, resisting the urge to shut the laptop down for good. "The video takes a while to load. I can only watch about five seconds before it loads again. She said something about an auction for VIP tickets. That means people want to attend this event."

Bear looked down at the trap. "They can have my ticket for free," he said.

"The invitations have already been sent. I am surprised we have not had more visitors," Ruth said, stretching her torso to look out the window.

"I'm telling you. Very few people know where I actually live, and the people who do know wouldn't be mouthing off to some government worker. They know I would find them out and pummel them," Bear said, allowing the trap door to slam shut. "There it works. Now maybe it will catch us something."

Ruth finally closed the laptop. "I will not watch that video load for one more second. I will go to Levi's house and use the HMS." She got up from the desk, and kept the blanket tightly around her. She walked to the living room and sat in front of the fireplace next to Bear.

"How do you feel?" Bear asked, gently bringing his index finger across her bruised cheek.

Ruth liked when he asked her how she was feeling. It forced her to analyze her emotional state. "I enjoyed Deborah's visit yesterday, even though she could not stay long. I would like to visit Esther before we leave for the Gala."

"We still haven't figured out how we are going to sneak you in," Bear said. He pushed the trap to the side and brought Ruth into his arms.

"I have contacted Cindy. She says she knows what we can do. She did not give me specifics, but I trust her," Ruth said, leaning into Bear's arms.

"I'm glad we donated that food," Bear said. "I am praying for those sick people that Li and Zach are taking out of the labor camp. I'm surprised Levi let Pilar stay, but I can see she is needed there now."

"I miss her," Ruth admitted. "I enjoy talking to Reyna, but she is a lot younger than I am. I listen to her mostly."

Ruth sat quietly leaning against Bear, and they both stared at the fireplace.

"Where's Grandfather?" she asked.

"Who knows," Bear sighed. "He likes to wander on days like this. It is beautiful outside. I miss being out there."

Suddenly, Bear turned Ruth around in his arms, so she could face him. "I was thinking that we never went on our honeymoon," he said.

Ruth smiled. "That's an old tradition," she said.

"I know, but you said people are going to be coming here looking for me, so why don't we get away for a week. I want to take you to Enchanted Rock."

"Isn't that where you had your last fight?" Ruth asked.

"Yes, but it's amazing there. I'll pack my truck. I'll put a mattress in the bed of the truck with a tarp, and I have plenty of food to bring. We can just enjoy nature and being outside," Bear said, enthusiastically.

"I don't know," Ruth hesitated. "I have never really lived outdoors before."

"This place is as close as you'll get to living outdoors. You're only one step away. The only difference is a sponge bath and no HMS or computers. C'mon. If I'm going to be stuck in the city for this stupid Gala, I want to be outside for a while," Bear petitioned.

Ruth looked into Bear's dark, brown eyes. "What about the house?"

"*Aha-enah* will watch everything for us. People won't bother an old man," Bear insisted. "They'll see that I'm not home and leave."

"It would be nice to get away before people find you," Ruth agreed. "Will you set up a toilet for me?" she asked.

"Of course, anything!" he said.

"Okay, when do you want to go?" Ruth asked, feeling excitement build.

"I want to go now," he said.

"Shouldn't we wait for Grandfather? Plus, I want to tell Reyna we won't be home," Ruth said.

"We'll wait until he gets home, and then we'll drive past Levi's house on the way out. I want to trade for some baked goods anyway," Bear said, getting up. "You pack our clothes and whatever bathroom items you need, and I'll pack everything else."

Bear reached out his arms and pulled Ruth up. "And make sure you pack plenty of warm blankets. I know how much you hate being cold."

"My first honeymoon," Ruth whispered.

"Why didn't you tell Deborah the truth about how you got hurt," he asked, as he stared at the blue and yellow bruise across her cheek. The skin around her eye was still swollen, but she could see out of her eye now. "She knew you were lying."

"I did not lie. I was hurt by an accident," Ruth said.

"Yes, but not in the river," Bear countered.

"I did hurt myself in the river," Ruth said. "I got a few bruises from the rocks."

"Yes, but not on your face," Bear said, seriously.

"It is not a relevant issue, and I know Deborah likes to coddle me. She is about to have a houseful of very sick people to care for, and I did not want her to worry about me or jump to conclusions," Ruth said.

"I'm a grown man. I can handle the consequences of my actions," Bear insisted.

"I avoided the topic because I wanted to save myself the trouble. It had nothing to do with saving your feelings," Ruth said.

"Okay, I understand. I just think you might have done more damage than good," Bear said.

Zach tried to be careful driving the van, but now that he was so close to Bear's house, he couldn't help but drive fast through the rough terrain. He was less than a minute away from the clearing that led to Bear's property. He'd had more than enough time during his ten-hour drive to think about exactly was he was going to do and say when he got face-to-face with Bear. When he finally made it through the clearing of trees, he saw Bear packing up his truck.

"Where is she?" he said out loud. He looked in the passenger seat. There she was. Bear was taking her away. He knew he had messed up, and now he was running away from his problems. "I can't believe it," Zach said. His hands gripped the steering wheel and he pressed the gas. He didn't care how the large van flew over the uneven path. He slid the van to an abrupt stop, blocking Bear's truck from behind. The wheels of the van spun dirt all over Bear's truck, hitting Bear in the face. "You're going to have to get around me first," Zach said, jumping out of the van.

Bear's face held a stunned expression as he tried to get thick clumps of dirt out of his ponytail with his left hand while holding blankets under his right arm. "Is that you, Zach?" he yelled. "What are you doing here?"

Zach's body lunged in Bear's direction. "Where are you taking my sister?" he yelled, swinging his fist at Bear's jaw.

Bear easily sidestepped Zach's fist. "What are you doing, Zach?" Bear demanded.

Zach instantly turned around and dove at Bear's legs below the knees with his entire body. Bear tried to stop him with his left hand, but he was unable to prevent Zach's shoulder from knocking him off balance. The blankets under his right arm flew out as he fell to the ground. Both men tumbled across the dirt.

"We just washed those blankets!" Bear shouted.

Zach pushed off the ground and tried to crawl onto Bear's torso. He needed to land a few good punches, but Bear pushed his foot into Zach's gut and threw him back several feet.

"Zach! Why are you attacking Bear?" he heard Ruth yell. He looked toward the voice and saw his sister. Deborah had been right. Her face had been slapped and her eye was still a little swollen.

"You are going to get hurt!" she shouted.

Zach felt rage pour into his veins. "You beat my sister!" he screamed, getting up and facing Bear.

By now Bear was already on his feet. "Zach, it's not like that!" he yelled, holding out his hands. Zach saw the one that was bandaged. The one that Bear had put through a window to save his sister from being kidnapped. How could he use the same hands that saved her to hurt her?

"You've beaten every woman you've ever dated, and now you've beaten your wife!" Zach yelled. "My sister! The only family that I have left. Look at her face!"

Bear looked at Ruth. "You see? Didn't I tell you to just be honest."

Zach used that moment of distraction and ran full force toward Bear's body.

"That's it," Bear said. He grabbed Zach's outstretched hand with his left hand. Then he stepped back, bringing Zach's hand up and twisting his arm under his armpit. Zach hunched over and yelled in pain. "You know what this is, Zach? It's a standing armbar, which I am doing left-handed. Most men have to use both hands, but here I am using my weaker hand. I can twist harder, and make the pain hurt more."

Zach groaned louder and fell to his knees.

"Bear, let him go!" Ruth yelled.

Bear looked at his wife, sighed and dropped Zach's hand. "I really do miss training my men."

"How could you do it?" Zach said from where he kneeled on the ground.

"Do what?" Bear asked.

"Hit her," Zach answered. "Deborah told me about Ruth's face and that her ribs are bruised."

"Well, did she also to you that it was an accident?" Bear yelled.

"How could that be an accident," Zach yelled, pointing at his sister's face.

"He was asleep, Zach," Ruth tried to say calmly. "He was completely asleep. Ask Grandfather. He was being attacked by demonic spirits. He was trying to fight them off. I prayed over him and they went away. But he was really hurting."

Zach looked at Bear. "Is this true?"

"Yes, Ruth didn't say anything because she forgives and forgets so easily. I told her to tell Deborah, but she didn't want to bother her. I knew this exact thing was going to happen."

Zach looked from Ruth to Bear and stood up. "Then where are you two going?" he asked, still not believing.

"We're going on our first honeymoon," Ruth said and smiled. "To Enchanted Rock. I'm going to be staying outside."

"So you aren't beating Ruth?" Zach asked again.

"Zach," Bear said, holding up his right hand. "I broke every bone in my hand and tore ligaments and skin to save Ruth. Why would I purposely hurt her?"

Zach stood speechless.

"Sounds to me like you let an old busy-body fill you with worry," Bear said. "Didn't my five years of being away from women, making those stupid videos, convince you that I had changed?"

"Yes, I did believe that you had changed," Zach said.

"Yet, one little incident and you lose all faith in me?" Bear said.

Zach looked at Bear. His eyes stung with tears. "I'm sorry, man. I just heard that Ruth was hurt, and I know your history with women, and I ran with it. Please forgive me. I was so confused, thinking that you had hurt her. It felt like you had hurt me too. I didn't mean to lose faith in you."

"It's okay," Bear said. "I lost faith in myself too. But Ruth is teaching me how to let go of the past."

Zach walked to Bear and stretched his arms out. "I should have asked you first," he said and wrapped his arms around Bear's shoulders. "Thank you for saving my sister. I'm proud that you're my brother-in-law."

Bear patted Zach on the back with his left hand. "I hadn't thought of it like that. We are brothers. I've always thought of you as my brother."

When Zach released Bear from the hug, Bear quickly wiped his eyes. "The fact that you would fight me to avenge your sister makes me respect you even more."

"Do you think I had a chance?" Zach asked.

"Against me? Not one bit, but I was impressed by your passion," Bear said, chuckling.

Zach walked to his sister. "It's so nice to see you, Ruth," he said, bringing her petite body to his chest. "I've missed you."

Ruth looked up at her brother. "Pastor Tom told me that you helped save Randall's life."

261

"We all did, but he left yesterday afternoon. He took Pilar's truck and vanished. But he did leave a note, apologizing," Zach said, gently squeezing his sister one more time before letting go.

"Do you think he'll come after us?" Bear asked.

"No, we didn't tell him anything. The note said something about going to find his family," Zach said. "It felt really good to forgive him."

"Will the sick people be arriving at Rohan Gupta's house tomorrow?" Ruth asked. "Are you not supposed to be there?"

Zach smiled sheepishly. "Yes, I need to leave almost immediately to get back, but I need a few things."

"What do you need?" Bear asked.

He looked at Bear. "I know you donated a lot of goods from your shed to help us, but can you also spare some gasoline? I'm already on empty. Also, I'm a little hungry."

Bear stood for a moment and then laughed so loud that the echo of his laughter bounced through the trees and along the Trinity River. "Yes, you can take some gasoline. And I'm sure we can get some food packed up for you."

"Great, thanks, guys. I really should get back before Pilar gets too worried," Zach said. "I didn't tell her that I was leaving."

"If I know Pilar, you are going to be in big trouble when you get back," Bear said, smiling. "And I'll be on my honeymoon."

CHAPTER FORTY-ONE

"Deborah told me what you left to do. How could you think that Bear would do that to your sister?" Pilar asked, while waiting for Zach to exit the van. "After all that he has done for her, you would make presumptions like that?" Pilar had been sitting on the porch all evening waiting for Zach to get back. She received a note from Ruth, telling her that Zach was on his way back. The night sky was cloudy, so the darkness swallowed up the small town. When she finally saw headlights, she ran to the curb.

Zach sat in the van and looked out the window. He left the inside light on. "Look, Pilar, I have already embarrassed myself enough for one day. Bear almost killed me. I'm tired of driving. It's late. I just want to go to sleep. We have to pick up the people in the morning and I'm just worn out."

"Can you get out of the van, please?" Pilar asked.

"Yes, I can do that," Zach said, opening the van door. He got out, and when he shut the door, everything became dark. He felt Pilar lean into him.

"I'm not mad that you left. I think the fact that you would drive all the way back to Levington to make sure Ruth is okay is sweet. That's what brothers should do. Although, you could have saved time if you'd have just written to her. I'm angry because you didn't think to tell me first," Pilar said. "Deborah let me in on your little secret."

Zach began to say something but stopped. He wrapped his arms around Pilar. "You're absolutely right. I should have told you first. I've gotten so used to not being accountable to anyone. I apologize. So did you tell Deborah about what happened?"

"Yes," Pilar said, "She felt awful, but she doesn't know Bear like we do."

"Deborah meant well. She was worried about Ruth. Ruth should have explained what happened, but she forgives and forgets too easily, like Bear said. I also think she tends to neglect the fact that there are people around her who really care about her," Zach said.

Pilar leaned back. "So that's it? No excuses? We're not going to get into one of our arguments?" she asked.

"No, I think I like this better. If I want to have a relationship with you, I need to start acting like it, right?" Zach said.

Pilar looked at Zach's face in the dark. She could barely make out his features. The beard made him look stronger and more mature in some way. "You want to have a relationship with me?" she asked.

Zach chuckled. "Have you ever seen me with anyone else?"

Pilar thought. "No," she acknowledged.

"I realized that what we used to have is dead. Whatever our relationship was before can never be again. There's too much hurt and confusion there," Zach said.

Pilar placed her head against Zach's shoulder. She liked the fact that he was taller than her. Many men in her village did not reach her height. She had always been a tall girl, but Zach made her feel diminutive in a good way. "I agree. I finally had to let it go," Pilar whispered.

"But that doesn't mean we can't start something new. We can get to know each other as friends again, like we were doing at your dad's house. I liked that," Zach said.

"I did too," Pilar agreed. "I missed having you home. I know it sounds strange, but I'm glad I was kidnapped and brought here. While I drove my truck and Randall had his gun pointed at me, I felt so much peace, like I was where God wanted me to be. He was using that horrible situation to move me. It's what helped me to go back and get my truck. I wasn't there by accident."

"I still don't know how much I actually rescued you," Zach laughed. "You weren't far from the village by the time I got to you. You would have made it there eventually."

"But you would have missed me waving my bra in the air like a white flag," Pilar said.

"Yes, that image will always be in my mind," Zach jested. "I loved seeing you so out of your element. You looked so vulnerable at that moment."

"I did have a gun by my side," Pilar said. "I wasn't that vulnerable. If I hadn't recognized you, I might have shot you."

"That's the second time someone has said that they almost didn't recognize me. This beard must really be throwing people. Maybe I should shave it," Zach said.

Pilar reached her hand to Zach's chin. "No, I like the beard. You should keep it," she said, feeling the soft bristles.

Zach felt a tingle, igniting from her fingertips and down his spine.

"You're tired, aren't you?" she asked.

"I'm not used to driving for long distances anymore. I'm beat. Where's everyone sleeping?" he asked.

"Deborah has the couch, and the rest of us have pallets on the floor. We are keeping the rooms empty for the people coming in the morning," she said.

"Is my pallet next to yours?" Zach asked.

"Mine is in between yours and Li's. He says he's done enough sleeping next to you. Something about keeping warm at nights and sleeping under a tree," Pilar said.

"Don't remind me," Zach said. "A pallet on the floor will suit me just fine. I'll wash up in the morning. Right now I just need to sleep. Did Pastor Tom leave yet?"

"He left earlier this afternoon. He needed to get home. He's worried about this *Grand Opus Gala* that going on," Pilar said.

"What's that?" Zach asked as he began to walk toward the house.

"Do you mean Ruth and Bear didn't tell you?" she asked, grabbing hold of Zach's hand.

"No, they didn't have time to talk. They're going on their honeymoon," Zach said. "What's a *Grand Opus Gala*?"

"Ada Armel is organizing the event of a lifetime. There are one hundred representatives around the world who have been invited to present their life's work to the World News during this three-day event. It's only a few short months away, starting New Year's Eve."

"Well, it sounds like a good thing to me," Zach said, confused. "The World Government will be more distracted, so Li can cause more damage."

"But you don't understand," Pilar said. "Bear is one of ten Colonials that have been summoned to represent at the Gala."

Zach stared at Pilar for several seconds. "They invited Colonials?"

"Yes, ten of them. It's brilliant, actually, because more Colonials are plugging back into their HMS," Pilar said. "The video of Bear fighting at Enchanted Rock has the most views of all the representatives."

"Bear won't go," Zach said.

"He has to," Pilar insisted. "Everyone summoned must attend."

"What about Ruth?" Zach asked. "Are families allowed to be present."

Pilar nodded. "Yes, because the representatives will be there for about a month before the actual event. They've taken over an entire building, calling it the Grand Opus Building. That's where the representatives and their families will be staying."

"Ruth can't go," Zach said. "She'll definitely be found out."

"You were willing to take her with you to rob the World Bank. What makes this any different?" Pilar asked. "Remember how Bear begged you not to take her, but he finally yielded because he trusted you?"

"Yes," Zach said. "I remember."

"Now you need to trust Bear and whatever decision he and Ruth make," Pilar said. "They are married, and they will do what's best for each other. We shouldn't meddle."

Zach shrugged. "I think I'm done meddling for now."

"Good," Pilar said, grasping Zach's hand tighter. "Now let's get some sleep. We are going to have a busy day tomorrow."

"Sounds good to me," Zach said, matching the strength of her hand with his and leading her to the house.

CHAPTER FORTY-TWO

"Please remember, Deborah, you are about to see a situation that you do not agree with and that will anger you, but any reveal of emotion will compromise our position. We are here to help the sick, but they think we are taking these people to use for our experiments. We have to treat them like they are almost inhuman. Otherwise, the government workers will think something is wrong. We will figure out a way to free the rest," Li repeated. "But we need time to form a plan. Do you understand?"

"You keep telling me the same thing, Li. I used to run a foster home. I know what hardship looks like," Deborah insisted. "I can see the people behind the gate, working the cotton. I'm fully capable of handling myself." Deborah secured her sweater. Despite the cold weather, sweat collected on her brow.

"We'll see. The men are all working the field, so we'll only see the women and children and some of the elderly on the facility grounds," Li said. He sat in the front seat of the van. Deborah sat in the passenger seat. They had cleared the entire back space of the van to fit as many people as possible. He hoped they would be able to get everyone in. The van was parked in front of the entrance gate, and he waited for one of the security guards to come to him. He recognized Officer Jackson walking up to the gate. The officer took a set of keys from his belt and unlocked the gate. He exited the gate, closed it and relocked it. Today he wore a jacket over his uniform. Cold air appeared with each breath as he neared the van.

He walked up to the driver's side window of the van. "Where's your Bodyguard and who's she?" Officer Jackson asked.

"I needed to make room, so my Bodyguard is waiting at our facility. This is my nurse," Li said nodding to Deborah.

"You like your staff old, don't you?" Officer Jackson asked.

"They tend to be more discreet when it comes to my work," Li said.

"Whatever you say," Officer Jackson said. "Mr. Stanton says you have something for him."

"Yes," Li said, reaching into his pocket and pulling out a folded piece of cloth. "Let him know that there is more where that comes from." He handed the cloth to the officer.

Officer Jackson pulled the fabric aside and saw two blue earrings. "I've never seen anything like this," he said. "What are they made of?"

"Those are sapphires set in platinum. Very rare and expensive," Li said. "Where are my volunteers?"

"We had a slight delay," Officer Jackson said, folding the fabric back up and placing the earrings into his pocket.

"Why might that be?" Li asked. He feared that they had been found out.

"One of the mothers won't let her sick daughter go. We don't want to move them because the girl may die, and we know you want your volunteers alive—at least a little. We're trying to figure out how to separate them," Officer Jackson said.

"Where are they?" Deborah asked.

"They're over there just a few yards away. The girl's mom was working the cotton when she saw her daughter being carried out. Before we knew it, she had her daughter in a deadlock grip," he said.

"Let me talk with the woman," Deborah said. "I can be very persuasive with Colonials. I'll simply explain that we are taking care of her daughter."

"She'll know you're lying. The laborers here don't believe nothing we say," Officer Jackson said. "We can't lose this one. She works hard because she thinks we are caring for her daughter. If she loses her, she may stop working like some of the others do when they lose family."

"Don't underestimate my assistant. She has worked with Efficientists and Colonials for many years. She can be very convincing," Li said.

Officer Jackson took off his hat and wiped his brow. It wasn't hot outside, so Li knew his sweat was from worry.

"Okay, I will give you one minute to talk with her. Otherwise, we'll bring the girl back to the sick room," he said. "Get out of the van, and we'll walk in."

Li got out of the van. He prayed silently that Deborah would have more self-control than Pastor Gupta had. As they neared the gate, the horrible smell overwhelmed him. He looked briefly to Deborah, but her face showed no expression. Officer Jackson opened the giant lock and let them through. They waited behind the gate for him to relock it.

Li looked around and saw the familiar sight of women at looms, pulling together threads of cotton. The kids and a few other women were picking through the cotton for debris. To the right about twenty yards away, Li saw the sick people he remembered from the darkroom on the first floor. In the daylight, they looked worse than before. They were so thin that their bones could be counted. Many of them had bald patches on their heads. He could see them itching and knew they were infested with fleas. They smelled of human waste and rotting infection.

He glanced back at Deborah. She still showed no emotion. When they got to the group of sick people, they stopped.

"Where is the mother?" Deborah asked, instantly.

"Right there," Officer Jackson pointed to a woman holding a toddler who looked pale and weak.

"These people are severely underdressed for the weather," Deborah snapped.

"That's not my concern now," Officer Jackson said without hesitation.

Deborah walked over to the woman. The woman squeezed her daughter tighter and pulled her away from Deborah. Deborah slowly got down on the ground and sat next to the woman. She motioned to the woman to come close to her, so she could whisper in her ear. Li watched as the woman listened. She nodded her head. He could see her grip on the young girl loosen. Deborah continued to whisper. Li saw tears welling up in the woman's eyes. Finally, Deborah pulled her head back. "Do you understand what I've told you here today?"

The woman nodded and mouthed the word yes.

"Officer Jackson, would you be so kind as to carry this one. Hold her tight. She's extremely cold," Deborah said.

Officer Jackson walked up to the lady. At first, she didn't want to let go of her daughter, and she looked at Deborah with pleading eyes. "It's okay. Hand her to the officer. I'll take care of her," Deborah assured. The woman finally loosened her grip completely and let the officer take her into his arms.

"Okay, easy enough," Deborah said, slowly getting back up. "Now, let's get the rest of these fine folks into the van."

Li walked up to Officer Jackson. "I notice we are missing a few people," he said.

"A few of them got well enough to work," Officer Jackson said, adjusting the girl in his arms. Li could tell that the officer didn't like holding her. "One of them died. There was nothing the medic could do. He was an old man and ready to go."

"This group will work for now. But remember, I need many more volunteers, but only the sick," Li said. "And make sure they have blankets next time. We have a long drive."

"Ain't nothing I can do about the weather being cold," Officer Jackson said. "Now let's get these people into your van. Too many of the laborers are wondering what's going on."

Officer Jackson led the way back to the gate entrance. The other officers carried and guided the sick behind him.

"Keep working!" Officer Jackson yelled at the onlookers gawking at them. They all began to work.

Li looked at them one more time. He saw Hispanics, blacks, whites, Asians—women and children of all different races with two things in common: they were both poor and nomadic. He realized now how important Pastor Tom's vision of uniting the Colonies truly was. They were stronger when they were together.

Another officer unlocked the gate and opened it for their group. Li walked straight to the back of the van and opened the double doors. Officer Jackson came up first. "They're going to be crammed in there. How far do you have to drive?"

Li would not tell him they were going to the town only thirty miles away. "We have a complex about two hours north of

270

here. It's a secret government facility and the location cannot be disclosed."

Officer Jackson appeared to be insulted. "Believe me, I don't want to know what research you all are doing. Best to stay clear of stuff like that. I don't think these people will make it that far," he said.

Li took the young girl from the officer, surprised by how little she weighed. "That is precisely why I brought my nurse. Don't worry about us. She will ensure my volunteers stay healthy enough until we arrive."

Officer Jackson laughed. "These people are a long way from healthy, don't you think?"

"Please let Ted Stanton know that I will be able to pick up more volunteers when they are ready," Li said after he placed the young girl in the van. He and Officer Jackson moved aside as the other officers helped the other sick people into the van.

"We talked to one of our sister facilities. They will be sending at least a dozen people. It will take a week or more to get them here, though," Officer Jackson said, patting the packet where the earrings were located. "And Mr. Stanton will be expecting some more in trade for them too."

"Of course," Li said. When all the people were in the van, Li closed the doors. The officers were quick to get back to the other side of the gate.

Li got into the driver's side and closed the door. He quickly started the ignition and turned on the heat. He thought about how he should have left the van running, so the air would be warmer. Deborah was already seated in the passenger side. He put the van in reverse and backed up slowly to make sure the people in the back compartment were not jostled too much by the movement. When they were a distance away, he looked toward Deborah. Her face was wet with tears, but she made no noise.

"What did you tell that mother?" Li finally asked.

Deborah wiped her face and looked back toward Li. "I told her what every mother would want to know. I explained that we were Colonials who found a way to rescue people out of the labor camps. I told her to stay strong and pass the word on that there were people praying for them and planning how to get them out. I told her that I loved Jesus, and I would do everything I could possibly do to save her little girl."

Li's mouth fell open. "You just risked our entire operation."

Deborah looked sternly at Li. "I just gave those people hope. Believe me. They will not let this secret slip out."

Li looked back at the road, saying nothing. Gradually, white flurries began to flitter across his windshield. "Is that snow?" he asked.

"It sure is," Deborah said, straining her neck to look into the sky. "I haven't seen snow in many years."

"I have never seen snow," Li said. "It hasn't snowed in the city since before I was born."

Deborah smiled. "You know what I read this morning?"

"From the *Bible*?" Li asked.

"Yes," she nodded. "The Holy Spirit brought me to Micah chapter three."

Li looked over at Deborah. "What did it say?"

Deborah thought for a moment. "*I will gather together my people who are lame, who have been exiles, filled with grief. They are weak and far from home, but I will make them strong again*. That's verses six and part of seven."

Li looked back at the road. "It's interesting that the verse uses the word, *gather*," he said. "The World Government is *gathering* people for evil and now we are *gathering* people for good."

"Very true," Deborah agreed. "And by God's grace we will keep *gathering*."

CHAPTER FORTY-THREE

Cindy threw the door open, "Tom, they're here! They're here!" Cindy yelled. She grabbed Ruth and held her tightly in her arms. "Wow, Ruth! You feel stronger than before." Ruth smiled and said nothing. Cindy was used to her quiet mannerisms. She gripped her slender arms. "Your biceps. I feel the muscle in there."

"Living outdoors takes a lot of work," Ruth said. "The first night I was exhausted from putting up the tent."

Cindy looked toward Bear "It was strange not hearing from you guys for over a week! But I envy you. Some days I would love to just get away into the wilderness, but I doubt if Tom would ever leave his HMS and computers. He loves keeping up with the World News, and now that Pastor Rohan has set up his computers, Tom's network is becoming more widespread." She leaned in and gave Bear a hug. "You are as muscular as always," she said patting his arm. "How's the hand?"

Bear held up his right hand. "I had to get rid of the bandage, but the skin has healed. I have some movement now. I gripped sticks and rocks while we stayed at Enchanted Rock, so my strength is coming back slowly. There's no permanent nerve damage, so I'll be back to normal in a few more weeks."

"That's good news since you're going to be in the *Grand Opus Gala!* I can't believe it. I know I shouldn't be excited about it, but Ada and the World Government are really making a big deal about it all. I've seen the pictures of the actual summons. Did you get yours?" Cindy said.

"Cindy, this is the opposite reaction we are supposed to have for this Gala," Pastor Tom said, walking into the entryway.

"No, that can't be true. God created these people and gave them their talents like Bear's talent to fight. Even though the World Government doesn't recognize God, I do. And when I see the representatives, I see God's imagination and ingenuity," Cindy said, defensively.

"I know. But I've never seen you on the HMS so much as you have been since Ada Armel declared the Gala," Tom said. He gave Ruth a gentle hug and walked to Bear, grabbing his shoulder. "So how's our representative? Are you ready for the Gala?"

"It's not happening for six weeks yet," Bear said.

"Yes, and a good thing too from what's going on at the labor camps. Zach and Li got another group of sick people in yesterday. They found homes for all their previous sick, except for the young girl they are saving for her mother. God is just providing for them with one miracle after another. They ran out of food, and Li had a prophetic word that a farmer would be bringing food, and that night he did! Another day they needed more medical supplies, and a neighbor found out about what they're were doing and fetched the medical supplies that he had stored in his attic for over five years. God has just been moving!"

"Is Li still working on his hack to equalize the money points?" Ruth asked.

"He works on it during the few hours he has off from helping the people. He said it's harder than he initially thought. It seems that Neil Elder has strengthened the safeguards for the World Government. They still haven't discovered our use of the computers, but they've made security even tighter," Pastor Tom said. "Come on in. Cindy has lunch ready for you both. Once we're done, we'll take a look at the Trading Center. It's expanded a lot since you've seen it last."

"I apologize," Ruth said, following Cindy and Pastor Tom to the living room. "We stopped at the farm first, and Esther served us breakfast. I am extremely full."

"She served the best pecan pie," Bear said. "After eating off the land for a week, the pie tasted sweeter than honey."

"She served you pecan pie for breakfast?" Cindy asked.

"We ate breakfast first," Bear said, smiling. "Then the pie."

"That's okay," Cindy said. "I thought that might happen, so I'll pack it to go for your drive to the city."

The four of them sat down in the living room. Ruth looked around. "Where are your kids?" she asked.

"They finished school already and begged to go outside. It's such a beautiful day, so I let them. But I'll bring them by before you leave, so you can see them. They have grown. My oldest is now fourteen. Can you believe it?" Cindy asked.

"Time is just flying by," Pastor Tom said. "Levi wrote that you stopped by the bakery before you left."

"Yes, we celebrated his birthday," Bear said. "Ruth made him a few gis like the ones she makes me."

"People have been talking about those gis," Pastor Tom said. "I might have to get me one too. Did you happen to retrieve your summons? They have your name listed as delivered on the World News website."

"They gave it to my grandfather. We got it before we went on our honeymoon," Bear said. "I'm glad we left to Enchanted Rock because my property has been swarming with people. I didn't think they would find me, but they did. But several of my men have come out to guard my house and shed. And *Aha-enah* has shot his shotgun a few times. It seems to scare people off."

Pastor Tom laughed. "I'm sure it does. Can we see it?"

Ruth picked up a bag she had set on the floor. She reached in and pulled out a black envelope. "Here it is," she said, getting up and handing it to Cindy.

"This is the first time the World Government has used paper invitations for anything since the Second Civil War," she said, taking the thick envelope. She slipped the summons out and held the corners with the tips of her thumb and index finger. The paper was black linen with metallic lettering. "Wow," she gasped. "It reads, *The Shaman, you have been invited to be one of the representatives at the Grand Opus Gala. Please check in at the Grand Opus Building by November 20th. Sincerely, Ada Armel*."

"They should have written *required* to be a representative, not *invited*," Bear said.

"What do you think about all of this?" Pastor Tom asked Ruth.

Ruth thought for a moment. "Neil saw that the public ratings for the Efficientists were down, so he allowed Ada free rein to create excitement."

"You know," Cindy interjected. "Many people think those polls dropped when Eve Pallue died." Cindy noticed that Ruth looked away. "I'm sorry. I didn't mean to offend you."

Ruth looked back at her. "I am not offended. I am relieved I do not have to do their bidding anymore. Public support was the thing I hated most about my work. I am glad I never have to do another PR event again."

"Well, you're about to be in the public eye again," Pastor Tom said.

"Not I," Ruth countered. "The Shaman."

Cindy shook her head. "No, Ruth dear, you will be in the limelight as well. Some of the other representatives have already arrived, and their families are the first thing they are looking at. The World News will be watching you too."

"But the World Government allows families, but they don't draw attention to them," Ruth countered.

Cindy looked at her husband. He scooted up in his chair. "This Gala is changing a lot of things about *Life Plethoricity*— even the ideology of *Life Efficiency* is changing."

"Neil is allowing this?" Ruth asked.

"Ruth, Neil wants only power and control, and he'll do whatever it takes to get those two things," Pastor Tom said.

"Do you think Ruth should stay at the farm while I go to the city?" Bear asked.

"No, that is the worst idea," Pastor Tom said firmly. "You need your wife by your side because the enemy would like nothing more than to isolate you both, so you'll be easier targets for temptation and stress. No, you two need each other's support during this time because a lot of things are going to take place."

"That is why I have a surprise for you," Cindy said. "Ruth, come with me to the Trading Center. I have just what you need to keep your identity safe," Cindy said, getting off the couch.

"And Bear," Pastor Tom said, getting up as well. "I have an old printing press that I got from Rohan Gupta, the pastor who helped Zach and Li with the sick at the labor camp. I'm trying to make copies of some of Ruth's work to have in case I find someone interested in them. Can you help me print copies for a bit?"

"You have my writings?" Ruth asked.

Pastor Tom smiled. "Of course, I have all of them. You didn't think I would just let them all float away into the void, did you? I always made copies before I deleted them."

"I see her typing for hours every day, but I've never seen what's at the other end of all that time she spends," Bear said. "How much work does she have?"

Pastor Tom whistled and thought. "She has written several hundred thousand words. All of her writing would probably make up half a dozen books at least. Ruth writes in droves."

"We aren't making copies of all of it?" Bear asked.

"No, I've chosen some work that will appeal to the Efficientists who keep dropping rank. I get quite a few of them at the Trading Center daily. They're having trouble integrating into Colonial life."

"Do you have my work here?" Ruth asked. "I have never seen it all together. I started writing when my mother was still alive."

"I sure do," Pastor Tom said. "I keep it in our bedroom closet. I don't want to leave it in the Trading Center in case something happens over there. Let me get it." Pastor Tom said and got up, disappearing down the hallway. He came back carrying a large box filled with a tall stack of papers. He set it down on the coffee table in front of the couch. "Here is half. Let me get the other half," he said, retreating back down the hallway. He reappeared with a bigger box and set it down next to the other.

Ruth and Bear got up to inspect the contents.

"Ruth, that's a lot of writing you've done," Bear said, lifting the edge of several sheets to look over the print-covered pages. "I never realized."

"It does not look like much to me for a year's worth of writing," Ruth countered.

"Ruth, that's because you're actually living life now," Pastor Tom said. "Not just producing. This much work for a person with a marriage and a job, like your sewing, and a person who knows how to rest and enjoy friends is a lot. You've done very well."

"Speaking of work, I think it's time that I get to work on Ruth's look," Cindy said, turning to Ruth. "Are you ready for your makeover?"

"I am ready," Ruth said.

Bear looked toward Cindy. "Don't do anything too crazy. I like how my wife looks."

"I promise I won't shave her head," Cindy jested. "Her hair has grown so beautifully long since we met her a year ago."

"So what color do you want to be, Ruth? Blonde or red?" Cindy asked, holding up two bags. They stood in the Trading Center looking down the beauty aisle. "A local lady mixes these herself, and everyone raves about them."

Ruth thought for a moment. "Red," she answered simply.

"That's what I thought," she said. "I'll dye your hair today, and then I'll give you an extra one. There are no directions, so remember what I do today. You'll want to dye your hair again in four weeks. That should get you through to the end of the Gala. But I have something even more exciting," she said. "Follow me. I traded for them right away when they arrived. I put them in our office."

Ruth followed Cindy to the office. "Everything has expanded. You must be very busy."

"You know, we've even started giving store credit. Someone will bring something by and if we know it will sell, we'll give them store credit to trade for whatever they want or use it for later. We don't need money at all, as long as people trust us at our word—and everyone trusts Trinity Trading Center."

"No money points required," Ruth said.

"Those are no good here. No matter what the World Government does to gain the interest of the people, I still don't think Colonials will trust the money point system again. It comes with too many strings attached," Cindy said as she entered the office.

Ruth looked around. She noticed the HMS connected to a generator. "That machine started it all," she whispered.

Cindy looked to where Ruth was staring. "What? Our HMS?"

Ruth nodded. "I found my mother on that HMS. Jonah found me on that HMS. And because Pastor Tom let me use it, I was able to meet her before she died. I doubt if Zach would have believed I was his sister if Mom had not confirmed it to him. I look too much like my dad's family."

"One machine can produce so much good, yet so much evil," Cindy said, placing her hands on her hips.

"Like most things in life," Ruth added. "Vessels can be filled with good or evil, but it is up to us which we choose."

"You know," Cindy said, smiling at Ruth. "You are a brilliant woman. I miss your writing. Will you write again?"

"I brought my laptop," she said. "And I think there will be an LPS in our apartment. It will be nice to use one again. I am also bringing my sewing supplies."

"Yes, make yourself some outfits that beat Ada Armel's. Everyone is constantly talking about what she is wearing," Cindy said. "It will show her up if a Colonial creates clothing better than her own."

Ruth thought about her old image consultant. "A little friendly competition might be nice," Ruth said. "But I would not want her to recognize me."

"Well, she won't after I get done with you. Here is what I've been saving for you," Cindy said, reaching for a box that she placed on a high shelf. "I had to put it up here to make sure my two girls wouldn't find it. They wanted to try them, but I wanted to save them for you."

"What is it?" Ruth asked, curiously.

"They are green contacts. I have a little more than six weeks' worth, so you have to be careful with each one. We are making you a redhead with green eyes. With the muscle that you have gained and your complexion is much darker from being outside, no one will ever recognize you," Cindy said. "I can't wait until Bear sees your transformation!"

Ruth hesitated.

"What's wrong?" Cindy asked.

"I do not want to dye my hair or wear contacts," she whispered. "I spent years transforming my image for people. I do not want to do it anymore."

Cindy thought. "I totally understand, but how can we disguise you?"

Ruth thought. "May I look around the Trading Center? I have an idea of what I can create in order to hide my identity."

Cindy smiled. "You can take anything in the store that you need."

"Thank you," Ruth said. Then her cheeks blushed slightly. "There is one more thing that I need."

"Yes, anything, Ruth," Cindy said.

Ruth tried not to squirm. "Do you have a pregnancy test that I can have?"

Cindy's eyes shot open. "Ruth, do you think you might be pregnant?" she asked in a hushed, excited voice.

"It has been over a month since my last period. My breasts feel sensitive, and I have been feeling nauseated. I thought it was the food I was eating, but I am not sure."

"I can't believe it," Cindy said. "Does Bear know?"

Ruth shook her head. "No, and I would like for him not to know yet. He tends to become overwhelmed, and the Gala is expecting a lot from him. I would like to wait until it is over, but I want to know before we go, so I can be prepared."

"I totally understand," Cindy said. "And yes, I have pregnancy tests. I get them from the Colonial hospital just to have in case I have a young lady come in asking for help. Let me get one right away. You stay right here. I'll be back in less than a minute."

"Thank you," Ruth said. She watched Cindy leave. Her gaze returned to the HMS. So much had changed since the day she first used it. She had lost everything. Yet, just over a year later, she had gained so much. She gently rubbed her lower stomach. Now, she had so much to lose.

CHAPTER FORTY-FOUR

Grandfather sat on the chair he had placed on the grass between the house and the shed. Less people were showing up at the house for the last two days. He had sent the other men who'd been helping him keep watch home. He didn't need help from *Ne'aw-ze*'s men anymore. He could protect the house himself. He kept the shotgun across his lap. He reached down into a box that was next to the feet of the chair and pulled out another piece of banana bread. He thought of Pilar's little sister, Reyna. She spoiled him more than Pilar did. She had brought him sweets three times this week. He always smiled and eagerly took the box. Now that *Ne'aw-ze* and his *baynit* were gone for six weeks, he hoped Reyna would keep the sweets coming. Maybe the next animal he trapped, he would give to her.

Suddenly, he heard a car coming up the hill. He grabbed his shotgun. When the car came into the clearing, he saw a woman driving with a young girl in the passenger seat. He set the shotgun back on his lap. The women were probably just wanting to meet the Shaman. He would let them come up to him. He watched the car closely and continued to eat his banana bread.

The woman and the girl seemed to be arguing. The grandfather could see hands pointing and moving as they talked. Women loved to talk with their hands. He guessed they finally came to some kind of agreement as the car came to a stop because the young girl crossed her arms and stayed in the car while the woman got out. She looked at him and saw the shotgun.

"I'm not a threat!" she yelled with her arms up in the air.

Grandfather stared at her face. He could tell she was speaking the truth. He moved the shotgun to the ground.

The woman walked slowly toward him with her arms still up. She stopped about five feet from where he was sitting.

"Are you *Aha-enah*?" the woman asked. She must have been in her mid-thirties. Grandfather could see the lines around her eyes and the grey in her hair.

"Only my grandson calls me that," Grandfather said.

"I know," the woman said, putting down her hands. "I'm an old friend of Bear's."

"How do you know him?" Grandfather asked intrigued. Most people looking for his grandson asked for the Shaman.

"Oh, we dated briefly when he fought on the circuit," she said.

"My grandson is married," Grandfather said.

The woman raised her left hand. "So am I."

"Where is your husband?" he asked.

"We own some property—much like this place," she said looking around. "He stayed home with our other kids."

"My grandson has gone to the Gala in the city. He won't be back for six weeks," Grandfather said.

"I knew it was too late, but my daughter insisted we try. I'm sorry to bother you. Can you let him know that Cassie came by?" the woman asked.

"Is that your daughter?" Grandfather said, motioning to the girl walking up to them.

"Shayla, I told you to stay in the car," Cassie said sternly.

"Is this his grandfather?" the young girl insisted.

"God, help me," Cassie said. "Yes, this is *Aha-enah*."

Grandfather dropped the bread he had been eating and quickly stood up. He walked up to the girl and stared at her face. He felt his hands shaking. "Why does this girl look like my daughter?" he demanded.

Cassie covered her face with her hands, trying to cover her weeping.

"Because I am your great-granddaughter. The Shaman, or, Bear, as my mom calls him is my father," the girl shouted. "And I demand to meet him!"

"Shayla, he is not here," Cassie said. "And your dad and I will not let you go to the city to find him."

"He is not my dad!" Shayla shouted.

"He is the man who raised you since a toddler. He has cared for you and given everything to you. Yes, he is your father!" Cassie shouted back.

Shayla looked back at her great-grandfather. "All my life, my mom would never tell me who my father was. She only told me he was a fighter and that he was no good. But then I saw his video on that Gala list. I knew the Shaman was my dad!"

Cassie interrupted. "Look, the only reason I brought Shayla here was because I found some videos that Bear had done recently. He's a Christian now?" Cassie asked hopefully.

Grandfather nodded. "We all are."

"So he's a decent man now?" Cassie pressed further.

Grandfather nodded. "He is good to his wife and to the men he trains. The town here respects him."

"What does that matter, Mother? I deserve to know who my dad is," Shayla insisted.

"No," Grandfather interrupted. "The innocent don't deserve to know the terrible. Your mother has done right by protecting you from who my son was. But he has changed. Now he would make a fine father. You would like Bear and his wife, Ruth."

"Do I have any brothers or sisters?" Shayla asked.

"Not yet, but I believe they are trying," Grandfather said.

"I don't know how to get in touch with Bear. Will you let him know that we came by?" Cassie asked, handing Grandfather a piece of paper. "We don't have an HMS, but my neighbor does. He can use this name to find us."

Grandfather stared at the piece of paper. "I will give this paper to the baker, and he will help me contact my grandson."

"Please, let him know that I really want to meet him," Shayla said. She stood awkwardly for a second and then walked up to the old man and wrapped her arms around his neck. "I look so different from everyone in my family. I finally see myself in you."

Grandfather felt his face heat up with embarrassment, but he didn't mind the hug from his young great-granddaughter. Her hair was black and thick like his daughter's hair once was, and her eyes were dark as night. "How old are you, Shayla?" he asked.

"I am fourteen," she said.

"Do you know where your bloodline is from?" he asked.

"No," she said, shaking her head.

Grandfather puffed up his chest. "We are Ka'to Indians," he said. "Be proud you look like us."

"Here she is!" Cindy said, presenting Ruth to the two men standing in the Trading Center. Their hands and clothes were covered in ink from working on the printing press.

Ruth walked out of the bathroom wearing an Italian masquerade mask. It was black and gold with white, black and red beading and long black feather coming out of the upper left side.

Bear inspected his wife. "She's wearing some kind of fancy mask."

"Isn't it breathtaking?" Cindy asked. "I don't know how she created it so quickly and with the simple items she found at the Trading Center."

"I recognize those feathers," Pastor Tom added. "They come from the tail plume of the pintail duck. A gentleman brought it in just last week."

"Look!" Cindy exclaimed. "She even sewed decorative beading on the edges."

"I took a few other items, as well. I want to make at least two more masks, so that people think I am simply making a fashion statement and not hiding my identity," Ruth said.

"Ada Armel will probably steal your idea," Cindy said.

"That is what I am hoping. If she likes the idea, more people will wear them. I will not stand out as much," Ruth said.

Bear stared at the mask. "The mask is a good idea. I didn't want you to change your looks. You look good to me the way you are."

"That is the perfect thing to say, Bear," Cindy said.

Pastor Tom turned to his wife. "Do you mind if Bear and I wash up now? We have ink all over our hands, and I don't want to touch anything."

"Sure thing," Cindy said. "I have everything set out in our bathroom at the house."

"Ruth, get ready to go. We will leave once I clean up," Bear said.

"Wait. I have something for you," Ruth said, walking back to the bathroom and picking up a bag.

"What is it?" Bear asked. "I can't touch anything. My hands are stained with ink."

Ruth reached in and pulled out a pair of new moccasins from the bag. "I made these with the two rabbit furs you gave me. I saw that your other shoes were getting old, and I want you to have nice ones to go with the outfits I have made you."

Bear stood silent, staring at the moccasins. "My other shoes were a gift from Naomi when I moved back home. She had them made for me."

"I did not know that," Ruth said. "You never told me."

Bear shrugged. "I didn't find it important until now."

"Do you like them?" Ruth asked unsure.

"Yes, I just never would have believed, Naomi's daughter would be giving me a new pair. I will wear them today as we drive into the city together."

"Ruth," Pastor Tom interrupted. "I'm noticing that you don't use a lot of contractions while you speak. The way you talk sounds very formal. If I were you, I would try to integrate more of a causal vocabulary into your speech. Someone might guess that you're not a Colonial."

"I've gotten used to it, but Pastor Tom is right. You sound like an Efficientist," Bear said.

"No, she sounds like Eve Pallue," Pastor Tom said. "Even Li, who was an Elite Efficientist doesn't speak like Ruth."

"I have noticed that, as well. My goal is to speak very little while I am in the city," Ruth said. She thought of the life growing in her womb. Her identity had to stay secret in order to keep her unborn baby out of danger.

CHAPTER FORTY-FIVE

Randall stood, staring at the solid wood door of the large estate. One of the pillars to the entryway had fallen, and the balcony on the second floor above him swayed uneasily in the cold breeze. Yellow weeds groped along the cement porch beneath him. He would have driven off thinking no one was home if it wasn't for the puffs of smoke coming from the chimney. He adjusted the leather eye patch over his left eye socket. He had traded it for the last can of fuel he had left. The food and water stored in the back of the truck had gotten him to his destination. He didn't want to steal that young lady's truck and supplies, but there were worse things he had done. She'd get over it. He had to change his life, and that change began here at his grandfather's estate.

He felt the gun tucked in the back of his jeans under his shirt. Renegades might have taken over his family's estate. He didn't know if anyone from his past even lived here anymore. But he needed answers. He needed to know who his Colonial family was. He had visited this estate a few times growing up, and the divide from *Life Efficiency* to life in the Colonies was difficult for him to reconcile. He loved being on the estate, shooting with his grandfather. But his father always wanted to go back to his work with the World Government. The arguments between his grandfather and father were brutal. The visits back to the estate became less frequent until they stopped altogether when he was still a boy. By the time he was thirteen, his mother was done with *Life Efficiency*. She wanted to live in the Colonies. She asked him to go with her, but he wouldn't leave his father—the man he idolized.

When his mother left, his father did more jobs for the World Government away from home. Randall went on all the jobs except one: the last one. Randall was seventeen when his father never returned home. Randall searched for him for almost a year. He finally gave up hope. He was too young and the world was too big for him to find one man. He went to school, joined the World Police and, finally, became a private Bodyguard to the most renowned name in *Life Efficiency*, Eve Pallue. If his father were alive, he would have contacted him to praise him for his achievements. Instead, silence was proof that his father was dead.

Randall brought up his fist to knock on the door. Suddenly, he saw an image of flames eating away a church. He knew that more than one father died at his hand. Did taking another man's father ease his own pain? It didn't matter anymore. Zach Daniels had forgiven him. He was never good at carrying guilt anyway, yet somehow parts of him normally dead were awakened. And the images of the fires from his past were eating away at him just like those flames ate away at the church.

He finally pounded the solid door with his fist. "Open the door!" he yelled. "I am Randall Hunt. Grandson of the estate's owner."

Randall waited and listened. He could hear footsteps. He pounded on the door again. "Do you hear me?" he yelled. "I am the grandson of John Hunt! My father's name was Trey, and my mother's name was Lisa. Come to this door and speak to me!"

Randall waited again. This time he heard deadbolts on the door shaking. From what he could hear, there were locks up and down the inner seam. He had to laugh. Many of the windows of the old estate were busted in and the outer walls were crumbling. If someone wanted to enter the house, he could choose from one of many access points other than the front door. When the door finally opened, he stared down the barrel of a shotgun. An old man held the shotgun at chest length with his index finger on the trigger.

"How do I know you are who you say you are?" the old man said.

Randall instantly knew he was looking at his grandfather. Nothing had changed besides a more weathered face and whiter hair. "Grandfather John, it's me, Randy." Randall held his hands up.

"What happened to your eye?" his grandfather asked, motioning to Randall's face.

"They had to remove it," Randall said without adding any details.

"Are you carrying?"

"Yes, it's tucked in the back of my jeans. I didn't know if you still lived here. I thought maybe you had been taken over," Randall said.

John Hunt stared at his grandson for a long moment before bringing his gun back into both hands, pointing away from Randall. "Many people have tried, but I get rid of them quick enough."

Randall put his hands down. "Are you the only one here?"

"Your grandmother died a few years back. Your two uncles and your aunt and their families have never condescended to visit me. Only your dad would come around, but then he stopped coming just like the rest of them."

"His job became more demanding," Randall said.

His grandfather laughed. "Son, you don't know much. Your dad only visited to see if he could find more oil on the estate. He would leave you with me and go drilling holes in my land, looking for that black gold. He always thought he would strike an oil well, but he finally gave up. That's when he stopped visiting."

"He never talked about oil to me," Randall said.

"Of course, he didn't. He was the type to keep things to himself unless they were so. You look just like him. Not an inch of your mother in you except that light eye of yours," his grandfather said. "What color is that? Blue? Green?"

"Hazel. Where is my mother?" Randall asked, trying to calm his voice.

"She came 'round here when she left your dad, but what was I going to do with her? She didn't bring my grandson now, did she?"

"I stayed with Dad," Randall said.

"I know you did, and you worked for that corrupt government just like he did. And look what it cost him."

"You knew he died?" Randall asked.

288

"Yes, Colonials are not all stupid. Someone caught wind of who he was and what he was doing and decided to take him out of business," his grandfather said.

"What about my mother?" Randall said, changing the subject.

"She stayed here for a few months, but then this band of nomads came through. She decided to go with them. That's all I know about her. Those people have no clue what's going on in the world. They live off the land and constantly move. She probably doesn't even know her husband died."

Randall stood, staring at his grandfather. He didn't know what to do next. It was all a dead-end. How could he find change when he had nowhere to go?

Randall was just about to go when his grandfather spoke up again. "Your mother left you a few letters and a box with some stuff in it. Why don't you come in for a while? I got some fresh bread and meat I can warm up for you."

"She left me letters?" Randall asked.

"She had been writing you letters. I think she wanted you to come back to her. I told her I wouldn't bring them to you in the city, but I'd save them if you ever did make it back here."

"I'll take the letters and the other box and be on my way. I don't want to eat your food. From the looks of it, you probably don't have enough to even feed yourself," Randall said. His grandfather looked poor. He wouldn't be a burden. He would try to find somewhere else to stay.

"Don't worry about me. I'm rich. I pay people to bring me food from the village nearby," his grandfather said.

"How could that be?" Randall asked, looking around.

"I keep a low profile to let people think that I have nothing. It works for me because they leave me alone," he said.

Randall laughed. "Okay, whatever you say."

"Don't believe me. Well, I knew where the oil was all along that your daddy was looking for. I just didn't want my Efficientist son selling it to the World Government."

"Why are you being honest with me? What makes you think I won't sell it to them?" Randall said.

The grandfather grinned. "You wouldn't be on my doorstep with a missing eye if you still worked for the World Government. Seems to me, someone wanted you dead just like they wanted your daddy dead. Now you can come in here, and I'll show you what your family is worth. Or you can leave to go find your nomadic mother."

Randall looked at his grandfather, the man who brought him joy as a child but caused his father such grief. "I'll come in. But I'm not promising you that I'll stay."

John Hunt opened the door wide to his estate. "No, I think you'll take one look at what I got on this property, and you'll stay."

Onoma Series:
Eve of Awakening: Book 1
Bear into Redemption: Book 2
Mark within Salvation: Book 3
Hunt for Understanding: Book 4
Straight to Eternity: Prequel Novella

I hope you enjoyed this fiction series. If you like this book, please write a quick review on Amazon. Also, if you enjoy my writing, check out my other non-fiction and fiction works on my website, www.alisahopewagner.com.